JUST ABOVE

A Tony Spool Novel

JOCK KEEL

Pequod Press

Just **ABOVE**

First Edition

Manufactured in the United States of America

V 10 9 8 7 6 5 4 3 2

ISBN: 978-0-937912-61-4

On the cover: Alan Gutierrez, *Just Above*

Pequod Press
P.O. Box 80
Boalsburg, PA 16827
www.PequodPress.com

For the daring warriors

of the SAS

Love nothing but that which comes to you
woven in the pattern of your destiny.

—Marcus Aurelius

Rain cuts the place we tread...
We shiver uncomplainingly,
And taste upon our lips, this minute,
The emerald kiss,
And breath on breath of indigo.

So is there missed a certain godliness
That's not without its woe,
And not without divinity,
For it can quicken or it can kill.

—Dylan Thomas

ONE

SUMMER 1999

Tony Spool had some unfinished business to take care of.

A minor traffic violation, three years back, was all. A hundred or so dollars and a couple points on his driver's record. Really wasn't much of anything. Not at first, it wasn't.

But Tony just couldn't get it out of his head. He felt violated by it. As time wore on, it meant more and more to him. It got to be about false justice, about betrayal of the public trust, about preying on the innocent. About right and wrong, really.

It got to be all about a new civilization he dreamed of.

And he saw a chance to teach a harmless lesson to the wayward law that might wake them up. As a sort of warning.

So now Tony drove his jet-black BMW 850 coupe down the Parkway from Atlantic City, careful not to exceed the posted speed limit, slowing down slightly as he came up to obvious speed traps, smiling an odd smile behind the tinted windshield, lost in the refracted sunshine.

At Cape May, he pulled into the loading lane for the seventy-minute ferry crossing to Lewes, Delaware. Forty-seven minutes to kill before the next sailing. Okay, good timing. Tony turned off the engine, losing the AC, but the car's interior would remain cool for a while. Outside the temperature sizzled in the high 80s.

He selected the second album from his CD changer, *Brother's Keeper*. Yeah, those bitchin' Neville Brothers out of New Orleans! Tony grinned openly now, but his face remained invisible behind the darkly tinted glass. He set about tinkering the mood for the job to be done, like an artist, flashing through his mind, the delicacy of it all, the lovely irony.

He picked out his two favorite cuts, put them on Memory and Repeat. One of the all-time hot beats in Tony's collection of adrenaline pumpers, "Fearless," filled up four shimmering minutes, giving him its usual lift. Tony's mind buzzed as he listened raptly to the words, but nothing could go wrong. He was resolved.

Next up was "Bird on a Wire." Tony shivered, hearing it again. So connected! Wondering, as he always did, how Aaron Neville could know him so well.

As he listened, Tony smiled evilly to himself.

The song ended and Tony's eyes opened like a slow yawn. He touched Pause. The car was warming up. Movement outside his space was merely that of tourists walking to the shops and toilets inside the terminal.

No threat.

He touched Play, and drank in the words one more time as the CD changer repeated cut number one.

He touched Stop on the CD interface. Nodding, feeling the perfection of the mood down to his bones. This was a small part of the right fight. There was nothing to fear.

Twenty-eight minutes till the sailing. So he closed his mind to all but philosophy and the echo of the words he had just heard.

At five minutes before sailing, Tony turned up the AC till it blasted the heat from his black monster. The rush cooled him down, going over and over in his mind his plan for the day, just like it was the real thing.

He reached behind the passenger seat.

On the ferry, he locked his Beamer with a zip from the infrared remote, and carried his small handbag up the steel steps to the men's room on the second deck. No eye contact with anyone. Proceeding directly.

He locked the door of the small private cubicle, set his bag on the toilet seat, and removed a freezer bag containing some of the instruments of his trade.

Over his close-cropped, thick salt-and-pepper hair, he adjusted the deep-black hairpiece of luxurious curls. It would be noticed, no doubt of that. Next he glued into place a gorgeous black moustache. Unctuously folding his gray Italian silk shirt, he replaced it with the one he had just bought for cash in a casino in Atlantic City, a gambler's silky gold print with black dice. Who would forget seeing him? Underneath was a black sleeveless T-shirt, and an underarm holster.

Slipping on latex gloves, pulling out the Beretta .380 auto with its squat noise suppressor, Tony slid it into the holster. Then drew it quickly. It sat deep in his fingers, part of him, an extension of his mind.

He ejected its ammo clip and stared at the ten odd-looking bullets. Mounted on the shiny brass wasn't lead that would kill but a slug-shaped gel that would stun as it turned to liquid beneath the skin.

A purple bruise would remind the recipient of it for weeks.

Tony smacked the clip into place and slid the Beretta back into his holster, smiling at it, approving of its efficiency in the task ahead. Snug and waiting. He removed his gloves and placed them in his trousers pockets.

Then Tony zipped up the carrybag, unlocked the toilet door, and made his entrance upon the stage of public recognition.

Walking to the back of the ferry, kidding around with the bar guy about the heat outside, ordering a ginger ale with four cherries and lots of ice but no straw, strutting to the cushioned captain's seats at the back of the lounge, complimenting a young mother on the beauty of the baby she held to her as she passed him, Tony set himself out for view in one of the seats, his black silk-trousered knees wide apart, his eyes happy and closing, his curly black eyebrows at rest.

After a few moments Tony's eyes slipped open and he watched sleepy Cape May dwindle behind the ferry's wake.

It was such a peaceful ride, all the way across.

Upon disembarking, Tony's 850 steered cautiously through the tourist berg of Lewes and out to the highway over to Rehoboth Beach. Outlet malls taking up miles of useless sand along both sides of the road—sucker traps, Tony thought.

As he reached the town center, a congested maze of vehicles and holidaymakers jamming the streets, Tony slipped off his blue-tinted Revos.

His fingertip touched a dash button, bringing up the car's GPS-Navigation system. Entering the state, then the town, and zooming in to where he now sat, Tony memorized the electronic street map, and soon selected an ideal location.

He turned right just before the promenade, proceeded two blocks south, and parked in front of a vacation rental.

He walked south again, away from the promenade, up a side street, searching. In the middle of the next block of vacation homes he saw it. House appeared quiet, holidaymakers probably at the beach this time of day. He approached the house, ringing the bell. He would ask directions to the Italian bakery five blocks away. But no answer. Perfect.

The Ford Ranger was powder blue, with no cap over its open bed. Virginia plates. Tony's hand reached for his car keys, before he noticed the door was unlocked. In a second he had the ignition on, slipped open the rear cab window all the way, and rolled quietly off down the street.

The powder-blue truck entered the main east-west thoroughfare, a broad boulevard divided in the center by side-to-side parking spaces, a row of them in each direction. Tony aimed the Ranger towards the beach a couple of blocks away, and at the busiest intersection made a short left and pulled up immediately to a Stop sign.

A confusing clutter of traffic and commercial signs stared at him, including two small ones reading NO LEFT TURN. Their denial went against a driver's natural instinct to continue turning left in order to head out of town, away from the beach. To go straight, instead of turning left, meant getting lost in the town's side streets.

It was nothing but a revenue trap.

When traffic cleared, Tony hung a slow left at the NO LEFT TURN sign, and sailed slowly on down the avenue away from the beach.

Nothing happened.

This same traffic violation was just an innocent error on Tony's part, but a common mistake, three years ago. Tony's mind had been halfway around the world, planning a mission. Three years ago, amid the throng of vacationers, of sports utes, minivans, convertibles, walkers and joggers, those jerkwater cops were all over his silver Porsche Carrera in a matter of seconds. Thieves. Criminals with badges, weren't they.

So, they missed him this time, he'd give it another try. No problem.

Out toward the gas stations, heading away from town center, he made a legal U-turn and drove the eight blocks back towards the beach.

This time he pulled into an open parking slot in the center island, sat there a few minutes watching the action, and suddenly backed out into the path of a slow-moving green Ford Explorer, getting an irritated honk out of its driver. Then he glided up to the revenue trap.

He made a legal left, stopped briefly, then made the illegal left—and this time, right away, a cop on a bicycle yelled into his window to pull over. To irritate the cop, and position himself, Tony made a lazy U-turn before stopping in front of the Italian bakery.

Tony watched the bicycle cop mouth the truck's license number into the mike attached to his lapel, then carefully set down the kickstand. Tony got out of the truck. A few passersby glanced his direction, he noticed. His gold gambler's shirt glinted in the strong sunshine.

"What's the matter, officer?" Tony asked quietly.

"You made an illegal left turn. Posted twice."

"Didn't see it. Too much confusion."

The bicycle cop took out his ticket book.

"Oh surely, officer, you're not gonna write me a ticket for *that*." Tony's voice was firm but moderate. What an actor, he thought.

"You have to obey the law wherever you go."

"I always try to," Tony saying, easing his shoulder muscles, relaxed now, in control. Counting on help from above for a flawless performance.

A backup cop, walking, also in his early twenties, approached behind the bicycle cop.

"Back in your vehicle, *now,*" the new cop was saying.

"Why? Is it against the law to stand beside your vehicle?" Tony asked, the irritated tourist. Tony liked the tone of his voice as he said it. Came out good. He dropped his jaw at the cop.

"Get back in your vehicle, right now. *That's a direct order!*" The new cop got a mean, self-important stare on his face. He fingered his billy club.

Tony stared back himself for a moment, nothing menacing, just to irritate, then shrugged a visible resignation and got back in the truck. Completely in charge of the situation. In the rearview mirror, he watched the backup cop plant himself squarely behind the truck. Tony made a great face at him in the mirror. Maybe he shoulda been an actor after all. Coulda made a *lotta* money at it, maybe.

At his window now the bicycle cop demanded to see Tony's driver's license, registration and proof of insurance.

"Of course, officer, no problem," Tony uttered, his shoulders without tension, his hands dry and steady, the latex glove on his right hand slipping inside his gambler's shirt, sliding out the Beretta. "Yeah, I got it, here it is, officer..."

The kid with his hand out next to the truck window, the summer cop off guard as Tony pressed the muzzle hard into the kid's chest, with a single noiseless pull, Tony's left hand holding the kid's belt, watching his startled eyes, smelling his Coca-Cola breath, holding his limp body against the truck's door, then taking a single steady shot out through the open rear window of the truck's cab. Hit the other kid perfect, right above the sternum. Kid's heart would pump the gel into liquid in seconds, do its job.

Tony chuckled to himself as he ejected its clip and parked the empty Beretta under the seat, pulled the bicycle cop's floppy body to hang into his window, then slid quickly out the passenger's door as a few holidaymakers looked toward the cop behind the truck slumping to his knees, falling onto his face as though he had fainted in the heat. Tony was away from the truck and into the Italian bakery within moments of shooting them both. Most of the passersby were too absorbed in themselves and the scene to notice anything.

Tony smiled nicely at the bakery clerk, said breezily to her, “Hey, how about two chocolate canoles and a cafe latte, okay?” and as she turned to get them he stepped down the hall into the men’s room. In seconds the trash receptacle concealed Tony’s hairpiece, moustache and gambler’s shirt. Tony hated to part with it, but he dumped the holster into the trash too, emerging from the gent’s in his plain black T-shirt a different man.

A crowd started to gather by the street outside the bakery. Tony walked rapidly to the rear door. Locked. No problem. At the front of the bakery people were beginning to stare out the windows. Tony slipped through them, out the door, to the left to the next corner, left again, and two blocks to his Beamer. He patted his left pocket, feeling the latex gloves and the ammo clip.

Oh yes, very nice, he thought, reaching the car. Beautiful performance. Tony’s gaze heavenward settled upon the subtly textured, mulberry gray leather of the Beamer’s ceiling, his eyes at peace, his brow smooth as the finest marble, smooth and dry and cold.

“Thanks for the cool, Lord,” he whispered.

He smiled wanly as he turned over the 850’s ignition, sat a long moment listening to the power behind its hum, slipped on the gray Italian silk shirt as the AC kicked in, taking care not to rumple it, then slid the tranny into gear and drove slowly out of town, his luminous blue-tinted Revos aiming almost due west, gleaming in the sunshine.

Feeling happy beyond words, Tony Spool eased the big, black BMW 850 coupe along the highways of the peninsula at a couple of miles per hour under the posted speed limit, stopping for tomatoes at a roadside stand once he crossed the toll bridge into Maryland.

Wondering all the while what those cops would think happened to them when they woke up.

TWO

If there was anything Susan Spool was obsessive about, it was time. Time management, she called it. Punctuality was her gig.

When Susan married Tony Spool seven years ago, waiting for him at the Presbyterian church, when he hadn't arrived an hour prior to the ceremony Susan called his cell number. After a few moments a recording informed her that the cellular customer she was trying to reach was away from his phone.

Shower, Susan thought. Tony was always taking showers. He loved showers, probably because he'd never had one as a kid. But an hour before his marriage? Nerves, Susan chuckled to herself: Tony always cooled his nerves with something cold. He took chilly showers, cranked up the AC, and took all his drinks with lots of ice, another mild rebellion against his past.

Well, fifteen minutes more would still be fine. So in fifteen minutes exactly, Susan rang him again.

"Tony?"

"Hi, doll. I know, I know. I'm standing here dripping. Be there in twenty. Love ya!"

"Make it fifteen, Tony." Her voice sounded decisive.

"Fifteen it is! Hug ya later," Tony finished, clicking off the cell. He sat in his darkened den, dressed in a gorgeous white tux, the screen of his laptop PC before him, finishing his e-mail. In moments the mail was off, the message file deleted. Tony wrinkled up his mouth as the screen went dark, pursing his lips, thinking tenderly of his wife to be, forgetting the e-mail.

In the little dressing room at the church, Susan thought of Tony. He always made her laugh. He was a card. She thought he loved her dearly. She loved him deeply, had for two years.

Susan stared at her reflection in the mirror, adjusting this and that, fidgeting really. She was ready for this. At this moment she wanted to be Mrs. Tony Spool more than anything else in the world.

Will I ever look this pretty again, she pondered. Her normally wispy, pale brown hair had been done at a beauty shop, for the first time since she'd graduated from college, to a swept-back look. With her fine features, it made her look a little like Grace Kelly in those old 1950s flicks. Susan bared her bottom teeth in a grimace at her image in the mirror. She was ready for this! She glanced at her watch. Tony better be here in eight minutes, she bossed him in absentia.

Her lips softened, facial muscles relaxing. Would Tony be pleased? She cocked her chin, giving the mirror a coquettish smile. She turned to a body profile; she was soft and lovely, her wedding gown silky but discreet, not overly fancy. Yes, Tony would be pleased; she was the perfect bride, about to marry the most wonderful guy in the world, perfect if he would just be more punctual, perfect for Susan nonetheless.

And Tony had gotten to the church seventeen minutes after she told him make it fifteen. For the next seven years their marriage seemed the perfect match to all who knew them. And plenty of people did.

* * *

Tony saying "I picked up some Jersey beefsteaks... I'll make us Tomatoes Napolese. How are we on supplies?"

"Short on bread and onions. Get Vidalias," Susan said back into the portable phone by the pool, lounging in the shade. "Where are you?"

"Maybe half an hour away. Just rounding Baltimore on the ninety-five. Where are *you*?"

"Out by the pool. I just had a dip. Now I'm drying off."

"I'd like to see that."

"Well, you will when you get here. Speed up!"

"Drying off *au naturale?*"

"No tan lines, baby! Just the way you like it."

"Listen, dove. Only thing's speeding up is my heart. Stomach too, maybe. I have to stop a few minutes for those groceries, or we could go out *after*, but I really wanna make you my tomatoes."

"Umm… I can't *wait*. See you inside an hour. Drive safe."

"Always. I hardly ever speed in America, you know that. Ta, love."

Susan could just see Tony picking out the best of the elephant garlic cloves, finding just the right loaf of crispy Italian, oh, maybe they didn't have mozzarella in the fridge but yeah, he'd buy some anyway, don't worry, smelling each item with that sensitive nose of his. Susan loved Tony's nose. Strong and full, rounded in the sexiest way at the tip, Italian she guessed, from his mom. He sure had his mom's hair, judging by Tony's photos of her.

Smiling about Tony's nose, Susan picked up the iced drink by her side, dripping some condensation drops onto her tummy. Momentary goose bumps. The iced orangeade tasted heavenly in this heat. She set the tall glass next to her pink chaise lounge and picked up a plastic bottle of tanning oil, thinking of Tony's nose as she rubbed it gently, softly, over her private parts, lingering in the hair, her eyes closed, the tiniest smile on her lips. Rolling over onto her belly, she drifted into somnolence, she couldn't help it.

"But hurry, Tony," she'd purred into his cell phone a few moments before. "Do hurry home to me."

Tony's black 850 picked up speed as he joined the Beltway, with Annapolis at his tail. Well, he thought, he was on ninety-five *now,* so what if he was a few minutes premature, telling Susan where he was? Coming west from the bridge over Chesapeake Bay, instead of south from Baltimore, the distances were right, his timing perfect. She'd never suspect the discrepancy, and anyway it made no difference, he could have taken either route, but the ninety-five from Jersey was more direct, made more sense, unless one *wished* to take a ferry ride.

He had bought the "Jersey beefsteaks" a few miles west of Annapolis. He'd make a point of telling Susan he had bought them at one of those sandy little farm stops off the Black Horse Pike, the ones with the weathered rough lumber for sides and awnings faded to pale, nondescript colors from too many summers in the sunshine.

Tony stopped at his favorite deli, in the suburbs of D.C., Virginia side, near his house. Thinking of Susan, no tan lines, drying off by the pool, almost backing out of the deli parking lot after putting the trans in neutral. No, hell with it, that would just get better and better with anticipation, thinking of it plenty, turning off the engine.

Twenty minutes later he nosed his black bombshell around the corner of his tree-lined lane. Sycamores and boxelders towered over flowering dogwoods. Tony and Susan lived in one of the toniest houses in toney McLean, next to a senator and a political publisher, neighbors mostly in government or leaching off it, lobbyists and the like. There were even some executives in the neighborhood from the real world of earned money. They were *all* pretty boring, Tony felt, though he usually found the genuine people among them, and his antics at social events invariably made him friends. Well, not friends exactly, but close enough. Certainly close enough for Tony's needs. Just the right distance.

So when Tony parked under the shade trees in the circular drive and came in through the front of the house, Susan didn't hear him. She was in yummy land. Depositing the groceries in the kitchen, he spied her on the chaise, face down over her folded arms, nut-brown bottom skyward.

Slipping off his shoes, noiselessly crossing the pool's cement skirt in his socks, admiring her body, taking it all in. What a babe, Tony reflected. Lovely and desirable. And just smart enough.

Her tall iced drink had a watery circle around its base, on the pool deck.

Tony's gaze caressed Susan's curves, top to bottom, eyes riding like a rollercoaster gliding on velvety skin, gazing finally at the soles of her feet, loving them. Approaching, kneeling and ever so delicately touching the padded metatarsal arch of her left foot with the tip of his tongue, then the same spot in the middle of her right sole. Her fanny moved, just a hint of awareness.

Settling his lips around the distal tip of the big middle toe on her right foot, sniffing the tanning oil on her skin, caressing her ankles with his fingertips almost without touching her, arousing her from her nap, worshipping his lover, his sweet wife, Tony fell into her arms, gray Italian silk shirt and all, as she turned over to wrap herself around him. And then, right there under the summer sun, they did it.

That's what Tony always said. "Let's do it!" he'd say. Deep down she preferred to call it making love, but Tony's expression meant something very special to Susan. Besides, it was Tony all the way.

* * *

Appearances certainly can be deceiving. Standing at his kitchen sink, chopping Vidalia onions and pressing garlic cloves, Tony Spool looked for all the world Italian. His complexion was on the swarthy side, though without the olive tint of his mother's skin, his mother second-generation away from Sorrento on the Bay of Naples. He had *the look.* And then there was his first name.

"Tony, not too much garlic," Susan called from another room. "Pleeese," she whined.

"Right, not too much garlic." Tony stirred a couple of large, squished cloves into the pool of olive oil starting to sizzle in the frying pan, knowing the secret wasn't how much but how cooked, caramelized not burned, slow and rhythmic, like sex should be.

He stood in bare feet on the cool marble floor, hairy chest still damp, shorts only halfway to his knees revealing an athlete's legs, his salt-and-pepper hair drying in the air, still a little dewy from his shower. His big hands worked expertly at the chopping block, making fast work of the basket of "Jersey beefsteaks."

Despite all this, despite his appearance, he was only half Italian. He loved to play it up, had traveled in Italy a lot, was gaining an edge on speaking the language. But his father was English. A Yorkshireman from Scarborough, a roving beverages salesman who had moved with his Italian wife down to Sheffield to put distance in the family. And that's where Tony grew up, at a distance.

"So," Susan asked, in loose flannel sleeping shorts and a tan T-shirt advertising the University of Colorado, "tell me all about your vacation at the shore."

"Two nights gambling in Atlantic City isn't a *vacation*, doll face," Tony turned towards her, "it's a *holiday*. But it was fun. I like watching the human species, observing people practicing their foibles. It's a great hobby! Made a few bucks, too."

"Oh? Your investment in time produced some results?" she said, towel-drying her hair.

"You could say that," Tony replied, his eyes lifting from the tomatoes softening in olive oil in the skillet, gazing out the broad window heavenwards, searching the late-day, brilliant sky for a sign of approval.

"So you're ahead?"

Tony's gaze snapped back to his tomatoes. "Yup. Eight and change."

"Eight hundred?"

"Thou. Eighty-four hundred really, but deduct gas, food, hotel and it was about eight thou."

"*Tell* me." Her voice sounded a mock-pleading as she shook moisture out of her hair.

"Okay," he said, gesturing towards Atlantic City with his wooden stirring spoon in the air, "so after rippin' up these little Jersey backroads, I pull into AC and park for two days at Bally's, leavin' my baby in the VIP section, fifty bucks to some guy to watch it for me but heh, I tell him, I could be back any time, in and out, that's me, tryin' my luck up and down the boards." Tony did his little swagger across the kitchen floor, Susan laughing.

"And when I came for the car two days later, this jerk's still watchin' it, afraid to leave I guess. Suppose he thought I was Family?"

"Oh, Tony."

"All right... so there really isn't that much to tell you. I did the usual. Watched the suckers for a couple hours, my customary treat. Some guy dropped ten grand at one of Bally's roulette tables, daytime no less, nobody wins till ten p.m. at least, some big-bellied guy in loud clothes, plenty of gold chains with a wad of Franklins this thick musta been," Tony showed, holding his thumb and index finger wide apart. "Some cocky storekeeper from Philly probably, down with the Missus to show off how much he can afford to throw away, chiselin' like hell back home for every dime."

Susan shushed him gently, getting some iced tea from the fridge.

"At ten grand I couldn't take any more, I caught his eye and said to him, right in front of the dealer changin' out some more of his C-notes, 'You haven't a clue how to play this game, have you?' I says to him. Got a dirty look from the dealer with that remark. So I thought screw it, I've seen enough, I do a little shopping, come back later. The tables were no good anyway. Wrong time of day."

"I've cut up some fresh lemons for your iced tea," Susan interrupted, wanting to change the subject of the big loser from Philly.

"Yeah, hun, just like I like 'em... So it being midday, I decided to wander around the stores on the shopping pier. And know what? The best store there, the one with those great European clothes, where I bought that jacket last year? Gone. Out of business. Just like that."

"Recession's over," Susan mocked, reciting one of his favorite quotes from the electronic media, "and no inflation in sight."

"Yeah, no recession, no inflation, just desperate people, anxious about their futures."

"Somebody should do something," Susan said, making conversation.

Tony looked askance at his wife, realized hers was a vacuous comment, and said back at her "Somebody should indeed."

"Okay, so the clothes thing was a dud. Where'd you go next?"

"Right off the pier and straight into Caesar's, but then I thought no, too early, first have a bite to eat. I walked down the boardwalk, lovely day and that sea air tingling my nose with its freshness, to that coffee shop I like in the Taj. Corned beef with melted cheese, chips and dill pickles. Just what the doctor ordered!"

"All this cholesterol was two days ago and you're still alive?"

"Very much so! I'm telling you, it invigorated me. I'm back in Caesar's, they have one of those Planet restaurants there now, you know? I'm walking the tables, noting all the losses, when suddenly it hits me that table five is doing a lot of repeating. After four rolls I realize that, not only is it repeating, but the third dozen numbers are paying out, consistent like."

"Tony, you didn't, not before 10 p.m., you know better."

"Oh I know better, all right. Listen, babes, nobody knows nothing about roulette, except maybe to stay away from it, that's the smart guy, the winner. These tomatoes are softening down to perfection; slice that bread for me, will ya?"

"And set the table?"

"Thank you. Good idea, that! So I buy two hundred in dollars and play both street bets and singles, and I'm hittin' right away, slow at first, little wins, then a coupla slammers that brought over the pit boss. I cashed out, fifteen hundred to the good in fifteen, maybe twenty minutes. Screw them!"

"But you didn't stop."

"No I didn't stop. But I quit roulette. Enough's enough, I thought. Let's stroll down the boards all the way to the Hilton, used to call it the Grand, sort out what went down. A warm evening, half an hour I get there, I'm ready for a *large* iced tea, which I got. They put a taste of orange juice in it, California style. Really refreshing. I figure it's time for some blackjack."

"You gave it back."

"I gave back *half,* cut my losses but enjoyed it for two hours, sat around one of the bars with a cranberry juice watchin' the ponies, finally had dinner at that oyster place, went to bed early, tired from the drive and all the rest."

"Best move of the day," she added.

"First thing next morning, yesterday, I try the Taj, blackjack, and wow oh wow am I hot! I play for hours, never better. I'm up a lovely six G's, suddenly I can't draw anything, gave away a few hun, upped and outta there. Funniest of all, I'm passing roulette on my way to the cashier, get a feeling, you know? The ball's spinning. It's gonna hit eight, my mind's saying, I whack down fifty just before the call, and eight it is! Seventeen fifty payoff. 'Cash me out!' I brag, 'I'm not dumb! I'm goin' home.'"

"But it's yesterday, what, mid-afternoon? *You* leave?"

"Never looked back, nice clean new hundreds in my pocket, eighty of 'em. I'm psyched, but I'm smart too. Went to a movie to cool off, that dinosaur thing, had a late casino supper, smelled the salt air and went to bed with the hotel AC cranked to the max, buried in covers. Never feeling better! Not a care in the world, slept till ten."

Susan kissing Tony on the nape of his neck, taking the skillet from him, pouring the sauce of Naples over the sliced Italian bread, gooey mozzarella winding through it, watching him eat, loving his nose, glad to have him back home, his little tryst with luck over.

"That's what vacations are for," she heard herself saying. "And now you're properly rested for tomorrow afternoon's 'social occasion.'"

"Hey, Susan?" Tony mumbled, ladling Naples into his mouth, his eyes finding hers.

"Yeah?"

"Let's hit the sack early tonight, know what I mean?"

"Tony Spool," she said. Then she said, in a low voice, "I can hardly wait."

"Isn't anticipation wonderful?" Tony projected her way, in a whisper. She squeezed his nose lovingly.

THREE

"Bless me, Father, for I have sinned."

Early Sunday morning, going to be another warm summer day, and Tony sat inside the dark confessional, on the hard oak bench, his hands folded in the manner of a religious man of simple needs. He wore casual but expensive clothes. He was not a man of simple needs.

"Yes, my son, I know," the priest's voice drifted in to his ears.

"You know?" Tony cocking his head, leaning a bit more forward into a sitting fetal position, squinting into the dark mesh through which the voice had just emerged. He could see a vague form, nothing more, on the other side of the paneling.

"We are all of us sinners, my son," the priest replied in a monotone.

Tony settled his back against the oak bench, peering into the black corners of the confessional box, collecting his thoughts, recalling the ornate exterior of the confines he now found himself in, and the blackish brown knob of the handle on its door, the worn wood by its mortise, the scuffed-up bottom of the door itself. Many, many sinners had sat here in this place. *He* had not been in a confessional in years, had only tried for his mother's sake. He was not a Catholic.

He said nothing for a few moments.

"Tell me about your sin, my son," the voice came to him once again.

"Thank you for coming out early," Tony began hesitantly, "for hearing me. I know... I know it's customary to listen to confessions on Saturdays. I didn't want to wait, though. I felt anxious."

"That's what I'm here for," the priest replied kindly. "Lighten your burden."

Tony thought a moment. "Well, it concerns my wife," he began quietly. "I haven't been true to her, haven't loved her fully. It bothers me, but I can't have helped it."

"You've slept with another woman."

"No, not that. Not since I married her. Something else."

"Tell me."

"I can't reveal myself to her, what I really am or do, not at all. It never bothered me before, but I love this woman," he shivered to himself, "*completely*, I love her more than I ever knew I could love anyone." He gasped inaudibly.

The priest waited in silence.

"I *know* I cannot ever tell her everything about my soul, and she's happy with me, very, and I'm adept at keeping this thing from her, she'll never suspect... but somehow it feels like a *violation* of our love," Tony finished abruptly. This is not what he'd wanted to say to the priest; it had just happened. It surprised him that he had said it. He knew better.

"Well," the priest intoned, "perhaps in time you will have a revelation from God, and be able to tell your wife about this. *God* already knows it."

"What's that?" Tony asked into the mesh. "A what from God?"

"A revelation. Our Lord will reveal the way to you, how to act."

Oh yes! Tony thought, yeah sure, so why am I talking to this guy about Susan? I'm here for a *revelation* from the Lord. I'm here to talk *to the Lord.*

"Not a cardinal sin, my son," interrupted the priest's voice. "It's good to be so concerned, though. You're a moral man. Ten Hail Marys, to start. Pray for an answer every day. You'll succeed..."

Tony got agitated on the other side of the confessional wall. He was breathing loudly. He didn't want to hear this nonsense. He wasn't here to do penance. He was here for *a sign*, for further instructions from the Lord. At times these signs had come to him in churches, wherever he happened to be around the world, walking in off the street. Sometimes they came to him in his sleep, troubling him, awakening him in the dark. He sometimes perceived these signs in airplanes, peering out his window while flying through the pitch-black heavens in the middle of the night, when most human beings were safe at home in their beds. He had even sensed these signs while at sport or in the gym, pumping adrenaline. Odd, how they came to him, usually unexpectedly. Today he was *seeking* one out.

Maybe that was the problem, thinking more clearly now, hands releasing their clench on the oak bench, breathing a little calmer, eyes coming back to focus from their vacant stare into the black corners of his confines.

There was enough inexplicable movement, respiratory distress, inside the confession box that the priest put his eye near the mesh. Dark inside, but not so dark that he couldn't distinguish features. The priest recognized those features, thought he had seen them before, but he did not know the man beside him. Not a parish member.

"Are you all right, my son?" he asked into the mesh, softly.

"Yes, Father, yes, all right now. Dizzy there for a moment or two. I'm sorry. I don't know what came over me."

"Good, good," the priest said to him, cupping his hands around the words as he spoke into the mesh. "Be calm, my son. You will succeed if you pray. Are we finished for today?"

"Finished?" Tony asked, genuinely puzzled. "No, not finished, Father. But enough for now. You're right. I'll pray on it, await the Lord's guidance."

"Very good, my son. Jesus loves you. Go in peace."

* * *

When Susan woke up an hour or so later, Tony was already sweating a bit from his sit-ups, doing them just off the breakfast nook. He wore only a tank top and skivvies, counting out loud almost to himself "fifty-six, fifty-seven..." but hearing Susan pad barefooted across the parquet floor behind him.

"Good morning, sleepyhead," he grunted through a crunch in his abs, smelling her now beside him, fragrant as bougainvillea in a warm mist, but musky too, a hint of the sex they had enjoyed some hours ago.

Her eyes glittered ever so softly at the top of her body, standing over him, watching him exercise. "Just up yourself?"

"No. Up a couple hours. Took an early drive. Ready for breakfast?"

"Am I! But it smells... uhm... healthy."

Over in the kitchen Tony had some strawberry jasmine herbal tea steeping in a green glass bowl, Susan going over to inspect, some sort of bran it looked like in a puddle of warm milk, fresh apricots and bananas sliced and laying in two fancy, flowered bowls on placemats, and a tall uncut loaf of odd bread on a carving board with a large mound of butter nearby.

"Butter?" Susan suggested, touching the edge of the dish holding the yellow mound.

"Gimme a break," Tony grunted again, getting to his feet. "A concession to good old England, not to say a dish of gladness in the midst of all this nonfat madness." He rubbed his chest.

"Milk?" Susan asked again, with a finger in the bowl of bran, tasting it then, her tongue rebelling through her lips.

"Rice milk!" he intoned. "Nonfat. No value except wetness, to soften the various brans mixed therein?"

"Ah, and the bread. The bread!" Susan gleamed with delight. "They had it again at the deli! You devil, you didn't tell me last night!"

"I can still have a few little secrets from you, can't I? Let's eat!"

"Now this is an important afternoon, and you've had your fun," Susan began at the table, "so behave yourself. No pranks!"

"Wouldn't be ole Tony there among the stuffed shirts, would it, love, unless we had some foolishness. Hey... they *need* a laugh or two!"

Susan's look suggested she sort of meant it, munching away at the bread full of grains, nuts, who knows what all, mumbling "*Toneeey*!"

"No problem, no problem, just a bit of banter, insignificant chatter, maybe a touch of market wisdom thrown in for good measure. The usual. What else can I talk to them about?"

"Well, there'll be others from State, and you know they can't talk shop, no matter how much they'd like to," Susan was saying, Tony's mind on other things really, but listening.

"Bunch of blowhards, the lot of 'em. Maybe I can talk casinos?"

"Let's leave the dishes till after church," she was saying, moving away from the table, Tony slicing down another chunk of that bread, drowning it in soft butter, a smile on his face, the viscous waves in the butter reminding him of something. He crunched into the buttered bread with relish.

"Yeah, sure, sweets. I'll be right with you. Pick me out a tie."

* * *

And so there they sat, eighth pew, left of center, Susan in a new lilac-and ginger-colored summer dress, Tony attired in pinstripes and a tie. *A tie.* Tony never wore a tie, Susan thinking, seeing it just at the edge of her vision, trying to listen to the minister. Tony thinking, half an hour, another half at least to go, turning and smiling gently at Susan.

Tony did not consider himself a member of any organized religion, yet deeply religious, so listening to the silver tones of a silver-haired gent of ageing appearance plying the faults and the goodness of Washington's elite was, well, irrelevant in his mind. A waste of time? Perhaps, except that his being here pleased his wife, and that was reason enough to be trapped temporarily inside this stone edifice. He looked around the pews to front and sides, noting other heads drifting in and out of consciousness, smiling. They were human, too.

Tony shifted his shoulders, rubbed his wrists a little, felt some stiffness in his hips. Smiling again. Almost beaming. Couldn't help it.

Thinking of Susan. What a welcome home he'd gotten!

Thinking all this through the sermon. What was that he said up there, words from the sermon penetrating his thoughts, "... look for the mark of evil and set it out, cleanse it from the earth, do justice unto the Lord."

Tony's attention returning to the pulpit, his gaze floating upward, to the distant high beams of the church's ceiling.

'The mark of evil,' Tony repeated inwardly, 'the *mark* of evil.' He listened more now. An unpleasant message playing off the tongue of the minister. But *God's* message.

The silver-tongued voice droning on, "And in Psalms fifty-seven we hear the Lord's messenger praying for deliverance from his enemies, 'I cry to God Most High, to God who fulfills his purpose for me...'"

Tony's attention riveted now upon the lips of the minister. *Purpose for me. The Lord's messenger.*

"And so, my brethren, God reiterates the position of strength taken from faith, saying 'What can flesh do to me? All day long they seek to injure my cause; all their thoughts are against me for evil... My heart is steadfast, O God, my heart is steadfast!' says the Psalmist, and from these holy words we must all take heart. We must rely unconditionally upon faith."

The gold and white vestments of the preacher still, like a statue standing there, an image of God, but now his fingers flattening the pages of the huge Bible before him, his right index finger slithering across the printed columns.

"The Lord describes evil men as having 'venom like the venom of a serpent, like the deaf adder that stops its ear, so that it does not hear the voice of charmers or of the cunning enchanter.'"

Tony smiling wanly in agreement with the good book, with God's own message, the word of God spoken through that silver tongue *directly to him,* to keep from being swayed by the voices of enchanters, charmers who had evil in their deepest, darkest souls. Venom.

Susan's eyes lowered, coming up on the expression on Tony's mouth, and loving him she too smiled.

The man in white looked solemnly out at his audience.

"And just a few verses farther on, in Psalms fifty-nine, we listen to the supplicant crying out against the tyrant Saul, 'Awake to punish all the nations; spare none of those who treacherously plot evil...'"

Tony thinking of yesterday, the smooth ferry crossing, the jerkwater cops blaspheming the law, twisting the peace of God for profit, "just doing their jobs," Tony now smiling, still intent upon the minister's words. More than a practical joke, he thought. A lot more. Yesterday's warning was a modest gift to a new civilization. An act of faith.

"'Rouse thyself, come to my help, and *see!*' Wake up!" the minister interpreted, "and understand the presence of evil."

Tony's mind drifting now to this morning. What was it? A revelation from God, the priest had advised him. *A sign.*

"'... spare none who treacherously plot evil,' concludes the Psalmist." A pregnant pause from God's magnificently robed spokesman as he looked over his flock, some eyes focused upon him, others averted.

"And Our Lord's own words, from Jeremiah fifty-one: 'Behold, I will stir up the spirit of a destroyer against Babylon... Spare not her young men; utterly destroy all her host... for this is the time of the Lord's vengeance, the requital He is rendering...'" *Spare not her young men,* Tony heard.

But he had.

"And finally," the minister pointing his finger upward, then across his flock, "in Our Lord's judgment on the evils of Babylon, He tells us to 'Sharpen the arrows! Take up the shields!... Prepare the ambushes...'"

Tony soaking in the word of God, nodding to the verses.

"'You are my hammer and weapon of war... *Set up a standard on the earth...*'" Tony hearing, zoning out then, spoken to as an apostle, savoring his *sign...* wanting more than ever to set up that standard.

Feeling Susan nudge him, holding the offering plate for him to take, smiling at her, vacant, finding the envelope containing their check in his pocket and delivering it into the plate, passing it on, deep in his own thoughts, hearing nothing more till the choir's united voice rang out the final song of the service, jarring Tony to consciousness.

"Go and serve the Lord..." came from behind him, as the ministerial procession reached the exit of the narthex, Tony staring forward, his eyes like darts, staring at the crucifix hanging over the chancel, loving his Lord, sure that commandment had been aimed directly at him by God.

Around him, people standing now, greeting each other, showing off their finery, diamonds, golden trinkets, jiggling their car keys.

Wondering, had the Lord spoken to anyone else but him?

Susan tugged at his sleeve. Turning into the aisle, Susan whispering to Tony, "What was *that* all about?"

Tony found himself in an odd mood, looking at the sheer magnificence of the huge Episcopal cathedral, his eyes spraying like gunfire past the chattering faces of some of the most powerful private and public men in D.C., their wives and listeners nodding in quiet solicitude. Three hundred dollar shoes, watches costing thousands.

Normally these pomposities irritated Tony deeply, though he had never, to his knowledge, revealed his feelings. These were his and Susan's neighbors. Tony was a liked guy. He'd long ago vowed to keep it that way.

But today Tony's psyche was distant from these social gestures of self-importance. In fact, Tony was far, far away. *He'd been spoken to, and in a church again. What had his mom called it? An epiphany?*

* * *

A standing lunch, Tony called it. By which he meant that he and Susan stood around in their kitchen, propping up the cabinets, small talk squeezed between munchies. Not a proper lunch, but a sort of snack. To keep off the pounds. The 'social occasion' of the day a few hours off as well.

Susan slipped the pancake flipper beneath a sandwich on the grill and said "Convince me this is actually good for me!" to Tony.

"Think about it," he said back. "Thinly sliced crazy bread, laced with olive oil, little white chunks of feta cheese layered with roasted red peppers, fried on a low fire in just a hint more olive oil. Tuscany oil, with its delicate nuttiness. Tastes like paradise, and it's *absolutely good* for you, mostly mono-unsaturated fat, healthy fat, a meal fit for, well, me and you."

"But basically grilled cheese."

"Grilled cheese, but not grilled cheese. Just enjoy."

And in a few short minutes Tony's had been devoured and he was at the sink washing, not the dishes, but his golf clubs.

He had bought a special brush for cleaning club heads, and used it now, removing grass stains and dried bits of mud, saying "Maybe I can get up a foursome for later in the week, at the party today?"

Susan shaking her head, like shooing away an annoying bug in her face.

"Oh, Tony, what I wouldn't give to have as little to think about as you do. I know you've earned it, but honestly, Tony." Smiling that Susan smile.

"Careful of what you wish for, Suz," he mumbled back, wiping a thin film of oil down the shaft of his titanium driver, holding it out away from his face like a shotgun, as if looking down the barrel. He emitted a sharp little whistle and selected the next club for its bath.

Susan's loving smile was suddenly broken by a strange scene flicking onto the face of the kitchen TV. Shushing Tony, she nudged up the TV's volume with the remote. "This was on before. Listen to this, Tone."

". . . one of the strangest crimes against law and order yet to blot the American landscape," a reporter's voice was saying as the minicam scanned a blue Ford Ranger, then zoomed out to show a stretch of yellow police ribbon wrapped around it, then panned over to the reporter, his square jaw and movie-set hair filling the screen now as his excited voice recounted the story of two young police officers apparently the victims of an inexplicable mock-assassination in a sleepy little beach community. "Madness in the sunshine!" pronounced the reporter's voice with a melodramatic air.

“Moron,” Tony said under his breath. Susan giving him a funny glance.

Now they had one of the victims on, his belly wrapped in white bandages like a mummy. The kid Tony had mugged at in the rearview.

“So I go, ‘Back in your truck *now!’* And the perp does what I tell him, you know? But it was a setup, I guess. Like a trap.”

“So you saw him up-close? You could identify him?”

“Yeah, this close, from me to you. I told our chief, had a funny accent. Puerto Rican, maybe. Dressed like a Rican, too. We’ll get him.”

“Why do you think he didn’t actually kill you?” the reporter asked.

“Screwed up, is all. Gun misfired, probly.”

“Two times?”

“Yeah, well... who knows?” said the kid.

Susan asked Tony out of the side of her mouth, watching the TV, “What kind of lunatic would *do* something like this?”

“Just awful!” Tony said, exaggerating the *awful.* “Isn’t anyone safe from these practical jokers?”

Susan turned to Tony as the TV filled up with a dreamy ad featuring images of a couple of happy-go-lucky retirees strolling down a sunset-perfect beach somewhere, thanking their stockbrokers in voice-over thoughts.

“Oh, Tony. Honestly!”

“It’s a big joke, that’s all it is, don’t you see?”

“A joke.”

“Looks like a practical joke. Brilliant, in a way!”

“It’s no joke, Tony. I’ll tell you what, though. This kinda thing proves how much we need more cops, more gun laws—more protection.”

“Protection from what?”

“From creeps like that.”

“No, Suz, a *creep* would’ve killed ’em. This guy just scared ’em. Know what? I think maybe it was supposed to be a lesson. That’s what it was. They thought *they* had the power, you see? Had the badges and all. But this guy, he was the one with the real power. He had *all* the power, he could've done anything he wanted to them, but he held back."

Tony stopped, saw that look Susan sometimes got on her when he spouted his ideas on things, then added, "So the joke's on them. Maybe, if they think about it hard enough, they'll be better cops when they grow up. He's given them another chance, see—a chance to be *real* officers of the law. What do you think? Could be it, couldn't it?"

Looking at Tony through slants in her eyes, Susan let out a sissing breath. "Well, joke or not, I feel a chill after watching that. Scary stuff." She snapped off the TV and said quietly, "I want you to hold me, Tony."

Tony wiped the golf club he still gripped and set it down. Then he put his arms around his wife's shoulders, his nose brushing hers, looked deep into her hazel eyes, feeling her softness as he wrapped her up, and kissed an ear, telling her beneath his breath, "Thank God I've got you, Suz. Without you, you know, I'd be a raving lunatic myself."

"You sure would," she whispered, hugging him back. And feeling safe again, she closed her eyes.

FOUR

What's in a name, Susan reflected next morning as she washed her face and scrubbed her tiny, pearly white teeth with a soft-bristled brush, smiling at her own features.

She stopped brushing, pouted, and studied her image with a quizzical look. Tilted her head, trying to see it, what Tony had first told her, that her beauty was heart quickening. That's what he'd said, those words.

She thought back to her first innocent blush of teenaged discovery, when she'd tried to figure out if her nose was on straight. What she'd decided was that her eyebrows were too thick, but her mom wouldn't let her trim them. Pencil-thin eyebrows were the rage back then, and she wanted them. Her mom wouldn't relent. The eyebrows stayed.

Seeing them now, those eyebrows Tony loved so much, she giggled at her reflection, remembering something else she hadn't thought of in years: how she scared herself in a mirror the first time she saw her pupils dilate, sure there was something wrong with her, seriously wrong, some terrible disease in her brain. But then they did it again—her hazel irises changed shape, widening and narrowing in dimmer or brighter light. Silly. She wasn't a freak.

So she'd decided at fourteen that she wasn't exactly ugly. Maybe someone besides her mom and dad would call her pretty someday.

Until Tony, most men had more or less ignored her. So for years she never gave much thought to how she looked. Tony told her most men would be intimidated by her beauty. She had a hard time with that.

Still staring at herself in the mirror in the morning, her lips glistening with tiny white bubbles as the brush waited in suspension inches away, the unfinished tooth-brushing made her lose the present in the mirror all over, and she relived the moment when she changed herself the last time, signing the papers following her wedding ceremony. She'd begun to write down in the book 'Susan Cummings,' but writing the capital 'C' stopped her, and she placed a period after the 'C' and wrote out 'Spool.' How she loved being Susan C. Spool!

But 'Susan' was the only one of her names that went back as far as she did. After college, majoring in Political Science and English, the first picked to land a job, hopefully, and the second to gratify her soul, she hadn't managed immediately to locate a career job in government, but instead became a copy editor at a Beltway publishing company. Boring work after a while as it wasn't about poetry or literature of any kind but about the formalities of government, legislative agendas and such. But at least it was a start. It was where Susan bloomed out of the plain little shell she'd decided to live in while in college.

And then when her parents both died suddenly, together, in Susan's early twenties, she'd decided she was free to be whoever she liked.

She'd been adopted at birth by Stan and Sophia Stryeski, the finest parents anyone could imagine, giving and caring, protective and doting parents who had saved and done without for years so that their Susan could go to college. Susan thought of them as her angels, still watching her steps, and she hoped giving their approval to her choices, her way of life.

But when they died as she was crunching through her third year at the publishing house, Susan knew it was time to reinvent herself. She took the last name of her favorite poet, took as well his famous double initials as her own, becoming Susan E. E. Cummings.

And as her grief for her parents dissipated with time, Susan gradually left her academic shell behind her. She changed her hair. She bought nice clothes and a newer car. She started swimming and tennis. Tennis took her to parties and a social life, but no serious relationships. She quit her job, using her inheritance to live on while she searched for a career in the federal government, something of value, something that would have made her mom and dad beam with pride.

Her parents' final gift to her was the most dear of all. Freedom to be herself, to live a full life.

A girlfriend from college told her one day about a job opening she'd just heard about, an Information Officer position at the Department of State. Background in Political Science and English a must.

Susan worked her considerable charm on the people interviewing at State, she studied hard for and passed the appropriate exams, and took up her new life with gusto, arriving ten minutes early every morning, often staying late, getting into it sometimes to the point of exhaustion, forgetting her dull past, trying to put her parents and her childhood to rest. But work, Susan soon discovered, wasn't a cure-all. She needed something more. She needed love.

And then, in her second summer as the new Susan, she flew to Athens late in August for a cruise of the Greek islands, something so many of her college friends had talked about, something Susan had always hoped to do herself. It was impulsive, not how she usually did things. After she got the idea, she decided against it. But a little voice kept after her, urging her to do it. Nobody else she knew could get away on such short notice. Her married girlfriends had husbands to be with, or even children. So she went alone. Which was all right. It was something she wanted to do for Susan. Susan E.E. Cummings.

And on the second morning at sea, approaching Mykonos, the man of her dreams had simply walked up to her at the bow rail, had stood silently next to her and watched the sea with her a moment, before saying in the nicest voice, and still looking out to sea, "I'm Tony Spool."

Susan always thought, later on, that he knew he would find her there.

* * *

After she had told him her name, and watched in delight as his lips became a happy crescent as he learned it, she said, "So, what are you, a Greek god or something? Odysseus?"

"Noohoho," Tony said breezily, looking toward the approaching island of Mykonos. "The gods reside over there," pointing at the white-washed landscape ahead, dotted with windmills, Susan following his tanned arm with her eyes, noticing the strength in his muscled arm, extended off to sea, bristling with silky black little hairs, and the elegant small watch on his wrist, but no wedding band. "Sorry to disappoint," he went on. "I'm a fairly prosaic guy."

He turned then and looked her fully in the face, and Susan saw them for the very first time—those brilliant, estoril-blue eyes, an astonishing sea blue she'd never seen in anyone before. Of haunting intensity. They pulled at her immediately, drew her into him. Like beacons flashing from a lighthouse, warning passing ships to beware. She had a hard time looking away from their light, it was so appealing.

"English?" she quizzed. He'd uttered just a few words, but she figured.

"Yep, British. A Brit. And a very lucky one, having encountered you... a moment I'll never forget!"

"And you're here alone... on this boat full of couples and families? On a vacation?" It was just too good to be true. She held her breath for his answer. She was sure a half dozen kids would come out of nowhere in an instant, yelling 'Daddy! Daddy!' And of course a gorgeous woman.

"On *holiday*," he answered to her closed eyes. "And yes, alone. Until now"—seeing her eyes open, looking into his again—"at least, I trust I'm no longer by myself on this glorious trip!" These words sang with enthusiasm.

"No," Susan responded in disbelief, letting out a pent-up breath slowly. "No, I don't think you are."

He took her hand. His felt so firm. So masculine. She looked down at her pale little fingers sticking out from around his—long, angular and golden brown—sensed their power, and wondered at the things they had done.

Looking again into his eyes she found an enchanting, calm smile all around them. Noticed his thick, curly black eyebrows and long eyelashes, his tough manly skin like kid leather, smooth but rugged, and tanned like a seaman's, as if he lived outdoors, at one with the elements.

Tony Spool's smile infected her mood, and she realized she was nodding happily as she heard him say: "Then you'll accept my invitation to explore this wonderful place with me? You know, seeing you standing here at the railing, I'd hoped that might be what would happen—and now it has! How delightful for us both, don't you think, Susan?"

And so Susan's plans for a pensive vacation, with plenty of free time for planning the next stage of her life, with the intention of engaging only in the most meaningless chitchat with her fellow tourists, ended abruptly as she stepped into the cruise ship's launch with this stranger, this Tony Spool, to begin an exploration of the heart.

* * *

The launch pulled up to the bright, whitewashed concrete dock, and as Tony held out his hand to help her find her feet again, Susan saw all around her something of a fairyland. She was astonished at the clarity, the pale blue clarity, of the Aegean Sea, even here by the shore. Darting schools of drab tiny fish, and not so tiny but vividly colored wrasses and angelfish, raced around the pebbly bottom, all of three feet down but in water so clear it looked as if you could reach out and touch those pebbles, raced zigging and zagging beneath the bright blue hull of the launch, which seemed suspended in the sea's crystal membrane, rocking and floating in a spatial heaven on earth.

Susan walked along the dock apparently mesmerized by this.

"First trip, heh?" Tony interceded. "It *is* a marvelous place."

Susan just loved the way he said 'marvelous.' She didn't think she had ever met anyone who used that word, certainly no one she knew back home, and most decidedly no man. This man lent magic to the word.

And over the next two hours Susan Cummings and Tony Spool wandered around the tiny island together, Tony advising Susan not to buy postcards at the first shops along the seafront but to wait for the shops a couple of streets away, telling her she'd save money that way. Same postcards, better value for the drachma.

It was cool, how smart he was. Worldly, isn't that what it was called?

Not yet touching each other as they strolled, they set out on foot down the brown curving beach, lapped by the gentlest blue waves, only inches high. Up along a slope rising off the beach, the brown sandy soil held endless whitewashed island buildings—private hotels and tiny stucco homes and red-domed churches—all seemingly at rest against an earth that lazed like a sun worshipper whose head languidly touched the faultless azure sky and whose feet were constantly tickled by the bacchic blue-green waters of a bathtub sea.

Life went on lazily and happily around Susan and Tony as they walked the timeless sands of Mykonos.

Just off the beach, beyond the squat bulkhead, they could see tourists slumping along in the heat, inspecting with a sun-blanched stupor unique to the Aegean the street displays of bright pink and blue postcards and colorful tourist books, silkscreen-imprinted T-shirts and handmade leather belts, poking heads into shop after shop, some of the wanderers disappearing up winding white lanes that meandered listlessly through the hilly town.

Little boats bobbed off the beach, tied to their anchor lines: white ones with striking blue stripes and fire-red hulls, blue wooden rowboats with white oars, curious square little cabins on brightly painted fishing boats whose U-shaped hulls hadn't changed in two thousand years. Time captured itself in them, as in their masters—now, at midday, at rest in their white houses spread upon the grottoed hillsides.

Tony bought Susan a cold cola after they'd paced the streets for half an hour under the brightest sun imaginable, and she ran the iced can along her forehead, its frosty aluminum dense with drops of condensation, smiling gratefully at him. Her scalp was damp with sweat, which beaded and trickled down her nose. He wasn't even perspiring.

They climbed one of the steeper whitewashed streets, coming at last to an ancient, desolate churchyard, and Tony took her picture in front of a stucco wall that nearly blinded them with its whiteness in the sun. An old wood door, uneven in shape, hung on two rusted ancient hinges at one spot in the wall; it had been painted countless times to a thick, carmine red.

Susan and her Tony explored another lane, and near its crest they rested on a black-painted cannon, stuck for no apparent reason in the middle of a tiny courtyard, protecting nothing but the sandy soil and the golden brown weeds. Susan watched Tony stretch out his feet in a pair of the most gorgeous leather loafers she thought she had ever seen.

He smiled softly at her, seeing her looking at him, then told her of Mykonos, hinting at its legends, told her it was the isle of lovers and of the gods. The gods here approved of lovers, he said to her. It was easy to believe him, there in that courtyard, sitting with him alone beneath a sky the color of the purest pastel blues in a Matisse painting.

And as they climbed the squat hill at the island's point together, to walk among the curious stumpy windmills which had known renown for centuries, Susan realized how much she enjoyed being with this Tony Spool, this charming Englishman. She found herself thinking of him already as *her* Tony. From the start, she felt absolutely comfortable around him.

At a tiny taverna they stopped for lunch, for what she discovered was the best four-cheese pizza she'd ever tasted, a crisp Greek salad of simple delight, and a tiny glass of retsina wine. Sitting there under the shaded lattice, the sea before them and the brilliant hills of the town behind, Susan thought she might actually be falling in love—not with paradise but with a man she had met only hours before.

As they ate and chatted easily, she found herself studying the face of this wonderful, kind man. She liked him so much! But something else was happening to her, deep in her groin. His sexy nose made her squirm secretly: it was rounded, fleshy but not fat, chiseled like on a Roman statue, moist but not oily... oh, God, she thought, it was *delicious!*

As the food filled her senses, she found her heart filling up, too, and a surprising gladness slowly invading her soul for the first time since she'd become alone in the world, since losing her two guardian angels.

Her loss seemed to be fading like spots slowly disappear after staring into a glaring light, leaving a beautiful, new light in their place—shining within, distantly but distinctly.

While it gathered in her soul, this new light, a lulling fragrance from the sea whiffed tenderly at her.

Now she focused on his lips, fractured by tiny muscles expressing the most subtle movement, fringed by whisker stubs, and of a color somewhere between pale tan and the pink of clouds catching the sun's fleeting rays as it dipped into the western horizon.

Watching those lips, she realized that Tony was saying "I don't know anything about you, Susan. Please tell me."

And, watching those lips settle and bunch together, looking up into those blue eyes that were so startling and so beautiful, there was nothing in the world she would not have told him, at this moment.

"A career girl... waiting for love to find her," she said into the eyes.

"Ah, well now," Tony whispered back to her, his lips twisting into the most wonderful little smile, "methinks we may have taken care of that—what do you say?"

Susan blushed, felt heat in her face, dew in her eyes.

"I can't believe this is happening to me," she answered. Then she giggled like a schoolgirl, embarrassed. "Pinch me!"

"Well, I always believe the emotions sort themselves out. Tell me about Susan Cummings, her life so far."

"Not very exciting... wonderful childhood. Great friends in school. Some sports, field hockey in high school, swimming in college. Just varsity stuff. University of Colorado. Major in PolySci and Lit. Fond of poets and soft music, crazy about great singers."

Susan found she had fired these facts machine gun-style in Tony's direction. He seemed enchanted by her every word, looking dreamily at her with those mysterious blue eyes of his.

But suddenly she stopped, and a sadness overtook her face as the old blinding spots flashed again into her soul.

"What is it?" Tony asked, seeing the pain.

"Oh Tony! I lost my parents two years ago. I came here to celebrate their memory. It still hurts every day," she added softly, squeezing the bridge of her nose between her eyebrows.

Tony took one of her hands in his.

"It's all right," she said into those eyes, and watching his mouth, to read his heart: "they've brought me here, they've brought me you."

She liked what she saw in his lips when she said this. She squeezed his hand.

But immediately there came a hooting from the cruise ship anchored out in the deep harbor, killing the mood and snapping Susan out of her melancholy, confusing her senses. She told Tony in a decisive tone, "We shouldn't be tardy, and we must not miss the launch. Let's go!"

But Tony calmed her, put his arm reassuringly around the shoulders of this lovely girl he hardly knew, beginning to *adore* her, touched by her as he had not been touched in the past by any of the women he had known, never really expecting to find such a wonderful human being wrapped in such a perfect package. He hadn't till now believed that inner and outer beauty could come so perfectly together like this. It was something he had searched for, all his life. And here he was, holding it in his arms. Perhaps his life was savable after all, he felt.

And in the following days, as the cruise ship visited a succession of gleaming island dots in the Greek world sizzling under the August sun, exploring them together and spending the evenings on the ship in each other's company, Susan and Tony came closer and closer together, fell deeply and completely in love. Each with the other. Each for a special, selfish reason.

On the last day of the cruise, the ship sailed into the vast harbor of a place of legendary beauty which had exploded out of chaos eons ago. The waters off its port were so deep that no anchor could reach bottom.

A rocking launch carried a hundred passengers at a time to the modern cement dock at the base of its steep, forbidding, rocky hills.

While others ran to get in line for the funicular cars, Tony and Susan took to the ancient path that zigzagged up the hills for hundreds of yards. They passed donkeys and hardier tourists going up and down the stony lane.

In a little while, after catching their wind again, they strolled arm in arm through the dazzling white streets in the town of Thera, nestled along the crest of the crater of this blown-out volcano of antiquity called Santorini. Surrendering to its ageless charm, they spent two hours wandering its awkward rocky lanes, up one and down another, stopping often to rest at lookout points high above the harbor. The whitewashed brilliancy blinded the eye, the hilly homes stared silently at the sea, and the town's terraced streets teemed with tourists. Susan and Tony hardly saw any of it.

White rooftops and church domes and canopies over open-air tavernas shimmered in the sun, and a delicate haze spread out over the sea to an indistinct horizon. The brown rim of the ancient volcano arced in a semicircle, enveloping the harbor for miles, losing the present day in its mythic past.

As their precious time alone here came to a close, Susan and Tony stopped abruptly before a window of one of the seemingly numberless jewelry stores of the town, and their eyes fell in unison upon the least pretentious, but most sparkling, diamond ring in the display.

A wisp of sea breeze touched their close faces, damp with the heat.

Susan's eyes searched Tony's, asking him. Their blue pools held her heart. She watched his lips, then tasted them for the first time. He kissed her, first hardly brushing his lips against hers, then eagerly and passionately, enfolding her lips in his own, and at last, holding her shoulders firmly in his hands and her soul in his eyes, he said ever so softly to her, in a whisper only an angel could hear, "Let's do it..."

And so began their extraordinary romance.

FIVE

It appeared to be a palace, a white marble palace of some sultan, some king, or even a movie star.

Susan steered with special care, with deliberate slowness, through the high-arched gate made of wrought iron and painted in gleaming black and gold, showing off artistic symbols of power, lions *passant*, their extended claws and fierce growls fixed forever in metal, and images of crossed swords of medieval style beneath a crown studded with jewels, the "jewels" of iron painted emerald green, ruby red, and intense silver enamelled to suggest the sparkle of diamonds.

Tony expected to see Queen Elizabeth and her entourage at any moment now.

They rolled up to a portico and Susan stopped her little Mercedes in response to the white-gloved direction of a valet parker.

"I love this car, Tony," Susan thanking him again, "and it's already paying dividends on my career. People notice."

"I bought it for your career, and because it was as lovely as you, darling," omitting that its champagne color reminded him of her hair and smooth tawny skin, its sleek curves of her graceful body, its assuredness of her soul. Tony found his door opening in the care of white gloves.

Susan clasped Tony's hand as they approached the mansion.

"And besides, I wanted to get you out of that death-trap you were driving. Something runs into you in this baby, you walk away."

"Isn't that the Speaker of the House?" Susan said, gesturing with her head towards a man surrounded by sycophants like hyenas circling downed meat.

Tony sighed as they approached the greeting line at the top of the steps.

"If you happen to spot the *President*, let him know I'm getting up a foursome for Wednesday, will ya, hun?"

"Now, Tony. Don't."

"I was just thinking, Suz... you know, what a shame the hostess isn't somewhere inside, front door shut, and some bushes nearby?"

Susan shushed him with her eyes, knowing what Tony meant, seeing him running through the familiar routine of his favorite practical joke, ringing the door bell of someone expecting them for dinner, then hiding in the shrubs as they answered the door, watching them shake their heads, close the door again, usually peeking out a window to see who might be there, then surprised to see Tony's beaming puss inches from their face, looking in at them looking out.

"Just don't," Susan warned.

* * *

Appearances can be deceiving, they say. And so it was here, not the palace or mansion of some head of state, but an ego-booster of a Washington banker, formerly CEO of a savings and loan currently in receivership under the auspices of the Resolution Trust Corporation. His newly reborn S&L was now called a bank, and he was called a banker. His former creditors would be duly obliged by the federal agency. He himself enjoyed the elite privileges of a "friend" of committees on banking, international commerce, tax law, and the environment. His bank made modest but steady contributions to the "campaign war chests" of legislators from both parties. He was a true Washington success story, and his house and gardens among the most splendid in all of Georgetown.

As he and Susan approached the head of the greeting line, Tony reflected on this banker. Tony had read quite a bit about Ira K. Greenblatt and his escapades in the world of finance. Tony regarded him as a thief of the public trust. Tony had even considered him as a target, but had abandoned the idea as futile, knowing another just like him would step into his place. Tony sighed again. And steeled himself.

"Mrs. Greenblatt? Or is it *Sophia Loren?*" Tony pronounced towards the banker's wife, at the head of the line. "I should think the latter!"

"And ah… you must be Tony Spool!" she said in response. "You naughty boy, your reputation precedes you, I'm afraid. Do try to let *me* be the life of *this* party. However, your compliment is well received, let me assure you."

"And sincerely meant," Tony put in for good measure, nodding in her direction, seeing a woman in her late fifties pretending to be thirty-five.

And in moments he and Susan had passed the threshold, finding themselves amid a swarm of chattering black ties, business suits, and mostly expensive gowns. Susan as always was attired for the occasion. But Tony was alone in the crowd in his mulberry-colored Armani jacket, his Italian slacks of silky complexion, his textured *cupro* shirt buttoned to the neck, and the most beautiful pink-and-yellow bow tie. His shoes of deep black patent leather gleamed. His shirt sported an elegantly monogrammed "TS" over its pocket.

Some of Susan's people from State approached them right away, others looking their way too.

For Tony and Susan Spool, obviously rich, obviously well connected, had become a hot couple in Washington society of late. It behooved anyone wanting an advancement to be known by them. Tony enjoyed the irony of this new position he found himself in, relishing the fun he could have with these stuffed shirts because of his independence from them. He fired up the charm everyone expected of him as he settled in to take the room.

Susan said Tony's way, "This is Doree and Bernard, and Georgie and Adeline. My closest colleagues at State." They all shook hands. "Looks like we represent the State Department here today," Susan said, looking around.

"Monitors of world peace, you lot?" Tony began with them, thinking the one introduced as Doree had a lovely muscularity to her arms and thighs, shown off by her elegant silk pants suit. He admired strength wherever he found it. It was sexy, too.

Bernard said, "Well, hardly, Mr. Spool," running his hand over his balding head of graying black hair combed straight back.

"Now, now. Don't be modest," Tony rejoined. "And please call me Tony. Everyone does. My Susan's told me all about your admirable qualities, about how much she's enjoyed working with all of you since her promotion last summer."

"She's a great boss, and friend," Doree contributed, smiling at Susan.

"Same here," Tony said. "We're great friends, and she's in charge!"

"Tony..." Susan injected.

"It's serious work, though," Adeline chirped up, "and we do our best, along with your Susan, to help make the world safer."

Tony's left eye faltered ever so slightly, uncontrollably, taking in this second woman, her brown hair pulled into a taut ponytail, looking plain in her department-store clothes, without makeup, not even lipstick. Not much fun, this one, Tony thinking, saying "I'm sure of it, I admire the stamina all of you possess... I myself could not *handle* the stress. And I don't like deadlines, either: too much like work!" he pronounced with obvious self-mockery.

Georgie said "Susan's told us a little about you, how you've been lucky in life. About your cars. Yet we've never met." Georgie was dressed in a dark pinstripe suit and happy multi-colored tie of the latest fashion. His hair was light blond and bushy, cropped in a serious manner but still so full he seemed more of an outdoorsman than a paper pusher. Tony liked him immediately, sensed he wasn't particularly comfortable at this party.

"Ah, well, the Lord's smiled upon this miserable soul now and again,

I'll admit. Mostly in bringing me Susan," he kept up, taking her right hand in his left, their arms dangling.

An awkward moment of silence ensued. Tony smiling at all four of Susan's colleagues. They stole furtive glances around the room.

Tony reached a hand secretly into one pocket of his jacket, catching the eyes of the pretty Doree, winked at her and stated matter-of-factly, "What's this doin' behind your ear?" He produced a gleaming gold coin in his fingertips as though it had just formed itself out of thin air.

"What's that? How'd you *do* that?" Doree asked, thankfully innocent of this old magic move.

"It's a double eagle," Tony answered, "Twenty gold dollars, one of your own, I mean American. Pretty and bright as yourself," Tony's eyes capturing Doree's in their bright blue pools, rolling the coin over the knuckles of his right hand, the other State people closing in on him now to see the trick. They all watched his hand work the coin over his knuckles, little finger forward, then disappear beneath his palm to reappear at the small finger.

"How *do* you do that?" Georgie in the bright tie asked, reiterating, watching Tony's hand with considerable focus, his face one big smile.

Tony rolled the coin one more time beneath his palm, saying, "It's the simple art of deception, that's all," all five fingers turning up before them, rising slightly in a sort of gesture the Pope might make in giving a blessing. The coin had disappeared.

"Oh, neat!" exclaimed Doree.

"Yeah, real good," Georgie complimented. "I wanna learn that!"

"I've also got your wallet!" Tony said in response, raising his thick black eyebrows, producing it in his left hand. "You've gotta keep an eye on Tony Spool, you know."

Bernard, with the balding head, asked "What kind of work did you say you used to do, Mr. Spool?" Beaming Georgie reclaimed his wallet.

"Oh, magic of a kind. Numbers, mainly. Banking, money, boring drivel. I'm through with all that; now I'm what we call in Britain a *sportsman*, happily married," beaming towards Susan, "wallowing in domestic bliss by night and the evils of the golf course by day."

"A duffer?" Georgie asked gleefully.

"More an expensive habit, wouldn't you say?" Tony asked him back, adding "Something on the order of a sickness!"

"That's golf, all right," Georgie admitted, laughing at himself.

"Tony Spool, a man of many talents," Doree said Susan's way, a happy face watching her colleague Susan and her husband, wishing she'd gotten there first, Tony smiling back and squeezing his wife's hand again. Georgie was still smiling. Only Bernard and Adeline found themselves beyond the charm of this British jokester, their poker faces expressionless, not impressed by his cheap magic tricks, dismissing him as of no interest to people of serious natures.

"Any other hobbies?" Bernard asked solemnly, his thin face peering like a falcon at Tony's wide-open expression.

Starting to say something more, Tony heard a sort of rustle behind his back as the din of chatter in the room seemed to be nearing him, filling his ears, turning with Susan in unison to see the approach of the host and hostess, brushing their way through mere mortals.

"Tony," the hostess fairly yelled his way, speaking as though she'd known him for years, "Tony Spool, this is my husband!"

A man of great stature held out his hand to shake Tony's, dressed in a white brocade tuxedo, jeweled gold stickpin on his lapel, his graying hair short-cut and smoothed down. Bifocals on his nose.

"I'm Ira Greenblatt," said the suit.

"Pleased," Tony replied.

Shirley Greenblatt gave a look of reproach at Susan's four colleagues, especially at the harsh-looking Adeline, standing by her and Tony. Why did her husband always insist on inviting such lowlifes, supposing they might one day be of use to him?

"I understand you're a fellow banker."

"Used to be. Different league, though. Private stuff. Retired now."

"Well," Greenblatt retorted, a pause after the word for emphasis, "once a banker, always a banker at heart, no?"

"I suppose," Tony agreeing in obeisance. "Just a private investor, though, I'm afraid, these days. Living off interest on my funds, a modest income by your standards."

"Money be damned!" growled Greenblatt. "Once you have it, it's of no importance, right?" looking all around him for the room's approval, and getting it, rolling up his nose and shaking his head, Tony taking in more of Shirley Greenblatt while listening to all this, a woman of luxurious proportions, hair bobbed just above shoulder length, probably dyed to the color of henna, maybe not even all of it her own, her face taut from various tucks. Her evening gown shimmering.

"Glamorous outfit," Tony said her way, right past her husband. "It suits you. Versace?"

"Now you be careful with my wife!" Greenblatt blasted at him, chortling. "She'll have you for hors d'oeuvres!" And many laughed in the background.

"Not Italian," Shirley Greenblatt minded Tony. "French, custom made, for me," winking towards her husband, asking him "What was the name of that designer in Paris?"

"Louis something. You know, whatzisname? I have it in my checkbook somewhere."

"Well, he's famous. Does lots of film stars... and these threads, they ain't made outta fake gold!" She flashed the folds of her gown for all eyes to see.

"Better not be!" the banker barked, "not for forty G's!"

"Stop it, Ira," Shirley scolded her husband, dragging 'stop' out to three syllables, loving his bragging, taking Tony in her arm away from him and from Susan. "And I *am* ready for some hors d'oeuvres, I can tell you!"

Tony looking back over his shoulder at Susan disappearing in the crowd, shrugging his shoulders, Susan smiling her okay back at him.

Flashing an immense rectangular diamond ring in Tony's face, Shirley Greenblatt said into his ear, "Oh I'm not the hot bod I was twenty years ago, but I've still got the instinct and the passion, you know what I mean, Tony? I'm not one to pass up an opportunity," she growled luridly in his ear, holding his hand to her hip, Tony trying not to flinch. "You know what my Ira used to call me, Tony? He used to call me his *jaguarundi*, his wildcat!"

Tony for once was speechless.

"Come this way, Tony," Shirley Greenblatt insisted, pulling him along by the hand through the swirling orbs of Washington socialites in her great room, "come and meet my senator!"

A massive, larger than life man stood there, cigar in hand, in beautiful black attire, holding court. But Shirley Greenblatt possessed him.

"Sam! Meet my Mr. Gorgeous, Tony Spool," she insisted, waving off those around the senator.

"Senator," Tony said at the man, extending his hand, but it was not taken.

"Tony… oh yes, Tony *Spool*, connected to State by marriage—the best way, I might add!" he snorted at Shirley Greenblatt. She winked back approval. "So, Tony, what do *you* think of cholesterol? We were just deciding to make it illegal, all of us." And the senator popped a couple of hors d'oeuvres into his mouth.

"Export it to the UK," Tony suggested. "We don't mind it a bit over there. It's kind of a national pastime."

"Atta boy!" the senator thundered. "A man with his head on straight, I can tell right away."

"To be safe, though," Tony added, "I eat a little yogurt and fat-free stuff. Don't know what the payoff will be, do you?"

"A few more years, that's the payoff, my boy. But *boring* years!" he bellowed out. "I like excitement myself. If it don't taste good, I don't want it!" His turgid lips pulled at the end of his dead cigar. "But I understand you're in money," he said, continuing, looking around him. "Now that's something we all find exciting."

Shirley Greenblatt said, "Like the stock market. Right, Sam?"

"Oh yeah! I *love* the stock market. What about you, Tony? You in stocks?"

"Too wild a ride for me, at this point," Tony answered truthfully.

"The wilder it gets, the more you like it!" came from behind the senator's shoulder, the voice of banker Greenblatt. "We have a lot of our capital in stocks. Best way to prop up the old P&L statement, heh senator?"

They all smiled roundly, except Tony.

"No," Tony admitted, not liking any of these people, gamblers with other people's savings, "no, I'm not in stocks right now. Right now I'm in interest. T-bills."

"Oh dear God!" Shirley Greenblatt shrieked mockingly.

Senator Sam Winterbern, Republican from Idaho, stared histrionically at Tony, his mouth wide open, a vast grin coming on his face, exclaiming abroad, "Oh yeah, folks! Here's one for you! Investing in government debt! Shall we name him a patriot?"

Tony stared blankly at him.

"Tony, Tony!" the senator said back at him, seeing his expressionless face, more soberly now, handing out his wisdom, "Get in stocks! It's a sure thing. We're all in it together, Wall Street and us. Our friends will get us out in time, don't worry."

The senator held annoyingly onto Tony's silky Armani jacket with his greasy fingers, grasping at Tony's psyche with his greasy morals. Tony smiled anemically at this bloated farce, hoping someone, even Shirley Greenblatt, would rescue him, thinking of the Lord and wishing for just a moment, fantasizing he knew, no chance of it, wishing he could dissolve this slob back into the puddle he had hatched out of.

At which Shirley Greenblatt contributed her only thought of the day. She said, to Tony, in a genuine question, "What are you, then, at leisure?"

"Absolutely," Tony said emphatically. "Absolutely! You've read Thorstein Veblen's *Theory of the Leisure Class*, Mrs. Greenblatt?"

Shirley Greenblatt looked as if she'd stubbed her big toe.

Her husband jumped in with "Thor—what?"

The senator grabbed more refreshments off a passing tray, and handed a glass of white wine Tony's way, Tony taking hold of the tall slim crystal glass, now asking the senator "You've read Veblen, haven't you, Senator?"

"A hundred years ago," he replied hesitatingly. "He's pretty dated."

"Oh, I beg to differ, not dated at all, Senator. Bit queer perhaps, even in his time..."

The tone of the party around Tony had quieted down considerably. His response to the senator and the banker had not been of the required nature.

"One of *those!*" Shirley Greenblatt suggested, knowingly, hoping for a new pavement of discussion.

Tony frowned at her, rolled his head side-to-side, then smiled at her, saying quietly, "'Queer' in the old-fashioned sense of the word, *Shirley*. You know. Odd, touch mad by everyone else's standards, a contrarian thinker."

"Personally I'll take the modern version, myself," she concluded for the group. "Easier to deal with." And they all started chatting away with each other over nothing.

Tony tried to think of something witty to say, but nobody was listening to him anymore. He'd been dismissed, as he'd hoped.

Then he found himself rescued from these bores, but it wasn't by Shirley Greenblatt. Doree, the pretty colleague of Susan's, hooked an arm unexpectedly around Tony's elbow as he stood there, feeling alone, looking alone.

"Take a walk with me," she suggested.

Tony raised his eyebrows in a facial sigh.

"Thank you. Really, thanks."

As they reached a balcony overlooking the banker's vast gardens, aglow now with the colors of late summer flowers, and green everywhere from the moist climate, Doree told Tony "You know what *un*official Washington calls Shirley Greenblatt? We call her Shirley 'Spleenshat.'"

"Yeah," Tony agreed, "a good one, that!" He chuckled at the joke. "*Nice* lady..."

Doree looked adorable in her pants suit. Her hair was jet-black, and she smiled a lot.

Tony considered her fine anatomical qualities while they chatted each other up, immediately admiring her zygomatic bone, producing those high cheeks of classic beauties. In Doree it was as good as it gets.

"So what was that I heard, about your being of the leisure class?"

"Not me," Tony saying. "I was talking about a book. But there's no fault in being idle; believe me, it's a great pastime. It's the preferred pastime of all good philosophers. Even Bertrand Russell praised idleness."

"Oh, yes, Bertrand Russell. I read that in college, in my sophomore year," Doree answered. "That was quite good. Don't suppose many here have ever read it."

"Well, I particularly like Russell," Tony volunteered. "He was an interesting cogitator," while saying this, at work analyzing Doree's structure, which he found entirely pleasing, moving her about the balcony with his own body movements, for a better look, taking her eyes occasionally into his.

He saw enough to appreciate thick femoral bones and musculature beneath her pants, giving her naturally well-muscled legs. Strength again. She turned her back to him, admiring the gardens, maybe pretending to?

"How about a little info on yourself as a cogitator?"

Watching Doree's finely toned gluteus maximus as she turned, imagining the curve of the small of her back, at the base of her spine, Tony thought of her not sexually but as an athlete, a strong female, certainly a candidate for a vivacious life, perfect for the new civilization. But caught in a bureaucratic bog, he sighed inwardly. She deserved better.

"Tony?" she asked, for his eyes seemed far away.

"Oh, there's not so much to talk about. Susan may have mentioned it, I'm retired now, pension from the British bank I served, a few lucky investments," Tony offered, still musing over Doree's physical nature.

"So now you're free to be at leisure, to enjoy yourself."

"Exactly, you got it. And why not?" running his eyes easily across her pelvic girdle, seeing a hipbone with a broad iliac crest, producing nicely flared hips. A mature woman, a great candidate. Lesser men might have seen an object of great sexual desire; Tony managed to apply his considerable knowledge of anatomy to this woman, this excellent example of feminine beauty, of physical grace, much like his own Susan.

But his chain of thought he found interrupted, as well as his conversation, as a bitchy Shirley Greenblatt reappeared, stealing him away with the hissing words "No man-baiting at *my* party" directed towards Doree, waving her off with that big diamond flashing. "Excuse us, darling, but my senator wants to see Tony again," taking Tony inside the great room now, taking him to Senator Winterbern. And then the senator took him aside, out of earshot, gripping Tony's left bicep forcefully.

"You understand," he insisted in a low voice, "you never heard anything about Wall Street here, from me. I'm telling you as a friend, but also because you're new to this circle." His mouth worked on some delicate foodstuff.

"Oh, I never heard anything like that," getting a smile from the senator. "And I couldn't, could I? I mean, collusion would be illegal."

The senator frowned, demonstrating his superior influence over this Tony Spool character, loosening his hold on Tony's arm.

"Listen, Tony," he advised, "the *proper* people are just above the law, just a smidgen above. The law is the law, but it must be worked with, however unyielding it may appear, massaged you might say, to the comfort level. Its principles of course must be guarded, indeed *protected* against abuse by the majority, against sheer anarchy." The senator smiled easily now.

"We must stand in the light, willing to fight," Tony intruded.

"Poetic, but true enough, true enough. You've got it, Tony, I think you've got it. Vigilance on behalf of the law is crucial. We must guard each other's backs."

"And enforcement?" Tony asked, already figuring the answer.

"Well, enforcement must be rigid, even harsh, if society is to be prevented from breaking down altogether." The senator touched his bulging lips with a napkin, in a dainty gesture.

Tony stared at this man, this overfed monster in Brooks Brothers clothing, considering how civilization might be better off without him. But he uttered only "And your point is, Senator?"

"My point is, Tony," finished the senator, starting to wheeze now, "we in Congress have the law on our side. We reshape it every working day. More than that, more than anything, we have the *power* behind the law. Having only the law, you know, is meaningless . . ."

"Finally found you!" Susan's voice came to him, nearing him and the senator, a welcomed relief. "Ready to go? I see you've been having fun, but I have to get to work tomorrow, eight a.m."

Both of them shaking the senator's hand, a satisfied face on the senator, now working their way to the portico where they'd left their car, Shirley Greenblatt's stident voice telling someone nearby about their other house, the mansion in Beverly Hills, which they used in the winter, when 'Lion's Lair' was closed up, its gardens dead in the cold, ignoring Tony now, writing him off, and his wife as well, no matter what Ira wanted. They bored her. She turned her back their way, Susan and Tony's.

And as they got into Susan's car, Tony looked over at his wife, saying, "If that wasn't a labor of love, I don't know what is!"

* * *

Just passing midnight, hours after he and Susan left the party, Tony sat alone in his dim office, in a contemplative mood. Susan was sound asleep upstairs, tucked in safe and sound as Tony liked it, and the rest of the house was dark. Only a single halogen light broke the blackness in Tony's office, and in Tony's soul.

Having trouble putting aside the sour mood the party had created in him, feeling melancholy and angry at the same time, he had been listening over and over to the Adagio in G Minor reputedly written early in the seventeenth century by the Venetian composer Albinoni. It was Tony's favorite of all. He usually discovered a profound, but odd, strength in it. Tonight it worked on him gradually.

Like him, the adagio was deceptive. It sounded like a product of the Renaissance, but it was really a modern work, an impostor.

If only he could get permission, an official okay, to do the senator, he was thinking, *if only*. Knowing it would never happen. Fantasizing, figuring his approach to it in detail, working it out in his mind. Knowing too that such an act carried considerable risk with it, and to what end? Only another like the senator would step into his absence. It would not lead anywhere worthwhile. Nothing but impulse suggested assassinating the senator; no sign had directed his thoughts to it.

But under the influence of the rising strains of Albinoni's adagio, lulled by its lilting lyricism, Tony slipped into something of a trance, thinking how painful, how agonizing, the senator's death should be. Like the devastating heart attack the senator deserved.

Tony's choice, above all, would be the garotte, holding the lumbering, panicking body close to him as he strangled life from it. Suffocation for a rapacious brute. That would be true justice.

As the adagio began to repeat itself, he suddenly felt relieved, dismissing Senator Winterbern as meaningless, knowing besides that killing anyone had to be swift, immediate. All his training taught him that. He'd let the coming heart attack take care of the senator. Maybe it would be painful enough.

He slid aside the built-in maple bookcase beside his desk, sliding it on its swivel axis, to reveal a massive gray safe. Spinning open its five-tumbler lock, he retrieved a small leather case holding trays of coins, each one snuggled in a leather-lined, two-inch-square hole made of green velvet. Portraits of Nero and Commodus and other Roman madmen looked out at him from the ensconcements of the top tray.

Tony moved aside two trays, and from the third he picked up a gold piece measuring an inch and a half across, but so thin as to almost disappear when held sideways. On its face Tony admired the austere visage of Queen Elizabeth the First of England. She wore a protective ruff about her neck, a bejeweled dress, and a crown. Her nose in profile seemed bony and gaunt, even in gold, her face slightly oval. To Tony, her mouth always seemed fixed in a pensive, half-puckering smile.

She was nearly four hundred years old now. But to Tony, her political cunning, her famed ability to say just enough but never, ever reveal herself to anyone, made her always young, and forever inspiring.

And that's what Tony found in her now, absolving his former thoughts. She had remained in control amidst a host of scoundrels and threats in her own time. She had led a significant life.

Tony put her down gently into her soft green velvet home on his coin tray, touching her face with his fingertip. He sealed up the safe, and hid Elizabeth from the modern world again. She was one of his secret treasures.

Weary from the day, a day of forces ripping at his psyche, Tony touched the keyboard of his sleeping laptop PC, customarily his final act of the day, and found he had an e-mail. He was too tired tonight, he'd close down and read it in the morning. But no, maybe it was important.

He called up the message. It couldn't have been briefer. It simply said, 'Nine Ten Nine. Haberdasher.' It was not signed.

Sitting there, sleepy eyes upon the screen, having forgotten about God for much of the day, Tony felt the trill of blood flow back into his heart, and his mouth slowly transmogrified into a grotesque smile, his soul into a saintlike state of supreme wellbeing.

SIX

Funny how events coincide in life sometimes. Three of them worked out in just the right sequence for Tony. And in quick order.

Susan said, sipping decaf French vanilla at the breakfast table, "You're up early today. When did you come to bed? I was pooped and couldn't wait for you."

"Didn't expect you to," Tony mumbled at her over his shoulder as the toast popped up. "Here you are, mah dear!"

He spooned an omelet made of egg whites and red peppers out onto Susan's opalescent pink plate.

"Looks delish!"

"And... our magical mystery bread, toasted to perfection."

"Like our life. How could it get any better, tell me that, Tony."

"You could tell me State's sending you to Europe this fall, that would make it better."

"Why?" Susan asked, rolling out the word a little, wrinkling down her eyebrows over a forkful of omelet. "Don't tell me you found out."

"Found out what, love?"

"Don't be coy with me, Tony. You *know*, don't you?" She shook her fork at him. "Who told you? Doree? At the party? I'll kill her."

Eating his omelet, Tony chortled. "I don't know anything, honestly.

What are you talking about?"

"Well, why'd you say that, about going to Europe?"

"Because of the e-mail I got last night, just before turning in. I'm going to London, beginning of October. Board of Directors' meeting at the bank, some sort of emergency confab, probably over one of the currency crises in Asia. I *told* them to watch out, it's risky, these thrown-together democracies haven't the infrastructure—"

"Whoa, whoa," Susan charged into his verbal barrage, waving her knife bearing a swatch of butter at its tip. "Slow down, boy."

Tony found he had toppled his coffee cup. Brown fluid stained the Italian lace table cover.

"Oops," he admitted, watching the stain spread.

"So you're going, too?"

"Too?" Tony asked, genuinely.

"Doree didn't ruin my surprise?"

"Doree didn't say anything. What surprise?"

"Tony, hand me the marmalade." Susan rolled her eyes up toward the ceiling. She puckered her mouth, saying "Tony Spool," her eyes fastening now on his, still with a perplexed look in them, "you are exasperating, you truly are!"

He passed over the jar of marmalade and Susan spread it thick, very thick, over her toast. She took a big bite and munched it slowly, deliberately masticating.

Not eating, not moving a muscle, Tony watched her.

Washing down the toast with black coffee, she explained.

"I was saving this. When you've gone to England for meetings at the bank, I've wanted to go with you, but my job always precluded. This year, however… this year, not only isn't my job getting in the way, my job is *sending* me to London. In October. So there!"

Tony laughed out loud. "Well I'll be damned!" he exclaimed.

Susan laughed, too, lightening up. Smiling at Tony, whose intense eyes rounded softly, tiny crow's feet at their corners, his long black eyelashes outlining the glowing blue irises.

"How I love you, Tony! I don't think anyone could ever damn you, no matter what you did."

"So," he said, "a holiday together in the greatest city in the world."

"Not exactly," Susan corrected. "Some time together, definitely. But they're not sending me on a paid vacation."

"Of course. Me neither." Putting on a good face.

"Toast me up another slice, please. And I'll tell you about it."

* * *

When Susan left for the office, Tony washed up and then drove over to the golf range with his clubs in the trunk.

All the while he batted balls out past two hundred yards, he kept wondering at this coincidence. So Susan would be with him in London. If only he knew why London had summoned him. Would this make his duty easier, or tougher? Thinking it meant less to explain away, as well as time together. Maybe it *would* be a sort of holiday. He smiled secretly. Coincidence could indeed be sweet. Maybe coincidence would bring good luck, good luck and success.

Trying for three hundred yards, he broke down his swing to focus on the leverage of the stroke, and topped the ball. It sliced to the right maybe a hundred yards.

Just like life, he mused, frowning at his club. Saying to the driver, and then to himself, you sure don't need any special concentration: just do what you trained into your muscle memory, and loosen up, don't think too much.

Shaking out his shoulders he placed another ball on the tee, stood behind it looking out down the fairway at the "target," stepped up and swung almost without thinking. The ball sailed, seeming to pull higher and higher as it gained distance, landing in the center of the fairway right near the marker that was painted bright yellow and had the numbers "300" inside a black circle.

Tony stood there, no one else nearby, staring down the fairway.

Dense trees stretched along each side of the green. Sand bunkers marred the grassy path here and there. Obstacles. Traps. Clear blue sky smiled down on duffers.

Although pleased with himself, an odd sensation overtook him. He felt a curious sense of foreboding. This meant something, but what?

Inexplicably Tony's mind drifted to ballistics. Three hundred yards. Nine hundred feet. A high-calibre bullet could traverse the distance in a third of a second. He blinked. So what? A path right down the middle, he thought, true on to target. A dead shot. He blinked again.

A *sign*? Nah, dismissing it, shaking his head, shaking it off. How could it be a sign? It was a stupid thought.

He left the rest of the basket of balls unused where they sat around the tee, carried his clubs back to the car, and drove over to see his travel agent.

When he got home, Tony found the third coincidence waiting for him. First there had been the e-mail, which he told Susan was from the bank. Next came Susan's news of going to London at almost the same time Tony had been summoned to appear. That made two. And now the third: a catalogue from an auction house in London which Tony had opened and thumbed through distractedly, without interest, until he came upon the full-page color photographs of an item for which he'd been waiting for years. He stared at it blankly, hardly believing what he saw, then flipping the pages back to the opening of the sale. There he read: "At Christie's Auction Rooms, Wednesday 11 October 1999, 10 a.m. Sharp."

"Well I'll be damned," he said to no one.

He laughed out loud, in disbelief, realizing he needn't have even mentioned the e-mail to Susan, had he only waited another few hours. Going to this auction would have been mandatory for him, Susan would have understood that.

But now he had two excuses to be going to London in a few weeks. Thinking, wasn't life funny?

Coincidence, Tony decided, was a gift from God. Surely something significant lay ahead.

Tony found himself smiling like a schoolboy, almost giddy in anticipation of a good time, certain as well that, whatever duty he was being called upon to perform in London, it would be a contribution to the project that increasingly spoke to his psyche and taxed his energies.

In the kitchen, making dinner plans, he thought he perceived a high-pitched sound coming from his study, but when he went back to his desk all he found was the auction catalogue laying where he'd left it.

Turning to leave the room, a distant-sounding shrill made him look towards the desk. The room was still, quiet. The mysterious sound had been like a scream, but now was gone.

Tony saw the catalogue was open to the color photos again. Had he opened the catalogue? He couldn't remember.

He looked down at the photos illustrating a large gold coin with a waist-length portrait of a man wearing armor and a crown on his head, and holding against his shoulder a long sword.

Tony smiled at it. Below the portrait was the date, 1575, and in Latin the words 'Prepared for Either.' Indeed, Tony thought.

He mouthed over and over to himself the Latin legend on the other side of the coin: 'To Spare the Humbled and Subdue the Proud.'

He patted the photos, closed the catalogue, picked up the telephone and dialed a long number.

"Simon," he said into the phone, "Tony Spool here. Yes? You knew I'd call? I just *today* got the catalogue. Yes of course I'm coming! See you the day before the sale. We'll view the coin together. Yes, good... And, Simon? My wife's coming as well, after the sale... yes that's right! Unh huh, we'll *definitely* have a do, dinner or something. See you then. Right. Ta."

And then, happy as can be, Tony went about the rest of his day, making a scrumptious baked fish from a special Greek recipe for dinner. He and Susan turned in early, and made mad love for nearly an hour.

* * *

In the middle of the night, Tony's demons struck again.

The little boy yelled over and over, "Mummie, Mummie, Mummie!" Leather straps bound his small body to the bench. A huge man stood over him, brandishing a thin whip, lashing at his backside repeatedly.

"Defiance will not be tolerated at this school, do you hear me, boy? Defy me, and you'll have the switch to answer to! When will you learn?"

And as the leather stung his tender flesh, the boy's tears turned into a fury, his mouth into a vicious grin, and the silent words 'Die! Die! Die, you bastard!' stole the pain from his mind, and gave him endurance.

"Leave 'mummie' out of this, do you hear? This is between you and me, boy, between you and me!"

And as the lash flecked at his bloodied back, Tony twisted and yelled out in his sleep, awakening Susan next to him. Naked and sweaty, he awoke, and clung to her warm body. Clung for dear life.

SEVEN

Miles high, Tony peered down at the earth, using his compact Leica binoculars to see the icebergs from Greenland floating down from the arctic into the far North Atlantic. Brilliant, perilous dots sparkling like stars in the deep blue ocean.

The devil's stars, Tony thought, lowering his binos and adjusting his eyes to the dark cabin of the Concorde jetting at supersonic speed towards England.

Summer had ended in a blaze of heat which had persisted halfway into September. A dark suntan colored Tony's face and arms particularly, from repeated exposure on the golf course.

Looking at his forearms, nutty brown beneath the black hairs, Tony reflected upon the past month.

Susan would be among a small party from the State Department heading to London for a big meeting on October 13th. Absolutely top secret. They were all traveling in an Air Force jet scheduled to arrive the same day as Tony's auction appointment.

So Tony was alone today, alone with his thoughts. He and Susan had spent a lot of time together, these past few weeks, planning for any free hours they might have together in London. Susan shopped on Saturdays while Tony sharpened his golf game.

And now the trip was in motion.

Sipping his cranberry juice, Tony found himself smiling at a delicious decision he had made leading up to this trip, a promise to himself. Something special to anticipate. A moral decision.

One morning at breakfast, an article in *The Wall Street Journal* slapped him in the face, recalling discarded thoughts.

It seems the extravagant lifestyle of the Republican senator from Idaho, Samuel H. Winterbern, had attracted the attention of two aggressive investigative reporters, and their research yielded the sort of tantalizing, scandalous newspiece which the *WSJ* enjoyed placing on page one. A lifelike line-drawing of the swollen senator topped the story.

Virtually unopposed in his state's senatorial elections for over a decade, the powerful senator, it was found, had used his "campaign warchest" of more than seven million dollars on expenses that were hard to describe as campaigning.

The details had reawakened Tony's interest in the senator.

In its customary tongue-in-cheek tone, the newspaper catalogued the "minimal necessities" which facilitated Senator Winterbern's "grinding campaign schedule."

These included retainer fees paid monthly for five years to his personal consultant, a young lady in her late twenties whose principal preparation as political consultant consisted of several years as a skiing instructor in the Rocky Mountains. Her physical condition was explained to be "healthy," due to her conditioning on the ski slopes.

Thousands of dollars the senator had expended on theatre tickets for Broadway shows, excused as "entertainment" for political constituents.

Hundreds of thousands spent on takeout liquor at a chic Washington emporium made the expense sheets as "refreshments for fund-raisers."

Tony's eyebrows had actually raised upon learning from the article that Senator Winterbern had regularly, ever since entering office as a freshman senator, made small but continuous "reimbursements" from campaign funds to each of his four children back in Idaho. "Local canvassing expenses," the reporters had discovered among his vouchers.

Allowances? Tony wondered.

Most of the expenditures, however, focused on food and lodging. These included holiday-season visits to New York City, San Francisco, Honolulu, and even Paris and Amsterdam and Prague, among many others, all of which seemed somewhat distant from the senator's constituency and official job functions, noted the *Journal* article in a bemused tone.

Tony did not find amusing the one point one million dollars spent at hotels in those cities, nor the limousine bills into the tens of thousands, nor the several hundred thousand paid out to charter airplane companies listing "Mr. Winterbern and Miss Belinda Spittal" as the sole passengers on most of those flights.

As the list droned on through the dry-cleaning bills, country club memberships, car and boat rentals, inaugural-ball tickets, professional photographers, dues and subscriptions, music, artwork rentals, sports tickets, and detailed bills from expensive department stores, Tony's mind returned to his first encounter with the senator at the Georgetown party.

'The *proper* people are just above the law,' the senator had whispered into Tony's ear at the party. Tony's thoughts wandered again to the garotte, as he read the newspaper at breakfast.

The important senator, the reporters wrote dryly, held such esteemed positions as chairman of the Commerce Committee as well as seats on the Senate's standing committees overseeing Banking, Finance, Energy, and Appropriations. 'A powerful money man whose influence many seek,' the *Journal* explained to its readers.

Tony's decision was just about set when he read of Winterbern's bill for $11,292 at the London Hilton for five days during the week before Christmas last year, "not including food," observed the article coyly.

'Little old ladies who send in money from their Social Security checks don't have the slightest idea how their money is really being spent,' suggested the *Journal* reporters, who concluded with the following citations.

The ineffectual, titular head of the government's Congressional Accountability Office was quoted as saying: 'The rules overseeing campaign-fund spending for personal use were rewritten in 1995 by a committee which included the senator from Idaho. Those rules are open to the broadest possible interpretation.'

Furthermore, admitted the government's accountant to the *Journal* reporters: 'While Samuel Winterbern's spending habits are by no means unique to his situation, his flamboyant lifestyle appears to be almost in a class of its own. In fact, his spending is legendary inside the Beltway.'

Which, Tony decided that morning, made him the ideal target. Only this time there wouldn't be play bullets.

All that remained, in Tony's mind, was how and when.

And now, miles above the earth and heading toward an unknown assignment in his official capacity for Her Majesty's Government, Tony smiled wanly, recalling the Latin legend on the coin he hoped soon to own, which translated as 'To Spare the Humbled and Subdue the Proud.'

That would be his next mission, Tony had decided. In his unofficial capacity, once he returned to the States.

As the Concorde dropped to a lower altitude, Tony took up his Leicas again, seeing through them up ahead the tip of Ireland, and soon its green and brown hills passed under the jet's wings. With the Irish Sea coming into view, and the lush fields and tidy villages of England's west country just beyond, Tony Spool considered his mental state of readiness for the days which lay just ahead.

Wondering what cause had brought him that brief e-mail.

* * *

"Harry! Good to see you again!" Tony yelled over the noise in the reception hall at Heathrow Airport a short while later.

"And you as well, sir. Keeping fit, I see!"

"One tries, Harry. One tries."

"I'll grab your bag, sir. Follow me to the car, if you please."

Just outside, in the cooler air, lights beginning to twinkle off it as evening set in, stood the sleek S-class Mercedes.

"New one," Tony said to Harry's back as they neared the car.

"Yessir. Chauffeuring's been good to me."

"You look best in black, Harry." Tony getting in the car.

"Actually, sir, it's what they calls 'pearl grey.' Shiner, ain't she?"

"Fitting for your good self, Harry. I'm at the Dorchester again."

"Right chew are, guv."

"Always good to be home. I miss the accent!"

"So you reckon this is still home, sir, and not America?"

"Always a Brit, Harry. I love America—my life there. One *can* handle just so much golf, though, in all that sunshine!"

"Rough indeed, that."

"Proper golf, Harry, is with an unpredictable Scottish blow right in your face, salt air thick on the greens, mean clouds and forty degrees."

Harry turned to see Tony's face, to laugh with him. Harry's hair was billowy and whitening beneath a gray driving cap. He wore casual tweeds, no tie, and a mohair sweater. Chest hair puffed out around his collar. His nose was fleshy and slightly red. His eyebrows hadn't been trimmed in months, and their wildness offset his ruddy, clean-shaven face.

"Miss the cab, Harry? Be honest."

"No sir, I never look back. Everything's better. Life in general. It's a new deal, sir, this guv'mint. Best PM we've ever had. *Our Tony,* I calls him!"

"He seems a cracker, *your* Mr. Flair. Makes me think of coming back."

"You should, sir. You should!" Harry exclaimed. "It's the good old days all over again."

"We'll have a grand time, Harry, a grand time. A good solid week, we'll have. And the Missus is comin' over, coupla days from today. Unfortunately we won't see much of her, I'm afraid. Business, you see."

"Too bad, sir. I should like to serve her as well."

"You will indeed, Harry. But we each have work to do, separately."

"I see."

Tony settled back into the leather seats as the Mercedes negotiated the roads into central London. After a while he heard:

"Sir?"

"Yes, Harry?"

"The golf clubs, sir. You send them on ahead?"

"No, fraid not. I *might* get in a game, love to, but the schedule's not certain this trip. Too bad, really. Weather's perfect."

"Well, certain you'll have a successful trip, sir, golf or no."

"Yeah, Harry, successful. Maybe a run to Scotland at the end, if I'm lucky. . ."

"Luck'll be with you, sir. It generally is."

"Time will tell, Harry. Time will surely tell." Tony found his voice modulating, perhaps a touch of sadness in it.

Harry turned again to toss a smile at him over his shoulder.

"We'll have a grand time, sir. Don't you worry," Harry said as they rolled down the Kensington Road along Hyde Park.

Tony felt a sudden somberness overtake him as he gained a sense of settling in, of coming back.

Up ahead, on Park Lane, lay the magnificent Dorchester Hotel. Its pale yellow stone facade glowed faintly in the dying sun. As the car pulled up to the entrance, Tony wondered what else would be dying in the next few days.

EIGHT

Seven o'clock next morning, Tony faced the bracing British new day. Standing before the long, open casement window in Suite 309 of the Dorchester, the fresh air whisking his body. Staring out across Hyde Park at scattering nimbus clouds racing east high above the city, the end of a night of showers and wind. The new day at last.

A day promising clear blue skies, air slightly chilly: a balmy autumn day, if the BBC weather reader were to be trusted. A day of promises indeed.

Hair jumbled, attired only in boxer shorts, for now Tony still carried the long night with him. His chest and abs were dewed with perspiration. He smelled sleep on himself. His mind was preoccupied.

Just as he got into position for another set of situps, the telephone jangled out its dot-dash ring.

"Yes, hello."

"Darling, it's Susan."

"Good morning, sweetie."

"Tony, it's still last night here. Two a.m."

"Yes, of course it is." Tony replied absentmindedly. "Anything wrong?"

"No, I just miss you already, baby. I'm anxious about coming over, too. How was the flight?"

"The crossing went fine, good food and time enough for thoughts, planning. Harry met me with the car. You sure you're all right?" Tony asked.

"I've just been lying here, thinking about my husband. All of you. Rubbing myself. Needing you."

"Oh, honey."

"Tony?" Susan asked.

"Yes?"

"Were you thinking about me, too, when I called?"

"Nothing else," Tony lied. She hadn't crossed his mind, this morning. "We'll have a great time, what time we have together. We have lots of plans, remember?"

"I know. I'm just anxious. My first trip without you. I don't like it when you leave me. Silly, huh?"

"Not silly at all. Sweet."

Silence from both ends.

"Susan?" Tony whispered into the mouthpiece.

"Yes, honey?"

"Turn out the light. Rub yourself into dreamland. You'll be with me in a couple days."

"Sooner than that, Tony."

"Goodnight, baby."

"I'm with you already. You're right here with me, under the covers," Susan purred. "You're always next to me..."

Tony heard the phone slip into its cradle back in Virginia, then he carefully put down his end of the line, too. Sitting there, staring at the sheets. Love was such a hard thing.

He forced himself to do another hundred situps, in four sets. The shower awaited him. But first a good English shave with a badger brush and coconut shaving cream from Geo. F. Trumper's of Curzon Street, Mayfair. Just around the corner, but the Dorchester provided all the gear right here.

Again the phone rang. This could get annoying.

"Good morning, Tony," the voice said indistinctly.

"Yes, who is it?"

"It's Simon. Welcome home. Ready for me?"

"Ready for you? Simon, it's awfully bloody early."

"Now don't be cross. I'm eager for us to see the coin, is all. I knew you'd be up. No one sleeps in, traveling east."

"Simon, how'd you know where to reach me?" Tony asked.

"Darling, you *always* stay at the Dorchester! Right?"

Tony found this irritating. How far he'd come since the old days, when nobody knew his plans, ever. He'd become predictable. He sighed to himself.

To Simon he said: "Yes, I suppose I do... these days. So, all right, what's up?"

"Well..." Tony heard, fading away. Then the voice again: "Sorry, just passed under a bridge. I'm in my convertible Benz. These mobiles. Anyhow, *well*, I'm out and about, doing errands before going to the shop. I just thought we might have breakfast. My treat."

"When?" Tony asked into the receiver. Standing there, naked now.

"I'm twenty minutes away, maybe thirty, traffic's okay so far. Say thirty to be safe."

"Thirty minutes," Tony repeated. "Where?"

"Oh I thought downstairs, all right with you? They do the best full breakfast in the city."

"I'm not so sure I need a full breakfast," Tony said back, thinking of the fried eggs, the bacon, the veal sausage, the fried toast, the butter and rack of dry toast, the jams, the tea and cream. The fats. Thinking of Susan now.

"Of course you do!" Simon insisted. "Off to a proper start."

"Simon?"

"Yes?"

"Forty-five minutes. In the lobby. Drive around. Waste some gas."

"Petrol, darling, *petrol!*" And the merry voice disappeared.

Just finishing up with a final piece of toast, Tony said across the table to Simon, “I haven’t done that in years. Thank God Susan’s not here to see me.” Patting his flat stomach for effect.

“Susan doesn’t approve of eating?” Simon asked, looking askance and raising his right hand in the air above his head, twirling his index finger for the check.

“She’s the original American anti-cholesterol freak,” Tony answered. He wagged a finger of his own in Simon’s face. “Don’t you dare mention this, you hear?”

“How silly you Americans are,” Simon said simply.

The waiter approached, decked out in a stately black tux and stiff whites. A balding man in his sixties. Trim and beautifully dressed, still living in the Edwardian Age. Forty years at the Dorchester, in all probability.

“Yes, sir. More tea, sir?” he asked, enunciating each word as if it were deathless prose, picking up the teapot on the table, holding it over the immense florid teacup at Simon’s place. Huge teacups and large plates, fixtures of the Dorchester dining room.

“Just the check,” Simon said in his own stately manner, covering his cup with one hand, a hand sporting a bright rock of a diamond, a good three carats balanced in a delicate gold setting, on the pinky finger.

Tony’d been watching the clock. It now read eight forty-five.

As they left the dining room Tony said to Simon: “Tell you what. I need a few minutes in my rooms, to freshen up. Shall I meet you over at Christie’s? I’ll call my driver.”

“No, don’t be absurd,” Simon said back. “I’ll drive us. Wait for you here in the lobby. Take your time. I’ll make a few calls.”

And as Tony entered the lift, he looked to the lobby and saw Simon speaking into his cell phone. Doing deals, Tony thought. Smiling to himself. Tony liked Simon quite a lot. Urbane, accomplished, a real gentleman. A pro.

Standing again at the open casement window in his suite, Tony took his own cell phone from his right jacket pocket, flipped it open, and touched autodial number nine. It was all nines this trip, he mused.

Even open, the cell phone was barely bigger than a deck of playing cards. Tony had the latest model. His cell-phone number was secret. Most incoming calls were blocked.

A fine, very proper, female English voice spoke into Tony's ear, cheerfully asking, "Yes? Hello?"

"Oh, hullo, love," Tony said back into the tiny microphone at his lips. "Nine sharp. Kindly inform Sir Malcolm his tailor's ready." He immediately touched the *End* button, and closed the phone.

He stuck his head out the window, smelling the brisk clean air carrying a light humidity from the night's storm. Clean air tinged with the barest suggestion of diesel exhaust. Tony could smell it, from the busses and taxies. A fragrance, to his mind, bringing back fond childhood memories.

Immediately his cell phone rang.

Tony flipped it on, without saying a word into it. He heard: "Two sharp." Nothing more. The line went dead.

Tony smiled, visited the loo briefly, and remarked to the attendant on the elegantly appointed elevator what a fine day it was, a fine day indeed! Then he and Simon drove together over to Christie's in St. James's.

Simon parked illegally on the side street by the auction house, two tires on the street and two on the sidewalk. On the dashboard he placed a small printed sign that read, "Emergency Physician." Tony mentioned it as Simon locked the car with his remote.

"No, no fear. This is my *neighborhood!*" Simon scolded him.

Inside, Simon headed for the lift.

"Oh, no," Tony said, pulling at his arm. "We're walking up."

Simon shot him a disbelieving glance.

"The breakfast," Tony reminded him. "This will help."

"Help what?" Simon asked. "Give me a heart attack?"

"You're fifteen years my junior, Simon. C'mon!"

As Tony bounded up the inward-curling, cylindrical iron stairs, he heard Simon huffing behind him.

Tony smiled down at him as Simon neared the top step on floor three. "Soft Americans, huh?"

"Never mind, Tony, never mind. Must be a bit of a cold coming on, is all. I'm fit as a fiddle, you know."

"Good," Tony said. "I expect to hear you'll always be taking the stairs from now on. I shall ask, whenever I call over in the future. And I want the truth."

"Right," Simon said, rolling out the word. "Now let's see that coin!"

As they entered the Coin Department, a pleasant young man greeted them. He said, "Morning, Mr. Stinger. You're here early!"

"Buzz us through, that's a good lad," Simon said back, pushing open the security door to allow Tony to go before him into the private inner room.

"Sir," the young man said in Tony's direction.

"Tony Spool," Tony replied, extending his hand for a shake.

"Ian," Simon said at the lad, "we're here for lot viewing. Just one lot, actually. Lot 199, if you please."

And in a few minutes it lay before them, splendid upon a green suede riser, gleaming in the halogen light shining down from the ceiling.

Simon turned his right hand palm up towards the prize.

"I've already seen it," he said. "Special viewing last week. Just for me. Your turn, Tony."

Tony slid the green suede pad across the oak table towards himself, turning the pad in a slow circle, the coin turning on it. He gingerly picked up the heavy gold piece with the fingertips of his left hand, bringing it close before his face like some delectable pastry. Then he turned it over, holding only its edge in his fingers, tilting it in the light, rotating it, drinking in its features with his eyes. He placed it back down on the pad.

"Wow," he said softly towards Simon.

"Decent bit, isn't it?" Ian said facetiously. Both Tony and Simon looked at him without expression.

"What do you think?" Tony asked Simon.

"Well," Simon exhaled his breath languidly, stretching an arm across the back of the chair upon which Tony sat, "fewer than fifty known, in all conditions, minted only in 1575 and 1576, this one's from the first year. Maybe the *very first* one ever struck. Certainly possible, judging by its condition, absolutely Mint State. I've seen over the years, what, maybe eight, nine pieces... nothing close to this in quality." He looked simply at Tony for acknowledgment.

"The crispness of the impression," Tony said, cataloguing the coin's qualities, "no real doubling in the letters, everything visible in the portrait, and the surfaces! Surfaces unblemished, original. The color of mustard. The perfect gold color. I can't imagine anything better!"

"What I like, particularly," Simon added, "is, quite frankly, the face. The strike is so full it shows every minute detail in the king's face, even down to his eyelashes. And it's the face of a *boy*, a mere lad caught in kingship, not protected by but entombed in that suit of armor, that crown on his head weighing him down, a slave to his throne."

Tony just stared at Simon in disbelief.

"What?" Simon asked him.

"I didn't know you had it in you," Tony answered truthfully. "That's not a very commercial observation, Simon. That's the observation of a poet."

Simon chuckled back at him. "Dear boy. That's why I'm *your* coin dealer! It's not all a matter of money, is it?"

"Even the British Museum specimen is sad by comparison," Ian pitched into the conversation of which he was not a part, trying to resurrect himself after his previous comment. "The Ashmolean piece is even worse, and the Royal Museum specimen in Scotland is a full grade lower. We reckon this is the finest one known."

"Thank you, Ian," Simon said rather coldly. "Have we seen enough?" he asked Tony.

"For now," Tony replied, picking up the coin one more time, holding it above the suede pad with the tips of the fingers of both hands now. "I'll have plenty of time to study it later." He replaced it on the pad and slid the pad across the table, saying, "Thanks to you, Ian. Much obliged."

"Have you collected coins long, sir?" Ian asked him.

Simon looked protectively at his client, then blankly at Ian.

Tony said, quite somberly: "Oh, I have some coins, Ian, but I don't collect coins per se. I collect *souls*. It's only their owners' pictures that remain on the coins, but it's just about all we have, isn't it, that's tangible. So I collect them, coins, as reminders of souls I care about."

"And what's so special about the soul of this queer little king?" Ian persisted. "I mean, he wasn't much liked in his day, was he?"

Tony continued: "Collecting souls isn't a popularity contest, Ian. Popularity is a superficial thing. I'm interested in this man, in part, because he wasn't popular."

"Pray tell," Simon joined in, seeing Tony was not to be stopped.

Tony took Simon's eyes into his own, held him, telling him the story:

"You got it absolutely right before, Simon. King James was a boy when this coin was made. He was born in 1566, so he was only nine in 1575, the date of this coin. He was but a year old when his mother, Mary Queen of Scots, was forced to abdicate the Scottish throne.

"While he didn't actually rule, of course, since he was a child, he was the best royalty Scotland had, and those who controlled him put his visage on this coin as a symbol of authority. The coin was a *challenge* to the English throne."

"How so?" asked Ian.

"You see the two objects he holds? A long battle sword over his shoulder and an olive branch out before his face? Symbolism. Scotland giving England a choice: war or peace, accept the sovereignty of the Scottish throne—our James here—or face up to battle. That bit of Latin beneath the king's picture says it best. The words 'In Utrunque Paratus' mean 'Prepared for Either.' War or peace, you see? Virgil said it first."

"Absolutely," Simon said. "What a magnificent coin! I see it anew."

"What's that got to do with the soul, sir?" Ian asked. "I mean, lots of kings threatened other people. It's what they did! Their job, like."

Tony looked into the eyes of this young fellow. He just didn't understand, did he? Well, it wasn't to be expected. At least he had the curiosity to ask the question. Tony helped him:

"This man's soul changed, Ian. He had a succession of souls, rather like the succession of his thrones, first Scotland and then England as well."

"I still don't see it," Ian admitted.

"The long sword he's holding over his shoulder, see, doesn't appear on many coins. For most kings, the crown was enough of a threat. Power was implicit in it."

"That's the key," Simon added. "Power."

"Right," Tony continued. "But these men who controlled King James as a young boy, these Earls of Scotland? They wanted their king to be a threat to England. They were challenging the English queen, Elizabeth, to recognize Scotland's independence from her control. Once they had that, *they* ruled Scotland, because they controlled James, the boy James."

"But surely Scotland couldn't defeat England?" asked Ian.

"True enough. But Queen Elizabeth was too smart to go to war with Scotland. She had other wars to fight. She knew war with Scotland was self-defeating, so she recognized James as King of Scotland."

"Nothing's changed, has it?" volunteered Ian. "These power-mad people today. Only the names."

"Not much," Tony admitted.

"But why's this coin so special to you?" Simon asked.

"Well, the boy grew up seeing himself as a warrior, being told he was. Like the ancient Spartans, trained for battle. But the problem was, you see, James was no good at it. He was deceived into thinking of himself as a warrior and a hunter."

"So he was a fool?" Ian asked.

"Did you know, Simon," Tony asked him, taking back his eyes now after letting go of Ian's, "that when King James went hunting for deer, stag they called it then, in the Scottish forests, when he brought one down he *thrilled* at cutting open the animal's belly and warming his bare feet in the beast's bloody guts?"

"Sounds a mess," Simon pronounced, "disgusting."

"Don't you see?" Tony quizzed him. "Thinking himself a warrior and a great hunter, he had cold feet. A tenderfoot, they would say in America."

"Gosh, I had no idea," Ian uttered palely.

"A poof," Simon said.

"But here's the soul bit," Tony kept going:

"When he was only sixteen, thinking of himself as quite the hunter-warrior king, one day those power-mad Earls confronted James. At one of the king's hunting lodges, a grand oak-paneled place out in the forest, they isolated him in one of the halls, and drew their swords on him. They aimed to kill him, and name one of their own as Sovereign of Scotland. The young King James, you see, was growing up, getting a bit too head-strong to be led about as they wished. So they decided to stab him to death!"

"My God," Ian nearly whispered.

"But it's all right, Ian, it's all right," Tony explained. "You see, James was young, he was misled, he was a little foolish, but he wasn't stupid. No, quite the opposite. Legend has it he was frozen in fear at the sight of all those drawn swords, unable to defend himself. But he wasn't entirely vulnerable. His own guards saved him, put down the Earls' rebellion. And then James became decisive, became kingly. He ordered all the Earls executed as traitors. Beheaded by the sword!"

"So James's soul was saved," Simon guessed.

"Oh no, not saved," Tony told them.

"Well, what then?"

"His old soul perished. James was transformed by this incident, this treachery. From that point on, swords so spooked him that he forbade all sharp-edged weapons near his person. He turned completely away from the ways of battle and hunting, and embraced learning. He became a man of letters. He came to value wisdom over power. He gained a *new soul!*"

"My God," Simon said to him. "What a story!"

"But," Tony finished, "a sword appears on many of his coins—with him holding it! He never again let the power slip to others."

"Fabulous!" Simon cheered. "Simply fabulous."

"This coin's a window into this man's soul. That's why I want it."

Ian extended his hand to shake Tony's. "You're a remarkable man, Mr. Spool. Thank you so much for coming by. I hope you succeed in buying the coin you want in our sale!"

"Oh, don't worry about that, my boy," Simon told him. "Tony Spool always gets his man, no fear of that!"

In silence for half a block, Tony and Simon walked side by side up Duke Street. By and by, they stopped. Tony looked up at the thick plate-glass window they stood before and read the gold lettering stencilled on it: 'S. Stinger' centered above 'CAMDEN COINS.'

"Care to come in for a tea?" Simon asked him.

"No, I must be going now."

"Soooo," suggested Simon. "My instructions?"

"The estimate's thirty to thirty-five. What's it worth?"

"Forty anyway. But who knows? The record's nearly that, but this coin's never crossed the auction block before."

"Well," instructed Tony, "try to win it at that level, be your usual cagey self, but don't lose it."

"The top, then? Hammer price, without fees?"

"Go to a hundred," Tony said quietly, and walked off up the street without saying another word.

* * *

When he reached the high end of Duke Street, Tony realized he hadn't even glanced in the windows of the numerous art galleries which lined the street. He had left Simon and the golden king James far behind in his mind. He had attended to his hobby. Now he needed to focus on the work which lay ahead, needed to change hats, needed to revert to professional habits.

His life could depend on it.

Like an automaton, Tony turned right onto Jermyn Street, and half-way down he crossed over to the health food cafe annexed to the little churchyard. He presently found himself seated on a cold stone bench out in the yard, beneath ages-old trees amid a neat labyrinth of well-walked paths. He might have been a monk in his sanctuary. He began to spoon the lemon yogurt onto his tongue, mindlessly, as his thoughts accumulated.

He was no monk.

Why had ASF called him back, he wondered. It was a life he had more or less abandoned, a *way* of life at least, for no one ever truly left the Service, did they. Retired—well, ordinary people retired all the time from ordinary jobs. CIA operatives in America seemed to retire, and then write books for big sums, or became security consultants. KGB agents used to *be* retired for good, when they burned out; but now they had become mostly redundant, perhaps spying on Russian drug lords, smugglers and money launderers. Or spying for them.

No one, that Tony knew of, had ever really left the British Secret Service; if they aged successfully, they remained on call, like Tony. In a way, it was like being in the underworld: once in, you never left alive.

You never really got a new soul. Tony thought of King James.

Then he thought back on all the people he had assassinated in his official capacity. All! Well, who could remember them all?

He remembered the first one, though. Could recall that man's facial details like he was peering in a mirror. It had been up-close and personal, not by intent but by the force of unpredictable events. It was a hardened face, a mean face, its eyes of fearful intensity, a coarse darkly whiskered face, an Arab terrorist among a cast of killers who had stormed the Iranian Embassy and taken hostages. Right in the *middle* of London. Two decades ago. Operation Nimrod.

He could remember the smell of his breath as he died. That close.

Tony was in the elite SAS branch at that time. He wore dead black, like his colleagues in the assault. When six days of "negotiations" with the terrorists holding the embassy at ransom reached a deadlock, the SAS dealt with the terrorists on their own terms. In seventeen minutes of chaos they took back the peace, killing all but one of the terrorists without a single casualty on their side. Black-clad SAS teams had abseiled on nylon ropes down the exterior walls from the embassy's roof, crashed through the heavy-plate windows with frame charges, exploded smoke and stun grenades and CS gas, and mowed down the terrorists mercilessly with wicked bursts of horrific firepower.

All except one. The one Tony took out with a knife to the throat. The one who had shielded himself behind a frantic young telex operator. The one that no one could shoot.

Britain had served notice to the world that terrorist acts would not be tolerated on its soil. Tony had served notice to his soul of what he had become in the name of justice and good.

After years of commando training. After climbing 4400 feet to the summit of Ben Nevis, the nastiest bit of rock in Scotland, on numberless training exercises. After gaining expertise with every imaginable weapon, till using it became second nature. After attuning his mind to the idea of paying out death. After all this... came killing the terrorist with a knife.

That kill: the start of Tony's special reputation in the Service. A tricky, skilled, talented kill done masterfully.

Remembering to this day the smell of the terrorist's final breath. A true warrior abhorred distance, dealt death up-close, sensed evil surrender like an exhaled breath, looked it fiercely in the eyes.

Tony had eventually left the SAS. Only to be "enlisted" in the Secret Service to travel the world under the guise of being a banker having international duties. The ideal cover in the Age of Finance.

It was only a matter of time till the Service needed him to perform the skills he had been trained in. And then again. And then again and again.

And his final elevation to the ASF.

A zinging sensation in Tony's occipital bone brought him out of his revery. He found himself mechanically rubbing the base of his skull behind his right ear. The plastic yogurt cup lay empty on the bench beside him.

He suddenly looked over his right shoulder, and spied a wizened figure peering at him, leering at him. Maybe thirty feet away, seated on another stone bench. Tony looked away, then back. The devil's own stare, flashed into Tony's mind. How long had he been there?

The man's clothing, in marked contrast to Tony's rich Italian threads, was grim. Dirty gray trousers, a ragged, patched and filthy coat, what appeared to be a cravat at his neck but aged and worn and spotted, now little more than a rag. Unshaven. Unkempt gray hair sticking out here and there beneath a stained knit cap. Liver spots on his hands. Ragged, dirty fingernails. Skin the color of ash. Tony took all this in quickly. A large, aged paper bag bulging with who knew what, on the bench beside him. All his worldly goods?

The old man still stared at Tony. A threatening stare, the look of a thief or a night prowler? A menace to the innocent?

Tony rose suddenly and walked straight up to his tormentor. Stood before him. Looked down at him, seated there. The man's body didn't move but his eyes slowly rose to meet Tony's.

"Something I can do for you?" Tony asked him. His voice was severe.

The sweetness of the old man's voice jolted Tony. He said: "No offense meant, sir. I was lost in my memories. I saw myself in you, many years back."

Tony's soul wandered.

He took a new fifty-pound banknote from his pocket and placed it softly into the fist of the old man's right hand, cupping his hand protectively over the old man's for a moment.

"Have a lovely day, pops," Tony said ever so softly.

The old man opened his fist and saw the money.

"God bless you, son," he said, looking back at Tony's face, "may God bless you all your life."

NINE

Sometimes you have to do all the wrong things for all the right reasons.

Tony walked out of the little churchyard in something of a trance, the words of the bum ringing in his ears. 'May God bless you all your life.'

Lost in his thoughts, he nearly walked into the path of a taxi speeding down Duke Street, crossed in a hurry, and found himself before the window of one of his favorite art galleries.

In the window, staring silently back at him, he faced an immense bronze statue of a stallion, its eyes wild with fright, its mouth wide open showing huge teeth straining forward directly at Tony's face, its mane flying in the air, its hooves carrying it away from the source of its imaginary terror.

Tony stared at his image reflected in the gallery window, the wild horse just beyond.

And then suddenly Tony snapped out of it, realized he had gone too far, turned around and at the corner headed left and fairly trotted up the block and across Piccadilly. Proceeding apace through the Burlington Arcade he glanced again at his watch. Thinking, close timing. At the north end of the covered shopping street, its glossy black painted storefronts baroquely decorated in gold, Tony found Harry waiting with the car.

A few minutes past one. Closing down, but okay. Should be okay.

"Where to, sir?" Harry asked.

"Off to work now," Tony told him somberly. "To the City, Harry. The bank on Lime Street, quick as you can."

"Midday traffic, guv. . ." Harry reminded him.

In spurts and halts, the big Mercedes cut through little byways and along major roads, down the Strand into Fleet Street through heavy traffic, Harry taking all the shortcuts he knew, till they pulled up in front of a modern skyscraper faced in black marble and gleaming mirror-like windows. So tall it appeared to lean backwards from the street.

As Tony left the Mercedes he said, "Take some private time, Harry. This is a big meeting, international problem. Tied up all day, I reckon. I'll manage by myself. Call you in the morning. Ta."

And watched Harry drive off in the direction of the river as he entered the skyscraper.

He emerged almost immediately and hailed a passing taxi.

Handing the driver a twenty, Tony asked him, sounding as American as he could, "Any chance of making it to the Tate Gallery in fifteen minutes?" His watch said one twenty-eight. The normal fare would be about seven pounds.

And off the taxi flew, throwing Tony from side to side, forward and back, in the slick bench seat, as the driver crossed London Bridge almost in Harry's wake and threaded his way through all the little streets on the south side of the Thames, avoiding the worst traffic in central London, passing the Imperial War Museum, crossing back over the river at Lambeth Bridge, and drawing up along the Millbank and to the Tate in eighteen minutes.

The day was bright under an October sun.

Still following procedure, Tony walked up the sloping cement steps of the museum, only scattered tourists about, paid the entrance fee, and inside he passed down the long gallery, barely noticing the Zen-like freeform stone sculpture taking up most of the center of the large room. He turned a couple more corners, and came to it.

Always the same shock. You turned the gallery corner and found it glaring at you. Its effect never altered.

Tony stood facing the painting he had always found both disturbing and fascinating. How appropriate, it always seemed.

The meeting place.

The woman's posture would never change. Forever she would lie on her back, nude, thighs open, arms bent over her head, her very essence bared for all eyes to assess. Her own eyes swept across the picture, averted, yet they captured everyone's. Everyone forced to see her fully exposed genitals, her breasts sagging away from youth, her whimsical face, her languid posture, in an attitude of submission. A humbled goddess, adored but wounded. Plucked from grace.

Behind her, also facing the world, squatted Stanley Spencer, his knees drawn up to his shoulders, his genitals just as bare as hers, sagging too, his posture a pure expression of languor, muscled but used up, his frowning face the face of someone who just knew, challenging all to dare to expose themselves, too.

The maker, the godhead, Tony thought. The spymaster.

It was two o'clock precisely.

A voice behind Tony said quietly, almost inaudibly: " 'See ourselves as others see us.' "

Tony looked over his shoulder at a face from his past. He turned back to the painting and said, "Sir?"

"James Joyce."

"Oh I see. Yes of course."

"All great artists bare their souls," said the voice. "This one does it unblushingly. Nothing much left in secret."

Not looking at the voice, Tony replied, "*Nec tecum nec sine te.*"

"Explain," said the voice.

"Samuel Beckett, sir: 'Neither with you nor without you.' It's supposed to be a picture about worship, but I've never been convinced that

Spencer had a soul. The perfect modern artist, in that sense. You agree?"

"A lonely man," admitted the voice. "A stark viewpoint."

Tony turned around, faced the voice, and they shook hands. The voice's hand grip was very strong.

Tony said, "Like ours."

"Come, walk with me," the voice commanded quietly. And they turned away from the nude couple transuded in oil, and walked silently together to exit the gallery.

Outside, they strolled down the river embankment, the water just to their left, Tony following the other man's lead. They entered the walkway across the Vauxhall Bridge by themselves, neither saying a word till they reached the center of the river, where they stopped. No other foot traffic appeared on the bridge.

Sir Malcolm Goodge looked like anything but a killer. He looked like someone's favorite uncle. Short, slim, slightly puffy cheecks giving him a sort of jovial look, a neat angular nose above a bushy white 'Kitchener' moustache, and a ring of snow-white hair around a shiny, tawny pate.

Facing downriver, not looking at Tony, he finally said into the slight breeze coming off the water, while nodding to his right, "That's our destination this afternoon, Captain." His voice was that of an aristocrat, firm and authoritative and in perfect diction.

Tony winced inwardly at hearing his rank again. His ears hadn't heard the word 'Captain' applied to himself since his last visit back. But instead of saying anything, Tony looked along the bridge to the far side of the river at the building on the Albert Embankment.

It looked more like a fortress than an office building, once you really studied it—an impenetrable, terraced modern castle. Multiple levels of pale yellow Gloucester limestone with rounded battlements jutting out here and there, some faced with green bronze the color of an ancient Roman statue, and expanses of mirrored glass to blind watchers like moats reflecting the sun. Each story a little smaller than the one beneath it.

Tony looked now at the other man on the bridge, standing next to him. He said, "Sir?"

"You know what it means, Captain Spool. Follow me."

And again in silence they walked the rest of the bridge, leaving behind its fanciful, long crescent steel buttresses painted rust-red and approaching the entrance to another side of life. Cameras inside the brick and green-bronze wall around the building tracked their progress along the pavement.

At the tall gate, on the side of the building away from the river, both men stopped. The camera rotated to face them, a good twenty feet above. Then the metal lock clicked open, at the sound of a buzz. And the man at his side said, "You first."

Tony's eyes read the name chiseled into the Gloucester stone above the imposing, green bronze door. The building was labeled 'BRITISH HOME BANK,' but nearly every Londoner knew it was the home of MI6, the Secret Intelligence Service for foreign affairs.

As he crossed the threshold, Tony steeled himself for the world that lay beyond.

* * *

Through a glass, darkly. Tony thought of this as he stared through the narrow, dark-tinted, one-way window of the room in which he waited, alone, high in the fortress. Beyond lay the river, the quixotic bridge he had just crossed, the Tate Gallery, and the protected world.

He thought of the painting again. At this moment he felt like the nude woman, adored but in the grasp of the artist behind her.

Tony had entered that indigo world another time.

He let out a slow, deeply held breath only he could sense the release of. He knew he was being watched at this moment.

He strummed a finger across the vertical blind at the window, picked up the mud-colored coffee mug from the sill where he had laid it, and sipped at the hot, rich black liquid. With a dead expression on his face, he looked around the room, seeing oak bookshelves filled with row upon row of volumes of all sizes, some looking like same-binding sets, some four or five inches thick, some pencil thin. Reference books, reports, monographs. A library. A specialized library.

But it was a small room. And quiet. Linoleum floor, wood paneling between the bookshelves made of closely set narrow grooves running vertically, ceiling tiles filled with confusing dot patterns.

No dust. No lint. Clinically clean from bottom to top.

But full of bugs, electronic bugs everywhere. So quiet Tony could hear his heartbeat.

He had never felt more isolated in his life.

Tony took another sip of the hot liquid. He warmed his hands on the thick, plain mug. He felt the coffee warm his stomach.

He consciously straightened his posture. Thought of the old man in the park, so vulnerable. Then of the terrorist bearing the devil's own face. Then of the senator...

The door opened softly and a woman entered and closed it behind her. She said, "Tony," seeing the distracted look upon his face.

His eyes met hers. She'd always had the most beautiful, sparkling eyes, he remembered, seeing her again.

"They want you now. Please follow me."

"Thank you, Nora. I'm ready."

Tony followed the petite woman down the hallway in silence. Closed doors bearing only numbers stood along the outside wall. The inside wall was nothing but solid wood paneling.

As they walked, Tony noticed her brisk step, her strong calf muscles, her pretty brown curly hair bobbed around her ears, the dangling gold earrings. He thought of his new civilization, and a smile came to his lips.

Back in the little library he had just left, the coffee mug sat on the window sill.

They came to an elevator. A uniformed guard stood by, a Royal Marine, holding a black Beretta submachine-gun with a long ammo magazine, and a pistol on his belt. His face was expressionless. He did not look at them.

The elevator went up one level to the top floor of the fortress. They walked down a short hall to a door with another Marine, similarly armed, standing beside it. He opened the door and closed it behind them. They stood, Nora and he, inside a tiny cubicle, a mantrap. The opposing door then opened, and Tony followed the woman through it.

She escorted him to a plush seat at one end of a beautiful, highly polished, oval conference table made of English oak, then took her seat next to a man at the other end of the table. A portable notebook computer sat on the table before her, ready for use.

The man next to her, opposite Tony at the long end of the table, began to speak. He said: "Good afternoon, gentlemen. Thank you all so very much indeed for being precisely on time today. We have a great deal to cover."

His voice came to Tony's ears not that of an aristocrat, but more one of the common man, a good solid Labour Party voice. It was calm, steady, most English, lilting at the end of phrases and sentences.

"This meeting of COBRA has been in planning by the Ministry of Defence for months and is absolutely top secret. Aside from the Prime Minister, no one outside this room is or will be privy to any of the information you hear this afternoon. You shall soon see why. But first, as this is being recorded for the PM's review as well as for the record, introductions are imperative. Also, some of you have never met."

The speaker cleared his throat and sat taller in his seat.

"My name is Samuel Noone, special under-secretary to the PM for home affairs, and liaison to the MOD. To my right is Sir Wilfred Nuttle, head of MI5." Noone halted abruptly, did not avert his eyes from his papers.

Sir Wilfred glanced toward the speaker, but said nothing. He wore narrow gold-framed spectacles, although seated was obviously tall, quite thin and patrician-looking, seemed to Tony perhaps in his early sixties, and his hair was reddish mixed with patches of white. He might have been a barrister.

"To Sir Wilfred's immediate right is Brigadier Denys Groat, recently appointed new Director of Special Air Service Group." Again Noone halted. This time he smiled briefly at the officer.

The Brigadier scrutinized the table, stopping to peer especially hard at Tony. He alone was in uniform. He seemed to Tony perhaps Welsh, mid-forties, short brown hair showing a little gray. He held himself rod-straight. He barked out "Gentlemen!" in a tone that was cold as ice. He still peered at Tony. Tony noticed the unusually fancy, solid-gold insignia on his lapel, a winged dagger bearing the enameled motto "Who Dares Wins," and smiled gently at him.

"And next to Brigadier Groat we have Tennyson Bruce, head of MI6. Although our discussion does not immediately concern going beyond our shores, as you shall see we may encounter that possibility."

Bruce said: "I certainly appreciate being consulted, Mr. Noone," and nodded graciously.

"MI6 have assisted our *inquiries*," Noone hastily added. He bobbed his head towards Bruce while saying "And we thank you, sir, for your gracious use of these facilities today."

Tony saw Tennyson Bruce as an aristocrat, heard the Etonian accent in his few words, decided immediately his clothing was Savile Row, couldn't help but notice the sternness of his countenance, knew he had been head of foreign intelligence at least since the invasion of the Falkland Islands. His slight build belied his reputation for dogged belligerence.

"And," Noone went on, extending a pointing hand towards Tony, "our man of the hour, Captain Antony Spool, one of our deepest operatives. You've all reviewed his dossier, so no further introduction will be forthcoming."

Tony felt compelled to lift his bottom ever so slightly off his chair, and he nodded at Noone across the table, saying nothing.

"To the Captain's right is of course Sir Malcolm Goodge, whom you all know. He has had the final word in deciding upon Captain Spool for the current mission.

"And of course," continued Noone, "perhaps the most trusted of all civil employees inside the intelligence community, Sir Malcolm's secretary of many years, Miss Nora Horsey."

All the men smiled towards Nora without saying a word.

As Noone picked up a glass of water and sipped from it, Tony glanced around the room, seeing elaborate paneling of mixed woods, finely carved and joined, a rich purple carpet with the Royal Badge woven in a pattern throughout, and a ceiling of gleaming, plain white plaster. There were no windows. The lighting was indirect and low. Tony figured this must be one of the most secure rooms in all London.

"Right, then," Noone went on. "I shall get directly to the point."

Clearing his throat once again for effect, he began the discourse: "One of the principal goals of the present Government is to make Britain a truly *united* kingdom. This was a primary plank in Labour's platform in the recent elections. It was a *promise* the PM made to the public, that he would try to solve the problem of Ireland. Solve it! Let me assure you, gentlemen," Noone said, raising his voice, "that this was not idle, political lip-service intended merely to gain votes!"

He looked sternly around the table at the faces of his audience.

"It has also been, let me assure you, the PM's *dream* to make this come true. His personal dream for years, in fact. Many of us have been behind him in this dream, and in his quest to come to power."

Tony thought he saw the speaker's bland white skin taking on a blush of color. The blue worsted suit, with its fine silver pinstripes, looked better for it, Tony thought. Here was a man of some conviction, perhaps.

No one interrupted the speaker, who was saying:

"And as you all are keenly aware, the PM has personally instigated and frequently attended an ongoing series of discussions with Sinn Fein, and with as many as six other faction representatives, in an effort to halt the war that has been raging in Ireland these many decades."

Tony noticed, in the exact center of the conference table, a tiny raised knob, perhaps half an inch across. Black. A microphone. He looked over to see Nora Horsey's hands spinning out the words they all heard into the keyboard of the little computer in front of her. Aside from this, nothing else distracted attention from the speaker, who was saying with increasing force: "And there has been progress. There have been brief periods of peace. We are confident the IRA want peace. We are confident, for the first time, there are people inside the IRA who are genuinely sick of the bloodshed, who *genuinely* seek unity, as we do. But the peace has never lasted long. . ."

Noone let out an audible gasp of exasperation. He stopped talking, he picked up the water glass in front of him and took a sip, and he looked at each man around the table with eyes of steel.

Sir Malcolm Goodge broke the mood. He withdrew a cigar from his lapel pocket and noisily twisted off its cellophane wrapper. Everyone looked at him. He looked only at the cigar, placed it in his lips and spun it gently, withdrawing it and licking the tobacco's pungency off his lips. He then moved his eyes level with Noone's, and nodded ever so slightly.

Noone went on: "I speak for the PM directly when I tell you, gentlemen, the Government is damned sick of this blood feud. Damned sick. *And we are going to stop it!*"

At this, Tennyson Bruce broke in. "And how is that, Mr. Noone? I for one would like to know how you are going to accomplish what no one else has been able to." The hard face, Tony thought, looking nonplussed. But Tony had the same question in his own mind.

Noone looked back at Goodge, lighting his cigar. As the tip of his cigar began to glow deep red, Sir Malcolm said to him:

"Tell them, Samuel." It was a quiet command.

"We are going to war ourselves. Not defensive. *Offensive.*" He stopped for effect, watched the faces of those watching him.

After a brief silence, total silence in the room, Sir Wilfred Nuttle joined the talk. He said: "MI5 has made a recent discovery, gentlemen," he told them quietly. "We have a mole deep inside the IRA, very deep indeed. It was he who led us to decide that the peace talks have been a true effort on the part of the IRA to find a peace, to bring us this unity of which Mr. Noone speaks." The old man's tongue, just its tip, ever so briefly flicked at the center of his upper lip. His little gold-framed spectacles were aimed at the tabletop. His eyes seemed closed in thought as he chose his words.

Noone interrupted, saying: "It was the reason the Government has offered Northern Ireland her own legislature in these peace talks."

"And the IRA responded most favorably," said Tennyson Bruce.

"But..." Noone said in a harsh voice, "but these damned private militias, who had representatives at our peace talks, these damned bastards betrayed even the IRA and began the killing again!" He pounded a fist on the table.

"It's these so-called splinter groups," Brigadier Groat said loudly. "Their specialty is vengeance killing, the bloodier the better. They'll go into a Belfast tobacco shop," he said even louder, looking toward Goodge's smoking cigar, "or a shoe store, any place chosen at random, and murder the Protestant owner. They'll then contact the local press to claim this act as theirs, as 'payback' for Catholic deaths."

Sir Wilfred Nuttle remained silent, his eyes closed. Only Tony seemed to be looking at him.

"And then some Orange extremists take their own vengeance," Tennyson Bruce continued the argument, "and murder a Catholic shopkeeper, shooting him maybe twenty times to make sure he's good and dead, or they'll abduct some innocent who's doing nothing but walking down the street one fine day. The Loyalist Volunteer Force, the Ulster Defense Association, or some other private army of Protestant killers, blood feuders. And on and on it goes, the cycle..."

"Senseless!" exclaimed Noone. He took a long, deep breath, exhaling it noisily.

He looked around the table. "For years we blamed one splinter group, one gang, especially. We always thought it was the Irish National Liberation Army which renewed the fight. A group, I'm sure you all believe, so feared that most civilians won't even mention it aloud. The INLA seemed able to kill at will, to penetrate anywhere. They even managed to kill the 'King Rat' himself, Billy Wright, certainly the most vicious of the Protestant combatants. They killed him *inside* Maze Prison, for God's sake! We don't *have* a more secure prison, yet they took him down right in front of us!"

"Which led to the murder of some Catholic teenagers at a dance club in revenge—using Micro-UZIs, if memory serves," said the Brigadier. "Quite a mess. Followed in due course by more counter-threats."

"My point precisely," concluded Tennyson Bruce for them all. "Derailing the peace talks, frustrating everyone."

"Well," Noone said, "they keep their political representatives at the peace table, yet they seem to feel compelled to strike back."

Goodge broke in. Peeved, he said: "Yes, yes. They kill their enemies, sometimes they even kill naysayers within their own gangs, blaming it on their enemies. But, gentlemen, let us hear out Sir Wilfred."

The old warrior's gold-rimmed specs leveled with his audience's eyes, and he peered down his nose. He said, again quietly:

"This mole of whom I spoke. We have just learned from him something most interesting. It startled even me." His voice trailed off.

Everyone looked at him, waiting.

Goodge put down his cigar. It fell off the edge of the ashtray. His thick moustache bristled as he said, "Christ sake, Freddy. Tell them!"

Sir Wilfred twitched. He opened his eyes widely and said, just a bit louder than before, "We've learned that the INLA now has its own splinter group, and may be a scapegoat itself for these far-right extremists."

He pushed his glasses up to the top of his head, looked straight and hard directly at Tony, as he told them all this: "The real killers, the worst bastards ever associated with the IRA, are in fact so secretive that only in these past weeks have we learned of their existence. They call themselves the Irish Free Volunteers Army, the IFVA. Their chieftain—the fellow, we now know, who arranged for Billy Wright's demise from this Earth inside our prison—is someone called Alex Allgood."

"Allgood indeed!" Noone hissed.

"We have no ID for him," Sir Wilfred went on, his chin bobbing a bit. "No clue what he looks like, who he is. We have no idea of his

HQ's location, even vaguely. We *do know* he's the most vicious imaginable *bastard!*"

Sir Wilfred smiled wickedly now. "And we know something *else* about him . . ."

"Mind your words," Goodge said gently.

Tony looked towards Samuel Noone, noticed him draw his right index finger across his bare upper lip. He looked across at Goodge, whose eyes were cast downward. Nora's fingers were poised above the keypad.

All eyes were on Sir Wilfred, who finally said:

"We know where he'll *be* four days hence. Friday the thirteenth. Lucky Friday for us. Unlucky for him!"

Tony throught he heard Big Ben sound faintly in the distance. Four o'clock, it sounded like.

"To what purpose?" the Brigadier asked bluntly.

"We intend converting Mr. Allgood to Her Majesty's personal custody," said Noone dryly.

"You're joking!" the Brigadier blurted out, startled. "Kill him? Where? How? By whom!" and he suddenly glared Tony's way.

Tony's eyes widened, eyebrows arched. He straightened his shoulders.

"Oh, we're not joking at all, Brigadier," Goodge interjected, his eyes twinkling now.

"I must agree," Tennyson Bruce said quickly. "With Brigadier Groat, I mean. This is surely unprecedented. Personal opinion aside, I must question this. Political assassination by another nation is just not done. Bad form."

"This is not *another* nation," Noone argued forcefully, "and neither is this a leader, a political leader. This is a thug we're talking about, an outlaw!"

"But wouldn't it be interpreted as vengeance, killing this man?" added the Brigadier. "And vengeance, in fact, as well?"

Noone rebutted immediately: "They can interpret as they will. But we shall not be avenging anyone here. We shall be paving the way for peace. This Allgood, this savage murderer, has been at the heart of the bloodshed. In his absence, peace may just have a chance to succeed."

"We shall be breaking the chain," Goodge added.

For the first time, Tony said something to them. He said: "You shall be purging evil, pure evil."

And Tony looked first at Goodge, and then at Sir Wilfred. The *duumvirate*, the joint chiefs. Tony understood now.

"A sentence for life, that's what you're initiating, in my opinion," Tennyson Bruce uttered brusquely, ignoring Tony's comment.

"Thank God I'm not a politician," the Brigadier said resignedly, blowing his breath out his nose. He looked tenaciously at Goodge. "How can SAS help?" he said.

"Oh. . ." Goodge said in a tone of voice affecting obeisance, and easing back into his plush seat, "direct your questions to Mr. Noone. ASF is but an instrument in all this." And he picked up his cigar and relit it.

"It seems," Noone resumed, "SAS is to have no involvement in the current mission. You, Brigadier, are here at this meeting so as to be fully briefed. SAS may possibly play a role at a later time, in case we do not succeed on the first attempt. So we thank you for your input," he added coldly, not looking at him now, "but your task here is simply to listen."

Denys Groat sat back in his chair, his face expressionless.

Tony sat back in his chair as well.

Noone continued: "Owing to our information-sharing agreement with CIA, we know this. We know that the U.S. State Department has arranged a secret meeting with several parties from Northern Ireland this coming Friday, here in London. The meeting will be at the U.S. Embassy at lunchtime. . ."

And suddenly Tony felt his soul drift. Susan, he thought.

". . . an informal luncheon meeting. Sinn Fein will be there, other IRA reps, myself standing in for the PM, a delegation from the States, and—we have learned—*Mr. Alex Allgood* of the IFVA will be representing himself as a political delegate of the INLA."

Everyone in the room was silent, listening. Tony felt ice on his heart.

"The mission of the U.S. State Department, we are told," continued Noone, "is to let the Irish delegations know, in no uncertain terms, that Irish terrorism must stop, and stop immediately. If it doesn't, State will use CIA to apply special pressure on American sympathizers who fund the Catholic cause in Ireland."

"And the U.S. Department of *bleeding* State," interrupted Tennyson Bruce, "believes this will actually make an impression on these terrorists?"

"Well," Noone admitted, "American naiveté is a most endearing quality to some. The PM has encouraged it. The Americans are the world's peacekeepers, you know." His tone took on a certain sarcasm. "They, however, do not understand the IRA as we do, nor do they know what we do about the INLA, or shall we say about Alex Allgood."

"Tell us the plan, Mr. Noone," Tennyson Bruce demanded, "do tell us the plan, please!"

"The plan," Noone continued with less emotion, "is quite simple, really. Brilliant in its simplicity. But a bit complex logistically. You are all here, fundamentally, for the security of British Intelligence. As well as to be sufficiently in the loop should a second mission become necessary."

Noone placed both hands flat on the polished oak, leaned forward slightly in his chair, straightening his posture. "For, you see... our window of opportunity is *very* tiny. We may *not* succeed..."

Tony noticed a fine crust of white rime had formed on Noone's lips, dried spittle. Usual cause, tension, Tony thought.

"Our chance is worth the taking, however," Noone continued, his voice beginning to sound strained. "The decision has been made to try. And our *best chance*, we believe, lies with ASF."

He paused, pushing his chair back a foot or so from the table. "Please, Sir Malcolm," Noone said, "please lay out the plan for us all."

"Needless to say," Goodge said instantly to them, with authority, "no one will be shooting at the U.S. Embassy!" He saw Tony's facial muscles relax. He smiled gently at Tony.

"You see, immediately following the luncheon at the U.S. Embassy, at which we expect all parties to submit verbally to State Department demands, our Alex Allgood will be going directly to a second meeting, which *he* thinks is top secret in his camp."

Goodge took a deep puff from his cigar, and tipped ashes into the bright glass ashtray on the table. He looked wistfully towards the ceiling.

In a sort of chuckle, he said, "The PM's office has requested of Archangel Special Force that Mr. Allgood not be permitted to exit that meeting successfully. . ." He allowed his words to diminish into a pregnant pause. His puffy cheeks had a distinct, but delicate, blush to them. He looked almost merry, with his fringe of white hair and his billowy moustache. "And we intend to comply with that request! If it's possible, it will get done!"

Tony looked upon his boss with a soft heart. The Santa Claus of death.

"And this is where Captain Spool comes into play?" asked Tennyson Bruce, a hint of challenge in his voice. "Or so I presume."

"Oh, indeed. Indeed!" Goodge turned to look at Nora Horsey, and asked in the gentlest of voices: "Miss Horsey, the screen, if you please."

Nora entered a command on her keypad, and an illuminated colorful map of central London appeared on the wall behind her.

"You see Belgrave Square," Goodge said, pointing with a miniature laserstick, "and Apsley House, just here," moving the pointer to the southeast corner of Hyde Park. "Until yesterday, Mr. Allgood's secret meeting was planned for Belgrave. Our shot was to be from the roof of Apsley House, a distance of barely more than four hundred meters. Still, a *difficult* shot, owing to the configuration of the streets. We reckoned our chance was three in ten."

Goodge looked round the table, all eyes riveted on the image of the map of London on the wall behind him, Tony's especially.

"But yesterday, we learned from Sir Wilfred's mole, Mr. Allgood's meeting plans changed." Goodge peered Tony's way. "You'll love the irony of this, Spool," he continued. "For you see, Mr. Allgood's secret second meeting, set for approximately three in the afternoon on Friday the thirteenth, will be at the Iranian Embassy in Prince's Gate." He moved his laser pointer appropriately.

Tony pulled his chair back to the edge of the conference table, sitting bolt straight. His blue eyes glowed, brighter than ever.

"And my vantage point, Sir?" he asked Goodge.

"Nine hundred meters away, Captain, directly across Hyde Park, from the roof of the Police Station beyond the Serpentine, just here." Goodge's laser beam touched the green spot on the illuminated map. "Dead easy by comparison with Belgrave Square, where so many three- and four-story buildings would have allowed a very, very narrow path for a bullet."

"Pardon me," intruded Tennyson Bruce's voice. "You're going to shoot across Hyde Park, in the middle of a weekday afternoon, through the heavy traffic on the Kensington Road, over a brick wall, and hit a man, what, walking a few feet from an automobile into a building... *only nine hundred* meters away!"

Goodge looked blankly at Bruce, who continued with:

"A man, unless I missed something here, for whom you possess no photograph, whose ID you lack?"

Goodge said quietly, "Yes, Mr. Bruce, that is precisely what we intend doing." In his left hand, his cigar had gone dead. He laid it down in the glass ashtray. He stood up, short of stature, tall on authority.

"Captain Spool will shoot from a recessed pod, on the roof of the Hyde Park Police Station, and will have an almost perfect, direct line of fire through the trees at the entrance to the embassy. We commenced trimming tree branches this morning. Mr. Allgood's car will intrude itself in the line of fire, but the target will most likely exit and walk from the pavement side of the car about twenty paces to the embassy entrance. The shoot will be a rear head shot. Captain Spool will have perhaps ten seconds of opportunity. Should the target happen to exit the car from the street side, we shall have even more time."

"And the traffic?" Tennyson Bruce asked. "And the weather?"

"Mr. Noone has already warned, and I'm certain no one here fails to understand, that the unexpected may happen. It often does. However, should interference occur, our second chance will be when Mr. Allgood *exits* his meeting. That will give us a frontal head shot, in any event."

"And the nine hundred meters?" asked Bruce again.

"Some twenty-nine hundred feet. The munition we have selected can traverse that distance in approximately one second."

"Untoward things can happen in one second, or less."

"Things can and do happen, that is correct. Our chance is just that, a chance. A chance most definitely worth taking."

"And the target's ID?" Bruce persisted.

"After Mr. Allgood appears at the American Embassy, we shall have his identity. Captain Spool will have it seconds later through his headset," Goodge answered.

"And the good Captain's security?" Bruce again insisted.

"He will not be visible from the ground. The shooting pod will be recessed on the roof. The Royal Parks Constabulary police will do the rest."

"And the weather, time of day if the entrance opportunity is missed?" Tennyson Bruce asked.

"You know my answer, Mr. Bruce. Same equipment you would use abroad. Two sniper rifles, one with dayscope, one with nightscope."

Goodge looked at Tony across the table. "You will have a full briefing tomorrow on all this, Spool. You are scheduled to commence at nine a.m. in Southwark, with our Mr. Merriless. Plan on spending the day there, hummh?"

Tony sat still, attentive. The soldier listening to orders.

"The only other information you gentlemen need, at this time," Goodge went on directing, "is that, should we miss our chance due to circumstances beyond our control, no shot will be fired, and Mr. Allgood will never have known what peril he put himself in. We should then, all of us, weigh further opportunities and strategies, possibly involving SAS and MI6. For you see, we know just one more thing about Alex Allgood."

Goodge looked once more in the direction of Sir Wilfred. He said:

"Tell them, Freddy."

The head of MI5, home intelligence, took off his gold-framed spectacles again, looking steadily out across the conference table. He said, his voice still low, steady, calm:

"Should Mr. Allgood unfortunately survive Friday the thirteenth, we know he is eager to make a trip abroad before year's end—"

Goodge jumped in here: "Possibly to talk up sympathizers for funding, or arms. Our intelligence here remains hazy thus far; our mole is listening, knows only there is a row between old guard IRA and Alex Allgood. It seems evident to us he remains the principal dissident in the IRA's decision to sue for peace. Mr. Allgood's support, gentlemen, appears to be drying up. No other reason for him to hazard a trip out of Ireland." Goodge halted abruptly, then added summarily, "But enough of this for now."

"So that's it, then," Brigadier Groat suggested. "Godspeed to you, that's all I can say."

Goodge rebutted: "Not quite all, Brigadier. Mr. Noone omitted one vital fact of your involvement in this mission."

"And that is?"

"You will support Captain Spool's security. The PM himself has directed me personally to order you to place SAS teams throughout Belgravia, Kensington, Mayfair—in short, the periphery of the area of our operation. Use appropriate restraint in the event of need. Usual uniforms. Be invisible, but be in vantage points across the area. Yours will be a surveillance role primarily, but you are directed to gently remove any intruder from the shoot location."

"You know how urgently SAS shuns publicity, Sir Malcolm," the Brigadier responded. "Are we to deal with the Metropolitan Police at all?"

"No. No. In the vaguest terms, the police will be instructed early Friday that a security operation will occur in that area of Hyde Park. We cannot divert traffic from the Kensington Road, lest our target become edgy at any unusual change. We can, however, and we will, 'thin out' movement along the line of fire as best we can."

Samuel Noone spoke up again, after listening for some time:

"Miss Horsey will provide you, Brigadier, with a packet of logistical details for your teams. And that's it. Further questions, comments?"

Tennyson Bruce at last: "Just one. For Sir Malcolm."

"Yes Mr. Bruce?" Goodge smiled at him dimly. His questions were valid ones, but he'd said enough already, overstepped his bounds on this one. Sir Malcolm would need to have a word with the PM about it, definitely a word.

"It's just this. Given the numerous sharpshooters in SAS, indeed throughout Military Intelligence, and even in your own ASF ranks, why choose Captain Spool for this mission?"

"Why indeed," Goodge answered, not looking just at Bruce but rather around the table at all the faces. He stopped panning to smile at Tony.

"Oh, a certain fondness, I suppose, entered into my decision. Captain Spool was absolutely my all-time best agent when he worked for me full time. He never, ever failed me. His expertise became legendary within the force, you know that. But, beyond all this, he possesses two qualities that cannot be found elsewhere."

Goodge looked over to his old comrade, Sir Wilfred, saying to him: "Tell us one of them, Freddy, will you?"

"It's obvious," Sir Wilfred proffered. "He's retired, or mostly so. No one knows anything about him, other than his 'banking' activities, nor have they for years now. And also he's an *American* citizen. What possible concern could he have for our Irish problems?"

Sir Wilfred averted his eyes then, looking away from Tony, from them all, looked only at the tabletop.

"And of course, should things go terribly wrong," he said in a husky voice, "although it's most unlikely they ever could—he has no link to British Intelligence. He is, in a word, expendable."

Tony sat expressionless, motionless in his chair. This was not news.

Goodge said very quietly: "Freddy… you do have a way of being direct, I must say. I should have said, myself, that Captain Spool's cover is foolproof. He's too valuable, in my mind, ever to be put into a position of becoming expendable. His person will be completely protected in this mission, believe me."

Goodge next looked over towards the PM's representative, saying to him, "And Mr. Noone, have you any idea of the other reason I've chosen the good Captain to carry out this difficult mission for us?"

Noone drew his right middle finger thoughtfully across his hairless lip, pursed his lips ever so delicately, and shook his head to indicate he had not.

Goodge: "It's so obvious to me, but I suppose none of you knows him well enough to understand this. It's so easy to say, really. But so difficult to realize. For, you see, Captain Antony Spool's qualities as an assassin make him practically unique in his profession. Beyond his technical qualities, I mean."

Goodge paused, to look Tony keenly in the eyes. And then he said, this Santa Claus of death said: "Just look at those startlingly blue eyes, gentlemen. Their intensity is not merely one of physical color. They are a Viking's eyes. They are conduits to a soul which will compel the Captain to kill our target, not just for us, not merely for justice, not only to pay for the lives this monster has stolen, but for and with a passion that is *religious* in nature!"

The chief of Britain's elite, top-secret assassination team stopped abruptly to look momentarily at each of his listeners. His bushy, snow-white moustache rose and fell with his breathing. Then he said: "Never forget, it is pure evil we are up against in this mission. Captain Spool already told you that in the few words he uttered here today. I am absolutely confident in the dedication of this man, that he will purge this evil—for us, of course... but also for himself."

Goodge halted again, his face aglow, then added this final, insistent thought:

"His *soul* will not rest until he has dealt wickedness the death blow!"

Tony sat with his eyes closed now. Sometimes the truth was so stark when you heard it out loud. His heart was troubled, but he could not, would not, allow it to show.

Sir Malcolm Goodge sat down with a soft whoosh emitting from his cushioned chair.

After some moments of shattering silence in the room, Samuel Noone stood up at his spot, looking at no one, and said with a gentle politeness that was almost Italian in its diffidence:

"Thank you all for your patience."

The last word withered away into utter silence. The bureaucrat seemed to want to say more, but he did not. Instead, he pushed back his chair and quietly exited the conference room. As did the other men.

In a few moments, Nora Horsey tapped out some further, nearly noiseless keystrokes and then closed the laptop computer's screen over its base.

She cleared her throat and said softly towards Tony, "My instructions are to escort you back to the library. As soon as possible, you will be driven to your hotel in a Mercedes that looks identical to your chauffeur's." Her voice trailed off.

And presently Tony found himself again in the little library, the clean room. As Nora closed the door softly behind him, he walked to the window. His coffee cup still lay there, on the sill. It was empty. He touched it. It felt cold. So cold.

And he looked through the narrow slats of the one-way window at the darkening day outside. Across the Thames, down there in the protected world of ordinary people, he could see figures walking to and fro, living out their lives.

As they passed along the embankment, these figures, they disappeared under the shadows of the trees as the day died away.

TEN

Merle Merriless had to be the most unpleasant human being Tony had ever encountered. And that was saying something.

However, an order was an order. So, he now found himself in the good hands of his driver Harry, sitting next to Harry in the front seat of the black-pearl Mercedes as they wended their way carefully through the avenues and side streets of Southwark, on the nether side of the River Thames, in the morning traffic.

Tony had closed his eyes momentarily as they crossed the Vauxhall Bridge, the same bridge he and Sir Malcolm Goodge had traversed by foot the previous afternoon, and as they drove by the Art-Deco fortress containing MI6.

Tony had had a good night's sleep, but it took some doing all right. Delivered back to the Dorchester Hotel by limo following the long meeting, Tony had fallen into a deeply troubled mood. He had taken a snack in the hotel restaurant, instead of a full dinner, had found some consolation in a half-hour's worth of the *Meditations* of that saint of Roman emperors, Marcus Aurelius, had then resorted to two tabs of Melatonin, and lastly had steamed himself into submission to the day's travail in the waters of a particularly hot bath bubbling with George Trumper's finest soapy concoction—a pink powder fragrant with French lavender from the Albion plateau in the Provence, the label had stated.

He awoke ten hours later relaxed and restored. Cleansed, Tony wondered, by the healing powers of the magical medicinal plant he had soaked in? Or had he simply knocked himself out?

But, in fact, he awoke so hungry for life that he had quickly showered and dressed, and had tucked in the Dorchester's best breakfast fare of two eggs poached on biscuits, bacon as only the English can make it, three links of veal sausage, and as many pieces of dense white breakfast bread toasted and cooled in a dainty 18th-century sterling silver toast rack bearing silversmith's hallmarks. And plenty of butter and cream tea.

Tony having thought, as he spooned on thick helpings of sweet strawberry preserves, what the hell, once Susan arrived here it would be back to browsing food. And it was indeed going to be some day today, needful of nourishment to sustain one's equilibrium in the face of Mr. Merle Merriless, longtime armorer for ASF.

He and Harry had by now entered the bowels of Southwark, an ancient neighborhood of row houses, schools, tiny shops, guildsmen's markets and businesses, warehouses, taxi depots, corner grocery stores, a confusing array of streets which intertwined with little apparent plan, and residents who mostly traced their lineage back many centuries within the confines of these hallowed roadways.

On the fringe of the river at the north side of Southwark could be found here and there a tourist attraction, and tourists sometimes wandered into the district to see such charmingly named things as the tube station called the Elephant & Castle, only to be disappointed at finding a dreary, deep-set, workingman's subway stop.

For this was a workingman's place. People of varying complexions and strangely diverse origins these days roamed the streets which bore the litter and refuse of work. It was not a place for tourists. And no tourist could have imagined the working place Tony and Harry now pulled up to in the Mercedes.

It was as anonymous looking a place as one could be, an apparent warehouse lacking in personality. The Mercedes pulled into a tight parking corral, walled off from its surroundings by high stacks of cemented dirty-red bricks. A couple of old minivans bearing dents and rust were jammed among the dozen or so vehicles, all of which were of English manufacture, with a sole exception—it brought a faint smile to Tony's mouth—the brilliant silver BMW M3 coupe. It looked brand new. No dents in its sides yet, Tony noticed as he left the Mercedes and waved Harry out of the lot. Harry had to back up gingerly and turn three times to maneuver the big car safely out of the corral.

As Harry drove off, Tony took to the metal and cement stairs on the exterior of the building, climbing them to the second floor, where he walked along an outside corridor bearing only one door at its far end.

The door bore no sign. Had no handle or knob. Was grimy and of mixed paint, as was the entire building. It had a keyhole and a small red button. Tony pushed it, smiled at the pinhole-camera lens he knew was hidden somewhere in the door at shoulder height, and shoved at the heavy door when he heard the buzzer come to life.

"Yes, come on in, Spool," Tony heard as the door opened enough to permit him to pass through. The voice had a whine to it, and sounded unreal, like an artificial voice driven by computer at the end of some telephone menu.

Tony found no face beyond the heavy door, just another mantrap like the one yesterday at MI6, but no handsome wood paneling in this one. Dirty metal walls instead.

"Close the door, Spool! All the way," whined the voice again. Maybe a kind of groan mixed with the whining. Tony pushed the outer door hard, and when it locked, another door to his right unlatched itself with a click.

"Come on, Spool. We're not all retired, ya know." His personality matches the building, Tony thought as he proceeded twenty yards or so down a dreary corridor, dimly lit by a bulb at each end.

The gray metal door at the far end opened with a simple twist of its handle, and as Tony prepared to greet the body on the other side of this door, it had already turned away, its muffled voice, real this time, saying,

"Well, let's get to it, Spool. I *do* have other things on my schedule today."

What greeted Tony inside the warehouse was far from the fanciful gadget manufactory of fiction. There were no imaginatively dressed servants of invention within these walls, no explosions or fireworks produced by ray guns or the like, no dummies being experimented upon.

What Tony saw once again, reviewing the place as he followed Mr. Personality to a lab room, were cameras in ceiling corners, dingy workspaces whose windows were crisscrossed with wire molded into the glass, closed doors behind which sat human robots laboring at computer terminals, and no other evidence of life. A grim sort of spot.

Mr. Personality waved Tony into a large laboratory—a place of engineers' workstations, several computer terminals, windowless drab cinderblock walls and metal partitions bearing not a single decoration to remind one of life outside, stools placed here and there, and a single large swivel chair before one of the computers. Tony noticed that the CRT at this one danced with colorful images of frag bombs exploding above the heads of a field of electronic soldiers, many of whom "died" as a bomb would go off over them. A bright red blob of "blood" marked the spot where each "soldier" had been advancing across the field.

"Take one of those stools by my chair," said Mr. Personality. He had slammed the green metal door closed behind them. The outside of the door identified its resident with a stained and dull brass plate which read in capital letters 'MR. MERLE MERRILESS, CHIEF.'

He noticed Tony looking at his CRT's screen saver.

"Kill 'em all, that's the goal," he explained towards Tony, nodding at the screen. "I've devised a game based on this matrix. Configured the software myself. In the real game, naturally, the soldiers *try* to elude our fragmentation bombs—"

"Naturally," Tony interrupted, his tone suggesting mockery.

This earned a dirty look as Merriless strummed on: "Yeah, they run to cover, they zigzag around the playing field... it's useless, of course. We kill 'em all, at the end of the day."

Tony looked curiously at this man, whose face was busy admiring the CRT screen, who now lit a cigarette and offered the pack to Tony, forced more or less to actually look at Tony at last. "Coffin nail?" he asked Tony.

Tony said back "Not for me, thanks all the same. You got the coffin part right."

Merle Merriless glanced and puffed away, looked at the screen again, pushed a few keys to bring up a new pattern, tossed the pack of butts on the workbench, and said in a deadpan voice, "Don't give a shit, really. Not that it's any of your sodding business."

Tony had a mean thought, which he held back. He faced a human being, more or less, dressed in a smeared lab coat, rumpled gray worker's trousers, a cheap cotton button-down shirt open at the neck, no tie. He was skinny, looked in his early sixties, had much subsided curly gray hair and a clean-shaven face streaked with depression but otherwise nondescript, and wore old-styled, plastic tortoise-shell eyeglasses.

"So," Merriless said to Tony's silence, "I imagine you've got yourself another termination order, judging by the equipment I've been ordered to supply you with. That so?"

Tony found the fairly cheery mood he'd awakened with was now gone completely. He tried to get his rump comfortable on the hard stool, but couldn't manage.

"I'm afraid I'm not at liberty to divulge what my orders might be, nor to what use, if any, I'll be putting this *equipment*, as you call it." Tony tried to say this in a nice tone of voice, but didn't imagine it came across that way.

Merriless gave no facial response. He entered some keystrokes and an image appeared on the screen. Just then a bell rang in the background, too.

Merriless rolled his swivel chair a few feet to the next computer screen, tapped a key, and a man's face filled it up.

"Yes, what *is* it?" Merriless said grumpily into a microphone by the screen, and both he and Tony watched the man's face start to talk. The face said:

"Am I speaking to a real person, or are you a computer?"

"Real, you sod. What is it you want?" Merriless said back into the microphone. Tony realized the face on the screen was at the outside door, where he had been a few minutes ago.

"Well," replied the voice outside, "I've got a load of goods addressed to someone named Merriless. Is that you?"

"Goods from where?" Merriless persisted into the mike.

"Admiralty," said the voice outside.

"Oh, you're *new*, aren't you?" Merriless said, more irritated now. "Drive your van round to the loading dock, rear of the building. Push the button there. A man will sign for the goods."

Merriless looked crossly at the retreating person on the screen, glanced at Tony with a disagreeable sneer, touched another key and a different view appeared on the screen, to which Merriless said:

"Charlie, a truly bright young sod will be at the loading dock in a couple minutes. Make sure he understands that if he ever rings at the front door again I'll have him sacked within the hour. You got that?"

"Yessir, Mr. Merriless," answered Charlie, his face now on the screen.

To Tony, Merriless said, "You see what I have to endure here, on my budget? Thirteen thousand quid for a receptionist. I told them, keep it, you must need it worse than I do, I'll answer the door myself. They kept it."

Tony nearly laughed at Merriless. Decided against it.

Merriless rolled his swivel chair back to the screen in front of Tony.

"Anyway," he said, blowing cigarette smoke over Tony's head, "here's the little darling *they* suggest you use. You're familiar with it, of course." The voice had taken on a snotty tone now. Whining and groaning and snotty.

Tony directed all his attention at the computer screen.

"Yes, familiar," he said.

The see-through image of a rifle rotated on the screen, turning steadily in its electronic state, floating in 3-D perspective as he watched it, the Computer Aided Drafting & Design program revealing the gun's inner mechanism, each of its parts and dimensions, even an imagined view through the barrel, the "eye" twisting down the rifling.

"Encourage me," Merriless ordered. "Pretend I don't know anything about this thing. Explain it to me."

Tony said dryly: "Accuracy International model PM sniper rifle, 7.62 by 51 NATO caliber, normal range one thousand meters, ten rounds, flash-suppressor built in, bipod under the forestock, stabilizing spike under the butt. UK manufacture."

"Oh, bravo, *Captain*," Merriless sniveled back, "retirement has not harmed your faculties as of yet."

"L96A1 is its technical designation," Tony added.

"Quite. What's it weigh?"

"Six and a half kilos, unloaded, without sight."

"And what's the customary sight?"

"Schmidt und Bender," Tony recited. "German, zooming in to 10 by 56. Accuracy International believe it's the best pairing with their rifle, has the highest daytime light-gathering capability, while zooming does not adversely affect the mean point-of-impact."

Merriless keystroked a new image onto the screen for Tony to observe.

"Oh, well, *there's* where you've fallen behind the times, Spool," he scoffed. "That scope was state-of-the-art nine years ago, when you took one to Pakistan with you. And never returned it, I might add. Came out of my budget till I bitched enough." He took a deep drag on his dying cigarette.

Tony looked at him with a blank expression.

Merriless noticed it and added insult to injury. He said, in an especially prissy manner: "Have a close look at the screen, Spool. You might learn something here today."

Tony peered with interest at the CADD picture on the screen, showing the diagnostics and innermost details of a rifle scope, its image rotating to illustrate all angles. Tony hadn't seen one like it before now.

"Yeah, that's right, Spool," Merriless jeered on, stubbing out his cigarette on the workbench, which was scorched in many spots with similar burns. Tony noticed a number of cigarette butts on the cement floor as well.

"The S und B zoom scope is scrannel these days. This one's the preferred darling," Merriless insisted, tapping the image on the screen with a nicotine-yellowed finger. He coughed a cigarette cough, as if on cue. Repressed a second one.

"Okay, inform me," Tony said coolly.

Merriless did: "Pilkington Kite image intensifier. No good at all under cloudy moonlight or in complete dark, but a mother in twilight or on a clear, starlit night. British... finally beat the huns at something technical."

"Better than infra-red?" Tony asked genuinely. "Or thermal imaging?"

Merriless taunted him: "As you certainly know, Spool, infra-red is detectible. You probably don't want your target saying to himself, 'Well, lookie there, an infra-red scope pointing my way. Jeez, I wonder what that's for.' Do you, Spool?"

"It's doubtful my 'target' will be equipped for such detection," Tony responded matter-of-factly.

"Infra-red's obsolete. We don't ever use it anymore. End of subject. And the coolant problem with T.I. was always a pain in the ass. Weight, heat, that shit." Merriless reached for his pack of butts. "Good system otherwise. SAS use it, okay?"

"Please," Tony asked nicely. "Spare me for a bit. There's enough smoke in the air as it is."

"My turf," Merriless almost snarled in reply. "Suck it in. You're getting paid, remember?" And he lit another.

Tony held back any reaction. This couldn't take that much longer.

"I.I., image intensification in case you don't get it, yields daylight vision as long as there's any light to be gathered. As I said, no good in total darkness. *They* tell me total darkness won't 'enter the picture,' in a manner of speaking, for the present requirement," he pushed, trying for a bit of levity. Tony didn't provide a smile. Merriless pretended not to take notice anyway.

"How's it work?" Tony said, returning to the scope.

"Electrons on a photo-sensitive plate. Forget the techs, you don't need to know." Merriless flicked the image away with a keystroke. The screen again showed the bombarded "soldiers."

Tony had about had enough of these put-downs. But he did not react. Reaction was what Merriless sought from Tony. Tony wouldn't give him the satisfaction.

"Weighs practically nothing, runs on two small batteries. No heat. I imagine the huns are pissed we outdid them on this," Merriless concluded, his deeply lined face adust with ugliness.

"Doubt I'll need it, though," Tony suggested, hoping for a reaction himself. "Daytime event, you see." He smiled brightly.

Merriless already had an answer to this, though, prepared like a good investigator:

"It's just the backup, on the second rifle. *Doubles* for Spool, sod the cost. You think these things are cheap?"

"It's not my department," Tony answered truthfully. "So, the first rifle *will* have the old scope on it?"

"Yeah, yeah." The armorer looked in another direction, mumbling.

"I need to handle both guns, with both sights," Tony suggested. "Not just imagine them on your computer."

"Right. C'mon down the hall, I have 'em ready."

And in a couple of minutes they entered a small room whose walls were chock full of rifles of many kinds, on racks, standing vertically. On a heavy wooden workbench in the room's center sat three rifles, each on horizontal perches made for them.

"Okay," Merriless began, picking one up, the one with the new scope. "Here's your Pilkington I.I. baby, the one for low light." And Merriless showed Tony its various adjustments.

"Got it, Spool?"

"Got it."

He handed Tony the second rifle, with the older scope mounted on it. "Not only Pakistan," he reminded Tony, "but Fonseca—Christ, all those other times. I've shipped these all over the world. You don't need to spend any time on this one," and he took it back out of Tony's hands almost before Tony got to touch it.

Tony said with some severity, "Do you mind? I *am* the one's going to use it, you remember?"

He recaptured the rifle, inspected it longer than need be, while Merriless stubbed out a smoke with his shoe and lit a replacement. He seemed to take pleasure blowing the exhaled smoke at Tony.

"Any changes at all?" Tony persisted.

"The zoom scale's been modified since you used that one in Pakistan, nine years ago, is all. See, here," pointing it out. "Nothing special. You'll get it quick enough, a *pro* like yourself." He fairly spat out the fortis sound of the 'p' in 'pro.'

At this, Merriless picked up the third rifle from the bench. He examined it lovingly, working its smooth mechanism with satisfaction.

"And this is?" Tony questioned.

"The better gun, which *they* have passed over in favor of the British item. Same calibre, but more advanced, in my opinion. Course, it's just my opinion; what do I know? Here, have a feel," passing it to Tony.

"H and K," Tony said, admiring it.

"That's right, Spool. Heckler & Koch PSG1. The old favored brand from your SAS days. But it's German... so, rejected." Merriless sighed.

"Certainly prettier," Tony admitted, aiming it, trying the trigger.

"Better!" Merriless insisted. "Like a BMW is better than a Rover. Just *better*. Clever friggin' huns."

Tony smiled slightly, remembering the silver car in the parking corral.

He handed the rifle back.

"Let's see the munition," Tony said with some insistence. "I'll have some time to familiarize myself with the gear before I need to use it."

Merriless withdrew a box from a drawer beneath the workbench.

"Twenty rounds," he showed Tony. "Ten per magazine. Course, a man of your skills, one should do it. But twenty nonetheless. Now listen up..."

Tony was beginning to get peeved at this hostile attitude. Still, he said nothing in response to the put-down.

"I'll make this as brief as possible, Spool. Nothing all that novel here, though Goodge thinks there is. We both decided against the Splat rounds: they break up too readily, as you know."

"AET profile, I reckoned, is what you'd have for me," Tony responded.

"Not the old AET, though." Merriless took a deep drag from his cigarette; its tip lit up redly. His eyes squeezed tight for the effort.

"Even with extensive barrel porting," he hissed as the nicotine hit his lungs, "the old AET round eluded total reliability." Like a locomotive engine, he puffed out smoke, right in Tony's face.

Tony looked down through the haze at the box of ammo. He picked out a cartridge to examine it up-close.

"I always liked the steel pin inside the hollow point," he said. "One to penetrate any body armor, the other to smash up the flesh." It was simply a statement of fact.

Tony looked up from the cartridge he held in his fingers to see Merriless focused on him with a crooked face. It was a look of disgust if ever there was one.

"You killers are a savage lot, sure enough," Merriless muttered. "Did you ever get to inspect the 'remains' after you got done shooting with AET?"

"I have, as a matter of fact," Tony said tersely. He'd really had it with these unnecessary judgments.

"Well, wait till you see what this new mother accomplishes," Merriless said back, more surly than before. "It's a brand-new AET profile, called a 'THV.' Ballistically, the design phenomenon is called 'reverse ogive.' The fore-end of the bullet still has your happy steel pin protruding beyond the casing. But the ogive shape causes a deeper, fanned-out rip into the body. You getting the picture, Spool?" His lips produced a twisted, ugly smile.

"Body-part disintegration," Tony answered, looking at the bullet again.

"Yup. You can't get nastier results. The *perfect* round, they say. Higher velocity. Energy spread out better. Pierces any armor. Has low recoil. Stops anything. Dead." Merriless was studying what remained of his cigarette. "And no reliability bullshit," he added tartly.

"Twenty of them, you say?" Tony reiterated.

"Fearsome enough, even for a bastard like yourself," Merriless smacked him in the face, verbally.

Tony'd had it.

"Not really," he said, getting nearer to Merriless's face. "In actual fact, I dislike guns of all sorts. I prefer to kill up-close. It's a personal passion, you see. Real *satisfying* to me. You'll never know, of course..."

"You're a heartless brute, Spool. A real turd. You and your sort."

Tony didn't hesitate a second. He said: "A greater man than either you or I'll ever know said this about it: 'No tears with those who wail, no quickening of the pulse.' He too killed plenty of people who needed killing."

"So why'd you quit SAS, Spool? Tell me that."

Tony wanted to snort at him, maybe swat him like a bad bug. Instead, he said, in a real calm way:

"You're referring to the terrorist I killed at the embassy? That Arab? That cold-blooded thug hiding behind a political agenda? Is that what you mean, *Mister* Merriless?"

"Yeah, that's what I mean. Scare you too much?"

"Oddly enough," Tony told him bluntly, "you're right. It *was* frightening at the time. Frightening how much I *enjoyed* depriving that chunk of crud of living another day, even another moment."

"One kinda man you can always trust, heh Spool? A dead man?"

"More than that." Tony said the words slowly and emphatically: "It gave me a sensual rush. A warrior hard-on."

"You're a real sickie, Spool, you know that?"

Merriless reached for his pack of cigarettes. Tony took it out of his hand and crushed it in his, clenching his fist.

"You want a real thrill some time, Merriless? Try killing a man with your hands. Take one of those blades you make, and cut his windpipe, watch him gasp and try to scream without a voice box, feel his hot blood squirt!" There was a hint of excitement in Tony's voice.

The armorer's face, stuffed with a dead cigarette, took on still-life qualities.

Tony continued, his audience in rapt attention now: "But you got the 'bastard' part backwards, see. It's not me that's the bastard. What I do, my job is to *remove* the world's bastards to keep little shits like you safe."

Merriless blinked hard, shook his head disapprovingly, said, "Christ, Spool! How do you live with it?" His eyes searched around for cigarettes.

"Professional training. Though one sometimes wonders if the target field ought to be expanded to encompass just plain ordinary assholes, know what I mean, Merriless? Relieve their misery."

"Point made." Merriless was doing a good job of recovering from his angst, grasping his usual attitude. He stepped back out of Tony's space. "Anything else we need to review here today, Spool?"

"Not with you. You got the delivery instructions covered?"

"Yeah, all covered. Pick out a good cartridge from that box for the first shot, Spool, when the time comes. Shame if they didn't all have a full charge. Mess things up, wouldn't it?"

"You wouldn't dare." Tony said this without any emotion at all.

"Why not? No snot outta my nose."

"I'll tell you why not. I might have my own private target list, and it might increase by one, that's why not."

Merriless acted as if he didn't even hear this.

"Time to leave, Spool. I have more important things to do today." He got up and went over and opened the green steel door.

"No, I'm not through here yet. I need to see Dithers. Take me down to his lab."

"Goodge didn't say anything about needing to see our Mr. Dithers," Merriless said coldly.

"Maybe not to you. I have my orders. They include Dithers."

Merriless shrugged, went over to a computer terminal on the workbench, tapped a few keys, and spoke into the microphone. He said: "Percy, do me the honor of stepping out your door. I'm sending Spool down to visit you. See he doesn't make any detours on the way down, humh?"

And then he stepped back to the open door and motioned Tony out into the dreary corridor. At the far end stood a diminutive man in a lab coat. Tony saw him. He waved gently at Tony. Tony started toward him.

"Ta ta, Spool," Merriless jeered, his old voice completely back now. "Do come back soon. All the best on that assignment, okay?" And he slammed the door hard as Tony glanced back at him a second, before proceeding on down the corridor.

Talk about contrasts. Percy Dithers was as different from Merle Merriless as day is from night.

Standing maybe five foot five, Dithers held out his hand and grasped Tony's warmly when Tony reached him. He wore brown tweeds beneath a tidy lab coat, and a twinkle in his eye.

"Back again, are we, Captain Spool?" he smiled benignly.

"Tony," Tony said back. "Okay, Percy?"

"Surely. Come on in to my domain."

He closed the door noiselessly and followed Tony over to the nearest lab counter, one of half a dozen jammed full of glass beakers and all the usual chemist's tools, as well as a variety of measuring instruments such as gas chromatographs. Computers, of course. But real chemicals bubbled and colored lights tracked them on living electronic charts.

Percy Dithers looked like a professor of poetry in residence at All Souls College or the like. Maybe forty, hard to tell for sure. Fine features, smooth pale skin. A receding hairline of light brown, neatly trimmed. Freckles. No glasses. Eyebrows delicate as angel's wings. Sensitive mouth, smiling still.

He was ASF's poisons expert. Among other things.

"What is it you need, Tony?" he asked again, quietly.

"I need something very special. For a very special, very deserving individual." Tony smiled, too, the same knowing smile.

"Describe this need, Tony."

"Well, I don't know if it exists, but I need something that works quickly, say in ten minutes, not instantaneously but quickly. Something that cannot be reversed. Something that can be held safely in the bare hand but that will dissolve rapidly in a cold liquid. Something without odor or color. Something that cannot be tasted. Something that might simulate a heart attack, kidney failure, that kind of thing—a natural-looking cause of death. Does it exist?"

Percy Dithers sneezed a mild wee sneeze. He withdrew a hanky from his lab coat and dabbed at his eyes.

"Just a second," he said to Tony allergically, and reached behind a bubbling beaker. He produced a small spray bottle with a squeezer on the end of a narrow tube, like a perfume bottle. He spritzed some fluid into the air, right at Tony. Tony flinched.

"Oh it's nothing," he hastened to say, reassuringly, "don't worry. A little air freshener I worked up. To overcome Mr. Merriless's tobacco smoke. You brought it in on your clothing. There, isn't that better already?"

Tony noticed the air did smell like the outdoors now, cleaner, for the first time since he entered the building. He also noticed that Dithers had fans going all over the laboratory.

"Much better," Tony admitted, amazed.

"I blow and vent," Percy said to him, almost in a giggle, "but Mr. Merriless presents a constant challenge."

"So I noticed," Tony said a little sourly.

"Oh, he's not the big bad wolf he seems." Percy let out a little shoulder shrug, made a cute upside-down smile with his lips as he leaned his chin out slightly, in almost a girlish gesture. "It's his wife, you know. A real nag. No wonder he smokes so. I'd fume, too."

"I never knew," Tony answered.

"Who really knows any of us, I mean really?" Percy chuckled. His right thumb and folded forefinger turned the tip of his chin in a motion that might be used to screw a small light bulb.

Tony noticed now that the walls of Percy's laboratory were not barren like the walls in Merriless's surroundings, but held many taped-down prints of famous paintings, mostly Degas and other French Impressionists.

"As to your special need, of course it exists!" Percy whispered loudly. "In fact, I get a surprising number of calls for concoctions along these lines. Sometimes the taste doesn't matter. Sometimes an odor is preferred..."

"Oh," Tony added, "and virtually undetectable in autopsy."

"Ah-ha! I have the perfect thing!" Percy said excitedly. But then he stopped abruptly, wrinkled his nose. "Speaking as a chemist," he began again, all emotion gone, "I should show you your options. I can make recommendations, but it wouldn't be right for me to choose for you."

And he got up and came back in a minute or so with a little sample case, like something a salesman of pharmaceuticals, or even of candy, might carry. He opened it for Tony and picked up a green pill. Held it out to the light, admiringly, between two fingertips.

"You might want to save this for another time, Tony, but this is one of my favorites. This sample here is sugar-coated and sealed in lacquer. It's a normally white crystalline alkaloid which is made from the roots and leaves of a plant that's common all through Europe, but it also grows in the States. The plant's called *belladonna*, nickname 'deadly nightshade.' Looks like a blackberry bush!"

Percy spoke ever so quietly but more enthusiastically again, like a university lecturer investigating the finer points of the symbolism in the poetry of Byron or Shelley or Keats.

Tony asked him: "The berries, are they poisonous?"

"I don't recommend them for pies," Percy twinkled in reply.

"What's it called, the poison?"

"Oh. Atropine. Very toxic, Tony," Percy said in a warning tone, his voice hushed. "Either by swallowing or by inhalation. Don't get it in your eyes, either. That wouldn't do, you know." He seemed almost charmed by these qualities of the poison he held in his fingers.

"What's it do?"

"Well, it makes the skin, mouth and throat become very dry. The face usually gets fairly flushed. The victim becomes quite cranky, Tony... and restless. Then the pupils of his eyes enlarge, like a frightened puppy dog."

"Is it deadly?" Maybe the question was stupid, but it had to be asked.

"Oh it can be, in the right quantity. Produces tachycardia: heart arrhythmia. The heart usually fails, but it takes a while." Percy looked hard at the little green pill in his fingers. "I don't think it's what you want."

"What else do you have?" Tony asked politely.

Percy replaced the green pill and picked up a yellow one, slightly larger, gleaming in its lacquer.

He smiled approvingly as he said: "The old standby. Strychnine. Another alkaloid, Tony, but it has a bitter taste. Might do, mixed in the right food—something spicy, say?"

"Deadly?" Tony felt dumb even asking. What else could he say?

"Hohoho, is it ever! Very toxic, I mean *very*—if swallowed or even if it touches the skin." Percy was getting excited again; you could hear it in his voice. "That's why all these are coated, in fact coated over and over. It wouldn't do, killed by my own medicine, would it, Tony?" All this in little more than a loud whisper.

He looked wickedly into Tony's eyes, answering the next question before it got asked: "Hits the central nervous system. Tremors, then stiffness of the face and legs—could look like a heart attack, couldn't it?"

Tony could only nod.

Percy continued: "Ends in convulsions. Only a top athlete, a physical specimen of that nature, could survive five of these convulsions. Would that be satisfactory for your needs?"

Tony thought a moment. "You say it absorbs through the skin? That could be tricky. What about dissolving in cool liquid?"

Percy put the yellow pill back in its place in the sample case.

He winked at Tony, picking up another pill, this one clear, like a gel. He rolled it between two fingers. It seemed pliant.

"What did I say? I said I had the perfect thing, didn't I?" His voice, though still very soft, seemed both insistent and more than a little threatening in tone now. A little ghoulish maybe.

"Yes you did," Tony agreed politely. One thing he definitely did not want to do was upset the master chemist.

"My invention, this one." Percy held it up to his nostrils, then offered it to Tony to sniff. Tony did so haltingly.

"No odor at all, this little potion. No taste. As you see, no color. The clear gel-skin is stable as long as a temperature of forty degrees Fahrenheit or higher is maintained. You said you wanted something undetectable, didn't you, that you could handle without protection but that would melt invisibly in a cold liquid—a mixed drink, I imagine, humh?"

"A mixed drink, exactly," Tony answered, eager to agree. "A highball, say, with ice."

"Oh," Percy suggested, "or a daiquiri?"

"A daiquiri, yes. Maybe a daiquiri."

"I'm quite partial to daiquiris," Percy said lowly, absentmindedly. "Banana daiquiris especially."

"What do you call it?" Tony asked.

No response.

He asked again.

Percy seemed absorbed, peering at the gel capsule. After some moments he spoke dreamily and melodiously: "At first I thought of naming it 'xycine.' It's in the strychnine family, you see. Both are derived from the same source, from *nux vomica*, which is the seed of a tree which flourishes in the heat of India. The seed is also poisonous, but only mildly so compared to its chemical derivatives. They're all alkaloids, of course."

Percy looked, peered at Tony. Said with more emphasis now:

"I especially like the delicious irony here that the seed it comes from grows only in really hot weather, but that my derivative of it only dissolves in cold." He sought approval from Tony.

Tony said promptly: "Brilliant, oh it's just brilliant, Percy!" Tony was getting the feeling that Percy Dithers was far more dangerous than Merle Merriless ever could be. Best to be on the right side of this civil servant.

"I'd like to take a patent, of course. But, in my position... It's only a matter of time, I suppose, until one of those Indian labs in the Punjab stumbles onto the same formula. Ah well, I'll always have the inner satisfaction of knowing it was mine first."

"You never told me its final name," Tony proffered hesitatingly.

"I'm calling it dyzine, after 'Dithers,' you see. Doesn't matter."

"And what symptoms does it generate?"

Percy suddenly snapped back into his previous, matter-of-fact attitude, saying coldly, "Oh, same as strychnine. It's pretty nearly undetectable, safe to handle, kills within fifteen minutes of ingestion—as I said, it's perfect."

Then he did the oddest thing. He popped it into his mouth. Tony reacted in a startle. Put his hand out towards Percy Dithers.

Percy produced the tablet on the tip of his curled tongue. Removed it with his fingers. Chortled thus: "I *told* you, can't dissolve at body temp!" He put it back into the sample case.

Tony let out a breath of air he hadn't realized he was holding.

Percy giggled. "The host will come a cropper, all right, don't you worry. How many do you want to take with you?"

Tony collected himself. "Umh, let's say one and a backup. Two tabs. Okay?"

"Whatever you say, chief," Percy said through a charming little smile. "I'll put two in a little glass tube, stuffed with cotton."

"Much obliged," Tony replied, grinning at the chemist because he really thought it wise to act grateful.

Then Percy said, "You're sure this is for a truly deserving individual?"

"Oh, truly deserving," Tony nodded.

"Gosh I wish I could be there to watch the magic," Percy said finally. "You will remember to let me know how it goes?"

"No fear of that," Tony said, rising to leave. "No fear of that at all."

* * *

Some ten minutes later, Tony strolled lightly down one of Southwark's little side streets. He found an oddly mellow mood had taken hold of him. Carefree like. He had the "how" in his trousers pocket, in the little glass bottle provided by Percy Dithers. Although the future remained vague, as always, Tony felt certain that the "when" would take care of itself. He had always led a charmed life in that respect: providence would provide.

He stopped short in mid-stride, on the sidewalk. He looked skyward at the bright day, and smiled broadly. Realizing he had been whistling a Jimmy Cliff reggae tune, an old favorite that always gave him a zestful charge.

He turned round and looked back in the direction he had come from. No, he couldn't see it anymore: he had turned one corner too many. He had left the house of horrors behind.

Pulling his cell phone from its holster on his belt, Tony flicked it open and touched an autodial number. It was the noon hour.

"Harry, it's me," he said briskly into the mouthpiece. "No, I've finished early. Tell you what. You know that little sandwich shop I like so much, over by Tower Bridge Park? Yes, that's the one. I'm headed there now, on foot. Pick me up there in, oh, let's make it an hour. What?"

He listened to the receiver.

"Yes, thanks. I'm having a lovely day. Turned out fine. How 'bout you?"

He listened for a moment, then said: "Excellent! See you in an hour, then." And he strolled off lightheartedly down the road.

It was a little past one-thirty when he stepped from the Mercedes at the top of New Bond Street, in Mayfair.

He smiled through the open driver's side window at Harry, saying, "You know what, Harry? Nothing on for tonight. And I'm in the mood for fish. How about joining me for some fried plaice and chips and mushy peas at the Seashell—say about eight?"

"Pleased to, guv," Harry hummed back. He was such a delightful man. "What about this afternoon? Where you headed, sir?"

"The afternoon's on me, Harry. You go take in a cinema, or whatever. I'm just gonna walk about town, enjoy meself."

"Certain, guv?"

"Certain, Harry. Hang around Mayfair, wander about a bit. You can collect me at the Dorchester at seven-thirty. Dinner for two gents in Marylebone! Sounds okay, doesn't it? We'll have Spotted Dick for the sweet."

Tony waved at Harry's beaming smile as the Mercedes inched its way into the traffic jam and crawled off down New Bond.

It has always been a fashionable avenue, lined with exquisite stores selling marvelous and exotic goods.

Tony found his mood soaring. He looked up above the tall rows of buildings as he strolled happily down Bond. The bright sunny sky billowed with puffy white clouds floating merrily, it seemed, past the building tops. He realized he was again whistling the strains of the reggae master's *Breakout*. They matched his mood perfectly.

He stopped in at one of the street's venerable Italian shops and purchased a Ferre jacket, two pairs of narrow pleated slacks to be made to measure, one in striped double-black and another in sandy tan, and finally a pair of Italian loafers of a softness rarely found. He had them shipped home, to avoid the "value added tax" imposed on local shoppers.

Passing a holiday agent's shop, he decided on the spur of the moment to extend his stay in Europe. A sort of treat for the upcoming triumph he was now anticipating with increasing excitement.

At the counter he told a pretty young lady, smartly dressed in blue to set off her golden hair and shining face, that he'd like to engage some bookings: "Can you arrange," he said to her, "a late-morning Sunday crossing of the chunnel for me?"

"Yes of course," she said while retrieving a glossy brochure from under the counter. "Every fifteen minutes, *le Shuttle* leaves from Folkstone, here," she pointed to the brochure's map, "and arrives in Calais thirty-five minutes later."

"Book me for 11 a.m. or thereabouts, if there's an opening."

"With automobile?"

"I'll need to hire one. I have a special request, though. Have you got a Ferrari by chance?"

"Checking the computer," she responded, at a keyboard. "Umh, we have two in our fleet... Oh, you're in luck! We have something called a 550 Maranello, here in London. Seven hundred miles on it."

"Absolutely splendid!" Tony told her.

"Rather dear, though, I'm afraid," she explained soberly, showing him the price on the screen for a daily rental.

"Ouch!" Tony said mockingly. "I'll have it for two days. Full insurance for the train and France, too. Mileage charge?"

"Fraid so... 33p per. Plus petrol, of course."

"Of course!" Tony agreed.

"And accommodation?" she asked further.

"Yes, book me a front suite at the Negresco in Nice, Sunday and Monday nights."

"In Nice, sir? That's some distance from Calais, you realize," she asked efficiently, politely.

"Hence the Ferrari!" Tony told her.

"Just checking on the computer, sir... Yes, you'd be out of luck for Saturday, but Sunday and Monday are available. About four hundred pounds a night, on today's exchange."

"Book it all," Tony said, flipping some plastic onto the counter.

"Yes, charging to American Express..." and she typed the numbers into her computer. "Deposit, sir?"

"No, prepay the entire amount."

"I've never seen a Black card before, sir. Something new? Gold, Platinum... first time I've seen black."

"Oh, it's been around," Tony said simply, not explaining.

"Right, then!" she exclaimed in that so-English way. "Give me a few moments and I'll have all the documents ready for you."

Tony thumbed through a travel brochure on the Italian lake district.

"All ready, sir," she hailed him back to the counter. "You pick up the Ferrari at our office by Victoria Station—"

Tony broke in. "I'd like it delivered to me at the Dorchester by 6:30 a.m. full of petrol."

"Yes, sir. Six-thirty at the Dorchester"—making a computer note. "And you're set for the 11:15 a.m. boarding on *le Shuttle* from Folkstone. They ask you to be at the toll gate at least twenty-five minutes in advance of departure. There's a boarding map with your documents. And, last, the hotel booking for Nice. A residual charge for vehicle mileage will be made against your credit card... and will there be anything further, sir?"

"Thanks awfully!" Tony said to her, collecting the packet. "Ta."

As Tony stepped from the booking agent's, he collided with another man on the street. They nearly knocked each other down.

"Heh, you okay, buddy?" came the American voice to Tony's ears. "Didn't mean to strike yuh. Geez, I was lookin' at all them fancy posters in the window there."

"Quite okay. You okay yourself?" Tony said back.

"Hell, it takes more'n a little bump just to get old Mikey's attention," he laughed. Then he rapped his skull with his knuckles and muttered, "Hello, anybody home!" Started tucking in his colorful shirt, straightening his red nylon jacket. Tony doing more or less the same to his Italian duds.

"Okay then," Tony said. "Nice meeting you!" The attempt at a joke was a mistake, it turned out.

"Heh, you're American, ain't ya?" The man started to tag along by Tony's side as he walked on, ambling sort of into Tony's stride.

"Formerly British, now American," Tony told him, not knowing why, except that the man's manner was so engaging.

He stuck out his hand Tony's direction, across his body as he stood to Tony's right. "Name's Mike Black. What's yours?"

"Umh, Tony. Tony Spool." They shook hands.

"Glad to meetchuh, Tony Spool! What a great name!" They were now several storefronts down the street from where they'd bumped together.

Tony saw his new friend was bigger than himself, maybe six-three or four, seemed in his sixties, had wind-blown white hair and a ruddy complexion. An American potbelly stuck out in front. His gait was easy and casual. He smiled constantly, looking alternately at the surroundings and at Tony. His clothing was strictly tourist, nylon and rubber.

"Geez, what a town, huh Tony?" he continued. "Lookit these fancy-schmantzy stores, will ya?"

Tony didn't reply. This was going in the wrong direction.

"Aw... I don't mean to be a bother, it's just that I'm free for the afternoon. I'm on a coach tour. How 'bout you, Tony?"

"Same as you, free for the afternoon. Now if you don't mind..."

"Bet ya know this town upside down, donchu, Tony?"

"A bit," Tony said quickly, stepping up his pace. His friend kept up.

"I don't hafta get back to the tour group till breakfast," he continued on. "See, this is our 'get to know London' free day. That means they don't hafta put out nuthin'! Free to them, see my point?"

Tony made no reply.

"Geez, it'll be supper time in 'nother hour or so. I'm gettin' hungry. Know any place good to eat, Tony?"

"Just pick any place," Tony said noncommittally.

"How 'bout joinin' me, Tony?"

"Fraid not. Previous arrangements."

"How 'bout a beer, then?"

Tony stopped and faced him. He was going to shine him on, but the man's smile was so friendly, he just couldn't be rude. Tony detected some alcohol on the man's breath.

"Look," he said, "nice meeting you, Mike, but I'm afraid I must excuse myself. Things to do, you know." He started walking. Mike kept up.

"Aw, don't let me bother ya, Tony. It's not really Black, ya know. Blaczewski. Pollock blood. The Bronx, rough town, ya change your name so they don't beat ya up all the time. So it got to be Black."

"Nice Yankee name," Tony said away from Mike, stopping to look in a store window. Mike stopped too, didn't look much in the window.

"Ya change your name in America, Tony? Italian, ainchu?"

Tony said nothing.

"Spent forty years in construction, Tony. Got beat up plenty, know what I mean? Aw hell, I did some beatin' myself!" Mike smiled on, Tony trying to ignore him. "I could sure use a drink..." He followed Tony as he moved on.

Tony picked up his pace again. Mike kept up, huffing at him. "Every time the foreman pissed me off, I belted him. He belted back plenty, believe me, but I'm the one always got fired. 'Mikey,' they says to me, 'ya gotta get ahold of that temper of yours.' Then they'd call me the next week and hire me back! Hard to get a good man, ya see..."

Tony nodded in Mike's general direction.

"What line of work ya in, Tony?" Mike persisted on the nod.

"Banking," Tony said.

"I can see it's been good to ya, Tony. I've been blessed with a good life myself. Can't complain. Lost the wife a coupla years back, cancer ya see. She always wanted tuh see London. I was too cheap. Now I'm seein' it for the both of us. She'da liked me doin' it. She'da like you."

Tony had turned right where Old Bond Street took over from the new, onto Bruton Street. Mike followed him, saying "No use bitchin' cause ya never know what's comin' next, right Tony?"

Tony stopped in front of the ornate, columned entrance to number

33 Bruton Street. Mike stopped with him.

Tony said, "I'm going in here, now, Mike, if you'll excuse me."

Mike looked at the window, with fancy gold lettering that announced 'HOLLAND & HOLLAND.' He said, "Oh, what's this, a gun store?"

"By appointment only, I'm afraid," Tony lied to him. "So, nice meeting you. Hope you enjoy your tour here in England." And he started in the door.

"Okay, yeah. Heh, you too, Tony!" The voice was happy, friendly. You couldn't help but like him. "Bye now," he waved.

And the man Mike Black walked off seemingly without a care in the world down the street, all red nylon and white rubber. Some might envy him. Tony, looking back on him a moment, closed the heavy mahogany and glass door behind him.

It was another world, this store. Tony's duds fit these surroundings: clublike and aristocratic: tawny walls offset with polished oak windowed partitions revealing specialized rooms, one devoted to the clothing of sport for the English gentry, another protecting a long rack of domestic and imported shotguns carrying ID tags attached to their trigger guards. The heads of impressive quarry taken on far-off safari in yonder days now festooned the walls here and there. Persian rugs relieved the highly polished oak floors. An armor-suited knight, frozen forever at attention, overlooked a mahogany table with a gold-tooled leather top, awaiting the proper client's checkbook.

Clerks in stiffly starched white collars, ties and prim business suits attended to customers throughout the store. One of them appeared intent upon measuring the barrels of a side-by-side shotgun for some purpose.

Tony sauntered among it all, exchanged polite gestures with a clerk or two, explained he was just looking, and then came to an inner room with a closed, windowed door bearing a painted plate saying 'GUN ROOM.' Tony tried the door handle. Locked. He noticed the security keypad, and pressed a brass button for admission.

A clerk in his thirties, possibly, wearing a white smock-coat, relieved the lock and welcomed Tony through the portal with a dubious face. He sized Tony up and down, then his look lightened as he recognized the expense of the clothes he saw.

"And how may I be of assistance, sir?" he asked.

Tony walked past him and went over to admire a glass-fronted gun case holding half a dozen large rifles. He touched his forefinger to his lip.

"Just thought I'd look at some safari doubles," Tony sort of mumbled.

"In from down under, sir?"

Tony turned to him. "No, America." Tony's mouth was drawn out long, appropriately without expression.

"Ah, America!" the clerk now said with a sudden enthusiasm. He shuffled his shoulders, as if among friends. "Been there twice myself, sir. Four years back, me and the kiddies and the better half we all did Florida. Caw, the kids spent a bloody *for-tune* in Disneyworld. I'm still in hock! Myself, I loved Epcot Center. Been there, sir?"

"No, afraid not," Tony said truthfully, looking back at the gun case.

"Oh, you shouldn't miss it!" The clerk's eyes seemed distant. "Now the better half, she hated the whole place. Moss-queet-oes, you see. Bothered her no end. Rather too hot as well," the clerk said, snatching a glance over his shoulder, an expression on his face suggesting he was about to reveal a state secret. "Two days and the pair of us we looked a fright, like as if we'd been in sauna the entire time!" He smiled widely at Tony now.

Tony said without interest, not looking at him, "Bit hot for me, too."

"Now, California, sir..." the clerk persisted, "ah, we all liked that! Did Los Ange-lese last August. Hot but dry. I could take that. We spent a day at that rollercoaster place, Six Flags Magic Mountain? North of the city proper. The kids, well they couldn't get their fill of that thing they call Colossus. The better half and me, we had enough doing it just once. You partial to rollercoasters, sir?"

"I've done a few... let me see that gun, there, will you?" Tony said, pointing in the case.

The clerk retrieved a set of delicate brass keys from his pocket, and with great care handed the rifle in question to Tony. But he went on:

"And Santa Monica, the Palisades! Better half says to me, she says, 'Steve, this is a bit of all right, isn't it?' Said she'd live there if I wanted. You know, if we could find the right place, after I retire, when the kids have gone."

"So it's Steve is it?" Tony asked.

"Oh, sorry, guv. Steven Squatt, at your pleasure," and he held out his hand for Tony to take. His dry skin shone faintly with gun oil.

Tony sighted the gun instinctively, held it away to take in the details of its engraving and fine stock, pulled it back fast to his cheek.

The clerk noticed Tony's way with the gun.

"You shoot, don't you, sir?" he inquired more professionally now.

"I have... other kinds of guns."

"Not a double rifle?" the clerk asked. "Nothing like 'em, sir. Two killer barrels."

"No, never have. I take that journal, though. Been on my mind, getting one of these for myself."

"The *Double Gun Journal*, sir? Oh, quite an elegant magazine, that! Some of the lads here really like that one, advertise in it. True sportsmen there, certain. H&H are in it, of course. I've sold a gun or two to gentlemen like yourself who saw our advertisements, come to London to see the best."

Tony handed back the rifle, pointed to another in the case. The clerk retrieved it, again with the greatest of care.

"A Holland & Holland .577 Nitro Express Royal, sir," he explained. "New, this one. We produce just a few each year."

Tony ran his fingers over the chequering of the superbly grained walnut stock, touched the tooling, clicked open the twin barrels. Didn't say anything. Just admired.

"A deluxe model, this one," the clerk continued to extol. "Notice the gold tooling of the leopard engraving," he pointed out, "and the buffalo horn fore-end tip. This would be a fine choice. Planning a safari, sir?"

"You never know, do you?" Tony answered flatly. "It would be enough gun, wouldn't it, for anything?" He looked at the description and generous five-figure price noted on the gun's trigger tag.

"No question, sir. Take down any of the Big Five."

"And what's the largest calibre?" Tony asked. "Just curious."

"We do make a .700 Nitro, sir. Not much call for it, though. Your occasional Indian royalty, sometimes a sand-dune billionaire. The cartridges run to about a hundred dollars each..." he finished, as if that settled it.

Tony handed back the rifle. The clerk wiped it down with an oil cloth, smoothing away the human touch, and eased it back into its resting spot in the gun case.

"That .577 might do," Tony said simply, without elaboration. "I'll consider it. On my next trip to London, maybe..."

"You sure you've never been on safari, sir?"

"I've done a bit of hunting," Tony told him vaguely. "Nothing very special, routine stuff. All sorts of weapons. It's mainly the double rifle that's outside my experience. So... you see my interest."

"Well, sir," the clerk said, looking sharp at him, "when you're ready, H&H shall be happy to assist in every possible way! We can even arrange your safari for you."

Tony accepted the clerk's offered card.

"Just about the ultimate sporting gun, isn't it?" Tony intoned, still looking at the double rifle he had just handled, gleaming in the glass case.

"Yes sir," replied the clerk, "it's a unique experience, shooting a double. If it's the savage beast you need to kill, good and dead, quick like, nothing compares with the Nitros for stopping ability."

"Oh it's the savage beast, all right," Tony agreed evasively.

"Them buggers," the clerk said under his breath, barely above a whisper, squinting his eyes for effect, "deserve a proper stopping!"

Tony ticked his chin to the left, chirped his lips in a gesture of agreement, and walked out without saying another word.

ELEVEN

Lightning combed the darkening heavens.

Susan checked her wristwatch, thinking about halfway there maybe, hopefully. Her eyes darted again to the illuminated Fasten Seatbelt sign, looping immediately back to the window on her right.

Flashes streaked everywhere through the ominous gray clouds making a Valkyries sea of misty waters beneath the jet. Susan's eyes jumped at a brilliant crazy long explosion as it streaked off under the nose of the plane, out of view, disappearing. Even the bluish black skies above the storm were turning sour from its intensity.

Just then a deafening, hollow explosion rattled the illuminated gray clouds, like a tin ghost dinning its empty armor as it skipped through the marshes of Hell. The sound roared into Susan's brain, forced her shoulders to lift and tighten. Her head sank, like a tortoise's into its carapace.

Her poor neck hurt, tightened in fear. Her eyelids flicked, jittering her vision. She remembered Doree, caught sight of her in the seat to her left. Sound asleep, oblivious.

Susan straightened her backbone, pushed her tail into the flexion of the airplane seat, and felt better. Rolled her head, to relieve her neck muscles of some tension. Yes, that helped.

A soothing voice intruded into her fears, clear and steady, saying

"Folks, Captain Michals here. We're, uh, encountering a bit denser of a storm than radar indicated. Undercurrents are pushing it higher. So we've started climbing out of it. Nothing to worry about..."

Doree slept through it all, Susan saw.

"We're now just to the southeast of the tip of Greenland," the voice resumed. "The seas down there, well just imagine a gigantic toilet being flushed. Something called the Irminger Current drags freezing waters south through the Denmark Strait into the warmer Gulf Stream, and you get perfect storm conditions. In the old days, the Viking sailors daring those waters called the tip of the continent 'Cape Farewell.' And they were kinda brave, those guys."

Another pause. Susan felt the jet pulling higher away from the lightning which still streaked wildly, far below. The bellowing thunderclaps lessened. It all seemed like a distant parade now, its sound and fury a comfortable measure away.

The voice again: "Okay, folks, we're at a good altitude now. Should be fairly smooth sailing from now forward. Sorry if we disturbed your rest! We'll dim the lights again, but keep the seatbelts sign on for a while longer. Sleep tight till breakfast, in about an hour." And Susan's thoughts fell among silence.

A tentative smile coaxed itself onto her lips, her head lifting. She clicked her jaw, it had been so tight.

Looking back and far down at the matchbox storm, now but a swirling thunderhead of gray and flickers surrounded by billowing white ocean, Susan thought of Tony. Thor's hammer, he would have told her. Nothing more.

How she missed him! They had rarely been separated during the seven years of their marriage. All of their vacations had been within America, places and things that Susan had always wanted to see and do. Tony had been everywhere in the world, so he always let Susan choose their precious holidays together. She felt comfortable in the States.

Okay, maybe she was a little jealous of him. He had plenty of free time. When the bank called him to London, or somewhere else, and it really wasn't that often was it, he had to go. It was right that he should. How many stuffy old British institutions kept retired officers on retainer, after all? Especially expatriates? It was quite an honor, being a financial consultant to a private London bank. It sure paid well!

Course, she mused, Tony didn't need the money. He was loaded. No, *they* were loaded! But he must be worth his retainer and his fees. Tony always seemed eager to go when they called him. Kept his mind alive. Must make him feel proud, too. Susan smiled inwardly at this. Her closed eyes slumbered now, her normally sparkling eyes at peace, her head dreamy.

Okay, she *was* jealous. She had wanted to go on all those trips with Tony, but never had. She had her own career to take care of, after all, just like Tony. The Department of State wasn't exactly the easiest place to get into, was it? She'd made steady advancements, okay they were modest but they were steady, she was getting nearer and nearer to top-secret clearance, she was paying her dues. Tony had already paid his; he deserved time for himself. When she reached his age, another fifteen years, she'd have her own dues paid. Meantime she did much more than put in her time, she gave extra every day, she did her absolute best. Yep, she nodded in the darkened cabin of the Air Force jet, her best!

She knew her parents in heaven would be pleased as proverbial punch at what she'd done with her life since they left her.

Feeling this way made her occasional separations from her husband easier to live with. Her working hours belonged to State. Her leisure time, her down time, she dedicated to Tony and their enduring romance.

The only drawback was that her vacation allowances, earned though they might be, tended to be quite limited. She still lacked seniority. And that had always meant she couldn't accompany Tony on his business trips. That was okay, though. She knew Tony missed her whenever he went away on bank business, but she also knew that he was an old hand at it; he always seemed to handle the separations better than she did. She figured he probably held his sentimental nature in check while he attended to business. It was the only practical way to manage, really, wasn't it?

Ohh, she'd be with Tony soon now—*imagine* them being called to work in London, *England*, at just the same time—it would be such fun. She drifted toward sleep. All their plans—those weeks of anticipation—looking for the perfect clothes on autumn Saturdays. Tony wasn't right about that, she commanded to herself, maybe dreaming already, she just wouldn't have enough time to shop in London as Tony suggested—all her free time was going to be by Tony's side, seeing...

Tony ambled along Curzon Street in the cloudy late noon hour. Storm coming, he wondered, noting the dwindling sun after what had been an especially beautiful autumn morning. Temperature dropping as well. High winds carried in pale gray clouds, amassing above the tall ancient masonry and old red brick buildings of Mayfair's crowded blocks. Londoners carried furled umbrellas, experienced anticipators. Tony's was home in Virginia, and he didn't care, October was supposed to be nice, end of decision. An English sprinkle reminded him deliciously of his childhood. You'd get a little wet, but so what? Live 'dangerously' or not at all.

Today a bit of wet couldn't obnubilate Tony's high spirits nor his optimism. Neither would a drenching, even.

What a moment it had proven to be! Tony had invisibly taken a seat in the back row, entering Christie's auction rooms just a few lots before his coin came up for bidding, and he had enjoyed watching Simon ply his trade with a skillfulness few might ever master. The punters never got their paddles in the air. Most of the dealers had faded away with rapidity. Then the telephone and computer bids fought each other, representing absentee buyers, and just as a smug hand holding a cell phone thought it had captured Tony's coin, Simon finally snuck into the contest, deftly stroking the air above his head with five widely spread fingers, jumping the bid by five thousand pounds.

And that was it. Done deal. The competition flagged under Simon's bold move and under his defiant stare carrying a unique air of insouciance with it, as though he were only just beginning to fan his interest, and the auctioneer called down Lot 199 to Mister Simon Stinger of Camden Coins. A brief applause let out, at which Simon emitted only a slow, long yawn, and patted at his mouth with the triumphant paddle.

The auctioneer moved on to the next lot, whereupon Simon removed himself noisily from his seat at the front ring around the auction podium, announcing his boredom with the remaining proceedings, and strolled casually out the aisle, the rolled-up sale catalogue in his left hand, an inscrutable look upon his face.

Neither he nor Tony allowed each other's eyes to meet as Simon exited his stage.

And still a good hour to elapse before London broke for lunch.

Doree bumped an elbow gently into Susan's ribs.

"Hey, sleepyhead, don't you want some breakfast?"

A stewardess stood by their row, serving the seats opposite theirs from her much-used metal hostess cart, its purple and silver paint chipped.

Susan rubbed her eyes. Smelling breakfast, she felt her stomach growl lowly. "Good morning, Doree," she murmured, running her tongue across her lips, dry as an old sock left in the sun from sleep, and tasting much the same. Coffee was going to taste great this morning! Strong black coffee.

"I'm getting excited." Doree secretly spoke into Susan's ear, hushing her vocal cords so no one else could hear.

"Me, too," Susan mouthed back, soundlessly.

Doree did a quick airplane exercise, pulling first one knee and then the other up towards her belly with her cupped hands, stretching her hamstrings upward off the seat. Then she dropped her meal tray for the approaching plastic platter. She'd eat it, whatever it was.

As Susan accepted her tray from the Air Force hostess, Doree suddenly looked past her out the window, as the cloud cover broke brightly to reveal an endless expanse of wine-dark sea, dotted with white caps.

"Look down there," she told Susan. "What are those white dots all over the blue ocean, I wonder?"

"Icebergs," offered the air hostess. "We don't often see them this far east, better check them out while you can."

As they ate, the brilliant dots thinned out. The restless eternal sea, miles below, seemed but a dark still pool this far away.

"Aren't they beautiful?" Susan muttered to Doree. "God's wonders are sure endless. I've never seen an iceberg before. Wait till I tell Tony."

And again her thoughts turned to her soul mate.

Weeks of waiting, and here she was, almost in England. A completely new experience awaited her.

Most of the commercial airline traffic left the eastern United States in the early evening and arrived at either Heathrow or Gatwick Airport outside of London in the early hours of the next morning. But Susan and Doree were on an Air Force jet, part of a small party of State Department people who found themselves seated among transferring military personnel and government executives from various offices headed for London as a destination or as a transfer stop to other destinations in Europe or beyond. They had departed from a military gate at Dulles Airport just before dawn and would arrive in London late in the afternoon. Less wasted time was how the schedule was explained to Susan and her colleagues.

Susan herself approved of the concept. She knew she would probably be pretty tired, though, by the time she got to hug her husband again.

Not that there would be that much hugging, Susan sighed.

Tony wasn't wild about the idea, either. In fact, he had wanted her to ask for an exception to State Department travel rules, urged her to ask permission to stay with him at the Dorchester, at his expense, even though she was in London on government business. But Susan was reluctant to ask, putting her personal desires aside for the sake of her career, and it being her first foreign trip for work. She had made casual inquiries about such exceptions, and her inquiries had verified her suspicions that an exception to the hotel rule would not be likely. This trip had a certain amount of secrecy to it, and security was a concern.

So Susan would be sharing a double room at the Savoy with her assistant in the Information Office, Doree. Intimate time with Tony would surely be slight. It didn't matter all that much. They'd both be home soon.

Let's see, Susan thought, she and Doree would settle in at the Savoy, she'd call Tony right away, she knew he'd be waiting at the Dorchester for her call, then they'd have the balance of the day together, dinner, and who knew what else... in Tony's suite. A romantic rendezvous, like.

Could she keep awake that long? Seven hours plus in the air, five hours of daylight lost flying east to England, another hour at least to get to the hotel, then maybe a quick nap?

She was *so* looking forward to seeing London, so hoped she and Tony could walk about town in the evening. She'd generate the energy somehow. That would take care of Wednesday certainly.

Susan went over the schedule once again in her mind. Managing one's time was so necessary in today's working world, she mused.

So, Tony had left home last Sunday. The Concorde, oh how Tony loved that airplane! It was so expensive. But time was money, he reminded her, and in his case it was the bank's money, so he invariably took Concorde whenever it fit into his travel plans. By Sunday evening Tony was safely in his rooms at the Dorchester. She called him when he woke up early Monday, which was in the wee hours of the morning for her, back in Virginia.

Then, he explained beforehand but she didn't listen carefully, any more than he gave homage to all the details of her days, he was to have two long, boring, business-meeting days—'confabs,' Tony said they were—that consumed both Monday and Tuesday. He had said, she recalled, something about seeing that coin he wanted to get in some auction, checking it out before his business day began, Tuesday most likely he said.

That brought her up to date. It would be such a long day, the rest of this day. And she had to work tomorrow, Thursday, but only through lunch.

Yes, tomorrow, Thursday morning, there was to be a hush-hush briefing at the American Embassy. That sounded kinda exciting, actually. She had been instructed that the afternoon, following lunch at the Embassy, would be free time. The rest of Thursday would be hers and Tony's! And Tony had mentioned something about dinner plans at a fancy restaurant with some people he knew, Londoners. That would probably be fun, too. Tony's friends rarely disappointed.

Friday was the big day for everyone. The reason State was sending her and her colleagues over here. She knew it involved some sort of liaison with the British government, knew it included big hopes for helping to solve the awful war that had been raging in Northern Ireland, knew it was important. She was looking forward to being part of the peace process. Her job would be to report on the activities, to marshal information about what would take place. She was looking forward to it. Peace was a wonderful goal!

But Friday was also going to be a day she would not see Tony much, if at all.

Because of the five hours' time difference between the eastern U.S. and England, and their separate work schedules, she had managed to talk to Tony only twice since he had gone on ahead of her. The first time was that early morning call she made to him at the Dorchester. The other time, his call came in during her mid-afternoon break, a surprise to her, really: it was something he rarely did, call her at work. Poor baby. He sounded so very tired, weary, that night: she figured he had put in a tough day. Not something he was much used to doing anymore.

He'd need to be at an all-day meeting at the bank Friday, he'd said, sounding exhausted. Said maybe there'd be time to see each other late in the day Friday, or maybe not. Something about currency devaluations in Asia, people in from all over for the 'confab' at the bank, maybe drawing out late into the night. He just wasn't sure.

But, he promised, all day Saturday was theirs! Susan would be free then, too. All the State Department personnel were being given Saturday at leisure. Their work would be done. They would all fly back to Washington on the Air Force jet Sunday morning. Tony would be home a couple days later.

So, some work, some fun together, then back to the comfort of their usual routine next week, as soon as Tony finished up his meetings. He promised they would all end early in the week; he'd be home mid-week—

Doree interrupted Susan's plan-making.

"Look," she told Susan, "we're reaching land."

They both sat peering out the jet's window at the quaint villages and the lush greenery now flowing beneath the wings. They smiled happily at each other. It was such a pretty landscape.

"Wow!" Doree said to Susan. "I can hardly believe I'm here. England, Susan, England! After work, I'm seeing some sights. Maybe Mr. Right will bump into me, like Tony did to you. Wish me luck!"

Susan held Doree's hand, giving it a little squeeze. They watched as the jet lost altitude and approached Heathrow Airport, seeing a huge gray stone castle below, smiling at their good fortune.

Susan thinking she just knew she was going to have a wonderful time in London. After all, Tony would be there!

His magnificent gold coin fixed in his mind's eye, Tony loped up Curzon Street, his soul singing in possession of King James, former hunter-warrior, transformed seeker of wisdom, a religious leader who oversaw the 'authorized' translation of the Bible which inspired millions for centuries. What a thing to collect, souls!

At the southern end of the enclosed parklet called Berkeley Square, Tony's eye caught the statue of the Nude Girl, and it made him smile, reminded him of his Susan. Though he always found Susan sexier fully dressed than any other female wearing nothing but her birthday suit.

He thought of her silky, long pale-brown hair, parted in the middle, swooping down over her ears, framing her coquettish face. Hers was the most natural sexuality Tony had ever experienced. She was just herself, didn't try to melt man's heart, just did. Those sparkling hazel eyes and that softly sloping nose set in bones Michelangelo might have carved. Her dense, arched eyebrows: how Tony loved to lick them with his tongue! The brilliancy of her small, perfect teeth. The curve of her mouth, pink and moist, always it seemed fixed in a suggestive, delicate smile.

Tony found himself standing before the Nude Girl, musing, feeling aroused. She did more or less have Susan's angular, sexy small shoulders. Just a few hours more, Tony reminded himself. Just a few hours more.

Thinking again of King James, Tony's mind fell to things literary. Wasn't there a famous bookstore just up the block? He'd wander over and check it out.

Smiling easily as he walked, the smile of triumph. And how Simon had triumphed. Winning King James for him, and for two-thirds of his maximum bid as well. He'd reward Simon with a commission of ten thousand pounds, instead of the customary five percent of the hammer price. Simon had well earned it, he had been magnificent.

Yes, here it was, the bookstore. Looked more like a gentleman's townhouse, but he knew what lay inside. The ornate door said 'MAGGS BROS.' He walked through it.

A comely young lady welcomed him. Funny, she looked like your stereotyped librarian. But this was no lending library. She was doubtless a master of the books, too.

Tony smiled openly as she approached, mostly at the tight bun she had tied her brunette hair into. Thank God, he thought. Enough arousal already.

He noticed a display counter, lengthy and of well-rubbed oak, showing off a group of large, color-covered volumes featuring castles and knights.

"I'm thinking of military history just now," he said to her. "Any recommendations?"

Her voice actually did arouse him a little, gravelly, accented by the English lilt.

"We've a few bits in stock, sir. If you'll follow me. . . ?" And she led him to a brass-festooned tiny elevator, built for two. Airy, with vertical twisted-brass bars for the enclosure. They rode it down one level, finding in the 'basement' long rows of bookshelves, packed with uncountable numbers of volumes. Tony looked somewhat agog.

The young lady noticed it. She said, "The first ten rows, sir. All tagged for country and century. Do you need some help?"

"I guess."

She laughed knowingly. "This is our main storage. We own land well into the center of the Square. These shelves run for over fifty meters in length. Something on the order of three million books?"

"*English* military history," he said lamely.

She took him to the appropriate row. "You can start here, sir. I'll just be upstairs, should you require me. There's a buzzer over there, by the elevator. Or just come up once you've done."

Tony noticed well-developed calf muscles as she ascended in the open elevator. Cut it out, he told himself, and turned to the shelves.

Twenty feet along, he got out of the Celtic period and the Roman occupation of Britain. Then came what looked like a mile of the Middle Ages. He stooped and ran an eye down one row; it disappeared into the dim light. So he took the elevator upstairs.

Another young lady came over to him as he stepped off the elevator. "Find what you wanted, sir?"

"Uh, no. Maybe you can make a suggestion or two."

"Of course."

"Name me some battles England won. Old ones. Anything stand out in our history of military conquests?"

"Well," she began, "there are so many. I'm part French, so my own interests turn naturally to engagements between England and France, my two halves so to speak."

"Okay, try me."

"Hard to begin, isn't it?" she offered. "Battle of Hastings, 1066. William the Conqueror? Duke William of Normandy? He built the Tower of London, the inner castle, you know."

"What about something later? Something England won."

"My own favorite," she said, "is Agincourt. October 1415? You'll remember your Shakespeare. *Henry V?*"

"Agincourt," Tony mumbled. "Okay, that sounds of interest."

The clerk could tell he didn't know the story. "You'll like it," she said. "It's a real man's story. Young Prince Henry had a reputation for being, what shall we say, a party animal? Strong drink, willing women. So the French laughed when, some few years later on, as King Henry, he sent them word that he claimed sovereignty over France. In answer, they shipped him a carton of tennis balls, implying he could handle the game, nothing much else. Henry invaded, took the port city of Harfleur, threatening to march into Paris, you see."

Tony stood listening. The female clerk kept brushing her loose hair away from her face.

"Well, the two armies met near Calais, by a castle called Agincourt. The English were outnumbered something like five to one, yet they *charged* the French army of twenty-five thousand. Cheeky, huh? They say Henry lost just under four hundred men, to France's eight thousand killed and another two thousand wounded. Henry's long-bow archers reduced the French knights to carrion. Tennis balls indeed. It's quite a tale, sir."

"Where can I read about it?"

"It's been told over and over again. Hundreds of sources. To this very day, the French won't talk about it. The best version for your needs, short but inspired, might be Churchill's."

"Do you have a copy?"

"It's a common book, sir. We probably have a couple hundred copies."

"I'll have one, please."

And so Tony walked across Berkeley Square a few minutes later with

Winston Churchill's account in his hand, short just six pounds. The wisdom of the ages, Tony pondered, for the price of a cheap lunch.

Following a leisurely, hardly cheap lunch at his hotel, Tony decided to take a nap. By tea time, which Tony normally ignored, he was deep into Churchill's lyrically told history of the battles of the Hundred Years' War.

He found himself especially impressed by King Henry V's boldness in taking a weary, small army plagued by camp illnesses into battle against a well-rested and seemingly invincible force of huge numbers. The long odds beaten by the power of the spirit of one man! As well as by a cunning understanding of military logistics. Agincourt, Tony mouthed to himself...

Although he never questioned where his own destiny led him, Tony was beginning to wonder why this battle, fought almost six hundred years ago, had come into his world at this moment in time. The power of the battle, though, had indeed captured his imagination as he relived it through Churchill's words. It was beginning to fascinate him, as was King Henry.

Just then the hotel telephone rang by his bedside.

It was Susan's voice he heard. "Mr. Spool," she said in her oh-so-feminine voice, "Mrs. Spool has arrived."

Tony came to life. He'd been worrying just enough about her that he was anxiously filling his mind with the tale of Agincourt. Thank God she made it safely, he thought immediately. But he said in a steady tone:

"Susan, my Susan! Good crossing?"

"Most of it. Bad storm near Greenland. But I saw icebergs!"

"Where are you now?"

"In my room, at the Savoy."

"I'll rush right over."

"I'm kinda beat, Tony. Didn't sleep that much."

"Sweetie, I wanna see you—soon."

"I'm dying to see you too, Tony, but I need a nap. I'll feel better then."

Tony took her meaning.

"Okay, right. Howzabout my calling for you at six?"

"We'll see some sights?"

"Of course we will. One in particular I want to show you."

"Six, then."

"We'll find a light dinner somewhere. Feel like Greek?"

"Maybe. I'll leave it to you. Nothing heavy, though."

"Nothing heavy. Greek appetizers maybe."

"Or something English. An English dinner," Susan suggested.

"An English dinner. Not the easiest thing to find in London, Susan, unless you want to do a carvery."

"Tony?"

"Yes, sweetie?"

"I'm near to falling down. I need to rest now."

"Six, then. Harry will bring me. See you in the Savoy lobby."

"Love ya, Tony."

"Me, too. Kisses."

"Kisses."

* * *

Of all the hotel lobbies in London, none perhaps possesses more drop-dead class than the Savoy's. Same can be said for its stately, long rectangular entrance. Harry's black-pearl Mercedes carrying Tony snuck in among gleaming Rolls-Royces and even a Maserati with Italian plates. But Tony noticed none of this; his mind was set on just one objective.

He saw her as he entered the glittering lobby, and despite the reserved air of wealth and status, and the elegant people, Susan fell into his open arms. They hugged, bonding their love once again. They felt each other's bodies, holding on longer than might be seemly. They said not a word, didn't need to.

Breaking apart, Tony took hold of Susan's hand and led her away. Outside, among the glowing lamplights, Tony motioned towards his car.

"Shall we ride?" he asked her.

"Rather walk. We'd be all alone that way."

Tony led her to Harry's window by the curb.

"Susan, meet the finest chauffeur God ever made. Harry, meet Susan."

She liked him instantly. Harry broke into a genuine, happy smile, said "He's missed you all week, missus. I'm sure pleased to finally meet you in the flesh." Harry's tousled white hair blew in the breeze as he removed his cap to tip it to her, an old-world gesture of an old-world gentleman. His infectious smile brought out the best in Susan's.

"Oh Harry, I've heard so much about you as well over the years. Thank you for taking such good care of my husband!" And they touched hands.

Tony said, "Harry, we want to walk. I'd like to call you from The City in a while, shall we say two hours. Would you hang round somewhere near?"

"You take your own sweet time, guv. Harry'll be minutes away. Bye, now, Misses Spool. You enjoy the evening! Lucky for you, the rain's passed."

"Bye, Harry," she said to his window. "I'm so pleased to meet you."

And with his customary wave, Harry pulled slowly out of the hotel's grand entrance, his tail lights fading to dim red dots as Tony and Susan watched him go, just standing there together on the pavement.

"'Guv' he called you, Tony. 'Guv'!"

"We've been friends twenty years, Suz, but he's from the old school. He respects me as much as I do him. It's the English way."

"I'm already in love with this country," Susan said simply. "It's hardly a wonder the finest man I've ever met came out of all this," and she looked expansively about her. They still held hands. She quickly turned to him and kissed his lips, rubbing her nose against his as she did.

"Hungry?" he asked, his voice smothered in her cheek.

"Not for food. What shall we see on this perfect night?"

"I have a plan," Tony told her. "C'mon."

They walked at a peaceful pace east up the Strand, one of the oldest streets in London. Shortly Tony led her up a narrow lane, crossing Aldwych crescent, and she found some elegant buildings in a row to their right.

"The Royal Courts of Justice," Tony explained. "But c'mon."

And they zigzagged through some little streets, opening onto a large green oblong square surrounded by rows of connected buildings just a few stories high, each with distinctive doors. Lamplights made Susan feel she had stepped back into the days of Queen Victoria.

"Lincolns Inn Fields," Tony explained. "Thick with lawyers' quarters."

"All the doors have different shaped glasswork at their tops. Why is that, Tony?"

"My marvelous wife," he said softly, kissing her forehead. "Before there were numbers for addresses, centuries back, it was how you told visitors to find your house on the street, by its shape you see. And, in the early days of private fire companies, you registered your house with the company you contracted with by furnishing a drawing of its fanlight."

Susan studied the delightful variety of doors and their windows as they strolled along. "This is so *romantic*, honey," she murmured.

"C'mon along, I'll show you the best one of all." And presently they came to it.

"Why the best?"

"It's a museum now. Relatively few people find it, but it's jammed with the treasures of an 18th-century 'gentleman' collector. Everything from a real Egyptian sarcophagus and Roman signet rings—the best in the world—to Hogarth's original drawings satirizing the London of his day. One of my favorite, private places."

"Who was he?"

"Sir John Soane; built the Bank of England. But you wanted to see the real London, and we're about to walk through its very heart. Ready?"

And as they strolled, sometimes holding hands, stopping to kiss here and there, he led her through ancient alleys and turngates, past twinkling pubs and cloistered restaurants, down a tiny lane which opened onto an immense granite building with a footprint nearly a city block long. "The Old Bailey," Tony said without further explanation as she stared up at it. And around the corner he mouthed almost inaudibly, "Newgate, where the gallows once stood."

And then she spied the dome high above them in the darkening sky, saying, "A church?"

Tony only nodded, leading her around towards its front, but her eyes soon shone with recognition and she whispered: "St Paul's Cathedral!"

". . . where Diana Spencer married Prince Charles," she heard Tony saying. "I thought you would find it special."

Susan actually let her mouth gape. Tony saw her splendid pearly teeth behind the loveliest lips imaginable. "Can we go in?" she asked.

And they climbed the long set of steps and presently found themselves inside its massive, soaring vault.

Tony sat at a long ancient pew while he let Susan wander to discover it herself, watching her, as in love as he'd ever felt. She worked her way down one side, her eyes heavenward, taking it in, then came slowly back up the center aisle through rows of empty chairs to where Tony sat. They had the church almost to themselves at this late hour. Only a few heads could be seen deep in the long oak pews, rubbed shiny over centuries. Susan sat down silently next to Tony, and touched the lobe of his ear with her lips.

"I'll show you something really special," he breathed back into her ear. "Come with me."

He took her by the hand and found the hidden stairs that led up a wall, climbing till they emerged mid-way up the vaulted chamber of the cathedral. A frail filigree railing encircled the dome, enclosing a narrow aisle hugging the wall, high above the worship pews.

He left her and followed the railing until he was opposite her, far across the dome beneath the spectacular ceiling, holding his finger to his lips as he moved off.

Finally he cupped his mouth and said in a faint voice, "Who loves you most?"

Susan could hear these words reverberate across the open air, coming to her ears clear and distinct.

She mimicked Tony's mouth cupping. "I don't know. Who are you?"

Tony paused unexpectedly for a moment, halting at the phrase. But then he looked across at Susan and whispered something.

"If you don't know, you never will. . ." came back his hushed words, each one a tiny sound with bell-like clarity.

They came together again around the circular rail.

"Oh wow," she breathed in his ear as she touched him, in a loving hug.

"The Whispering Gallery," he breathed, audible only to Susan.

"It's wonderful," she sighed back, kissing him, barely brushing her lips against his.

"But now, my own favorite." He led her carefully down the hidden stairs, holding her hand as they descended to the vaults beneath the cathedral's main floor. They came to a niche along one cellar wall.

They could speak in normal tones now. They stood in poor light before an unimpressive, dark-bronze statue of a man whose chiseled eyes were forever fixed in a peculiar stare, as if towards another world.

Susan looked at Tony with a question in her eyes.

Tony had rarely mentioned his passion for visiting holy shrines, having said little more than that he'd seen such and such a place in his travels. Now it was time, he had decided, to reveal one of his secrets to her.

"Lawrence of Arabia. T.E. Lawrence," he said ever so quietly, standing before the bust reverently.

"Lawrence of Arabia," Susan muttered to herself. "Oh! Oh yeah. Peter O'Toole. He was so handsome, with his golden hair shining in the sun. I remember it now. Riding those camels. Those little flags waving. I saw the movie once, on TV. It was a beautiful movie, but most of the kids in school made fun of it, didn't see it."

Tony frowned inwardly, said "Peter O'Toole is an actor. A great actor, but just an actor. Lawrence wasn't a pretty blonde. Fact, he was kinda homely. I brought you to see this because he's one of my idols."

"Is he buried here?"

"No, he's buried by the sea, far from here. But this is the real Lawrence's likeness. His is not a story for school kids, though."

"Why, Tony?" Susan had never heard her husband mention any of this before. Because it was important to him, she cared. But she did not understand.

"A human being of towering character, and marvelous talents. A warrior, bold even for his time, a time when English gentlemen still saw wars as a chance to show off, as adventures to brag about later. Lawrence was no bragger. He was a genius as a warrior, and a genius as a literary narrator. In civilian clothes he looked ordinary. But the inner man was driven to greatness. He was blessed with a glorious soul, Susan, an inner flame more brilliant than you could ever imagine, if you looked only upon his skin."

Susan had nothing much to say. But she wondered at this secret: she thought they had no secrets, she and Tony, nothing unrevealed, between them. She looked at him with searching eyes, peering into the brilliant blue pools which guarded a brain she loved but appreciated only slightly.

"He understood the nature of the world, you see," Tony began telling her. "I've memorized a short passage from his account of the Arab revolt in the First World War. It goes like this:

"'Some of the evil of my tale may have been inherent in our circumstances. For years we lived anyhow with one another in the naked desert, under the indifferent heaven.'" Tony's voice, Susan heard, sounded like a soft song. Lacking its normal strong masculinity.

She listened as he went on: "'By day the hot sun fermented us; and we were dizzied by the beating wind. At night we were stained by dew, and shamed into pettiness by the innumerable silences of stars . . .'"

Susan just looked into his eyes, her own moistening just a bit as she began to appreciate what he was saying to her.

"That's so poetic, Tony. I think I see what you mean."

"It's wisdom," he said simply. "As true of the world today as then."

"I think it's more than that, Tony," Susan said ever so softly, looking inwardly. "I think it's seeing... God. Seeing that God rules us, guides us. Does he do that for you, Tony?"

It was a question Tony asked himself endlessly. He said in answer:

"Lawrence was misunderstood by most of his contemporaries. A lonely warrior. I think of him, sitting there under the star-filled, coal-black heavens, in the empty, freezing desert night, a lonely soldier, seeing man's insignificance, knowing that man lives a meaningless life unless he finds a quest for himself. His quest was to be a victor over the immoral creatures who preyed on others: he wrote that evil men 'have lost the world.' Lawrence embraced this quest as a private—well, a personal religion."

"It's very touching, Tony. But I wonder, did he give himself up to God's guidance? Did he really have faith?"

"I don't know." Tony said in a lost voice. "I know he devoted himself to his quest, loved doing it till it ended."

"The movie showed him dying kinda young, didn't it? In an accident."

"Yes, a triumphant life ending tragically. But more than tragically, also sadly."

"Sadly? You said he was a great warrior."

"Yes, a great warrior, Susan. But with a singular flaw."

"Which was?"

"He never knew who he really was, really was..."

Tony stood there, limply, not holding Susan's hand now, pensive in a way Susan hadn't often seen in him before.

Susan took hold of his hand in hers. He looked at her. She leaned over and kissed him tenderly on the cheek.

She whispered in his ear: "Only God knows who we really are. God's in charge. I think your idol realized that, Tony. I think he was blessed."

He just looked at her. He couldn't speak.

She said, "I love you, Tony. I always have, since the moment we met. I know who you are. And God knows who you are, too, Tony. You don't have to save the world. All you have to do is be you. You're all I want, or ever will..."

TWELVE

Sort things out, sort things out.

The silent words reverberated through Tony's skull, rang like clapping bells from inner ear to inner ear.

Ambition, renewal, dedication, salvation, duty, love... betrayal.

His eyes wavered from their fixed stare at the back of the dove-gray leather driver's seat as the Mercedes sped along the motorway out of London into the far countryside. They noticed for the first time the rear of Harry's head; his fluffy white hair and pink ears were all that showed above the high leather neck-protector of his seat. No hat, Tony thought consciously, coming out of his trance. No hat. A tiny smile trickled across his lips.

Harry drove silently, his face lacking expression. He knew it was one of those times when banter was not wanted, when the friendly word would not enhance their friendship. Harry had seen it before, always left it be.

Love, Tony thought more clearly now, his eyes steadying. Would it be enough to save his life? Would it ever?

How impossibly mixed with love was this force called lust. He always managed, before Susan, to handle lust. Just human nature, his nature at least. It yielded pleasure, for him an intense pleasure that transcended mere physical release. Maybe he had it worse than other men. He wondered...

And he remembered last night. Harry driving him and Susan to the Dorchester, straight from her introduction to Lawrence. Club sandwiches and Polish spring water from room service. But neither of them touched any of it. Their hunger was not in their bellies.

Susan had wrapped her lips around Tony's fleshy nose, tickled his nostril hairs with her tongue, her fingers massaging his ears as her mouth engulfed his, exploring his cheeks with her tongue... and soon their clothing lay strewn on the floor, Susan working her thumbs down his spine, vertebra by vertebra, grasping his muscular round glutes as they stood embraced, pressing her breasts into his chest... and as she lay on the baby-soft bed's comforter, working her belly into it, her back arched to its full extension as her lover combed her long hair with his fingers, swooping it in rhythmic waves again and again, biting the nape of her neck with his lips as she buried her face in the pillow.

Tony moistened her silky skin with his tongue, slid his nose through the moisture down her spine, descended the hollow of her backbone, sent chills to the tips of her toes—aching for him, arching her posteriors, feeling his nose smoothing its way along her tender inner thighs, then...*doing it,* divinely, like a god from Mykonos.

Like a star's light beam reaching Earth from millions of light-years away, yesterday dissolved into sheer nothingness at that moment. Tomorrow was a mere dream, unformed, unknown. Time halted. Only now existed as they lay together, having copulated, hugged, then drifting into sleep.

But time, it seemed, had stopped only for them. The planets had continued to revolve throughout the night, and at 6:59 a.m. the bedroom telephone shrilly jeee-jeeed Tony's wakeup call into their unconscious souls, signaling another dawn for timeless human urges.

Quick showers as toast and tea arrived, soft promises in the rear of the Mercedes as Harry carried them to the Savoy in time for Susan's workday, tentative smiles and see-you-laters, a loving wave and she was gone.

Harry found Tony untalkative this morning, deep within himself in the back seat, freshly dressed in country gear most unlike his customary Italian duds, and wearing a troubled look on his face.

Probably hard to leave such a woman every morning, Harry reckoned, nodding to himself, concentrating on the road. He had his instructions.

They were headed due west now, nearing one hundred ten mph on the speedometer, out in the passing lane, to the bank's retreat a good two hundred and fifty kilometers away at an isolated stretch of coast on the Bristol Channel. Harry had taken Tony there before, numerous times.

Time was, Tony had taken it in stride, always used to be his usual talkative self, full of stories of his travels, asking all about Harry's homelife and hobbies. Jokes and good times.

That had all changed some seven years ago, was it, Harry reflected now as he drove in silence, noticing Tony staring out the window as the scenery flew by. His marriage, Tony's first so far as Harry was aware, had changed him. His mood, too. He'd seemed troubled like this, these past seven or so years. Not the old Tony at all.

Harry could sort of see it, though. She was a beautiful woman, a stunning creature. Just right for Tony was Harry's immediate impression of her. No doubt about it, they sure were in love. And seven years, too, Harry reflected. Humph.

Harry's thoughts had allowed his foot to relax, causing the car to slow to the nineties. Suddenly his thoughts were shattered as he heard Tony bark from the rear seat:

"Punch it, Harry! Really kick it!"

The Mercedes zoomed to one-forty and Harry noticed a more attentive Tony now, spied Tony in his rearview, not letting Tony notice. Tony's eyes busy studying diagrams or suchlike, was all Harry could see.

The undulating Berkshire farm country disappeared and soon the Mercedes took command of the passing lane on the M4 motorway out in the Wiltshire flats, hissing through its own wind at a steady 140 mph.

They zigged round Bristol on the interchange as mid-morning

approached, sailed south on the M5 at the constant speed, and in what seemed mere minutes but was actually forty miles touched the northern reaches of the county of Somerset. Once, when England consisted of many kingdoms, forty miles was nearly a week's march for an army. Modern man had reduced the distance to minutes, the army to a single warrior.

At Bridgwater, Harry left the motorway, slowing to half his speed as they flowed out the A39 highway and the landscape changed to browner and the earth to sandier. Eons ago, this land had been the bottom of a bay of the Bristol Channel, stretching now along to the north of this road.

"Harry," he heard, again in Tony's normal, gentlemanly tone, "open the back of the sunroof, will you? I want to smell the sea air."

As he did so, Harry noticed his boss smiling at him in the rearview, and Harry smiled back. "Not long now, guv. Made good time there. Straight out, or make a stop?" It was his customary question at this point in the trip.

Harry heard Tony yawn, watching him in the mirror checking his wristwatch. "My Hublot shows we're a bit ahead of schedule."

"My *Seiko's* accurate as well, then! So, we'll have our break?"

Tony caught Harry's twinkling eye in the rearview and chuckled at himself. Harry was so real. He loved him for it. "Day's glorious, isn't it? Stop at the usual place in Minehead. We'll have us a proper cream tea."

Tony saw Harry smiling frivolously in the mirror.

"You mention clotted cream to Susan, I'll deduct the tea from my tab!"

Harry said, "We had a wee business drive in the country so's you could shoot some sporting clays with your bank's CEO, strictly on-the-job, and all's we had all day was a tea with lemon juice, and split one dry scone with a taste of strawberry jam. That right, guv?"

Tony smiled back openly. "You just nod stupidly when I tell her we did the manly thing together. Gave back the tea to the sea from a cliff top."

Harry laughed at the mirror, gripping the wheel with his beefy fingers.

"You're a piece of work, guv. A piece of work, all right."

And the Mercedes drifted into the beautiful seaside town of Minehead, passing red-tile roofs, lush trees and grassy plots, peaceful homesteads. Brown-brick, smokeless chimneys poked the air all about.

Although late in the season, rivers of snapdragons and black-eyed Susans and suchlike hardy flowers still bloomed brightly everywhere in the mild, salty breezes. People sat here and there on the seawall fronting the beach and in the park. Retired folks, and day-resters, and late-season holidaymakers. Lovers and love's sinners no doubt, as well.

Tiny waves lapped at the long, curving seashore, where a scattering of attentive mothers kept watch over tiny children playing on the sandy beach.

As the Mercedes drew into a parallel-parking space by the seawall, Tony gazed out his open window at the vast horizon. Cirrus clouds spotted the unending blue skies. The sea air smelt sweetly fragrant. And the day seemed like a day made for angels to sing.

Their tummies full, Tony and Harry walked back across the street from the two-story, white stucco bakery with a gay red-tile roof. Harry began to wipe the insects off the windscreen and Tony strolled off along the seawall. Hands in his pleated trousers pockets, he stopped to look down on a young mother with her two cubs playing idly in the fine brown sand, one of them some thirty feet away, stabbing her toes at the water's edge.

The woman noticed him looking at them and called out "Janey, come back to mummie!" and touched the back of the little boy playing next to her, digging a hole to China. Her face betrayed a hint of concern.

Tony smiled over the seawall at her. "Cute little nubbins, ma'am. Never had any myself. God's sure blessed you. You take care of 'em, hear?"

He saw her shoulders relax, her face loosen its concern.

"Thank you, sir," she called back. "They're my little dears. Can't be careful enough, these days, can you?"

"They'll be all right," he said over the seawall.

She looked so tender to Tony, so innocent, so vulnerable. A sweet face framed in wispy, pale brown hair. *Mummie*, he thought, turning away. But the dulcet scene pulled at him, caused him to smile back at her again, wave a friendly wave. He called out pleasantly to her "Have a nice day!" as he left the seawall. And got a furtive glance in return. That's the trouble in the world, he reflected: trust has been stolen so often by the violators.

As he walked back to the car, he thought of the old man in the park in London, the bum who gave Tony his blessing. Vulnerable out there on the streets all alone. With that kindly voice.

"Okay, Harry," he said, settling into the driver's seat. "I'll take the wheel for a bit. Can't remember how long it's been since I've driven. Just a few days, I guess, though."

Harry sat next to him, on the left, as Tony edged the Mercedes into the single lane heading west out of town. They still had plenty of time. He drove slowly, 30 mph, thinking of how much safer his new civilization would be for the fragile old men and loving young mums, wishing he could snap his fingers and bring it full-blown into existence.

Knowing, alas, how many monsters continued to prowl. He could eliminate them only as fast as time and opportunity would permit. Knowing his path lay straight and true, straight and true. *Knowing it!*

Harry said, as they passed the point of town, where dense trees covered the hill of the promontory and a long jetty projected out to sea, "Lookit them boats, guv," pointing fingers at the protected harbor. Small mahogany fishing boats bobbed in the near-still waters, their sides painted bright white. "That's the life, ain't it, guv?"

Tony nodded, said "If the fish are running..."

"No," Harry said, "no, I mean just you and your boat, out there on the water, chattin' with God while time goes by."

"You have a romantic soul, Harry."

"I might retire to it, guv. A few more years. City life, it can wear on you. I can see myself, guv, floatin' out to sea, not a care in the world."

"If you want it, Harry, you'll get it."

And at this the road turned landward, the two friends settled in for an easy rolling ride as the Exmoor Forest began to press in on the road, Harry with his head back on the leather rest, his eyes closed, a gentle snore purring from his lips, and Tony's eyes looking ahead down the highway and to the business of the day.

Twenty minutes or so out of Minehead, Tony aimed the Mercedes off the highway, down a one-lane hardened gravel road through the light forest which led presently to an opening in a little meadow fronting the sea. At the far end of the meadow stood a solid, single-story building made of neat large blocks of local stone. A hunting lodge, an executive retreat, it looked like. But it had no windows or doors facing the meadow. And its roof sloped sharply down towards the ground, like that of a military bunker.

As the Mercedes drew up to it, two men appeared from around one corner of the lodge, each with a leashed Doberman, black and growling fiercely. Each of the men also wore pistols on their belts, and carried black-as-night Beretta submachine-guns with long ammo clips projecting from their undersides. They wore hunting gear.

"Two hours, Harry," Tony told him, leaving the car. This was the part of the trip that made Harry uneasy. These bankers, he reflected. Big effing deals, them and their secrets. He slid across the seat into the driver's position and closed the door. The dogs barked fiercely outside, the two men held them at bay, and Harry drove off slowly across the crunching gravel and back up the forest lane.

"Morning, Captain Spool," said one of the dog-handlers. His Doberman yanked hard at its leash, snarling at Tony. "He's waiting for you, just through the gate if you please. On the porch."

Tony closed the gate to the high chain-link fence, forcing the heavy hasp into place, and walked over to the veranda facing the sea. The metal fence extended all around the perimeter of a long beach, attaching to each forward side of the hunting lodge. It ran into the sea a good fifty meters on each end.

Sir Malcolm Goodge sat in a lounge chair facing the water, a little marble table beside him. He sipped at a tall glass and then placed it by feel on the table.

"Orange juice?" he asked Tony, his eyes at sea. "Fresh this morning from Spain."

"Just the same, sir. I'm fine."

"I've always wondered," Goodge said, studying his fingernails now. "Your driver, where's he go during our meetings? Ever ask questions?"

Tony sighed inwardly at the routine. In the required confident voice he said: "There's a pub he favors down in Combe Martin. Been going there, what is it, sir, sixteen years now since the lodge was built?"

"That's right, sixteen."

"I think he may have a lady friend there... Harry doesn't say much. He never asks questions. He thinks you're a snobby banker who likes to boss me around"—Tony watching Goodge raise his Santa Claus eyebrows a hint—"and I tell him we shoot clays with your prized Purdeys, that I humor you, tell him I coddle your favor this way."

"And no questions?"

"Not from Harry, ever. I trust him like a father."

Tony appreciated of course that Goodge regularly ran security observations on Harry—on everyone he needed to know about—and possessed an imposing database of Intelligence backgrounds. This was mere idle chatter. A further thought occurred to him, adding to his side of it: "Loyalty like Harry's is a human factor of precious rarity."

"So..." Goodge uttered, going to where his mind already was: "How did it go with Mr. Merriless? Usual surly greeting?"

"Went fine. We understand each other. His attitude is none of my concern. He's the one lives with it."

"Ah, well," Goodge said, his eyes vacant, "glad all is steady. We're all looking forward to tomorrow," this last word upbeat. He cleared his throat, and seized Tony's eyes with his own. "Instructions all clear?"

"Clear, sir."

"I expect we should get to it, then." Goodge got up from his lounge. He wore hunting tweeds, high brown leather boots. He smiled at Tony through his bushy white moustache, saying "Shall we?"

And they walked side by side in silence down a little flagstone path to the beach, where several wooden crates stood beside a cement shooting pod holding a pair of scoped rifles and some boxes of ammunition. A man clad all in black stood there waiting.

"You know our Jack Rush, don't you, Captain?" Goodge asked in a manner of introduction. "Down from Southwark with the gear our dear Mr. Merriless rigged for our event."

Jack Rush looked the epitome of a commando, from fatigue boots to brush haircut. He held out a pair of heavy-duty ear protectors for Tony, another for Goodge. He said, "First we'll try normal seven-six-twos, all right, Captain Spool? Don't want to demolish the targs immediately. Last, some THVs. Scopes are all sighted, sir."

"Right," Tony said, looking out to sea, where he could barely make out some mirror-bright, silver-colored circles, far away.

"Nine hundred meters," Goodge said, pointing, setting his hearing guards in place on his head as Tony did the same. "Let's kill 'em!"

And so Tony settled into the shooting pod, and practiced with both sniper rifles until he was placing neat little, two-inch groups, over and over. As he filled one steel circle with holes, he moved to the next. Goodge and Jack Rush watched through spotting scopes for over an hour. Not once did Goodge mention he'd never had another sharpshooter demonstrate such consistency. But neither did Tony expect compliments.

Each time Tony selected a THV cartridge, and sighted to a crisp reticle in darting two-second glances down the scope before touching the broad, gold-plated hair trigger, he watched the inch-thick silvery steel targ out in the water disintegrate at its center.

Finally he rose to his knees, rubbing the palms of his hands with each opposing thumb.

They all took off their headgear.

"Impressive MPIs, Captain Spool," said Jack Rush at the end.

"That fractional click, to adjust to my eye," Tony said back distractedly, looking out to the targets at sea, "made the difference."

Turning to Goodge he said: "MOA for nine hundred meters is a bit tricky, sir. Think I've got it now." His lips pressed into his front teeth as he nodded at his own conclusion.

"It's a long shot," Jack Rush added. "Pushes the limits, doesn't it?"

Goodge rubbed his ears, evidently sore from the headsets. He looked earnestly in Tony's eyes.

"Just keep it firmly in mind, Spool. One shot, one kill is all well and good for your ordinary situation. Tomorrow..." he paused for effect, "unless everything's perfect, no shot at all!"

"All right," he said at Jack Rush, "pack it up. Delivery at the appointed hour, all clear?"

"All clear, sir."

And Goodge did the unusual, he put an arm round Tony's shoulders, prompting them both up the path to the lodge.

"We'll have a Jameson's for luck, you and I, and I'll leave it with you, Captain."

"Right, sir," said Tony to his boss in a sober mood. "I imagine we'll put out his lights good and proper!"

* * *

By the time Susan finished "lunch" at the American Embassy, two o'clock was nearing. As were Tony and Harry, flashing back east on the M4. At about Hounslow the traffic backed up.

Susan learned what an embassy lunch meant. A touch on the lavish side, the buffet. As she watched overfed bureaucrats overindulge in creamy lobster dishes and almond-chocolate mousse, she couldn't help but think of how her husband would react to the spectacle. She decided it would be best not to mention any of it to Tony. Not a word.

At about quarter past two, Susan found herself back in her room at the Savoy. Doree was busy rubbing her belly, laying on her bed, complaining of overeating, but everything was so scrumptious you just couldn't resist could you, and now it was naptime, she let Susan know, yawning, food-drugged.

Susan had the shower going, to her roommate's fading annoyance as she succumbed to the rich food, sprinkled herself down in record time, picked out a casual but elegant skirt and blouse ensemble Tony had particularly liked from her pre-trip shopping, fluffed her hair with a dry towel instead of a hairdryer, giving it that "lived in" look Tony liked most, and told an unconscious Doree, lost in pillows, she'd be back late, but not real late.

The Savoy's doorman whistled for a cab, a maroon one it turned out, to Susan's delight, and shortly she was engaged in a conversation with a most courteous gentleman of somewhat indistinguishable age and Indian descent. In truth, after Susan informed him this was her first time in London, the conversation became an occasional question on her part and a constant chattering on the driver's. Attired in a checkered gray and purple turban, a multi-hued cravat at his neck, and a rather dated Nehru jacket, he sported a matched set of oily, graying mustachios which twisted awesomely to ends some half-dozen inches in length. He kept turning round, looking back at Susan in the passenger seat, smiling, smiling, smiling. She found herself under the charm of the lilting song of his words.

He pointed out theaters around the Covent Garden, passing his card to her through the Plexiglas slot separating their seats and suggesting he might procure good tickets to hot shows on short notice. At her request, he drove slowly down Great Russell Street for a look at the British Museum, set back behind its high iron bars. They turned up the Tottenham Court Road and the driver worked his way deftly over to Regent's Park, circling the green oasis till they drew up to the Zoological Gardens at the north end.

She found Tony waiting by the entrance, in his best Italian threads. It was just three, the agreed-on hour.

"Ah," intoned the driver as only an Indian could, "a rendezvous of some romantic implications perhaps?" smiling larger than ever at Susan as she waved to Tony from the cab.

"My husband," she informed him drolly, sounding sorry to disappoint, but he merely rolled his head and shrugged happily and wished her joy. "Pretty lady," he had called her a number of times.

Tony had supplied her, back home, with all sorts of travel guides to London. The choices were all hers, he had insisted. Limited time, so what was paramount in importance to her as a first-time visitor? In her top six choices was the zoo, no matter how many times Susan rearranged the list. So the zoo it was on this their free weekday afternoon together. And the zoo visit was to be followed, she had told Tony, by a nice leisurely walk for some window-shopping. Down Regent Street, she'd hoped.

"Darling," Tony said, kissing her on the lips. "Everything all right?"

"Everything's just perfect!"

"Even the day." He looked up at the blue sky. "Remarkable luck, this weather. October can be glorious, as now. Or it can be a disaster."

Warm breezes carried the odors of the city to their noses and sunshine filtered down upon them.

"How was your day? What'd you do today, Tony?"

"Oh, this and that mostly. Boring stuff. Bankers' business. The Asian crisis persists, currencies depreciate, businesses fail and lives change." Tony looked at his watch. "So," he announced, changing the topic. "Three hours till closing. Time enough, I should imagine. What shall we see first?" he asked as he paid at the North Gate entrance, and they faced a litany of possibilities. Posted signs tugged at Susan's desires.

"What to see first?" she asked herself aloud. "Can't miss the pandas. Or the tigers. Or the elephants..."

"Nor the reptiles!" suggested Tony.

"Ugh. Oh Tony, don't let me miss the penguins!"

"We shan't miss anything. Let's begin by walking down the Canal."

And under an October sun as fine as could be imagined, with a light crowd about, they wandered along and Tony watched his wife enjoy the aristocratic cranes, honked at the geese to make her laugh, made faces at the great apes, it being suggested to him there might be wiser eyes inside the cages, stepped warily through the eerie simulated Moonlight World where bats and flying foxes seeped out of invisibility only as outside eyes adjusted to darkness within, and like animals of prey sized up the hoofed beasts—antelopes, zebra and giraffes, finally the llamas and the camels.

"Like Lawrence rode," Susan said to Tony as they left the camel pens and came to the tunnel leading to the southern side of the zoo. "No doubt," said Tony.

And there they found Chia-Chia, the zoo's favorite inmate, the giant panda. Susan stood for the longest moment, Tony watching her watching the creature consume stalks of bamboo with unwavering devotion, as one might engulf stalks of celery stuffed with cream cheese, never getting enough.

Tony found himself staring at the vipers in the reptile house. The crocs and alligators lazed, moving not a muscle. As did the rhinos and elephants, excepting the twitching of ears. They caught Susan's penguins at feeding, slurping up fish thrown at them like kids at an ice cream shop, making Susan giggle as Tony enjoyed her joy.

They were feeling the thirty-six acres of zoo lanes by the time they came to the tigers. Susan found herself holding onto Tony's arm as she stood only meters away from the cats with nothing between them, no bars or cages, nothing apparently but air and a deep moat and the cats' dislike of a soaking.

"What keeps them from leaping or swimming across, Tony?" she asked, in wonder of the beasts' restraint in their simulated natural setting. "Is the water electrified or something? It's scary. That big tiger there looks like he's thinking of how I'd taste."

"No," Tony laughed at her. "And I don't imagine he's thinking of anything, except how good his full belly feels. Gives you a real sense of what it must be like, though, doesn't it, facing one of these brutes in the wild?"

"No safaris for me, Tony. This is close enough."

But the pelicans and flamingos changed her mood, and they soon sat down on a lovely sculpted cement bench by the parrots to rub their feet, both of them.

"Think I've seen it," Susan said after a while, looking a bit bushed. "Thanks, Tony!"

"Quite a few blocks' walk down to Regents Street," he reminded her.

"Maybe a taxi most of the way?" she asked.

"Maybe a taxi," Tony agreed, and they headed for the exit at the South Gate of the zoo.

Nearing it, they passed the birds of prey, and Tony found himself oddly taken by them, stopping in front of an aviary-like setting with a sign identifying its inhabitants as Peregrine Falcons, native to Wales. He found their profiles of sharply pointed, curved beaks, created to tear and kill, noble looking. Susan saw his fascination.

"Tony?" she said, ready to go. Still he stared at the birds.

"What is it, Tony?" This was unlike him.

"Don't you see the power in those jaws? The confidence in their eyes? A beauteous sense of dominance, see it?" Tony momentarily lost in himself.

"I guess I do," Susan said vaguely.

The nearest falcon turned its head, peering at Tony with both eyes, right at Tony.

"A *beau geste*, you see?" Tony explained, Susan at a loss, not taking his meaning, his compulsion. "A kind of magnificence as a killer..."

A rare lapse of character for Tony.

Though, coming back, he noticed enough concern in her eyes that he started to laugh, as if at himself, said in a voice of clearly feigned coyness, "I should write ads for motorcar companies, shouldn't I, darling? Schmooze the masses!"—and then they laughed easily together, Susan feeling comfortable again, Tony still thinking about the *beau geste* as they walked away, arm in arm, exited the zoo, and hailed a cab down to Oxford Circus.

The day's brightness had begun to fade and streetlights began to twinkle in reflection in the windows of some of the world's finest shops, and Susan told Tony, see, there really wasn't time, was there, or energy, to explore the wonders of these stores? Just time to enjoy them for what they were. Just take in their status and enjoy the setting, wasn't that right?

Tony could only agree. Shopping in general interested him but little.

Susan insisted they go in Hamleys, though, the gigantic toy store. But they were both tiring, so the fleets of toy ships and airplanes, the legions of games and noisy amusements slipped by, they cruised the aisles of several floors arm in arm dreamily, just happy to be together, and emerged with but a single purchase Susan insisted on, a lovable brown-and-white-and-black stuffed animal labeled 'Lying Dog' because it was shaped to look like a floppy-eared beagle at rest, which Susan said she intended to call 'Stinkie' and keep at home in Tony's den, to comfort him while she was at work and he was alone, in need of happy company.

Tony carried it in a big Hamleys plastic bag as they hailed a taxi.

* * *

It was just six and working London was going home. As they rode in the taxi, Susan asked when they were going to dinner, and where. Tony said you'll see but it wasn't time to eat yet. Susan asked when people ate dinner in London, and Tony said "Late." Susan told him, generally without specifics, about the buffet lunch at the embassy. She hadn't eaten too much, she said, tempting though it looked, but really wasn't hungry yet. Tony said he hadn't eaten much all day, didn't mention the cream tea or even the drive out to Somerset for that matter, and said he wasn't very hungry either, not yet.

And they had some time to kill.

So Tony told the very cockney cabbie to burn up a twenty. They drove round the Wellington Arch in stiff traffic and out to Knightsbridge, Tony pointing out Harrods for Susan, huge and bejeweled looking, the Victoria & Albert—"I'll take you there for a day someday, the most beautiful museum!"—and up Exhibition Road, only Tony noticing the

Iranian Embassy on their right as they passed Prince's Gate road, then the opposing Royal Albert Hall and the Albert Memorial, Tony explaining, and down the Kensington Road and right and slowing as they passed along by Kensington Palace—"Where Princess Di lived," Tony told her, Susan's face saddening—and continuing along Kensington Palace Gardens—"Millionaires Row, the richest street in all London," Tony let her know—and turning right on the Bayswater Road with Hyde Park on their right, and back down Park Lane past the Dorchester—"I know where we are!" Susan exclaimed upon seeing it—and slowly out the tree-lined, "royal" red-paved Constitution Hill to Buckingham Palace, where the taxi waited while Susan gawked through the gold-painted monarchial crest on the glossy black bars separating the public from the palace grounds.

In due course, the taxi carried them over to the Queensway for dinner at one of the apparently countless restaurants lining that elegant avenue.

"The King of Siam," Susan said. "Is this where we're eating, honey?"

"You bet. As good as it gets—heh, there's Simon!"

And as they stepped from the taxi Simon took Tony's hand, turned instantly to Susan and said "Oh it's Susan isn't it? So charmed to meet you at long last!" And he kissed her hand.

"Susan," said Tony between them, "Simon Stinger, my numismatic genius and mate."

"But, come," Simon insisted, "we're all inside already, at table, holding two special seats!"

They soon sat at a large round table with more people than either Susan or Tony had expected. The room glowed with mirrors and the colors and garnishes of Thailand, a kaleidoscope of gold and red and indirect lights and gleaming reflections.

Faces beamed at them.

No one ventured to speak first.

"Introductions," Simon said, sighing loudly. "Susan and Tony Spool, of Virginia, the USA. Let's see . . ."—and he pointed out faces to them—"Bayard Finchley and his wife Jaine, and that's Ian McKennough, and Klaus Rothkin, and Martin Weller, and Theo Boots and Linda, and Nikos Papandrapous, and last but most my own darling Bridget. Coin dealers all, I'm afraid," he laughed loudly through his unique, infectious smile, ". . . and companions."

Hellos all around.

"An even dozen!" announced Martin Weller, finishing the table count with his chubby fingers waving. "A baker's cheat!"

Simon turned to Susan at his left and whispered, "Martin likes to eat."

But Martin couldn't have heard him across the table anyway, as the decibel level rose steadily with the arrival of more eager diners at the tables round about them. The heavy dinner hour just beginning.

Tony sized up the table, almost without thinking:

Ian McKennough, sounded Scots all right but who knew these days, in his thirties, rapidly balding, clear fair face, studious looking, well-tailored double-breasted blue suit, good tie. Klaus Rothkin, did Simon say, enigmatic German, possibly underworld, greasy black wavy hair, heavy nose and jowls, dark whiskers to match the personality in all probability, smoking heavily, looking weary. Nikos Papandrapous, was it, looked Crete, thin and gentlemanly in a gorgeous brocade black-silk suit, a slim black cigarillo ever at his mouth, his hands turning over baby-blue worry beads endlessly. Bayard Finchley, cockney Londoner more than likely by his figure and style, self-made most likely, a cocky but appealing smile always on his lips, looking pleased with himself for some reason unknown. His wife, once quite beautiful without a doubt, still very appealing, well made, expensively dressed. Theo Boots, heavy in body, costly suit ill fitting, balding and in glasses but otherwise not easy to sort out. His companion, well that was obvious. Simon's charming wife, Bridget, perfect for Simon, attentive and supportive, liked by everyone. And then there was Martin Weller.

As he was sizing them all up thus, Tony said across the table to the round but short man directly opposite him: "Where you from, Mister Weller?"

"Beverly Hills, Mister Spool!" was all he got for a reply. Tony guessed that summed it up. The diamond collar-stud in place of a tie was the giveaway, really.

Susan was looking around too, noticed the faces of the world's many nations, it seemed, at the numerous linen-covered tables, chattering away in a harangue of languages or chomping happily or in concentration studying the huge, colorful menu. She opened her own, and discovered bewilderment.

Simon saw it instantly. "Don't bother with the menu, Susan," he commanded, taking it from her fingers, "the ordering's all done already, by perhaps the most knowledgeable international gastronomist of all, our own dear Martin Weller."

Who beamed his ample round face at them from some six feet away across the table. And who explained in a deep, sincere voice: "And your money's no good here, Mrs. Spool; it's all taken care of."

Susan smiled back at him, as the first of many courses to come began to arrive on little boat-shaped, bright porcelain dishes placed discretely along the round lazy susan which dominated the broad table.

As they noshed down a host of odd and curious fare, captured from water and land and air halfway around the globe and brought to rest here in the center of London, the dozen diners fell into an insane cacophony of restrained shouts at each other, the same as the rest of the restaurant's denizens.

"Name's Bayard," said Finchley to Tony from his right-hand side. "Pleased to have you join us, you and your lovely wife!"

"Thanks!" shouted Tony. "Pleased to meet you, too! What's the occasion for everybody being here?"

"London Coin Fair, the yearly event. People in from the world over!"

"It's in progress?"

"Auctions all week. The Fair starts officially tomorrow. Most of the real business is done already, though."

Hearing this, Martin Weller caught Tony's eye. Weller shouted across: "The heavy hitters are done buying, Mr. Spool!"

"I see," Tony said too low for Weller to hear clearly.

Simon took over immediately. "Oh Bayard!" he shouted past Tony, for he sat between Susan and Tony, "tell our friends here about your run-in with the law!"

Those who hadn't heard the story already, meaning Susan and Tony, looked to Bayard Finchley, an outwardly robust and portly and always smiling Englishman, dressed in a beautiful suit, who launched gleefully into his tale:

"Hardly *the law*, Simon! Well, you see, it seems my shop's neighbors object to the noise put out by my security lights, which go all night, been complaining to the police for weeks, the silly buggers, just a buzzing really. But nonetheless, round comes this stunning black Jamaican bird one day last summer, I reckon she has some gear for sale, but no! Shows me her badge from the Department of the Environment, has all sorts of official forms jammed with a log of complaints, announces I must, *I must*, get these lights quieted down. I'm to call in a lighting specialist immediately, she tells me!"

Bayard Finchley is clearly enjoying his tale, Susan and even Tony listening politely, the others now keen to hear the story over again, too.

"So I says to her, very politely mind you, I says now just you wait a moment dearie, and I'll have my Tom fix 'em up good and proper like. Tom's got the extension ladder out already, you see, and this young colored lassie accompanies me to the front of the store, and we watch my Tom up there on the top rung give the first light he can reach a good whack with his hand, and what do you think? The sodding light stops buzzing, that's what!"

At this moment the rotund Martin Weller was busy yelling out to the waiter for more water: "Bring us three pitchers," he's barking, "with lots of ice! You've got some thirsty eaters here!"

"'No, no, no!' says the lass from Jamaica to me and my Tom," Bayard Finchley goes on. "'It's not fixed proper. You must hire in an electrical lighting specialist from our approved list. This isn't good enough!'

"'Don't be sodding *thick*,' I yell back at her. 'It's fixed!' Tom's going on to the next light from top of he's ladder, and whammo! It stops buzzing as well. But our good little toady from the West Indies, she's in a furor. Can't justify those salaries, can they, the bureaucrats, if anything's fixed up plain and simple!"

The Thai waiters arrived with a flurry just then, burdened with new dishes, main courses of substance, dead beasts dressed up for a party but hardly their own, Martin Weller bellowing for ice water again, as he'd been gulping it in unbelievable quantities along with generous helpings of food.

Bayard Finchley stopped narrating to help himself to the new platters and pass them on to his wife, seated next to him, who'd had nothing to say thus far and seemed with equanimity able to ignore her husband's tale. Probably heard it fifty times, Tony smiled to himself, having glanced at the woman.

"Go on! Go on!" urged Simon, relaxed in his chair, sitting ajar, lifting a fork to his mouth in a dainty gesture.

"Well, this wog's practically shrieking at my Tom to stop hitting the lights, for they're all going quiet now, you see, and she hurriedly scribbles out a citation for me on her papers, tearing it out of her form book for my signature, which I refused to give. She's frantic like, and I say, ever so shyly and politely to her, I say, 'You're just picking on me 'cause I'm pink!'"

"Oh, Bayard, for God's sake," interjected his wife, Jaine, hard at work on a bit of fried up pig, "you should know better!"

Martin Weller's howling now from his spot across the table, yelling over to Bayard Finchley, "Tell 'em the upshot!"

Finchley looks down at his plate and says in a long face, "Hauled into court, civil suit brought against me and my business by the wog, claims I've racially harassed her, wants recompense and damages."

"Und, tell zem," coughed in Klaus Rothkin through his cigarette, heard from for the first time now, his German English quite thick, "tell zem vhat ze judge tsay." He held his head in his hands, by the temples.

Simon leaned over and said in Tony's ear: "Klaus has got a

katzenjammer, a hangover. He started early."

But the story was ongoing:

"'Mr. Finchley'—his Honor lectures me from he's bench—'did you in fact utter those very words?' 'Yes I did,' I tells his Lordship. 'What's wrong with them?' 'Why, it's an *insult*, an affront, a racial slur, and you cannot, you *must not*, say such things, Mr. Finchley.' 'But, your Honor,' says I back to his High Holiness, 'I *am* pink! The good lady civil servant here from the West Indies may be black, or brown or whatever—I never called her a color nor anything else, not once! But I'm not *white* either, *I'm pink.* Pink in the summer, and gray in the winter. It's true, isn't it, your Honor?'"

"And what did it cost you?" asked his wife, Jaine, at this point in the story, busy inspecting her plate. "Tell them." A lovely woman, Tony noticed, lush dark hair, pretty face. Ever so slightly on the plump side.

"Two thousand quid!" Finchley harrumphed. With utter disgust in his voice, turning to Susan, he added: "There's justice for you! That's what's become of Britain at the end of the twentieth century, do you see? Sad, isn't it? What's one to do... I ask you!"

"One's to shut up, that's what one's to do!" Jaine Finchley barked at her plate, sorting through curious vegetables with a fork.

Through his own mouthful of morsels of grand flavor, her husband said, a bit more quietly: "I may have to pay up, but I'll be damned if I have to shut up! Not in Britain! This is *my* bloody country!"

"In defense of your husband, Mrs. Finchley," Tony offered, "liberty has its price, always. I'd have done the same myself, more or less. But it's not just Britain where freedom is under assault, it's *everywhere.*"

Bayard Finchley beamed now at Tony. He shot his wife a winning look.

Simon said lightly, "Bayard's a loon! Anything for a laugh! But he's right to have done what he did. And you're right, Tony, we must not keep quiet, mustn't we?"

No one answered the question.

Susan asked, to the table generally, but looking towards Finchley:

"What's a 'wog'?"

Simon answered for Finchley, letting him eat:

"In the old days of the British Raj, Susan, you had your British soldiers, regular army, and you had your British civilians all-round the Empire. Wherever the locals could qualify, you had your detachments of Empire soldiers. And you had your necessary servants, everyone who worked the mess halls, civilians who labored for the military establishment. Grunts. Their compatriots had uniforms, you see, so these servants wanted their own, to give them status round about their towns. Well, they couldn't have real military gear, could they, so a sort of uniform was rigged up for them to wear whilst on duty, and across the fronts of their jerseys we had printed the words 'Workers on Government Service,' and they came to be called 'WOGS' for short. It wasn't a derogatory term."

"So if Bayard called the Jamaican lady a 'wog' it wasn't an insult?" Susan asked in a naive tone, but maybe not so naively

"Well," Simon intoned, "not *really*..." but he was busy withdrawing something from his jacket pocket, and he handed it to Tony.

Tony put down knife and fork, and opened the white Kraft envelope, sliding a sizable silver medal out onto his palm. He looked pleased with it.

"The Kitchener bit you've been wanting," said Simon to Tony's ear. "Hope it's right!"

"Thanks, Simon," Tony muttered for his ears only.

"With compliments, of course," Simon added quietly still.

But Martin Weller was all eyes and ears now. He shouted over towards Tony: "A little thank-you from Scotland!"

Tony found this annoying and showed it on his face.

Simon glared across the table, while placing an arm around Tony's chairback protectively.

"Why, whatever do you mean, Martin?" Simon hooted at him.

"That's quite a coin Simon bought for you, Mister Spool!" Weller jousted back, stuffing a pork dumpling in his face.

"Don't take your meaning," said Tony in an even voice. "I don't collect coins, you see. Nor medals. I just like Kitchener items."

"Sure, sure..." Weller spluttered. Then he gurgled vehemently, "Waiter! Water, waiter! Water!"

Linda, a beautiful blonde with quite a figure and well dressed, sitting next to the man introduced as Theo Boots, asked Susan two chairs away: "So you're not in coins, Mrs. Spool?"

Simon intruded: "Susan's with the U.S. Government. Hush-hush stuff. Spies or something along that line!" He laughed breezily.

It was a throwaway phrase, of no meaning. Tony pretended to ignore it, looked busy concentrating on dissecting an unusual crab on his plate.

Susan smiled insincerely at Simon, while to the blonde she said, "No, not in coins, Linda. I'm just a *grunt* at the State Department. It's kind of a grind, I suppose... But you people all amaze me. I never realized anybody could make a living doing something like you do, not till I met Tony, who's told me about Simon. They're old friends. Tony's an American citizen now, but he's British, you see. He's known Simon for years."

When she said the bit about making a living, most of the table laughed knowingly.

"More than a living, Mrs. Spool, much more!" Weller hollered at her.

"And this is all you do?" she asked openly.

Simon took it up: "Well you see, Susan, it's a specialty career that the public at large just don't know anything about. Most of us here handle British coins, of course, and hence the London auction circuit. Klaus and Ian and Theo and Nikos deal in ancients almost exclusively, travel the world searching for what we call 'the right coins.' Martin buys and sells just about everything, except for ancients. We've all done okay at it."

"Mostly," Weller called across to her, "these days, I just jet around Europe and Asia buying for my own account. What else can I do with my money!" he exclaimed for all the room to hear, laughing exorbitantly as he attacked another plate of delicacies just brought hot to the table.

"And why is it you desire these things?" Tony questioned him suddenly. "I'm curious to know, what makes you tick?" A mild enough assault. Tony didn't even look up from the dead crab when he asked it.

Weller's face lost its flush, he let go of his eating utensils and gripped his heavy hands firmly on the rim of the linened table, producing a greasy stain, and then he grumbled daringly back at Tony:

"I only want what you and everyone else wants, Mr. Spool. *I want more out of life!* Isn't that why we're all here, yourself included?"

Tony's poker face was worth a thousand words. He looked up from his plate at Weller now, but in his mind's eye he pictured Senator Winterbern.

His look must have been intense to Weller, for suddenly Weller shifted focus to a plate of gleaming, caramelized duck, and he stabbed at it with his two-tonged fork, hauling a large portion to his mouth, gold dental caps gleaming as he seized it.

Tony calmly turned his attention back to Simon, sharing inaudible words with him.

Susan looked over at Bridget, seated near but not next to Simon. She said, "You in coins, too, Bridget?"

Bridget laughed happily. "No, and I know what you mean...it's hard to figure out unless you're married to one of them! I have a boutique myself, but Simon is zany for these old things, and I love him for it!"

The conversations were becoming twosomes now, as the noise got worse in the graying evening and the food took its toll. So Susan talked to the only person not engaged in chitchat, the pretty blonde named Linda, two chairs away. A bit of a shout, but not much.

She saw that Linda was in her early twenties, she thought, while the man she was with looked sixty-five, maybe older, so she said to her:

"Do you get to travel with your dad often, Linda?"

The girl giggled, not really embarrassed but obviously not used to explanations either.

She said simply, "Theo's not my dad. Not my husband either. Nor my boyfriend, if you see what I mean..."

"Oh," Susan said in a low tone. "I didn't understand, sorry."

"No problem," the man called Theo winked at her, "is it, bumps?"

So Susan decided to keep quiet. Tony talked solemnly to Simon next to him. The other men seemed to be swapping stories of money-making one after the other. And Linda and Bridget and Jaine, and Susan, contented themselves by picking at interesting tidbits of food remaining on the jammed lazy-susan, which went twirling round and round from eater to eater, but more slowly all the time and the evening eventually wound down.

Susan was suddenly feeling beat, saw the time on her wrist was past nine, and motioned to Tony till he got the message. They both had big days tomorrow.

Not long after, Susan collapsed onto her bed at the Savoy and Tony had gone on to the Dorchester in the taxi.

Wrung out from the long day, Tony found himself lying in the middle of the wide bed in his suite, alone again at last, the elegance all around him now invisible in the dark room, thoughts and memories of the day flooding his head, a confusing mixture of the good and the bad and the ugly.

His wake-up call was scheduled for eight, just in case he needed it.

Knowing he could sleep in till mid-morning if he liked, but figuring he probably wouldn't, physically exhausted from the long day's doings yet mentally eager, imagining he'd probably sleep fitfully but hoping not, maybe be up early, all refreshed. Hard not to think about the approaching day—lucky Friday the thirteenth.

An unseen smile captured his face as he fantasized for a moment on the new civilization.

Sort things out, Tony thought as the incoming haze of sleep began to take hold of him. *Sort things out. . .* He lost consciousness on the word 'duty.'

* * *

In the utter silence and pitch black, the little red digital numbers read three thirty-eight, but Tony didn't see them. Deep, deep in REM sleep, his eyeballs rolled violently as he fought with his demons.

The little boy could feel his dad's sinewy, bony frame but not any warmth, an odd coldness to his body… could hear his dad's sobbing as he held him, hugged him tight to his big cold body, could taste a salty moisture on their joined cheeks, could feel hands in his hair, big strong hairy hands rubbing his head, could remember with an astounding clarity feeling his dad's cold ears rubbing against his face, and after a while looking into his dad's swollen eyes and hearing his dad moaning. "It's your mum, Tony, your poor dear mum, oh how mummie loves you! But she's sick, Tony, very sick. Mum's body doesn't work like it should, you know how she's been falling down, don't you, losing her strength… and mum's going to have to go to a special hospital now, Tony, and we're not going to see her for a while, but maybe after a bit we'll have mummie back with us again, good as new, okay, Tony?"

But Tony never saw his mum again.

The little boy yelled over and over, "Mummie, Mummie, Mummie!" at the hollow walls.

And then the huge man with the thin whip made the little boy's flesh sting something awful as he stood over him and lashed again and again at his tender backside.

The little boy cried and cried. Not for the pain from the whip, but for his mummie. Where was mummie? Why had mummie gone away?

"You leave 'mummie' out of this, you hear me boy? This is between you and me, boy, between you and me!"

As the whip stung his flesh, lash after lash, the little boy's eyes suddenly widened, no longer frightened, no longer lost in their own inner dark, but intensely focused on the shadow cast upon the smooth wood floor. For the first time ever, they shone with a piercing light, a bright blue gleam that held terror itself in its pupils.

Tony twisted under the luxurious sheets of the Dorchester's wide bed, twisted and rolled and yelled out in his sleep. But nobody heard him. He was suddenly awake, naked and sweaty. He reached out but found no body to cling to. Then he lay still, staring into the black emptiness of the room, murmuring to himself, *Die, you bastard! Die!*

THIRTEEN

A brisk English morning, made for just being alive!

Dressed in his checkered black and gray headband, black rayon jogging outfit, and black Nikes, Tony felt keenly alive as he left the Dorchester, the hour barely five thirty, dawn cracking slowly but with an astonishing clarity through the night's void, heralding from an unseen horizon somewhere beyond the clustered buildings of the city.

Tony looked up as his feet touched the pavement to see the final remnants of the storm that had passed in the dark, its clouds vanishing into lighter and lighter gray as the day filtered in, the streets wet, the air dewy still and chilly, and Tony's nose now detecting that faint, sweet fragrance of diesel exhaust, from the lorries and buses and taxicabs just beginning to rumble yet again to life.

More than alive, Tony felt suddenly exhilarated as the crisp air penetrated his nostrils and struck his sinuses. The brooding sky animated his spirit. A peculiar but delicious refreshment penetrated his soul as the passing darkness lessened, and as the haunting memory of his nightmare merged with the cheer of the new day, the new day at last.

God's promise loomed.

Tony had gained the keen sense that a wondrous moment was fast approaching, for *the day* had arrived—the *Dies Irae*, the day of wrath!

A great day for civilization, Tony thought as his feet began smacking the pavement, seeking direction.

He turned up Park Lane, heading north under the trees parkside, his eyes peering up at their dark undersides, silhouetted against the lightening sky, then he jogged past the now-silent Speakers Corner, and headed out a leafy lane, in shades of green and gold and dying brown, paralleling the Bayswater Road to the north side of the park. It was no longer raining, but a sudden far-off crack of lightning recalled the storm. Tony ran on at a good pace, counting eighteen seconds. Three miles away, he smiled inwardly, from the count. His heart was pumping, he heard it distantly in his eardrums, and was gladdened.

Soon he was jogging through the heart of Kensington Gardens, saw the lovely old palace of King William the Third off in the mist to his right across the pond, and headed down along the Long Water, through the heart of Hyde Park, spying another occasional figure out in the distance.

He slowed his pace down the path running along the north side of The Serpentine pond as he neared its middle, then stopped for breath, hands holding his knees as he bent forward, the Police Station to his back.

Slowly he straightened his spine, as any athlete might, and his eyes swept across the water and the green, across Rotten Row, the ancient horse trail of kings and queens, and across the Kensington Road to the tranquil balconies of the white buildings along Prince's Gate. There among them he could make out the Iranian Embassy, silent, keeping its secrets, appearing as ordinary as the next building. But it wasn't. It had an appointment with destiny, and its moment was quick approaching.

Then the lone runner paced himself the rest of the way back to Park Lane and to the welcoming portals of the enveloping Dorchester Hotel.

Alone in his rooms, Tony stared at his image in the shaving mirror, holding the gleaming straight razor in his fingers, at the ready. Peering deep into the mirror, both eyes on their reflections, he was reminded of the Peregrine Falcon at the zoo, and wondered....

His revery was broken by the noises of the morning, not from the hallway, for the hotel's rooms deep set at the end of private halls are famed for their quiet, but rather from the street, for Tony had the balcony windows open. He always favored fresh breezes over air-conditioning, even over heating in cold climates. He lathered up with the rich facial cream provided by the hotel, and shaved his face slick.

The huge marble tub had been filling soapily, and now Tony slipped into it, letting his muscles relax, the balm work its wonders. His suite's bathroom was as large as many living rooms, mirrored in on all sides and on the ceiling so that the several gold-rimmed Italian marble columns surrounding the tub appeared as many, as in an emperor's villa.

As his tension dissolved, he began to read from his travel copy of the *Meditations*, forever a source of inspiration and wisdom.

And after half an hour's worth of this pampering, Tony stood drying himself down with dense tan towels, stood on deep carpeting amid the furnishings of an age gone by. Somehow even his finest Italian clothes begged insufficiency in these surroundings.

Soon he was amid the lobby's Promenade, more gold-braided marble columns rampant in the rich swirling imperfections of the stone, polished to jewel-like glory. Figurines suggestive of the grandest days of the Raj, recreated black-skinned servants of alabaster, stood as silent sentinels among the columns, and the high ceilings boasted of gold-leaf ornamentation such as a Caesar's palace might be jealous of. Tony was soon through all this, and seated in The Grill.

He took a long, leisurely full breakfast, pensive and evasive as the waiters called upon him for his requests. But they were used to this in their guests, and Tony's meal became satisfying, satiating, and rewardingly introspective.

An hour later, he smoked a large Cuban cigar in one of the silk brocade chairs of a nook in the lobby. Behind him, on the wall, a centuries-old, fanciful Chinese warlord lazed at his temple, with monkeys chattering and servants in attendance. To all of which Tony remained oblivious, lost in concentration on his forthcoming duties.

As eleven neared, he retired to his suite and chameleon-like changed his colors. The studied gentleman disappeared as the matte-black-suited modern warrior came to the ready. Boots, fatigues, cotton shirt, lightweight jacket, Kabar knife, H&K pistol, all were dead black. As was Tony's heart.

But a gentleman's cashmere overcoat concealed the killer beneath.

By eleven thirty, precisely, a Royal Parks Constabulary police van had delivered him to a private entrance to the Hyde Park Police Station. He and Jack Rush, dressed as a Bobbie, ascended the back staircase to the roof, and Tony took up his position on the recessed shooting pod, with Jack Rush and the equipment in the shadows as well.

In short order, all was ready. What remained was a test of patience and professionalism, several hours of tedium and concentration, and of vigilance.

As the day had brightened, and the forecast had promised no precipitation for the next twenty-four hours or so, the rifle with Merle Merriless's new Image Intensifying scope lay loaded and ready, but in the background. The backup piece.

Lying on the recessed pod, invisible to all eyes out in Hyde Park, and in deep shadows under its roof, Tony used binoculars to first survey the entire site.

The greens of grass and low bushes spread out all before him. The long pond called The Serpentine lay a short distance away, appearing as a broad beach from his perspective. Citizens and tourists were scattered hither and yon, mostly in isolated pairs or singles, walking the lanes of the park, lolling about in the mild sunshine on the grass, and strolling down the Rotten Row, which stretched from Tony's left to right out beyond the pond.

Through his spotting scope, set parallel to the rifle, Tony could see figures in taxis and private cars driving up and down the Kensington Road, on the southern fringe of the park. He could even see the figures' mouths jabbering away in passing vehicles, and could easily read license plates.

And just beyond the Kensington Road, he could see the windows of the white buildings which constituted the lovely avenue called Prince's

Gate. Amid them sat the Iranian Embassy. A curious smile crept across Tony's lips as he once again viewed its features, so familiar to him all those years back, in his SAS days.

He could count the window panes, make out shadows beyond in some of them, and could even discern the rivets in the poles holding up the tan awning which extended from the embassy's doorway out to the curb.

Under it a man would take his first final steps, a walk of the dead, Tony thought, smiling secretly.

Jack Rush sat behind Tony at his own invisible pod, bearing not a gun but another kind of armament, a portable computer, entirely of matte black, which linked him and Tony to surveillance cameras watching the American Embassy and the Iranian Embassy in turn. Rush flipped images on the screen back and forth, fine-tuning. It operated by modem running on a military radio and provided true-time pictures in living color of each scene.

Jack Rush whispered to Tony, "Digital Global up and running, Captain," placing the screen to Tony's side so they both could see it.

Tony nodded back in silence.

Jack Rush now placed a matte-black headset over his own ears. In less than a minute, he tapped Tony's boot, and Tony turned around to see the thumbs-up sign and the barest suggestion of enjoyment on Jack Rush's face.

What they had at their disposal was the latest high-tech secret listening system. It used an invisible infrared laser beam which could be bounced against any window, picking up vibrations from the window's glass to transmit back the sounds of human conversation.

Covert operatives were positioned along the route to beam the lasers at the windows of the American Embassy, next at the car which would carry Tony's target, and finally at the Iranian Embassy, should Tony's targ manage to make it inside upon arrival. Tony could then be prompted for an exit shot.

But Tony felt confident that an exit shot would not be needed. He intended taking advantage of the first opportunity, when Alex Allgood would get out of his car and begin that walk of the dead.

And so the two warriors set in to wait. Time passed slowly, tediously.

Tony looked at the luminous hands on the black face of his watch. The luncheon hour was underway.

He looked over to the computer screen and saw automobiles arriving at the imposing front gate of the American Embassy, only a few blocks away in reality, to the north of the Dorchester. He could request a zoom-in but there was no point. He knew Susan was down there, or else just inside. She would never be in harm's way, far from it, yet it was an odd feeling, knowing she was near as duty loomed.

So Tony turned his attention elsewhere.

Through his binos, his eyes crept out along the sight path, yard by yard it seemed, past citizens at work and at play, strolling the grounds languidly or marching off to some appointment or other, to fix the world or to enrich the self. They all needed protection.

The path the bullet would traverse was amazingly free from obstacles. Goodge had done his prep work well, for not a single branch or heavy bush intruded all the way down the sight path.

Sunlight played off the surface of The Serpentine, glitzy and bright, cheerful like. The green of the park stretched beyond the water, and Tony watched people merge into and then disappear from his field of vision, from left to right, and right to left, in the binos, when suddenly his eye caught a bright yellow reflection. What was it? He steadied on it, his eyes following it along the Rotten Row's sawdust path. It was a bonnet! A bright *yellow* bonnet, on a little girl's head. Her mother trailing behind, very near, trying to keep up as the little girl skipped down the path.

And then the trees and the green lawn and the bright yellow bonnet brought back a fleeting memory to Tony, causing a smile to spread widely across his lips.

Of course, the bright yellow marker! The marker for three hundred meters, back home at his golf course in Virginia. *That's* why he mysteriously envisioned, back there, many weeks ago, looking out to where his golf ball had flown, not a golf shot but a bullet true on to target, a perfect execution when he relaxed and took the shot naturally, a dead shot right down the middle—so long as he didn't think too much, just did it.

It *was* a premonition, then. It had been a sign after all!

How destiny called at him.

Tony took up his binos again, and they carried his eyes all the way to the front door of the Iranian Embassy.

As he allowed time to pass, Tony thought again of the preacher's message, when he all but called out in God's name for Tony to take up God's hammer of justice and his weapons of war, and Tony found himself slipping dangerously into a private revery about his new civilization. He blinked hard and pinched the bridge of his nose till it hurt.

Then he trained the spotting scope on the sight picture for a final time, right onto the curb where Alex Allgood should appear, in another thirty minutes or so. Two-thirty and counting.

He became aware of Jack Rush behind him still, silent, waiting too. Tony put his headset in place, over one ear, a replica of the man behind him, and they both listened together as a commanding voice intermittently narrated the proceedings. The computer screen showed automobiles at the ready in front of the American Embassy, then flicked to the scene in front of the Iranian Embassy, where nothing was happening, where only a few men in dark suits stood out front. In anticipation.

Tony moved to his shooting position, parallel with the spotting scope on the pod, and became one with the AI sniper rifle. The scope was zoomed in and focused on a sight picture which showed only a yard or so of diameter at curbside, front of the embassy sidewalk. Tony trained on an imaginary spot where a head might be, six feet off the pavement. His eyes made darting glances, of two or three seconds, at the targ, making sure of a crisp reticle. Then he closed his eyes, resting them.

The safety was off, a single THV cartridge at the ready.

The voice in Tony and Jack's ears came alive suddenly, beginning a steady narration. The voice was relaying what the Digital Global tracking system could not follow as well as binoculars on rooftops along the route giving moment-by-moment updates to the narrator.

"Cars filling up now"—the voice came to them—"starting to depart Big Eagle. Various parties . . ." Tony's eyes caught the scene on the computer screen beside him. "There's our boy now, emerging from Big Eagle. Getting in a blue Peugeot, rolling off now, four of them in all, confirmed by the voices in the car"—and Tony saw in the computer that three heads had gotten into the car. Three plus the driver, four in all. One of the heads was brighter, but it was too small on the screen to say why.

Again he sighted down the sniper scope, blacked out his eyes, waiting.

The voice in his ear said softly, "Your target, Haberdasher, is the one with bright blond hair, almost yellow, cut short, military style. And, Haberdasher, steady now . . . the targ is a *she*."

Tony's eyeballs not moving, his breath sure and smooth, muscles at ease.

"Passing the Hilton now," the voice continued, "a little traffic round the Arch, not slowing down much, proceeding west to the site." The soft but commanding voice in his ear. Tony's shoulders relaxed, completely. His facial muscles having no tension. His tongue soft against his teeth. A hard-on in his trousers, as nearly always. A delicious sensation of masterly power. A kind of magnificence, like the falcon at the zoo.

Yellow hair, he thought, then heard a forgotten fragment of experience, the words of the American tourist, Mike was it, yes Mike, even softer in his ear: '. . . ya never know what's comin' next, right Tony?'

Tony laughed inwardly at the memories.

"Past Sloane now, closing in"—the voice in his ear told him, Tony's eyes still closed, the picture ahead blackened.

"Car's turning off the K Road now, Haberdasher . . . the blue Peugeot, fifty meters to the site . . . take her, she's yours!"

Tony's earpiece went silent. He opened his eyes, his right seeing the sight picture clear as crystal, brilliance out of blackness, just as it should be.

Don't think too much, he heard in an inner echo. *Don't think at all!*

Tony's trigger finger lay a hairsbreadth from the gold-plated trigger, his thumb through the steady-hole, smooth and dry against the soothing polished feel of the stock. The black bore of the rifle lay invisibly ahead of his eye.

Blue in the sight picture—seeing it now! Leaving the Peugeot now, street side, facing Tony for a split second, long enough to catch the face of an Irish beauty. A true beauty. The crosshairs centered on her manubrium, at her sternum, then out, her back to him now, Tony adjusting the zoom a hair for the headshot coming up as a favorite meditation from Marcus Aurelius sped like a bullet itself through Tony's brain, *'Evil comes not from the mind of another'*—and the beauty didn't count. Evil was evil, no matter its gaze, beauty became hideous, no more no less than ugly... mini-seconds passed and he had it now, perfect, the reticle crisp, Tony's eyes darting for a constant focus, holding dead on the center of her skull from the rear, fuzzy yellow hair covering the parietal bone, filling the sight picture, Tony's shoulders loose, his whole body relaxed, no tension, his fingers like gel, pressuring the hair trigger, and the touch, the bullet away—just as a smear obscured the yellow targ.

What was it?

Tony's eyes had closed, in muscle memory, for a split second after firing, the professional follow-through, but now he had the zoom focus pulled back a fraction, saw heads turn quickly as the bullet's sound reached them, saw sudden chaos, someone down but not yellow hair, who was running hard out of the frame, under the awning into the embassy.

And then she was gone.

FOURTEEN

"The penny just didn't drop." The voice was unexpectedly sweet in tone but cool as could be, innocent of accusation yet somehow angry.

The words echoed into Tony's memory like a bullet ricocheting down a dark tunnel, a forgotten endless hole.

He saw not the speaker but a small boy, one hand in his father's, the other clutching a big old English penny, its bronze dark brown, worn nearly smooth. Walking the gentle hills of the tidy, tree-lined streets of the fair in the summertime, smelling the sea air, the sunshine glinting in the boy's eyes, a mild sweat on his skin, a determined look on his face, long ago. At Scarborough by the sea, with his dad and the memory of his lost mom.

Ah, there it was, the rusty old machine painted over to look bright again, shaped like a circus clown, 'A PENNY FOR A TREAT' painted in happy yellow letters along the brim of the cap over the clown's face, the little boy pulling away from his father's hand, rushing to push his penny through the slot, 'Now don't let's waste mummie's penny, Tony' came his dad's voice, kindly and sweetly behind his back as he pushed the penny into the hole watching King George disappear, but it didn't drop, it stuck behind the slot, the candy treat withheld, the penny not dropping down the cheap tinny chute behind the clown's mouth, and the little boy's eyes tearing up, his fist striking the clown in the face, but his penny didn't drop...

Just as suddenly he was back in the present, staring across an elegant desk made of teak inlaid with unusual woods, peering at the curiously dejected visage of the man to whom he had devoted himself for more than two decades, at the famous bushy white moustache which now drooped ever so slightly, betraying an emotion beneath, a rare event in Tony's experience, but it was only a moment before those enigmatic lips turned round again, upward into a wee smile, forced and insincere.

Tony said, seeing the doubt, "Sir?"

"The penny didn't drop on this one, that's all. No one's fault. Couldn't be helped. You did what could be done. Matter of chance, nothing more," the old man said in a somber monotone. His eyes looked kindly at him, Tony thought. "Odd situation," Goodge added as a kind of musing afterthought.

"I suppose so," Tony replied, dimpling his chin, nodding. "Nothing to be done, really, was there?"

"Absolutely right, Captain. We'll get her next time, that's all."

An awkward silence of confederates, the air around them still and heavy, as at a wake, the chief's resoluteness muted. Tony's, too.

Their immediate surroundings bespoke another world, another sort of fraud, trappings of practitioners of high finance, of the speculative spirit, soft lighting from unseen sources, dense dark green carpeting underfoot, rare woods from far-off savannahs and rainforests counterbalancing oiled English oak in the trim of the office, beauty from the savage world strangely elegant among the rugged wood of the homeland, an antique tickertape set on a pedestal off in one corner, beneath a gilt-framed picture of a bygone gentry on horse trotting among hounds after the fox.

And beyond this inner sanctum, ranks of cubicles suggestive of the mean and confining hierarchy of modern business, now-dead computer faces set amid banks of telephones, semi-private booths for salesmen whose daytime pitch was imitative of confidentiality, perpetrators of promises to the masses impossible to keep and dreams unreachable.

And beyond this boiler-room, made tidy and efficient by technology's advance, a gleaming chrome and glass entrance, just off the elevators, its bright plate-glass highly reflective and impressively etched with the frosted bold letters '*ANGLO SAXON FUNDING plc.*' Intended to impress but also to deceive. And even more, a double deception. Not so much the fancy offices of a mutual-funds operation as a shelter.

Far inside lay the heartstone of an 'ASF' of another fabric, where two lone men now faced each other as the day wore on.

"Who was it, then?" Tony asked finally, finding his voice again. "The deceased?"

"Ah, well that's curious, too, isn't it?" Goodge said as if awakening from a nap, and he stiffened his posture a touch, if that was possible as he always had the bearing of a military man, and his gracefully curved chair of rare woods protested the move with a squeak or two. "Chap named Dahoum bin Qibla. Bedu name, sort of thing might come out of the Empty Quarter, not what you'd expect at the front gate of anybody's embassy in London. Certainly not an Iranian name. So what was he doing there, that's the question, isn't it?"

A rush of inspiration born of memory buzzed at Tony all of a sudden, and he asked of the man across the desk:

"You're sure of this identity, sir?"

Goodge looked sternly at Tony for this. He was not used to being put to the question by anyone.

"Why is it you ask, Captain?"

Tony said, with widened eyes ablaze in blue, "Why, he was at *Karachi*, nine years ago, sir. *Somebody* by that name at least. Remember?"

And Tony saw it right away, saw Goodge's normal vibrant spirit return instantly. His boss's resolve spoke out in a loud voice, saying "Of course! I knew it seemed familiar, yet I couldn't place it. You're absolutely right, Spool, that *is* a name from Karachi!"

"And the ID is positive, sir?"

"Well... not much left, you realize. Nasty, those THV cartridges. But the police did a thorough check against the Iranians' claim of who it was. They're bringing charges, they say. Against whom, they haven't managed to enunciate as of yet. Scotland Yard are 'at work' on it. However, dental records checked out completely. Seems Mister bin Qibla had been a patient of a highly regarded, and expensive, dental surgeon in the Gloucester Place for some years, off and on."

"There would appear to be some sort of connection, then, wouldn't there, sir? Karachi, the Iranians, our *Alex* Allgood, I mean."

"Is it possible?" Goodge asked, mostly of himself. "Is it just. . .?"

Tony said, "What *is* her name, by the way?"

"Alex*andra*, it turns out. Goes by the name of Alex. Hence our confusion. Butch, one presumes?" Goodge said this in a distracted voice.

"Goes with the territory, sir."

"Appropriate in today's terrorist league, I reckon," Goodge mouthed in a faraway voice, then looked down from the ceiling, where his eyes had wandered, and started busily scribbling himself a note. He murmured in Tony's direction, his eyes upon his writing, "This connection business bears looking into. I intend getting to the bottom of this."

Tony watched him intently, unnoticed, till Goodge looked up from his notepad.

"What is it, Spool?"

"Just wondering, sir. Am I to have a chance to save my penny?"

Goodge folded his hands, regained the present moment, searching Tony's blue eyes, seeking the answer to this question in those estoril pools. He stared at Tony for the longest time before he said, nearly inaudibly, as if to himself, "Yes, I think so. And how is it with you, Captain?"

Tony said with an uncharacteristic hesitation:

"It's the question I've been asking myself over and over, since this afternoon. Haven't stopped pondering why I missed—"

"But you *didn't* miss at all, Spool. Don't you see it? Fate's intervened, that's what's happened, and maybe to our advantage, now we know of the involvement of this bin Qibla character." His eyes twinkled familiarly, Tony taking up on the energy quite suddenly, thinking anew. He felt alive again, the throbbing at his temples magically gone.

"So you reckon it was fate, not killing Allgood today?"

Goodge looked now at Tony in the way he always had, as a protective and guiding father.

"Surely you see what happened. Mister bin Qibla walked into the path of our bullet, and I suspect he's given us the clue to a mystery we hadn't even realized existed. So, yes, I believe fate works its wonders. I do."

"Well, then, *lucky* Friday the thirteenth after all, is it, sir?"

"Oh, indeed," Goodge smiled, quite broadly, his stained teeth showing beneath the white moustache, as they rarely did. "I don't see today's events in anything but a positive light. Fact is, as we sit here, I'm beginning to believe we have cracked into a puzzle that may solve a great many questions over in Whitehall. And, at the end of the day, they'll have you to thank for it. Your bullet did not go astray!"

Goodge watched Tony become himself at last, and then he asked the question a second time:

"Want to save that penny?"

Tony's face shone now. His scalp tingled as his short-cut, curly, salt-and-pepper hair bristled. A new vigor coursed through his veins.

"Oh yes, yes sir! What I'd like, what I *need* now, is some time to figure on it." His eyes gleamed in the room's low light.

Goodge saw it, felt it, stood up and came around from behind his desk. Tony rose, too. His boss put a reassuring arm around his shoulders once again, and asked into his ear, "And what are your plans for the moment?"

"A day out with my wife tomorrow, catching up on our lives, was my intention, sir."

"She leaves early the following day, isn't that right?"

"As you say, sir."

Wondering if Goodge knew everything they had done since arriving in London, he and Susan separately, and them together? He supposed so. Most of it, anyway. Not much eluded the wise old spy.

"After she's left, Sunday morning, I intend going over to Calais and south, a little journey of reflection. I had expected it to be a kind of reward for today, but it's turned out differently, hasn't it?"

They walked together from the sanctuary, and Goodge suggested, "Captain Spool, only time and the Good Lord will tell us that for certain, but in actual fact I expect we've had a *grand success* today—after all," and he actually patted Tony's back.

Tony looked at him with a trustful eye but there seemed to be nothing left to say.

They strolled down the long, oak-paneled hall, brass plates on doors, black marble here and there. Compatriots of silence. Near the top floor of the obsidian skyscraper on Lime Street.

As they neared the frosted glass partition, only the two of them about, nearly dark outside now, Goodge made useless conversation, saying, "And following France?"

"Home, sir. Unless I'm needed immediately, of course."

Goodge only smiled absentmindedly, and Tony knew where those thoughts were, mulling over the Karachi connection, so he simply added, "Get home and take care of some personal business, sir. Catch up, that sort of thing."

"I recommend it." A distant approval, as in his past.

The exit reached, Tony turned to face his boss, and eye to eye he said quietly, "Thank you, sir," and Goodge's moustache billowed overtop his unrevealing mouth. They gripped each other's hands vigorously. Tony so fond of him. A look of fatherly pride in the older man. Their hands released.

"You have yourself a good, healthy think in France, Spool, then come back to see me—on Monday evening, right here, shall we say eight p.m. sharp?"

"Eight it is, sir."

Goodge opened the heavy glass door himself. He said: "Big confab over the weekend, over in Whitehall. They'll all be there, Freddy and the lot. The PM as well now, I expect, thanks to you."

Tony's thick eyebrows arched, his face steady, his blue eyes aimed at the future.

"Recharge my batteries in the meantime, sir."

"That's it, isn't it? Do them good." With just a wee smile, though no longer forced or insincere.

Goodge closed the door and walked away without another glance, a firmness to his step, Tony saw, resolve in his posture.

And Tony smiled wanly to himself as the old spy disappeared into his asylum, looking through the reflective glass door from the outside, his own image before him as in a mirror, alone again.

* * *

Susan found herself with a girlish smile on her lips, a bubbly feeling in her heart, drinking in the fabled sights as she looked out the windows of the Mercedes, with Tony next to her and Harry driving, just past nine the next morning, breakfast in their tummies.

"Nothing like a balmy Saturday morning, like this one, eh, guv?" Harry said from the driver's seat. He had his window open, taking the breeze.

"Right chew are, 'arry," Tony said back at him, and they both laughed at each other, then Susan joined in.

"Cockney, right?" she said.

"Nothing like it, mum, nothing like it" was Harry's response.

Harry pulled up to the curb about halfway down Whitehall and Tony helped Susan from the car. She said, getting out, "That's impressive—what is it, darling?"

"Come round in forty-five minutes," Tony said into the window to Harry, and the Mercedes rolled off as Tony explained to Susan, following her finger, "That's sort of the heart of Whitehall, the Ministry of Defence and what's called the Admiralty."

"Like the Pentagon."

"You might say that. But come, something for you to see, and something for me," and he led her by the hand across the avenue and down a side street of what looked like row-houses, all in brick. They came to a guarded, roped-off spot and Tony said, "Number Ten."

"This is the famous 10 Downing Street?"

"The Prime Minister's office."

"Not very impressive, at least not to my eyes," Susan pronounced.

"The very idea, darling, the very idea."

Then he led her away and around the corner into a large cobblestoned courtyard, and shortly they stood before a grand imposing statue.

"Kitchener," Susan said, reading the plaque, "the guy on the medal Simon gave you at dinner the other night."

"Right. One of my heroes. Lord Kitchener of Khartoum. He took back the Sudan, very end of the last century, after the savages murdered General Gordon. The Battle of Omdurman."

Susan stared up at the statue.

"He walked these stones we're standing on," Tony added.

"A great warrior, like Lawrence?" she asked.

"Not so great a warrior as Lawrence. An aristocrat, a feared leader, a brave general, though."

"What's so special?"

"Oh, he symbolized British derring-do, at the height of the Empire."

"Empires aren't much admired these days, Tony."

"Yes, but every man is a captive of his age, darling. You do what you can do, in your time. In Kitchener's case, few men ever did more in a lifetime, and few have ever been so complex as he was."

"Complex? How?"

"In many ways. Determined, strong in every way, yet delicate in his sensibilities, a gentleman in the very age of gentlemen. For instance, while planning battle strategies in his command tent, he also received London sales catalogues, and, bidding by agent, built a grand collection of porcelains. The fragile in the hands of the powerful. It appeals to me, Susan, this duality—the glorious and the beautiful both given their due."

"Explains why you collect those old coins, I guess," Susan said.

"In a way."

"So my husband, the great warrior—of finance!—and the great collector, all rolled into one!"

Tony simpered at her. "You can be so silly sometimes, Susan," and he grabbed her hand saying "Let's go see the Horse Guards" and they walked a long way around the buildings, past the quarters where the palace guards stabled their mounts, and came back to where Harry let them off.

"Why is it called 'Whitehall,' Tony?" she asked as the Mercedes came into view, looking around her at the complex of buildings.

"I dunno. Why is it called 'Washington,' darling?"

She asked Harry once they were back in the car.

He said: "Called 'Whitehall' cause, back in the days of Jack the Ripper, your Victorian times, mum, the soot was so heavy over these parts, from all the coal-burning chimneys across the city, that they whitewashed the 'halls'—the streets, what they called 'em back then—so's the governors could find their way to work."

"Oh," Susan said to the back of Harry's head. "Makes sense, I guess."

"Drive us on to the Tower, Harry," Tony told him. "Susan's gonna get a whirlwind tour by yours truly, all before lunch! But show her what's up ahead first. Pass by slow as you can."

And Harry drove them to the end of Whitehall, around Parliament Square, Tony saying "Westminster Abbey out your window, dear" and down past the Houses of Parliament.

"Have you ever been inside Parliament, Tony?" she asked as they stopped before it.

"No, darling. You have to know somebody in government for that. I've seen the Prime Minister's Question Time on C-Span, though!"

"Oh, you!" she said back.

And Harry made a U-turn and drove them out by Westminster Bridge as Susan said "Big Ben" to herself mostly, and then up the Victoria Embankment and in a while she said again "Oh! The law courts, right?" to which Tony nodded, smiling as she had only seen them in the dark before, and then the roadway departed from its river view and after a bit Tony said, pointing out the window, "The Bank of England, darling," and she smiled back, assuming that's where her husband spent a lot of his time here, and Harry added, over his shoulder, "It's called 'The City,' this bit, mum, because it's where all the money decisions are made" and Susan smiled dumbly again at Tony, and in a few minutes Tony pointed out a stonework pyramid and told her "That monument marks the place where the great fire began, back in Charles the Second's time, the sixteen-sixties—it destroyed almost all of medieval London, which was made of wood" but they were past it before Susan could react, and then they approached the Tower of London.

Harry pulled up near the tourist entrance as Tony told him to come back in two hours.

"Are you ready, darling?" he asked Susan.

"Gee, the whole thing in two hours! I guess I'm ready."

As Susan looked at the massive walls, while hundreds of tourists milled around in the surrounding park and a few dozen stood in line to enter, Tony leaned back into Harry's window and asked him in a low voice, "That bit about whitewashing the streets, naming Whitehall after it, that true?"

Harry twisted his mouth in a funny way and said, "Sure, guv!"

In ten minutes Tony had paid and Susan was reading the self-guided tour in the brochure, between gawks at the walls and towers all around her.

"Built by William the Conqueror!" she said. "I'm like, wowed by this, Tony!"

"Bit of history, no doubt."

"I don't know English history like you do, honey, but William the Conqueror! I know something about him."

"What do you know?"

"Battle of Hastings, 1066. England became Norman, sort of French."

"And the English paid them back for it for centuries."

"How do you mean, Tony?"

"The Hundred Years War. Battle of Agincourt, in 1415, was another payback. I've just been reading about it. We trampled their hides."

"Unh huh. Everybody carried a grudge?"

"That's about it, yeah."

"What's this?" Susan asked, stopping before a huge iron gate in the stone wall, across a moat. The river lay beyond. "The brochure says it's the Traitor's Gate."

"Where they used to bring those convicted of conspiring against the monarchy, took 'em in through there—the iron gate's called a portcullis, which can be raised—and straight into there," Tony said, pointing behind them, "into the Bloody Tower."

"Built by Henry the Third, thirteenth century, the brochure says," Susan read from it. "What happened to them then?"

"They were allowed a few years' leisure to consider their prior actions."

"It's called the Bloody Tower."

"Sometimes they were spared the years," Tony told her.

"Let's go over there," Susan said, pointing to the biggest tower inside the walls, a mammoth affair.

"That's the part built by the Conqueror. They call it the White Tower."

"I get it," Susan smiled back. "Cause it's whitewashed, just like the street called Whitehall!"

What could Tony say? He said, "We English aren't so clever after all, are we? Just good at PR!"

They climbed lots of stone steps together over the next half hour, wandering through the four floors of the middle tower, Tony pointing out the mighty armor of Henry the Eighth's horse, set on a reproduction, and they walked along the nearly endless display cases of longbows and crossbows and early guns like blunderbusses, and in the basement vaults strolled around the cannons, mortars and early bombs, and finally emerged at the back of the huge tower, where Susan announced, "I feel like I've just done History 303 or something. Too much to take in, don't you think, Tony?"

And they sat for a few minutes on a wooden bench in the shade, craning their necks to see to the top of the tower. Tony rubbed his feet.

"How long did it take to build this place, Tony?"

"A good five centuries, darling. Most of the outer walls are early fourteenth century."

Susan was looking at her brochure again, while the sun glinted down on them through golden leafed trees and a cool breeze stirred the air.

"What a day!" Tony sighed. "Happy to be alive."

Susan was leaning over to kiss him on the cheek when she stopped, her eyes upon her brochure, and said, "Ohmygosh, we're almost next to 'The Block,' where they chopped off people's heads!"

"Let's go see it." Tony pulled her to her feet.

A plaque told of certain famous names beheaded on this spot and when, Susan lipping words from the brochure: "Lady Jane Grey. She was just a child, Tony!"

"Innocence in harm's way—or, in her case, in the way of ambitious men. Pity, but the way of the world, I'm afraid. Today they just steal your savings or your livelihood, don't bother with your life, not profitable enough."

Susan stared at the unimpressive sight, chains strung around some iron posts painted black, a big wooden chopping block in the center, in the midst of a grassy plot.

"Cold-blooded brutes, I'd say," Susan suggested. "Was it all the fault of those Norman invaders, Tony?"

"Hardly," he laughed. "The Anglo-Saxons before them weren't exactly pussycats, you know. Viking blood in most of them. Made the French look like poofs."

"Poofs?"

"Effeminate, darling. Softies. Dandies. Whatever."

"Let's look at something nice, Tony."

"How about the royal jewels?"

"Yeah. I'm psyched for that!"

And they walked to the long building behind them and got in a short line for the Jewel House.

"Don't blink when we get inside, Susan."

"Why?"

"Everybody gets the bum's rush past the jewels. Don't know why. They seem uncomfortable having lingerers staring at a billion dollars' worth of rocks, I guess."

And it was true. Uniformed guards kept repeating "Keep moving, keep moving" in a monotone, mindlessly, gesturing with gloved hands, and the crowd shuffled down the line. Susan said "Wow!" as they came to the biggest diamond, set at the front of one of several royal crowns, behind a circular glass case around which they walked. At the end they both jumped line and went around another time, everything sparkling before their eyes but one gigantic white diamond most especially.

Outside, Susan said, "What was that one?"

"I'm happy to find you interested, Suz. I'm quite keen on diamonds myself. That was one of my favorites. They call it the Koh-i-noor, which means Mountain of Light. Came from India hundreds of years ago."

Susan found it in her brochure. "Yeah, here it is. It's set at the front of the Queen Mother's crown. Geez! Says here it originally weighed 787 carats, but that it's been cut down several times. Only 106 carats today."

"Must have been magnificent, at the start."

Susan read on in her brochure. "Says here it was given to Queen Victoria in 1850, when it weighed 280 carats. Belonged to somebody called the Lion of the Punjab before her. Cool!"

"Another madman," Tony said without explanation.

Susan ignored this and asked him, "Are we going home soon, honey?"

"What do you mean? You're leaving tomorrow morning, aren't you?"

"Yeah. But what about you? I want to get home to our bed, our nice house. All this history's kind of upsetting to me. Besides, it's all past, over and done with. Fun for a while, but I'm ready to go home."

Tony considered this, as they walked arm in arm across the Tower Green in the bright noon-hour sunshine, said, "Well, I'd love to go home, today, but I'm afraid I have to deal with some more bank problems or I'll be history myself."

He saw disappointment in her eyes. He stopped and kissed her sweetly. She put her arms around him, and hugged him. Susan didn't care about the tourists watching them, if any were.

"You're not coming home tomorrow, are you?"

"Afraid not, sweetie. I should be on a plane Tuesday morning. We'll be in our own bed, together, Tuesday night," he said into her ear. "We'll make it an early night!"

"Toneeey," she whined for his ears only.

He touched her lips, comforting her like a child. "I know, I know..."

"Why?"

"Well, the world may be free of Norman invaders and warring kings, but the economic war never stops. Big trouble in Asia. You know about it. All over the television, in all the papers. And it's true. British banking's heavily involved, critical investments are at risk, and I've been asked to help. Something you can't do, turn down these 'requests.' There's a meeting in France on Monday, which I'll leave for tomorrow, while you're on your way home—lucky you! And then an evening meeting back in London, Monday. After that, I expect to be free for a while. It's just a couple more days, but it feels like forever, I know."

Holding each other's hands, they left the massive walls of the Tower behind them, happy to find Harry waiting for them, and they sank into the soft back seat of the Mercedes as Harry carried them safely out of history's reach through the crowded streets of central London, into Hammersmith and west down the Chiswick High Road, to a sight of a different kind.

* * *

"Just down the road apiece, minutes away. South side of Richmond, guv, by the cemetery. I'll have the mobile, case you want me."

"Enjoy those grandkids, Harry! We'll walk about till closing, so collect us here in the village square at eighteen hundred."

Tony waved him off as Harry and the Mercedes disappeared slowly down the tree-shaded lane, and he and Susan stood in the Kew Green.

"Oh, this is better," Susan said at once, brandishing a new smile. "I've seen enough crowds."

"Thought you'd enjoy a break, Suz. I stop at gardens all over the world when I travel. They always give me a mental cleansing. Haven't been to Kew Gardens for years, though. Well worth a repeat visit. I just know you'll love this place."

"I do already. Hey, there's a restaurant across the street! And I'm ready for lunch."

"No," Tony said suggestively, "I think you'll thank me for asking you to wait, and have lunch in just a bit at the Orangery."

"The what?"

"You'll see."

But they hadn't proceeded far down the lane when Tony stopped short in front of the window of a bookstore.

"Just a minute," he said, guiding her by the hand inside.

She followed obediently. She thought of their time in Greece.

He said to the clerk inside, "Spotted your Shakespeare exhibit in the window. Have a copy of *Henry the Fifth* by any chance?"

"Of course we do." She stepped over a few paces to the shelves and handed a slim paperback to Tony. "Five pounds, please. Than-kew."

Outside again, Tony slipped the book into his jacket pocket and took up Susan's hand again. He couldn't help but reflect that the whole of Churchill's account of Britain's birth had cost him six pounds used, but a new book not one-twentieth its size cost a fiver. No inflation, wasn't it, the official word fed to the public daily?

Susan's mood was infectious as they strolled down the narrow lane beneath the spreading, ancient chestnut trees, their pods all over the ground, as well as fallen leaves and an assortment of curious seeds from other trees, which crunched underfoot.

Tony was decked out in his best Italian casuals, while Susan wore the prettiest flowing dress she had brought, saving the best for last. A silk scarf fluttered at her neck, a present Tony brought her once from Italy. The pale greens and pinks and sandy tans she was wrapped in enhanced her loveliness, Tony thought, winking at her, squeezing her hand as they approached the gardens' entrance. Their day together, and nothing could spoil it for them.

Tony paid at the gate and they entered the broad, brown-gravel paths, the lawns still green and spreading out in all directions. The flowers were all gone now, but the perennials made for a peaceful exhibit, planted among trees of all kinds. Too late in the season for many tourists, so the walkers were few in number and, most probably, genuine garden enthusiasts.

Tony sighed and felt at ease. Susan looked happily at her husband, enjoying his relaxed appearance, his normal state but she hadn't seen much of it since she'd come to England. He had it back now.

"My tummy's growling, Tony."

"We'll put that right soon enough. Hard to take all this in on an empty stomach, I know. Just around the bend here, couple of quick turns."

And she saw it, the long building, high roof and arches before it, like a church back home. "The Orangery. That's what the sign says. What is it?"

"A garden restaurant with *browsing* food—just for you!"

"What a peculiar name, though."

"Honey," he said as they queued up, "gardens and palaces all over Europe have 'orangeries'—they're just old-fashioned hothouses. It was once popular to raise oranges and other citrus fruits in these colder climates. Before imports became so easy and quick. Now the airplane brings oranges to England every day, freshly picked in Spain and Israel. In the good old days, we either raised them ourselves or did without. The wealthy did not do without. The hothouses are all sunny restaurants these days."

Susan picked out a ready-made crisp salad in a big crockery bowl, doused it with olive oil and vinegar, then took a roll but no butter and a bottle of orangeade, looking at Tony as she placed it on her tray.

"It's not orange juice, dear," he informed her, taking a salad himself but with blue-cheese dressing, a crockery cup of homemade vegetable soup, a roll with two butters, and a bottle of water from the French alps.

They sat at a little round metal table next to an expansive, tall window made of old, unclear glass and framed in oft-painted white metal. A casement window, cranked open a few inches, allowing a gentle air to enter.

"I should have gotten a soup, too, Tony."

"No, we're here for the veggies, Suz. Enjoy!" He smeared butter all over his roll and dipped it into his soup.

"I missed you yesterday, honey," Susan said, dimpling her chin. "Where were you all day? I left several messages, but you didn't call till late."

Tony chomped at his salad now. "Gawd! What a day it was, Suz. All the fun ended after my early jog around the park." He looked away from her eyes and pointed his fork out the window. "Did you know that herbal medicine in Europe had many of its origins right here? One of these gardens dates from the seventeenth century."

"Unh huh. What did you do yesterday?"

"A lot of waiting mostly," he said truthfully. "Some big shot from abroad took his time showing up for a critical meeting that was arranged quite a while ago. Then the whole thing was screwed up anyway. But I managed to save the day for good Old England, as it turned out."

"Money makes the world go around, huh?"

Tony just returned her odd look, saying nothing.

"Where was your meeting?"

"The City. Why do you ask?"

"Just wondering. Thought maybe at that Bank of England place you pointed out this morning."

Tony laughed appreciably. "No, darling," he snorted affably, "I don't advise the governors of the Bank of England! Nobody does. My meeting was at my erstwhile employer's establishment, over on Lime Street. Sometimes we meet at another bank, over by the river, near the Tate Gallery—I should take you there some time. Next trip!"

"The bank?"

"No. The Tate Gallery. Lots of great things to see."

"Okay. If you like them, I will too. Want to hear about my day?"

"Sure," Tony said, his eyebrows raising. She rarely offered.

"I can't say much, some of it's secret, but we had a great meeting at our embassy. When we get home I'll be spending a lot of my time in the next few weeks on news releases, and we're gonna do some broadcast spots. The President may even talk about it at a news conference!"

"Talk about what?" Tony was finishing up his spring water.

"Well, all I'm allowed to tell anybody, for now, is that State is playing a new role in helping solve all the fighting in Ireland. The meeting was with both British officials—from Whitehall, I guess!—and some leaders of the arguing groups in Ireland. They all seemed very nice, a little suspicious of one another, but very nice to us. They really seemed to enjoy the big fancy lunch we put on for them."

"So you're hopeful of a peace accord at last, is that it?"

Susan smiled brightly. "Yep! We are. It was a great meeting."

"Wonderful. Let's hope it all goes smoothly from now on. There's been enough senseless killing in Ireland, that's for sure. And enough bombs in England as well. Perhaps they'll even reinstall the trash barrels in the railway stations!"

"Trash barrels?"

"Popular dumping spots for bombs. You've heard about it."

"Oh yeah. That would be nice, no more bombs."

"Indeed."

She reached over and held her husband's hands in hers. "I've had a wonderful trip, honey! Way too short, but I'll never forget it." She lipped him a kiss across the table.

"Nor will I," he said softly to her. "We'll come back, shall we, on your next vacation, and just have a holiday? No work for either of us. I'll take you to Scotland, make you take up golf—right where it started!"

"Okay, you're on!"

"So... I'll visit the gents' and you inspect the ladies' room, then we'll walk off these calories and enjoy our day in the gardens. There's plenty to see. Nothing like a relaxing conclusion to the work week."

And shortly they were wandering down around the garden paths, crunching the fine sandy gravel, under a sky beginning to cloud up here and there, casting shadows to play on the bright carpet laid down by the October sun. Susan liked the reproductions of Roman temples but most of all the large, metal and glass Palm House—"Now *this* is a hothouse!" she told Tony as they stared around at the indoor rainforest, complete with towering palms and ferns from all over the world—and then they walked all around the gigantic pond opposite it. Susan carried the brochure, leading Tony where she wanted to go next.

They stopped beneath the flagpole, with a huge Union Jack fluttering on top.

"Oh! Let's see the Pagoda—no, wait, we'll do the Temperate House next, okay?"

"Whatever you say, sweets. Have enough energy?"

"C'mon," she pulled at him. At the other end of the large building, leaving it, she said, "That was pretty boring, compared to the palm place."

Tony smiled. "In the age of cable TV, we've all become complaisant. That place is an absolute marvel, but not very dramatic, I'll admit."

In a few minutes, Susan stared up at the Japanese pagoda, which seemed to climb into the clouds when you stood at its base. Tony headed for a bench and took off his kid-leather Italian walkers, to rub his feet.

"Not as young as you," he explained to her. She walked around the pagoda several times.

"Wish I had my camera."

"We'll buy postcards."

Tony put his shoes back on, grabbed Susan's hand, and led her through a thicket of bushes, where he stopped and stood staring out into the distance, down the vast lawn spotted with ancient oaks. Susan turned to him with a question on her face.

"What's this, Tony?"

"This is the oldest part of Kew. The tourists don't bother with it, and they don't really want you to come over here. Not much to see. But plenty of history."

"What history? Looks like an empty field to me."

Tony smiled forgivingly at her, and kissed her on the forehead.

"It's the Old Deer Park, Suz. Where the kings of England once hunted, a private preserve for the stag."

And he stood still, holding her hand, his eyes looking backward in time. Susan stood silently. Tony thought of King James again, smiled to himself about his gold coin, remembered the story of the king warming his cold feet in the smoldering guts of the downed stag, and a shiver coursed through his body, recalling yesterday's shooting, the bullet finding the right mark after all, and Goodge's pleasure over it. He clenched his teeth and peered out at the park through mere slits in his eyelids, with an intensity and an anticipation he would forever need to hide. *He felt it now. He would pursue Alexandra Allgood to the finish!*

"Ouch!" Susan said beside him.

And he looked at her and then down at their hands, realizing he was squeezing her hand tightly, hurting her. He let go.

"Sorry, love." He leaned over and kissed her on the cheek.

"What is it, Tony?" She sounded concerned.

"Nothing, nothing. Just thinking, that's all. In my mind's eye"— all he could think of to say about it—"I see them out there, the royal huntsmen, the stag at bay, frightened by the hounds, the horse and the commotion, running for its life. Raw existence. Places like this, they make history live for me."

"As my dad used to say, you're really something, you know that, Tony? How many other people could stand here and see anything but trees and grass? Not very many! But that's why I love you," and she turned to hug him, threw her arms around him all the way, and put her lips over his, her tongue feeling its way, kissing him passionately. Her eyes were closed tight, her head falling back, resting in Tony's hands, cradling her. But his blue eyes flashed in the glinting sun, and continued to stare down the length of the old deer park, back at history and forward to his future.

"Let's do something different," Tony suggested as they rejoined the garden path by the Pagoda.

"Such as?" Susan felt horny. She wondered what he had in mind. She was giggling a bit, leaning into Tony. His eyes were elsewhere.

"There's a lot more to see and there'll be almost nobody on the trail where I want to go. It's all woodland, lots of trees and glades," and he pointed out the western section of Kew to Susan on her brochure.

"Lots of rhododendrons, it says, and a lake, and at the end of the lake a large garden of azaleas. Even some redwood trees back in the forest," Susan repeated, reading.

"Rhodies!" Tony said enthusiastically. "I really like rhodies, and some of them here are huge, hundreds of years old. It's a neat place."

"So what do you want to do different?"

"Let's not talk till we get to the end of it. Instead, let's *soar*, pretend we have no feet, no bodies, but spirits with eyes. It'll block out everything that doesn't matter, Suz. The rhodies will fly by, bright and colorful but in a wondrous blur. I do this sometimes, it's like chanting, and when we're done your mind will be clear as crystal. Wanna try it?"

"How do we do it?" She had a special sparkle in her eyes.

"We can hold hands, walk together, but you have to think *out of body*. You have no feet, no legs, no muscles, no skeleton, just a mind with eyes to communicate what you see to your soul. You'll see *everything!* Every bird, every plant, every living thing. But you won't remember any of them individually, just the experience. You'll feel more alive than you ever have! Ready?"

"Yeah. Yeah, okay!"

Tony grabbed her left hand in his right, reminded her not to look at him but to focus far ahead down the path, just on a spot, keeping it always in the distance, not on any one thing, and to square her shoulders and thrust out her chin, as if flying.

They started slowly, picking up their pace, walking and then jogging hand in hand, all alone, and the brown sandy gravel of the path suddenly lost its pattern, became a blurry path, their feet crunched no more, the sound disappeared as their feet ceased to exist, the air became a sizzling wind in their hair and ears, they lost their muscles, their bodies, only their minds following the eyes' images, the plants were no longer rhododendrons but mounds of green blurs, the trees not birch nor poplar nor chestnut nor oak but cascades of golden, crinkly light beyond the green blur, and the air filled their nostrils with a cleansing purity that scorched all madness and care into nothingness, and left the mind blank but for the images sent to it by the eyes focused on a distant point that was never reached...

And in no time they had left the lake far behind, never seeing it but only smelling its presence, and the giant redwoods of great age lost their centuries as the omnipotent floated past.

As Tony and Susan passed through the azalea garden, coming near to the main paths, she sensed again his hand holding hers, her feet on the gravel, and her presence in the world. He stopped and she did, too. He dropped her hand. She blinked repeatedly and shook her head. Her eyes came back to a normal focus. And she looked at her husband in a new way, leaning and almost falling into his supporting arms, out of breath.

"Oh, wow!" she breathed heavily. "Oh my God, that was great!"

"How's your head?"

"I've never felt so wonderful, Tony! You were right. I forgot I had a body. Nothing existed, no problems or cares, just the world in all its plain beauty. How did you do it? How did *we* do it?"

Tony swung his head side to side. He laughed. "Mind over matter, that's all it is. I believe the mind can do anything, if you just let it."

Susan's beauty seemed radiant to Tony now. Like a work of art.

She looked at Tony as if she wanted to eat him, and she found herself rubbing her legs together, leaning into him. "I wish we could do it right here, right this moment!" she breathed heavily into his ear, and made it moist with her saliva, tickling it with her tongue.

Tony pulled her away. "Later, later," he said commandingly. Still, her look didn't go away. So he said, "C'mon, we're back in the world again, we have to act civilized, let's walk it off down this path."

She did it reluctantly, but Tony was strong for them both. In a little bit, it passed.

Tony caught the time on his wrist.

"Half an hour to meet Harry in the Kew Green," he pronounced firmly. And he looked up and noticed for the first time that the clouds were starting to turn gray, the sun to fade. The air was chillier now.

Susan had drifted away, off the path a few meters. She was busy looking at what seemed to be blackberry bushes, among the magnolias and azaleas. Tony got over to her just as she picked some berries off a bush. She had them to her nose, smelling them.

"I'm starved after that experience," she said, seeing him, looking at the berries. "Think they'd mind if I ate some of these blackberries?"

Tony reached a hand out towards her, but a voice intervened.

"Wouldn't do that if I were you, ma'am," it said in a warning.

She stopped, and looked towards the voice. So did Tony.

A man in gardener's garb stood behind one of the bushes, nearby. He was all in tans and greens. Wellies, tweed trousers, green jacket to his knees, gardening gloves, wide-brimmed tan hat smudged with dirt, and a smile on his mug.

"They're not blackberries. They're a cousin, called *belladonna*. Those berries would do a number on your tummy, ma'am."

Tony looked in horror at the man.

The man's eyes wandered between Susan and the plants, not seeing Tony. He said to Susan, in the distracted manner of an academic lecturer, "You must be an American. Most Europeans assume that's whortleberry. The Scots think it's a heather, which they put in some of their ale. The Turks, they think it's what they call 'mad honey,' a narcotic they use to treat rheumatism." He ran on, cataloguing the botany, his attention on his subject. "The plants look very similar, but belladonna's a poison. See how shiny the berries are? No blooms this time of year, but the flowers are red and bell-shaped, quite distinctive. That's why we put labels out, ma'am, though you're not permitted to pick or eat anything growing here in the park, technically speaking. Most people abide, you know." His eye began to drift to Tony now.

"Sorry," Susan said lamely.

"Pity," said the gardener, rubbing his chin between two fingers, "for a pretty lady like yourself to eat any of those berries. The Italians, you know, they named the plant *belladonna*. Means 'fair lady.' Our English nickname is more descriptive; we call it 'deadly nightshade'—and deadly it is!"

But suddenly the gardener looked anew at Tony, and his mouth dropped open. Tony stared back at him in disbelief, couldn't help himself.

"My God!" the gardener said. "It's you, isn't it, Captain?"

Susan looked at Tony with wide eyes, then at the gardener.

Tony just stared at the man.

"B.C. Clive, sir. You remember me, surely?"

Susan said to Tony, "Captain?"

Still Tony said nothing.

"That's right," said the man, "we were in the Regiment together."

Finally Tony found his voice and he said, "No, sir. You're mistaken, my friend. I've been in banking just about all my life."

"Naw," said the gardener, insistently, his vision drilling into Tony now, "you're *Spool*, right? Captain Antony Spool—from, where was it? Scarborough? Why, it's been nearly twenty years, but I'd never forget you, sir. Not with your reputation!"

Tony extended his hand. The gardener removed his glove and shook Tony's hand.

"That's right," Tony said, "of course. Clive. Good man. You've been well?"

The gardener smiled quite a wide smile now. "As you see, sir," waving his hand around the gardens. "Couldn't be happier. And yourself, sir?"

"Married to this beautiful woman, very happy, and living in America. And I have been in banking for a long time now. The army's long past."

"Army!" said the gardener, Clive.

Tony grabbed Susan's hand, said, "Well, thanks for saving her life, and so good to see you again, Clive." And he started off, pulling Susan with him.

"Right," said Clive. "Well, keep good care, both of you . . ." He removed his hat and scratched his balding head, watched them pass under a huge Indian Horse Chestnut and disappear down a path towards the gate.

A few minutes later, Susan and Tony walked side by side down the long, curving lane leading into the center of the little village of Kew. Their feet noisily crunched the odd seed-pods fallen from the stretch of trees above their heads. They did not hold hands. Tony wore a strained mask upon his face as he glanced repeatedly at his wife, who hadn't said a word to him nor returned his look since leaving the gardens. Her lovely brow was deeply wrinkled, her eyebrows pushed into each other.

A late afternoon mist had formed out of the roving, high gray clouds, which had broken down the sunshine into ghosts of diminishing light.

As they turned into the Green, where Harry sat waiting for them in the Mercedes, Tony grabbed Susan's hand, pulling her up short. She turned and looked at him with something between anger and disappointment in her eyes.

"You've been keeping secrets from me, Tony," she almost cried at him. "You promised me, seven years ago, we would share everything in our lives. Everything."

"Suz. Suz, I have." His look could have melted thousand-year-old ice.

"The Regiment? Captain of what, Tony?" But her anger had turned into soft questioning.

"Suz, we share everything that matters, don't we? You don't share confidential information from your career. You're true to your loyalty. I admire you for it, admire you tremendously. I know what a temptation it is to want to share your days—share your secret thoughts with the one you love most in all the world. I do."

Now her disappointment was wavering, too.

"And I am loyal to my business duties," Tony was saying, "as I have to be. And so proud to be the husband of a woman who respects that loyalty."

Susan's moist eyes blinked repeatedly now.

"But, Tony, a 'Captain'! That's a big secret, Tony."

"It's not a secret," he said serenely, holding both her hands, "it's just old history. Stuff I'd rather remained forgotten, over and done with."

"I want to know everything about you, though."

Tony looked over to see Harry standing beside the car now. He held up his right hand with five fingers spread out. Harry saw it and got back into the Mercedes.

They stood under a multi-shaded green awning. The town center was deserted, the shops all closed, nobody about.

Tony looked her in the eyes till she saw nothing else, thinking of all the things he could never share with her, all the truths that would destroy them as a couple if she knew them, suddenly thinking of the priest in the confessional back home, and then he said, truthfully, "Susan, I just can't tell it all to you, much as I'd like to. It's too…painful."

"What is, Tony? Something you did in the army?" Concerned for him now.

"Yes."

"Tony, you have to tell me." And she put her arms around him, all the way around, hugging him to her tightly, for fear of losing him.

Finally he said in a whisper into her ear, "I was a commando, twenty years ago, and I killed a man in the line of duty…" He held her to him in the embrace, his eyes peering off into an unknown distance. They were bright blue in the graying light, and hard.

After a few minutes he heard her say, "I understand now, honey. That's why you have those awful nightmares, isn't it?"

"Yes," he lied almost in silence. And let out an audible sigh.

She released him, kissed him lightly on the cheek, then rubbed his nose with hers, staring up into his eyes, seeing them elsewhere.

"Tony?"

"Yes." Looking into her eyes now.

"Honey, I think we're *soaring* now, like in the garden." And she smiled ever so innocently and brightly at him. "And I love you for it! Thanks for sharing it."

He said, "Thanks for understanding." Nothing more.

They walked on to the car together, hand in hand. It wasn't far away.

"Maybe you'll feel like sharing it all with me some day," Susan spoke again as they reached the car. "When you're ready to . . ."

"Maybe," Tony said, and opened the door for her.

"You two all right?" Harry said over his shoulder, in a lilting question.

"We are, aren't we, Suzy?" They sat close together, snuggled in the soft leather in the back of the Mercedes.

"Yeah, we are!" Susan answered, smiling at Harry. Tony smiling as well.

But as the car left the Kew Green, in the darkening light, while Tony chatted with Harry, Susan's eyes drifted down to her lap and saw that her fingers were stained from the berries she'd picked in the garden.

Then she stole a furtive glance at the stranger beside her.

FIFTEEN

Loose ends. Tony hated loose ends. And now he had a bunch of them to tie together.

Starting with Susan.

When Harry drove them to the Dorchester, from Kew Gardens, Tony sensed a coldness in his wife he had never experienced before. They spoke easily to each other, but something was different.

He first felt it in the soft darkness of the Mercedes, as they drove back to London, night setting in. Susan held his hand in the dark car, but it had no life to it, no warmth; he squeezed her hand but the returned squeeze was barely perceptible.

Then she hardly touched her salad and French merlot wine in the Dorchester dining room. And she would not make love to him. Too tired. First time she had ever said that.

She asked Tony if Harry could drive her over to the Savoy. It was only nine, but she said she wanted to get to sleep early, had to be off about eight Sunday morning, back to the States on the Air Force jet. She had hugged Tony lightly, given him a kiss on the cheek, then left with Harry.

An hour later Tony dialed her room number.

"Hello." Her voice didn't sound sleepy. Something else.

"I know it's late but I couldn't wait," he murmured.

"Tony," she said back, sweetly. He smiled to himself.

"You may not be here but I can see your face and hear your voice tonight," and he pictured it in his mind's eye, her chin tilted into her bosom, peeking out from under her long, full hair, the ends of her mouth curling into wisps, just the tips of her teeth showing between her delicious pink lips, those bedroom eyes... that ethereal whisper on her tongue.

"I was thinking about you, too, Tony. I always think about you when I'm alone."

Tony smiled a different, private smile now.

"Are we all right, Suz?" he said into the phone after a few moments.

He heard a distant sigh, low and oh so quiet. A troubled breath. He knew he had her now. So he added: "I thought we were soaring again."

A laugh in the receiver. A genuine laugh, as of relief.

"What's been troubling you, Suz?"

"Tony." A pause. "Tony... you know. The secrets thing."

"I've been thinking about that, too," he said back, steady, a suggestion of confession in his tone, but his voice masculine, assured. "I guess it's best to talk out our past problems. Not keep them bottled up."

"That's all I meant, Tony." Her voice was the same as always now. Confiding, sharing. The soul mate's voice.

"I never intended to keep secrets, Suz. Just spare you the pain."

"Sharing your pain tells me you love me, Tony." The voice of concern.

"Okay," Tony laughed gently into the phone. "I know it's late, but are you ready for another confession? Can you handle one more secret today?"

He heard her laugh. "Sure I can," she said lightheartedly.

"You remember the other day, Thursday? We had dinner with all those friends of Simon's that night."

"Yeah."

"And you had your meeting in the morning, and then the lunch at the embassy? And I told you I was at the bank all day?"

"Yeah."

"I confess, I wasn't at the bank and I didn't work at all."

"You weren't? You didn't?"

"Nope. Harry drove me out to the seashore. My boss wanted me to target-shoot, on his private beach. We've done it before, plenty of times. He's crazy about shooting clay pigeons, and he likes me to shoot, find out if I measure up. He was a champion shot once, see. So I do what he wants." Tony thought, well all the facts were true, just out of order. Not lying, really.

"Part of your work," Susan said back in the phone, "if he insists."

"Harry says I humor my boss too much. I see it as part of the job."

"That's your confession?" Susan said then.

"No-hoho. Just the prelude. Ready for the secret?"

"Sure I am."

"Remember I told you it was all work, work, work and I hadn't eaten much that day at all?"

"You were starved by dinner time, I remember."

"It wasn't true at all. Harry and I stopped at a bakery on our little drive, ate tons of clotted cream on scones and drank pots of tea. Evil stuff! But the awful secret is something Harry and I did later on. I told him, 'Harry,' I said, 'you tell Susan about this and I'll get another driver!'"

"What?" Susan asked quizzically.

"Bursting with tea, we stopped at a lonely spot, found ourselves a cliff facing the sea, and standing side by side sprinkled all that processed tea back to nature. There you go, secret sins all out in the open!"

"Oh, Tony," Susan giggled into the phone, and he thought he detected a yawn after it, "that's the silliest secret I've ever heard."

"You wanted to know it all," he said laughing into his phone. "It's not *all* nightmares and bad memories, you know. There are some ugly white lies, too. You gotta take the good with the bad, you wanna hear all my secrets."

A short silence, and then:

"I couldn't sleep at all tonight, Tony," she told him quietly. "Now I can..." He heard another yawn.

"Suz?"

"Yeah, honey?"

"Just called to let you know..."

Sitting on his bed in the Dorchester, Tony held the silent phone in his lap for a few minutes, smiling winsomely to himself. Love *was* such a hard thing. And one of those loose ends tied up nicely as well.

* * *

Tony beamed as he admired the car, early next morning outside the Dorchester, parked in the center of the hotel turning, and drawing attention from the passersby on foot, and from all the cabbies.

"*Signore*," began the young man who had delivered it, for the hire company had sent their best Italian driver along with the Ferrari, "this automobile you have driven already?"

"Before?" Tony corrected his English. "You mean, have I driven this model before? No I haven't." He looked at the young man. "A few older models I have driven," he continued, in Italian, "but not this same car. Since only a year it has entered the marketplace, no?"

"Si," in Italian now, "so I demonstrate its features for you, yes?"

"Yes, but in slow Italian!" Tony replied, his hands making the sign for less velocity, and the driver smiled.

"Si, si, si. For you, I show in English, best I could."

Tony smiled back. "Okay, we do it in Italian and in English, but slowly for us both!"

And, their chins nodding in mutual respect, Tony and the driver went over how to drive a Ferrari, this Ferrari especially.

Shortly before seven thirty, Tony had his suitcase in its rear maw and the monster pointed out of the city, warming it up as he crawled through the lanes of fashionable Belgravia, imagining bored mistresses in some of the beds lying awake beside their wealthy keepers still snoring it off, in other apartments aristocratic youth frolicking in more accommodating beds, in yet others grande dames snoozing away their lives. For one and all, Tony revved up the nearly five hundred prancing horses, letting them gurgle in their own unique deep torque voices, as he wound round corners, east and south out of the metropolis, hoping to disturb each and every one.

He purposely chose the Vauxhill Bridge Road, nodded towards the Tate on his left as he entered the lanes of the fanciful bridge he and Goodge had taken on foot just days ago, but didn't it seem an eternity, smiled quietly as he passed the fortress, not looking at it, and shortly found himself coursing south down the Old Kent Road, gliding through the roundabouts at Eltham. Then Sidcup and Ruxley, past lovely country and villages still mostly asleep, and onto the M20 motorway, picking up speed out in the passing lane, almost no traffic yet, soaring through the heart of Kent at 140 mph, windows and sunroof open fully, the fury of the car's wind setting his spirits for the day ahead.

In no time at all, it seemed, the Ferrari 550 Maranello had carried its master near to the coast. He smelled the sea air, smiling in memory of the same delicious aroma over on another coast, with Harry driving the metallic black Mercedes the other day, his disappointments all behind him now, feeling the same intensity of purpose he had felt last time the sea's breezes had stirred his soul.

Downshifting through the high gears as traffic gathered and Tony saw up ahead the port town of Folkstone, where an even swifter transport awaited him and his monster.

At the terminal for *le Shuttle*, on a day of calm skies brightening out of gray, husky blues out to sea but still pale buttery colored over land where the sun broke through the high clouds, Tony loaded the car's CD changer with some of his favorites. They would play a role in psyching him today and tomorrow, an important role for him while he mused over the puzzle that was his future and helped lead him to discover both answers and his destiny.

The old hovercraft crossing to France took almost two hours, two hours of delight if you had the time and enjoyed the pace. Two long hours if the seas were rough. And the hovercraft, at first novel, seemed more a nineteenth-century vessel, quaint and earthy.

Just a glance at the Eurotunnel train proved its worthiness for the twenty-first century. A long steel muscle with a bright silver stripe through a blaze of yellow top and bottom. It would zip through the chunnel beneath the English Channel in thirty-five minutes while its passengers ordered up scones and tea and felt like they merely floated to another country.

Tony loaded the Ferrari himself, slipping its wide frame in through the slim doors of the train's ferry car.

The bulbous single eye of the train's pilot engine whisked its passengers to their destination at the port of Calais by the time Tony had sipped his Earl Grey tea and found the famous lines in his paperback copy of the Bard's play *Henry V*.

Le Shuttle's carriage doors opened up to allow the French sunshine to brighten the glow of his Ferrari's 'Ligurian Blue,' as the Italian delivery driver had called it—"Named, *Signore*, for the color beautiful of our sea which dances off the coast at Corsica, yes?" he had waxed ecstatic, causing Tony to smile sympathetically with a poetic soul in love with his culture. Tony turned over the monster's engine and eased it onto the road surface.

In no time at all, the Ferrari's gurgling valves torqued in Tony's capable hands, and he was heading away from the sea, aiming towards the north-south French E-road, about six hundred miles to go to reach Nice and another sea, but just before he came to the broad motorway he spied a sign reading '*Nord/Pas-de-Calais*' and something from his reading came to mind. He pulled off the tarmac and began searching for his roadmap. He couldn't find it, but there was the town of Hesdin, and he knew it was just north of there.

He put his Revos back on, their bright blue-tinted lenses concealing his own, avoided the E-road for now and took the 43 south, headed for the turnoff at St Omer and the 928 slow road southward, till he could locate it.

The air was lovely, the sun crisp but not glaring, the speed modest for now, and with his short hair hardly disturbed, his shirt barely fluttering in the breeze entering his windows and exiting through the tipped-up sunroof, Tony touched a button on the CD player and brought up the first song he had chosen for the drive, reminding him of yesterday and today and tomorrow.

Doing eighty or so, too fast for the road, but the sign caught his eye, and he braked hard, just now the only car on this stretch of the road, slammed to a stop, found Reverse, backed up to the turn-off and the sign. A tiny sign with an arrow pointing off the roadway. 'AZINCOURT,' it read.

Tony stopped the music, removed his sunglasses, rubbed his fingertips over his curly black eyebrows and into his eyeballs, massaging himself, restoring reality. As his eyes refocused on the world, he looked again at the sign. And then he peacefully slipped the tranny into first gear and headed down the narrow lane to a fight that was won four hundred years ago. Maybe it would help him understand the fight that lay ahead of him.

* * *

Tony parked the monster on the church square and walked a short distance to an eating establishment bearing the name *Kings Arms*. Curious for France, it occurred to Tony. Then the waiter, propping open the front door, said in English, with a strong northern accent, "First of those we've seen hereabouts! Beautiful motor, sir!" Pointing towards the Ferrari. Nobody at any of the little luncheon tables shaded by colorful umbrellas.

Tony smiled openly at the waiter. "Hire car, alas!"

"Ah… well. Beat the barrels, wot!"

"I shall try, my friend, I shall try. I'm surprised to find an Englishman here. How come?"

"You a Brit?" came the only answer.

"By birth. American now. I'll ask again…"

"Wish to order something, sir?" He handed Tony a menu. Tony didn't look at it, said:

"Bacon sandwich. Tomato mayonnaise. And a Younger's Scotch Bitter."

The waiter smiled now. "Okay," he said, looking over his shoulder for other visitors who might be French, seeing none. "Wife and me, see, we own this place. Bought it on the cheap. No Frog'd touch it. It's a lovely spot to live, this." He looked again for an interloper, still found none, so he continued: "They harbor resentment to this day, locals and the rest of them, incredible as it may sound. Our only customers are English, Americans, Ozzies, Germans and Scandies, the odd Spaniard. So I'm not clairvoyant, my friend. Guessed you'd be a countryman, you see."

"I see," answered Tony, his lips in a sort of pout. "I'm here to see the battlefield. Any chance, or is it paved over?"

"No, no. Still here. You're almost in the middle of it, you know. Private land, now as then. Another Yorkshireman owns the museum—"

"Yorkshireman?" Tony interrupted.

"Yourself, as well?"

"Scarborough."

"Ah!" The waiter shifted the menus he carried, stuck out his hand. "Robie, sir. Des Robie. Wife's Sally. She's from the Isle of Man. I'm out of the Dales, meself, see."

"Tony Spool," taking his hand in a friendly shake. "So the cultural isolation wouldn't bother either of you, would it?"

"That's it, sir. Tony. Precisely it!" In a lower voice he admitted, "Weather's better than home, I'll say that."

"And the bacon sandwich?"

"Yes, no problem. It's all traditional here. Our own Yorkshire cakes, real food, English teas. Sally'll do up a bacon sandwich—and the salad. Fraid you'll wait a long while for the Younger's, though!"

"No bother. Can you do a cold bottle of spring water and a lime twist?"

"You're right, there!" the waiter gleamed, and ran off to the kitchen.

And thus amply fortified, Tony briefly discovered the Yorkshireman in the museum gladly took his English money for the brochure on the Battle of Agincourt. Maps and displays in the little three-room museum explained the ancient fight, and the field of battle was reproduced in miniature, complete with metal soldiers. Arms and armor, longbows and arrowheads of the day, were on display. Tony studied them for a time before venturing outside and following a signposted walk down a narrow two-lane road along a field that led to the center of the action of 1415.

Tony retreated to the English position and tried to imagine himself as King Henry V, with a ragged band of sick soldiers, facing the French camp, thick with knights on horseback and thousands of foot soldiers. He peered down the grassy field, imagining the massive force between the forest to the left and right, hedging them in, no way out but a fight to the death, and a shiver ran down his spine even though he knew Henry had defeated what looked to be an overwhelming force of well-rested, fully armed, fierce opponents.

Unexpectedly a voice, an English voice, came from over his shoulder.

"'The fewer men, the greater share of honor.'"

Tony turned round. "Beg pardon?"

"Not my line. Shakespeare's," said the English voice.

"I've just read it myself," Tony replied.

"Hoot, mon! Thus ye ken, doth ye? Alan Mowress, sir, at your service. Do please forgive the theatricals. Always a sucker for an audience. Comes with the territory, after all these years."

They shook hands.

"Tony Spool," Tony said again. He probably didn't actually say his own name more than a dozen times a year, yet here he was, twice in an hour. "Scots?" he asked.

"Welsh, man! Don't mind the dialect. Comes with the territory."

"You said that twice. What territory?"

"Professor of linguistics, you see, but my passion's history. Hand in glove, though, aren't they? Right now I'm bogged deeply in the Hundred

Years War. Why I'm here, you see. First-hand impressions, nothing like 'em, is there?"

He wasn't looking at Tony, not at all. He was looking down the field where the armies had fought, centuries back.

"S'pose not," Tony said, also looking down the field.

Unexpectedly the man clapped Tony on a shoulder, said out loud, as if giving an order, "Well, let's not just *stand* here. Get a move on!" and stepped off the pavement and began trudging out into the field, heading towards a copse of trees up ahead.

It was just Tony and this stranger. No one else interested in 1415 today, it appeared. As Tony stepped out to follow, why he didn't know, he really saw him for the first time, and stopped himself up short for a moment. Oh, he'd be damned! From the rear, the linguistics professor looked for all the world like Percy Dithers, back in Southwark! Tony took off after him.

The grass a bit wet and muddy, Tony's Italians showing it already, he came up to where the man had stopped, middle of the field, pointing to left and right, running his finger back and forth at something out in the field, chattering away even before Tony came into earshot.

"... which is precisely why, you see," the professor continued, "Agincourt ranks at the very top of all the land battles we've ever fought, in terms of heroics."

"Why's that again?" Tony asked.

The professor turned to him, saying "The archers, man, the archers!"

Tony nearly jumped back. Even the professor's face looked like Dithers', with the same fairy eyebrows, same balding pate with light brown hair neatly trimmed, same odd smile. *Yee Gods*, Tony thought. But he said:

"Oh yes, the archers. Of course. Sorry, bit too far away, missed it."

"You should keep up, Tony," he scolded. And he again pointed down the field, following his fingers with his eyes. "King Harry's blood must've run cold when he saw these troops, standing here, morning of St Crispin's Day, don't you reckon, Tony? October twenty-fifth, chilly, wet, miserable affair all around."

"Was it?"

"Oh, indeed! Rained yesterday," he explained, meaning the day before then lost in his centuries, then catching himself, saying "Ha ha! It had rained on the *twenty-fourth*, you see. Conditions were not as we see them today, in the sunshine—no! The rain had turned these plowed farm fields all to mud, all round us"—twirling his hands around his body, to illustrate—"this was all mud, right where we're standing, you see. Halfway to the knee!"

"Tough way to fight, in all that armor," Tony interrupted. The professor's skin was finely grained, just like Percy Dithers' skin was. Freckles, too. Damn! Tony was staring at him, practically unnoticed.

"Weather intruded, 'tis true, Tony, 'tis true. Clausewitz comes up a mite short on that, doesn't he?"

"How so?" Clausewitz? Tony thought. *Oh yes.*

"Said only *fog* plays much of a part in battles. Fog indeed. Wrong again! As he often was... despite being German."

Uncanny, Tony thought, hearing this. *Attitude's even Dithers'.* Tony let it go.

"I've read Churchill's account of the battle—" Tony suggested.

The professor ignored this, and announced, "French foot soldiers took up the forward positions, Tony, all across the front there, from the trees left to the trees right. Behind them, the French crossbowmen, a small ranking—the major weakness in the French strategy. Followed by another huge force of foot soldiers—all but useless in the muddy field, wot?"

Tony remembered the display at the museum. He said:

"And a row of mounted knights at the French rear, I believe, Alan."

Which stopped the lecture.

Alan Mowress turned and looked Tony square in the eyes. No glasses, either, just like Dithers, Tony reflected.

"It's *Doctor* Mowress, my good man. Or *Professor*. Whichever you prefer, if you please. Wife called me 'Mowress,' never 'Alan.' Gone now."

"Passed away? You don't look old enough."

"Not away. Just *passed.* Doesn't matter!"

Tony felt the shock yet again. Hadn't Dithers used the same phrase?"

"Uh," he stumbled, "wasn't the battle won by the force of the English longbowmen?"

"That's right!" Mowress continued, leading Tony further out into the field, this time towards the dense stand of trees on their left. "Matter of fact, I'm preparing a major article on the archers. We know they flanked the field on both sides of the forest, there and there"—pointing for Tony—"and also they grouped in wedges right in the center, behind a fence of sharpened wood stakes, and protected by soldiers with pikes and swords. The key is, *most* of Harry's force were archers. And the English longbow carried far beyond the range of the French crossbow—*the* major advantage, of course..."

Tony interrupted again, trailing behind Mowress as he forged towards the trees still a hundred meters away. He yelled ahead towards Mowress, "Mowed 'em down, right, Professor? And they all piled up in the field, suffocated in the muck, couldn't get free in their heavy armor—"

Mowress stopped and turned abruptly towards Tony.

"*Yes-s-s,* Tony, that is correct. The hail of arrows wreaked havoc!"

"Thought so," Tony mumbled.

Mowress looked at him still, intently. Tony realized this man had on almost the identical brown tweeds that Dithers had worn. Different shirt, though. Argyle colors.

"What brings you to Agincourt, Tony, if I may be so bold?"

Gave him an odd look. Very odd.

Tony wondered himself, didn't have an answer, *actually* had no clue why he was even talking to this strange man. Instinct, nothing more. He had a desire to simply walk away, but didn't.

"Oh," he replied, allowing his eyes to sweep over the whole battlefield and suddenly realized a peculiar coincidence. This place, too, had dense trees stretching along each side of a run of green. Just like the golf course at home, where he first sensed his mission against Alexandra Allgood.

He smiled suddenly, remembering that *sign* at the golf range, but getting an even odder grimace from Mowress, like the look he saw in Percy Dithers just before the chemist had popped that poison pill into his mouth.

"Yes?" Mowress quizzed him. "Oh what?"

"*Doctor* Mowress, I'm merely an amateur historian. I sometimes take inspiration from places like this. They help me in my work."

"And what sort of work is that?"

"Banking. I'm a banker. Making money's a fight, too."

Mowress expressed silent contempt for this belief with a dismissive wave of his hand through the air. "Oh yes," he said breezily, "Sun Tzu, the MBA's trifling stab at history. All started with that American movie. Sun Tzu must be turning over in his proverbial grave, all I can say..."

"Probably is."

At this, Mowress raised what eyebrows he had and looked more deeply in Tony's face.

"Hmm... I was about to say something unkind about bankers, but I can see you *do* read, so forgive me, Tony. If you will." He turned back to the battlefield. "I suppose, in a way, banking is a modern war, now you mention it. But Tony, Tony, here we have the genuine article. Entire nations rose and fell in such places. Yet today's citizenry is blushlessly ignorant. Pity, a real pity."

"As they say, ignorance exists," Tony put in, his own tuppence.

"Yeoman archers," the professor ranted on, "nobodies individually, yet by King Harry's day they had achieved the status held by knights two and three centuries before them. And all because of the sticks they shot, farther and better than any other army. A *weapon* won this battle!"

"Not to my mind," Tony objected.

"Oh?" Mowress returned to see Tony now. "Do tell this pathetic, old ex-RAF flyer the significance of the Battle of Agincourt, will you?"

"Oh the arrows did the work, destroyed the ranks, drove the horses mad with pain, causing them to dump the French knights into the mud, all right. But it wasn't the longbow that won Agincourt."

"What was it, then?"

"It was the force of will. Confidence is always the deciding factor, Doctor Mowress. In banking. In any kind of war. Four hundred years ago, or tomorrow."

"Straight down the center, is that it, Tony?"

"How d'you mean, Professor?"

"That's what King Harry did, you know. While his longbowmen killed and maimed from a distance, French forces broke ranks because Harry led his men headstrong into the center of them! The French panicked, we won."

"But *why* did they panic, Professor?"

"That question begs many answers, Tony. No analytical article has ever been able to say for certain. Twenty thousand against five, why should they panic? Why *indeed?* Anyone who could prove why would break new ground."

"'We few, we happy few, we band of brothers'—that's the answer."

"Shakespeare. We all know that. How's that an answer?"

"I just read it in my paperback copy, in the chunnel this morning. It hit me, the truth of it."

"What truth?"

"You remember the scene in the play? The night before the battle, King Henry disguised himself and mingled with his men, listening to learn if they were behind him. Not realizing he was among them, they spoke candidly, from the heart. The king wanted to know beforehand the degree of his soldiers' courage."

"I remember that. Not every line, but they spoke only of winning, nobody complaining. That's where Harry's confidence came from. So what?"

"The king," Tony told the professor, "found in his men and in his cause what Shakespeare called the 'soul of goodness in things evil.'"

"Yes, but every side thinks God's on their side. It's trivial."

"Doesn't matter. The strongest passion wins. Royalty and archer and foot soldier alike, they all kissed the ground, giving thanks to God for their faith, and charged screaming madly into the huge French army, cutting it to ribbons. They charged to win the day *against evil!*"

Mowress stared at Tony with thought written all over him for a few moments, then said, "How is it you know this so well?"

Tony looked inwardly. "Don't know. I only know it's true."

"That *is* why the French broke ranks, isn't it? They were pitted against an opposition that looked ragtag, even pathetic, but that believed in itself—how did you put it?"

"The strongest passion wins. *Force of will* was what won Agincourt."

"I'll put it in my article, if you don't mind, Tony. We've rewritten Shakespeare, you and I."

"Don't mind at all, Professor. Thanks for the guided tour."

Mowress clapped Tony on a shoulder once again, as unexpectedly as he did the first time.

"Oddly enough, Tony," he said, in a humble tone, "for once it's not I who did all the guiding."

Tony smiled, not a word to be said.

"By way of thanks, may I show you where the castle stood that they named the battle after? It's just over yonder, through these trees."

Tony took him up on the offer. This was no Percy Dithers.

As they walked over to the ruins of Agincourt Castle, Mowress asked to borrow Tony's copy of the play.

"Ah yes, *here* it is," he said to Tony, showing him the passage. "Just an academic argument, Tony, but how do you explain this, then: You say *force of will* won Agincourt. Yet the French Dauphin also had the force of will. He speaks of what today's dreadful politicians would call empowerment. Readying himself for war, all cocky like, he says 'I soar, I am a hawk.' Pretty forceful self-empowerment, I'd reckon!"

Tony's chin bobbed in agreement as they approached the imaginary walls of the castle. "Absolutely, Professor. But it was King Henry who really soared with passion, wasn't it? The Dauphin fooled himself!"

"Reckon so. But why, Tony, why?"

Tony flipped through a few pages himself. "Here it is—this line made an impression on me. I dog-eared the page. King Henry tells a couple of his soldiers that the wicked—thieves and murderers, he says—'have no wings to fly from God.' No way can they escape holy punishment. And he says that war is God's vengeance on evil!" Tony snapped the book shut.

"The real hawk, then, was King Harry!"

Tony nodded, mostly to himself, as his eyes followed a bird high above what once was the castle. The professor jabbered on, but Tony wasn't listening anymore. Instead, he watched the soaring bird, imagined himself up there, soaring, and suddenly he realized that God had given him another mysterious *sign.*

Mowress, he noticed after a little while, had walked away, could be seen halfway across the field back to the village by the time Tony came to.

Tony smiled to himself, deeply.

No wings to fly from God. What could this mean? Best to leave it to God, he supposed, and circled Agincourt Castle twice on foot, clockwise. Two times. His lucky number.

* * *

Strictly speaking, of course, Tony knew that battles aren't won only by the force of passion. Cunning usually counted for a great deal. The cunning use of weaponry.

But the stop at Agincourt, was it destiny? You never knew when God would speak to you, did you?

Tony's heart was abeam as he nudged the gleaming, bluish green Ferrari down the French B-roads for a few miles, doing maybe fifty, warming up his horses again for the long ride ahead. The windows open, the sunroof tilted up, the day delightful.

As he entered the southbound lane of the major traffic artery, both the road and his hopes spread out before him, and he made the famous horses prance. Revos pointed dead south.

He pulled the first quarter mile in just over twelve seconds, gripping the wheel hard against the torque as his speed climbed over one-twenty, then settled into it at close to one-fifty, cruising then in high gear, a hum in his ear. Windows tight now, roof closed. Touching the CD button for a piece of music that seemed just right for the moment.

The sound rumbled at Tony like a steam roller, a rhapsodic pressure on his ears as Duran Duran sang of a perfect day, a day so idyllic that you forgot who you were, dreamed you were someone good, calling to Tony to be someone new. The music flooded into Tony's brain, into every cell of his body, its lyrics repeating over and over, praying for love to transform his soul, while the car tore away fifty miles of the journey to the south.

The air conditioning cooled the cabin as Tony's mind wandered from God's mission to his Susan and back again.

Outside, the countryside flashed by. Greens and browns. Farms and towns. Inhabited by common people, all needing protection against the menace. Like a swift bird of prey, Tony maneuvered the car around slower traffic, hardly taking notice, mechanically and in something of a trance. Seen from outside, it was a blinding speed.

Inside, Tony's eyes focused on the road ahead as they had at the shoot, in darting glances. A glaze frosted over them as the road passing beneath became mesmerizing, and increasing speed irresistible.

And at one-seventy-five the wheel pulled at his grip so much that he came out of the rush, relaxed his pressure on the gas pedal, and suddenly his eyes focused sharply again, his heart calming, and his speed dropped to just over one hundred. The Ferrari grazing now.

He stopped the music as his eyes fell to the center of the steering wheel, where a tiny black stallion stood on its rear legs, on a bright yellow circle. Yellow again. Tony smiled. Noticing the black horse outlined in thread-thin silver.

Then looked at the fuel gauge.

A sign by the side of the road announced 'DIJON 30 km' but

disappeared as quickly as it had shown up.

He'd stop for fuel on the outskirts, and wash his face.

Nearly halfway through the six hundred miles to the French Riviera, Tony felt calmer now, kept his speed at one-twenty.

How beautiful the world looked, how wonderful it would be when the new civilization dawned. He yearned for it, but knew that getting there required patience, determination, devotion. The monsters would fall one by one. Count on it.

Just as Jimmy Cliff sang "Breakout" to Tony for the third time, a little north of Lyon, Tony holding at an even hundred, first one and then a second vehicle passed him, in tight formation. Too tight.

Jimmy's Cliff's lyrics spoke of goodness, but that's not what Tony was about to witness on the road. Road rage, it was called nowadays.

Tony increased his speed, curious to see what was going on. And touched Stop on the CD changer.

Ahead of him, a pale-green Ford Explorer tailgated a gleaming red Mercedes. Speed over one-twenty, pulsating speed, but the SUV pushed at the more lissome Mercedes, following at what looked to be just a few feet behind. The Mercedes changed lanes without warning, the Explorer right on its tail, weaving around the few cars out in the two fast lanes. Then they did it again.

Tony dropped back a little, sensing the danger. He slowed to seventy. The lane changing was erratic, sudden, without warning.

Equally without warning came a spin as the Explorer chased the sleek Mercedes through two lanes, the Mercedes slipping out of a lane with a long truck just ahead of it. The Explorer didn't make it, twisting wildly as its front bumper caught the truck's rear. The truck continued on, but the SUV skidded sideways on its tires, slipping and then flipping and rolling noisily, end over end, until it came to a crashing halt against a bridge abutment, a massive concrete structure which folded the Explorer up into a mangled bundle. And then it burst into flames.

All the traffic behind it had slowed almost to a stop. Tony, too.

Up ahead, the dazzling red Mercedes screeched to a stop and sat alone in the open highway for a few moments before a dark-tinted window opened, smoothly on its electric glides. The driver stuck out an arm and made an obscene gesture towards the sizzling carcass of the sport-ute, then accelerated quickly and disappeared up the road.

Most of the following traffic picked up speed again and continued on. A few vehicles pulled over to the berm. Tony did, too.

But what could be done? The Explorer burned brightly, like a torch, and dark smoke began to rise from it. All was still. There was no life within. One by one, the cars on the berm gained the roadway once again.

Tony watched for a few moments more, then slipped the transmission into low gear. He drove on for some time in silence, doing about seventy.

Soon he came to the road which wound in two narrow lanes through the western side of the French Alps, followed an ancient path, and after passing by Grenoble, on its quieter south side, he stopped for fuel and a stretch. Traffic was slight. The road had a stillness to it here. A welcomed peacefulness. Mountains rose steeply off the thin highway, a mild breeze seeping down them, and on their faces gaggles of alpine trees confounded the eye with the dying glory of their turning leaves and brittle needles.

Tony found the gents and inside, with dulled eyes, stared into a poor mirror at the mask of his soul. Gaped at himself as at a stranger. He felt encumbered by his own humanity, wondering at the faded glass. He sought relief by splashing icy cold water on his face. He did it till his face numbed.

Back in the car, Tony lowered the windows again, turned off the AC, opened the sunroof to let the late-day sunshine freckle though the leafy sky onto the top of his head, warming him. The wind rustled in his stiff hair.

A day of promise and beauty. A day of senseless death.

Tony had an ugly taste in his mouth, and as he drove on he negotiated the Ferrari along the winding mountain road with great care, averaging forty to fifty, taking the curves cautiously, more so than he needed to, thinking often of Susan, wondering at God's ways, and listening to Jimmy Cliff's chanting voice, his melancholy longing, as he warbled repeatedly, asking Tony how peace could exist without justice.

SIXTEEN

Life's whys remained mysteriously on God's silent lips, Tony thought as he steered the Ferrari south through the mountains towards the French Riviera. His head wobbled indiscernibly in consternation at some of mankind's actions. The death he had just witnessed defied reason, yet maybe it wasn't a senseless, random act. Tony wondered. Maybe it fell within God's grand purpose. Who could know? Who indeed.

One thing *was* certain. Jimmy Cliff got it just right. He *understood!* There would be no peace without justice.

The Lord's messenger must do the Lord's bidding.

The new civilization beckoned.

Tony's mind settled on this as he devoted most of his attention to the road, which now drifted to the southeast, weaving at times like a meandering stream as it followed ancient tracks—tracks possibly laid down by the Romans, Tony imagined; he wasn't sure but he thought of it as he steered into the curves and accelerated on the short straightaways.

The scenery reminded him of the ride through the low Sierra Nevadas near Yosemite, in central California. Deciduous trees, many with hornlike leaves, tough and spiny, mixed among all sorts of evergreens. Rocky terrain with sandy soil changing to high mountains. Little streams, now mostly dry.

But this was not America, not the great West. It was ancient territory. The road here straddled the Provence and the Maritime Alps. Soft abundance on one side, the side of the magical lavender. Sparse and rugged towards the Alps. God's balance once again, Tony reflected as he stopped in a tiny village of just a few dwellings for refreshment, and to stretch his legs. He had covered nearly six hundred miles since lunch and Agincourt.

His monster stood waiting, cooling down, as he drank from a bottle of icy water. What was power, he mused, looking at the car, without control?

The smell of pines enlivened the cool air. Tony noticed a scruffy plant by his feet, among some shrubs, with delicate, pale yellow flowers.

As he looked down at it, a girl of perhaps twenty approached, coming from a tour bus unloading by the store where Tony'd got the bottled water.

She stopped near him, and he glanced at her. She smiled at him with a coquettish face, said "It is pretty, is it not, *monsieur*?" Eyes cast down, then peeking at him through long auburn lashes.

Before he could answer, she added "It is called woad. It makes blue dyes. We have just studied it in botany, *oui*?"

"Woad?" Tony simply said.

"A mustard, *monsieur*. The spice of life, *oui*?" Her eyes ate him.

Tony took a deep breath. How cruel temptation was. The girl's skin was smooth, her face blushless, her flesh spongy. The bloom of youth.

In his best Italian, Tony said "Sometimes we must do without."

The girl wrinkled her nose, not understanding, formed her lips into a silent kiss as she raised and dropped her shoulders, and bounced away towards the store, where others on her tour milled about. Her hips sashayed sassily. Tony watched them as she left him. The ice water was gone.

He thought of his Susan as he started up the Ferrari again. What was power without control? One of life's biggest questions.

Soon the road lost elevation and the sea was faintly in the air. Tony had the windows open but the air was heating up too, and drier. A simoom draft nettled at his sinuses, hot dust from faraway Africa, drifting in off the Mediterranean. Always something, wasn't there?

As evening settled upon the coast, the highway dropped sharply, in a long curving fall, Tony in the Ferrari gliding down through the green hills dotted everywhere with elegant homes and multi-story condos, all of pink and white stucco, all soft pastels, both sky above and sea below azure, an enduring draw.

Now his tires touched the clean boulevard at the western end of town. Royal palms separated the three lanes running in each direction. Balconied hotels rose to his left, and to his right stretched out a wide promenade, below it a pale-gray pebbled beach and, beyond, the vast blue sea, rippled only by tiny lapping waves. He had reached fabled Nice. Paradise of a sort.

The bright, metallic blue Ferrari commanded the happy road, drawing looks even from the most effete.

Halfway in, Tony pulled a gentle left at a break through the palms and glided to a stop in front of the Negresco Hotel. Its famous pink dome, capped in pastel blue, had watched over the goings-on for decades.

As soon as he had checked in, and stowed his gear, Tony stood at the open window of his suite, top floor of the hotel, facing the sea. The Ferrari stood in front of the hotel, adored in vigilance by the staff in turns. How far these French francs went, Tony smiled to himself, seeing the car's roof glinting in the day's fading sunshine. The Ferrari's blue was even more intense than the Mediterranean's.

The sea reached as far as the eye could encounter, and farther than that as well, all the way to Africa.

Its calm surface seemed so tranquil to Tony as he stood staring at it. No wonder these waters were called the Bay of Angels. It was how the world might be, free from predators. At peace under their watchful eyes.

Tony shrugged and changed into comfortable walking shoes.

The commercial Nice lay mostly out along the beach drive, to the south of where Tony was, down the boulevard, and in the busy streets behind the hotel. Streets lined with shops of every sort, Tony knew. So he headed off in the opposite direction, along the boulevard.

He worked his way on foot through a public garden ornamented with bronze statues, neatly pruned lollipop trees, tidy brown gravel paths, and a sprawling brown-and-white-striped tent. It had new automobiles parked under it. He continued walking and soon reached another public park, away from the beach, just distant enough from the center of things that tourists wouldn't go to the trouble to come here; it was the domain of locals, though few happened to be about at this hour, as dusk neared.

It was a park full of fountains. Few trees, little green, a modern French park of cement pools holding fountains which launched countless streams of water into the air with great force. Long rows of these waterspouts formed walls of water, spraying heavenward, or at least to the height of many of the surrounding treetops. A mist sprayed off the water wall, dampening the pavement of marble and cement in decorative formations. At the far end, curving banks of water shot up high into the air.

Tony sat on a sculptured aluminum bench, one of many, facing the walls of waterspouts. The air above seemed cloudy, so much mist rose off the fountains, like a huge plateau of white cotton out of which the fountains appeared to tumble, like a waterfall. His bench looked like an inverted mollusk shell, something out of Botticelli's mind, fancifully sheltering Tony from the mist falling out of the sky. He was almost alone in the park.

As he sat watching the fountains, soothed by their constant flow, seagulls would dive through the mist, then flap madly out of view. Scavengers on the lookout for scraps.

Tony's eyes closed, at rest with nature and with man for the moment. His mind drifted.

He thought of the bird he had seen soaring high above Agincourt Castle, then of the falcon that had peered at him in the zoo in London, wondering if any of it meant anything at all, doubting it, tired and near to dreaming after the long car trip, soaking in the calm of this place, restorative after the shoot and the stress of his official responsibilities. Was he aging? Those responsibilities had never been stressful in the past, they had been exhilarating. Was it being married now, having something to lose? Love was a compromise. Love had its rewards, but its costs as well.

As he drifted in and out of consciousness, he dreamed of a better world. Where rage would be unknown. Where mothers would not be in fear of losing their tots playing at the beach. Where greed would not overtake public servants. Where spies and assassins would be redundant.

A faint, high-pitched scream opened Tony's eyes, to see gulls flying madly in and out of the fountains' mist. Tony was slumped back deep into the fanciful seashell seat, relaxed, nearly asleep. He sat up as another scream came from the fountains, then above the mist saw a very large bird diving fast towards the fountainheads. It swooped at terrific speed and snatched a gull in midair in its talons, flapped its long wings slowly and majestically, climbing out of the park and finally soaring in the high winds. Tony's eyes followed it until it disappeared. He realized he was standing now.

He looked around. Nobody else anywhere in sight. The fountains spouted high, as before. The remaining gulls continued floating in and out of the mist. The world went on as if nothing had happened.

Tony thought the bird looked like a golden eagle, but wasn't sure.

Suddenly, standing there by himself, all the birds came together. The falcon, the bird over Agincourt, the eagle here. And the professor's line from Shakespeare folded them into a single bird. What was it? *I soar, I am a hawk!*

Goosebumps rose all the way down Tony's spine.

Just as suddenly, Tony felt he had the answer to the troubling question of Alexandra Allgood—that he would surely kill her.

He didn't yet know anything about the mission—not when, not where, not how. All he had was a vision: *I am a hawk!*

He would leave what it meant to God.

After a bit, Tony found himself wandering through the streets of Nice, and hungry. In the lanes behind the Negresco and its sister hotels, the menus on display—dishes listed in handwritten script on chalkboards—and the food itself on the tables outside the restaurants, busy now with many diners, started his stomach growling. He realized he hadn't really eaten in a long while.

The pizzas looked delicious, and the many breads, full of grains and nuts. But it would be imperative to be in top form if he was to defeat one of the world's most dangerous killers. So he stopped at a little place that featured fresh local seafood, and took a table inside by a wall.

Best to get back into professional habits.

A huge pot of steamed mussels arrived, soaked in garlic and lemon, as well as a tossed salad, with a great variety of greens and a tangy mustard-vinegar dressing. He dug in, but pushed the tray of wonderful-looking crusty French bread away from him. Icy water from the nearby Alps, with a twist of lime, relieved the intensity of the mussels.

One of the delights of dining in a small French cafe like this one was that the staff left you alone while you ate. Some might say the staff ignored you. But it was the French way, and at the moment Tony appreciated it to an unusual degree, as his thoughts were not on the table fare.

As he pried open the black shells and extracted the tasty, spongy yellow flesh of the mussels, the perplexity of the day's events became clear. God's ways were not so mysterious after all, he realized once again. All day, and in fact all during the trip, he had been witnessing small signs, leading to the vision he now embraced and which gladdened his heart.

The sea seemed at peace, nature appeared placid, compared to mankind's furies—whether on the road today or at the Battle of Agincourt. Man's nature did not change, not over centuries. Evil ceaselessly challenged good, but man's drive to kill for selfish reasons was cleansed by warfare, by God's own justice, sometimes by His special messengers.

Nature of course wasn't really at peace. Killers ate to keep life vibrant. And the world did not mourn the dead, not for long if at all. Strength and determination led to the future, spawned new generations.

As the pile of empty mollusk shells accumulated on the collection plate, Tony realized another truth about one of his heroes. Lawrence of Arabia had written that he found himself 'bowed to serve the holiness of victory.' Tony had always thought of that as just a pretty phrase. That was before he understood that God used warfare to cleanse evil. It was why nature's killers were both vicious and magnificent.

It was just how it is. It was why heaven seemed indifferent to death, why God's lips remained silent.

It was why Tony was who he was. A messenger of the Lord.

The waitress removed the used plates and the pile of mussel shells, and brought back a dish of icy lemon sherbet surrounded by juicy slices of bright orange tangerines and sprigs of fresh mint. A single vanilla cookie adorned the top of the sherbet. Tony ate it first.

He finished up dessert, his mind ahum with the joy of life, with renewed purpose, and he walked to the front of the cafe to pay his tab. The cashier was surrounded by scores of tiny, odd-shaped mirrors, glued to the wall and dangling from transparent cords as if suspended in air, and they reflected the images of the place hither and thither in all directions.

In one of the dangling mirrors, Tony suddenly saw himself, part of his face, saw his own vibrant blue eyes pass by in a flash, twisting gently in the air, and he steadied the shard of mirror with his hand, looked in it into his own eyes, remembering again what Goodge had told the assembled warriors at the conclusion of the meeting at MI6's fortress, and inexplicably an old Viking word came to mind.

The word was *shend,* and it meant to destroy—to kill in disgrace.

Outside now, Nice twinkled in the growing darkness of night. Windows, headlights, lamplights in the parks and on the boulevard along the beach, stars, and even a bright, gibbous moon far out to sea, they all invaded the shadows of paradise. Red taillights gave way to patterns.

Tony crossed under the lamplights of the boulevard and stepped onto the famous paved, broad English Promenade that parallels the beach. He walked westward, ambling among strangers.

He walked for nearly a mile, until the sea came nearer as the promenade and the beach narrowed. The strangers thinned out, too. A few pairs of lovers strolled by or sat on the benches, obsessed with each other. A same-sex couple stomped by in leather and chrome chains, cawing loudly in sync with their raw jewelry as it jingled to their stride, then fading away. Not meaning to look, Tony's eyes invaded the privacy of one bench as he passed it, to discover eyes closed and the sound of deep mewing.

He kept going, till he was almost alone. He faced the sea, while behind him lights shone dully in some of the windows of apartment buildings crowded onto the hill. Mostly the hill lay in darkness. The famous flowers of Nice had disappeared into night. And the azure sea and sky had blackened.

Tony's hands touched the cold metal railing of the promenade, chilled by the sunless air, as his mind turned to home. He could picture Susan's face and form. He remembered another night touching a rail and facing the sea.

The end of being alone.

How had he gotten there? A few days before, he had been in Karachi, had done his duty, had done it with as deep a satisfaction as he had yet known. Had gone on to Greece and the cruise, both to celebrate his success and to put it behind him. And then came Susan, out of nowhere...

Her innocence had moved him. Her beauty was complete.

Tony smiled in the dark, unseen by anyone. His fingers tingled as the cold metal cast him into the past, back to a moment of transformation.

She had accepted him at face value, had told him everything about herself, had opened her heart to him. Within hours of meeting her, he had fallen in love. He knew how dangerous that was, had never allowed it to happen before, didn't intend to let it happen when he approached her on the cruise ship. But it had happened. It just had.

When he had first talked to her, all he had wanted was the usual. Many, many women had fallen under his spell in the past. Somehow, he had fallen under hers. And then, mysteriously, he had a feeling that this woman might be his salvation.

It had come to him in an epiphany. You couldn't go searching for epiphanies. They always surprised you, seized your soul like fright.

He remembered it now, standing in that holy place, that Greek church in Santorini. They'd been walking by, he and Susan, like ordinary tourists, when for some unknown reason Tony felt drawn to its holiness, felt compelled to go inside. It was as if some force pulled at him.

Once inside, in its hush, the holy place transcended the outer world. Tony could recall, as if he were seeing it all over again, fresh and clear, holding Susan's warm hand, her dewy flesh, while they stared in awe up at the glorious ceiling decorated with images of God's messengers, a host of angels encircling the Holy Savior, betrayed by man's world.

He relived the guilt he felt as he had stood by her in that temple, his soul shuddering, knowing he didn't deserve to be loved by such a woman—but wanting it, wanting it more than anything else—and suddenly overtaken, his spirit trembling, *communing* with the spirits and defeating his demons under the dome of that church, feeling God's approval down to the marrow of his spine, dumbfounded by love, barely understanding it but suddenly he sensed his hardness melting under the beam of Susan's love, like ice dissolving, and realizing at that moment that God was speaking to him, giving him a sign—*blessing him with a new soul*—amplifying his powers and empowering his emotions all in the same humbling, shattering moment.

It was the first time he had questioned how he lived.

It was the moment of change when he knew he could—and must—do more. Holding on to that precious woman, wanting to protect her forever, needing her, he had first thought of the new civilization. He had first dreamed of making it happen.

The sea would forever remain part of his metamorphosis.

As the ship had sailed away from Santorini, that last night at sea, they stood alone at the ship's stern, and Tony remembered his fingers tingling from the cold metal as he let go of the railing to enfold Susan in his arms. Her warmth suffused him.

He looked from her loving eyes to the stars in the black, endless heavens, kissing her eyes and rubbing his nose against hers, sniffing her fragrance, pulling her into himself. And together they watched the twinkling lights of Santorini disappear from view.

And then his stare had settled on the viscous waves of the ship's wake. For a moment, just a moment, even as he held Susan to him, the black sea had turned deep red—into the blood of the wicked as they gave up the world.

SEVENTEEN

Only the shrill mating hiss of the mole crickets pierced the black isolation, their signals not coming from any one place but diffuse, emanating from secret spots among the turning leaves of birch and oak, and conifer, and from brush on the heather moor, but intense enough to imagine browning leaves quivering from their vibration. The only sound of night, and one of eerie insistence, the supplication of dying insects to their progeny.

Worn-out automobiles, three of them, none less than ten years old, rested now at one side of the cabin. Their hoods were still hot and a sort of steam rose invisibly off them into the chilling air.

The trees were numerous here, and still water could be sensed, ponds not far off, their mosquitoes dead by now. Low wooded hills spread for miles. A single, unpaved lane led irregularly through the trees to the old cabin. Its gray wood was not painted but aged. Its tin roof slanted unevenly; rust and accumulated debris interrupted the channels stamped into the sheets of which it was made, angled from the peak. Moss stuffed their ends, and dripped now. The edacious insects droned on.

A dull light came from the windows of the cabin where glass remained and peeked between strips of wood nailed over missing panes.

It was the only light, saving that from the gibbous moon, for miles and miles around. And the moon's light came shattered and in streaks through the trees, a sort of Halloween illumination. But Halloween was still a fortnight distant, and nobody here would observe it in any event.

This was the center of Northern Ireland, which had ghosts enough of its own invention. County Tyrone.

Inside the cabin, five figures occupied fairly threadbare easy chairs. Five of them, unarranged, as if thrown off a passing lorry. The dull light was that of oil lamps, three of them, two set down on the floor and one on a small table which tilted a bit to one end. Aged wallpaper remained on one wall, casting into the poor light phantoms of horses which once jumped but now sagged. It peeled in haggard disarray down from the ceiling.

Easy chairs but no one was sitting easily. A lanky man in his late twenties chewed at the tips of several fingers, one after the other. He had a cowlick in the center of his forehead; his red hair was unevenly shorn and uncombed. He hadn't shaved in days.

Three older men, only middle-aged but seeming older, held smoldering cigarettes, of which the air stank. Two wore driving caps.

Another man, with white hair and long white sideburns, leaned over the side of his chair, over its stuffed arm, to adjust the wick of a lamp on the floor. The room brightened somewhat, and he sat up again, without emotion on his face, in fact looking bored.

All of a sudden their faces all became strained. The noise of another vehicle came to their collective ears.

A rusted, beat-up Volvo chugged out of the lane. Only the wrinkled frown of the moon's coy profile witnessed its arrival. The men inside the cabin heard its engine switch off. They all looked anxiously towards the door.

A woman appeared, in a high tight skirt covering stockinged legs. A purple vest covered a crinkled blouse. Her feet wore brown boots. Her face was possessed of a beauty passed on to her by untold generations.

But it looked ugly now.

Without a word, she crossed the room and occupied one end of a broken loveseat, its stuffing revealed in places, its brown corduroy torn across the back as if cut by a knife.

She lit a cigarette and pulled at it, savagely. Her age was impossibly vague. She looked tough, her skin chalky, the color of cigarette ash. Her fingernails were short, unpolished. Her facial muscles tugged downward on her cheeks; her nostrils flared in anger. She ran a hand through her short hair, cropped to look like a boy's. Her hair was yellow.

The air remained unbroken by speech. Only the uneasy creaking of the furniture made any intrusion on the orgasmic squeal of the insects outside.

All eyes had evaded one another since the last two men had arrived some ten minutes before. Now they all looked in the same direction.

"Ahl hafta *gew*, then, that simple," snarled the yellow-haired woman suddenly, "won ti?"

The men looked at one another, all except the youngest man.

"Not worth it," said one of the middle-aged men through his cigarette.

"There's no uther *whey*!" yellow hair shouted back viciously. She stomped down hard on her cigarette butt, swinging a boot off the loveseat and herself into an upright position as her foot struck the floor.

In the silence, yellow hair shouted again: "Never gewhin' back, never see Lowndon agin!"

The man biting his fingers looked meanly through them, and he said: "We'll fock them bastids sure, them Brits! Their fockin' peace is done with! They can't git away with hit."

A grumble came collectively from the other men.

Yellow hair stabbed two tight fingers at the three middle-aged men, her eyes vicious. "Ahl teal yuh bouwt them Brits. It's a present for them buggars! A present *tamarrah*, right in their precious Lowndon! Yew four'll do it, tewh!" Their eyes were on the floor. "Yew will!"

Her ugly look twisted even more maliciously as she turned to the younger man, still biting his fingers.

"The *Brits*, was it?" she screamed, as if depraved. His shoulders jumped. He looked nervously at the oldest man, whose head twitched violently to one side, then back, his lips bunching together, showing stained teeth. His speech seemed frozen.

"Course the fockin' Brits. Who ealse!" exclaimed the middle-aged man seated closest to the door. But his eyes shrank.

"Ahl *teal* yew who ealse!" shouted yellow hair even louder. "Uhnly *one* knewh my timing, knewh to thu *minute!*"

The man biting his fingers looked wildly at her. His eyes darted to the others. They were immobile in fear. He forgot his fingers. He shouted, "Nehw, nehw! It's not so! Yew *knohw* that, Alex!"

But she already had slid the large automatic pistol out from cover beneath the loveseat's tattered corduroy pillow. Fingers braced himself into the back of his chair, pressed hard into it, knew what was coming.

"Only one knewh my timing was *yewh*, Colm! Only one!"

Ten loud bangs broke into the black of night. First one shot, then a pause, then two more, another pause, and then seven more bangs right in a row, so quick you couldn't count them.

The mole crickets ceased their vehement shrill for a few moments, then the leaves quivered again from their vibration. The edaphic world went on as if nothing had happened.

* * *

Tony watched the little white marble go round and round, spinning in its groove, while the numbers, set in black and red, spun in the opposite direction. Other eyes followed the ball, too. Mostly they seemed sleepy rather than anxious. Old hands at it.

At last the white marble struck a vertical canoe, causing it to whip and bounce over the circling numbers. Tony looked up, so as not to see it drop. That was always luckier. Turning a smooth black chip in his fingers, by twos.

Then he looked down to find out where it had landed, just as the croupier called out, "*Vingt-deux, vingt-deux.*"

Tony smiled now. Double twos. Again, one of his lucky numbers.

It was late, Tony had been playing for over an hour, so as the dealer raked off all the losers' chips, he said peacefully, directly into the croupier's eyes, "Cash out, thank you so kindly, gentlemen."

He watched the pit boss watching the dealer sort the chips and make big piles of black ones. No words were spoken till the dealer finished, then looking over his shoulder for the pit boss's okay, he announced, "Forty-one thousand three hundred francs, *monsieur.*"

About seven grand, U.S.

"*Grazie sette mille*, chaps!" Tony chirped at the dealer and the pit boss, both showing grim pusses, and scooped his chits into a plastic bucket. "See you again, then. And you good folks as well," he motioned towards the other players with his chin: "Thanks for the transfer of your assets!"

No sooner had he cleared his chips than they began covering the thirty-six numbers with bets, all over again. Nylon and rubber on some of them, Tony had already noticed, but the majority were showing off their finery, and there were even a couple of tuxes, as well there ought to be.

Tony walked away from the cashier's cage stuffing a check into his wallet, and strolled out of the casino through the grand foyer, all aglitter, indeed sumptuous. Completely paid for by those inside, through the years, though the scene wasn't nearly so frenetic as the palaces where one-armed bandits swallowed quarters and dollars by the zillions. As he tip-toed down the marble steps, leaving the casino, Tony reflected for a moment on his last stop in Atlantic City and smiled, but then the pizzazz of Monte Carlo relieved all that. This place was so gorgeous it almost deserved a license to steal.

His monster waited patiently on the circle around the fountain. Young couples strolled arm in arm past it, trying not to gawk, but a few older men stood about, arms folded over their chests, admiring it plainly. As Tony unlocked the driver's door, one of them said to him, "Now, mister, *that's* what I call an automobile!" His teeth showed, all of them.

One of the parking valets rushed over, seeing Tony at the car, to remove the little velvet cord which enclosed the Ferrari. Really, for his tip.

Tony whistled thanks at him, handed him three French hundred-franc banknotes, and settled into the driver's seat, touching the Auto Down button to lower his power window. The air would be refreshing as he drove.

And it was. He tooled in growling first gear slowly out the boulevard leading straight away from the casino, seeing its blue domed roof twinkling in its outlining red and yellow lights in the rearview, and at the end of the row of palms turned into the hill road, shifting up now, gaining speed, the right window and the sunroof open now, the breeze shuffling delightfully past Tony's face, through his hair, animating his silky shirt, now the wider road along the yacht harbor flew past, and Tony hit the horn a couple of times for effect, shifted down and up again twice for the noise to awaken the millionaires in their yachts, but soon enough the fun was over and the Ferrari took to the hills of Monaco and Tony worked the switchbacks, shifting constantly, till he reached the hilltop, and back over his shoulder the famous harbor and its denizens disappeared. The Ferrari settled in for the short ride back to Nice, humming, almost snoozing, at fifty or so.

* * *

Middle of the night, black as the proverbial ace of spades, the caravan of two cars drove at a hectic pace, had been going hard for a couple of hours at least, and now they were nearly there. In one of the cars the driver carried a particularly risky cargo, himself alone at risk at the moment, though the other car, with its two men, followed close enough to be in danger should the worst happen.

All three of them wore faces of fear, though, in equal allotment.

Maybe five miles out of Belfast, the cars turned off the main road, slowed considerably, then turned again, this time into an alley. At its end, one of the men in the second car got out and opened, sliding it sideways, a very heavy iron and wood door, on a rusted iron track, and watched the two cars drive into the gaping wound of a building. A warehouse, like, only it wasn't. It was a hideaway, and a secret meeting place.

The man who had opened the wide door closed it, flicked on an electric torch in his hand, and found the electrical panel. Low lights fluttered on, a good fifty feet up, among the beams under the roof.

They all rubbed out their cigarettes with their heels, deliberately smashing the butts into the concrete floor, making sure they were out.

The lone man without a cap went over to a notched board, next to the electrical switches, and removed a set of keys. Over in one far corner of the building sat a panel truck. He went to it, started it up, let the engine warm for a bit, then backed the truck over to where the two cars had stopped.

The other two men had been working at the trunk of one car. They began to remove stick after stick of dynamite, one at a time, handling them like birds whose wings needed mending, and putting them into a metal box, crudely seamed together, a homemade item from someone's garage, until all the sticks were packed in tight, neatly lined up, sixty in all.

Two of the men went over to the door, peeked through its cracks, checking the alley outside, which was black as could be, nobody anywhere, not even a stray cat, no kind of movement at all. They both held pistols in their hands, cocked. Old pistols, rusted, their bluing worn off the barrels and the cylinders, if there had been light enough to notice. There wasn't.

All around, mostly in the dark, inside the building, stood the implements of a whiskey mill. It smelled of disuse, nothing more.

The man at the box had been knotting a long fuse together, linking all the sticks of dynamite, and now he ran the end of the fuse through an inch-wide hole in the side of the box. When he was satisfied with it, he closed the iron lid of the box, worked three strong hasps into place over iron loops, and then ran a thin steel rod through the loops.

Despite the chilly night air, he dripped perspiration onto his work.

The steel rod had a Y at one end of it, holding it securely in place there against one loop, and a thin hole through it at the other end. The man threaded a metal pin through this hole, then twisted it with a wrench until it held tight against the loop at that end of the box.

He tried it, pulled at it, but the steel rod would not move. It would not be possible to open the iron lid without tools, without really working at it.

Anyone who did would never live to see the box's contents. Not once the booby-trap firing pin had been set in place. That would be later.

He whistled for the other two, and they came over to the panel truck. All together, they lifted the iron box into the back of the truck, slid it over the bed and gently lowered it into an integral toolbox in front of one wheel well, then locked the toolbox with a padlock. An identical toolbox was welded to the frame of the truck bed in front of the opposite wheel well.

"Time for a smoke?" one of the men asked another.

He nodded over to one corner of the building. "Just," he said, and they huddled over in that corner, far from the panel truck, smoking, taking a ten-minute break. The man who had rigged the dynamite wiped his face with an old rag. He looked grimy now, and they all looked wrung out.

Soon they were changing into workmen's gear, smudged work suits, old gabardine, gray and with the look of years on them. Faded red lettering across their backs read 'BLACKPOOL IRONMONGERS.'

They got in the panel truck, crowded together on the bench seat once they had killed the dim electric bulbs high up in the roof beams and secured the heavy iron-and-wood door, then drove slowly, quiet as possible and without headlights, down the alley, still in pitch black, until they gained the main road again, and made their way over to the ferry port.

* * *

A gray morning, with a promise of heat in the air. Misty in the town and over the beach, hazing out towards Africa. Most people weren't awake yet; those that were, well it wasn't the sort of place that encouraged early rising. The dining rooms of Nice mostly sat waiting to serve breakfast.

Tony carried a big white bath towel with 'HOTEL NEGRESCO' embroidered into its center in bold, capital letters. His togs chugged at the Promenade as he crossed it, clopped down a concrete stairway, and hit the pebbles. Ten meters onto the beach he kicked off the togs, dropped the towel.

It was like a pool, the Mediterranean. Hardly a ripple. Warm. Tony breast-stroked straight out, swimming swiftly and powerfully, refreshed from a great night and a stimulating yesterday. His black nylon swim trunks hugged his buttocks and muscular thighs as he glided through the water. Before he knew it he was out two hundred meters. He stopped, paddling gently, floating, his head bobbing as his cupped hands fondled the sea, and he twisted around to look back at the shore.

How beautiful it was. The green hills behind the seaside town seemed to undulate, like a mirage, coaxing the homes and other buildings in and out of existence, blurring their stucco pinks and whites into the very vision of peace, a place of people happy with the world, blending them all together so that imperfections, woes and cares, came to nothing, ceased to be.

How often did a man get a chance to forget the ways of the world, and just appreciate it as the Almighty might, looking in from afar?

Tony kept paddling in place.

God! he thought, almost aloud, it's great to be alive!

In a little while, he began swimming slowly towards shore, and soon he found the coarse bottom and his toes smushed into the gravel as he emerged from the sea. Standing there, drying off with the big white towel, he noticed some thin, elongated tracks in the slick sand. At the end of one he spotted their source, a lugworm, just burrowing, disappearing as its tufted gills folded like a hand closing slowly, finger by finger, into its body. A bubble popped in the moist sand where it had been.

Inside of an hour, while Nice still percolated out of night, Tony was at the wheel of the Ferrari. Driving slowly, politely, no horn-honking now, out the palm-tree-dotted byway toward the west end of town and the airport quaintly named "Cote d'Azur."

In the luminous, blue, perfect oval mirrors of his Revos, the road came at him, the reflected palms and blacktop and potted plants by the roadside running down beneath his eyes, refracting as in a prism, seeming less than real, and the intense blue pupils behind the lenses could have been those of a chimera, a monster whose power might best be left untested.

* * *

What sun could be seen through the moody clouds worried the three men standing at the ferry boat's bow, and standing alone. The wind whipped off the late-afternoon Crosby Channel, driving most passengers to cover inside the streaky glass windows where tea was available, but no scones and certainly no clotted cream.

They stood by themselves, smoking, nothing much to say, having had their tea early, to warm their insides. And to fortify their resolve.

The scared look was off their faces now, but fear seized them.

One of them signaled to the other two, by nods, that it was about time to get back to the panel truck in the hold. They trudged down the iron stairs as Liverpool loomed off across the channel, and in a while, driving off the gangway with other vehicles, in rows, their impression of the city was one of docks and ruffians and port police who gave them the usual going-over.

The cop thumbed them on, move the van, irritated to see them again.

A nice greeting after ten hours out in the Irish Sea.

The cop was used to seeing the banged-up, dirty panel truck. These damned Micks, why couldn't they get work in their own country—that's probably what he had in his head as he passed them through, heard the usual surly answers about scaffolds for construction to his official inquiries about the nature of their employment. Working for another Mick living now in Liverpool, supplying cheaper labor for the building trade. Well, get a move on, you're holding up traffic.

In no time they were out on the M62 motorway, headed due east towards Manchester, but they wouldn't get into rush-hour traffic, not this Monday afternoon. They'd head southeast any minute now on the M6.

Passing around Birmingham they caught the tail end of rush hour, got nervous in slow lanes for half an hour, then got around it, finally decided they needed a stop for food, halted for fifteen minutes for the gents and some bad burgers and chips and coffee, losing the daylight now, the Forest of Arden all around them. But they didn't care a turd for scenery. They didn't even notice their surroundings. Their focus was on reaching London in time for the fancy supper folks to be out and about, on the evening.

That was what they had been ordered to do, however impossible it might seem to cover so much distance, and with such a dangerous 'present.' If they didn't make it on time—well, they just would.

The panel truck was heavy with scaffold sections, coarse moldings, iron bits. It would all make for effective shrapnel.

The truck lumbered on down the M1 motorway, to the southeast, as fast as was safe without getting over into the fast lane, without incident.

By seven-thirty they had done it, had managed without sleep for going on two days now, some shut-eye on the ferry but no real rest, got in past the beltway around London called the M25, traffic not too bad, most of it leaving the city against them, not even seeing many police cars, everything going their way. In Camden, by the out-of-service tube station, they pulled over and the bomb expert went around to the rear, got in among the scaffolding bits, connected the booby-trap, all except the spring mechanism, tested the fuse wire again, and connected the radio receiver. He banged on the cab, and the driver carried on.

They came down Tottenham Court Road, slowly, made a left and plodded along High Holborn in stubborn traffic, came south on the Kingsway and rounded Aldwych crescent, then entered the Strand, and there it was, their excuse ready-made, scaffolding on several buildings, as they had been told. The driver parked in the end of an alley.

The economic expansion in England, fueled by the stock market, had resulted in what seemed to be construction everywhere. As if made to their order. An ideal cover.

The two men on the bench seat climbed through the cab's window, into the rear, where the bomb expert was already busy loading the spring mechanism to the booby-trap. It was now a delicate deal. The three of them removed their coveralls, carefully, with deliberate slowness. Underneath they all wore jeans and pullovers. They got out of the panel truck's rear door with great care, closing it quietly, barely on the latch, then walked in three different directions.

The bomb expert, the man without a cap, sidled into the evening crowd, and stopped across the street from the panel truck. He could see its taillights, their red plastic, unlit but reflecting the ambient light.

They came from the alley beside the Royal Courts of Justice, a large and impressive building fronting the Strand for nearly two blocks.

No, he thought, way too close. But everything looked a go. After a few moments he ambled off to a safer distance, stopping where he had a direct view of the bomb site. Now it was just a matter of waiting for the right moment—enough pedestrians on the pavements and some fancy cars to come by.

He fingered the radio-signal device in his pocket, feeling the textured plastic cover over the red button, smiling now for the first time in two days. A cruel smile, like a boy's pulling the wings off Japanese beetles in the garden while dad cut the grass and mom was busy cooking a nice dinner for them in the kitchen.

*   *   *

How sweet it was, not a mere smell but a fragrance to Tony's senses, any time a whiff of diesel exhaust reached his nostrils. It came to him now, in a fleeting memory of the happy days of early childhood, a weekend down in London with his mum, down from the hills and vales of Yorkshire. Just a wee lad he was.

Harry carried his suitcase, insisted on doing it, and now Tony was taking the front passenger seat in the Mercedes. It was where the aroma of diesel greeted him back home.

"To the Dorchester, guv?" Harry asked, starting the engine.

"Thought you'd seen the backside of Tony Spool for a while, hadn't you, Harry?"

"Naw! Any time you call, guv, I'll be here for you." He was steering for the exit lanes from Heathrow now, and repeated his request for directions.

"Nope, I've reserved a night at my club in Surrey. Soon as I get there I intend to practice some driving!"

"My neck o' the woods!"

"That's right. Horsley. Should make for a quiet night, Harry. Now, after dinner at the club, an early one, I've an appointment at the bank on Lime, so"—checking his wristwatch—"okay, it's just coming on two-thirty now"—thinking of his schedule, a quick freshen up, tee some balls, oh maybe nine fast holes if there's an opening—"so collect me at seven fifteen. That be all right by you?"

"What's that they say on American telly? Oh yeah. 'Whatever'!"

And they both laughed a good chuckle.

"And when shall I gather you up, guv? Any idea?"

"I imagine round about nine thirty. Stick close by the bank. I'll just ring you on the car cell. Hard to tell about these emergency meetings. Should be able to put Indonesia's currency right in ninety minutes, though!"

Again, a good chuckle from them both.

"Gettin' in the game at long last, eh, guv?" Harry guffawed.

"Everything else is just an excuse, isn't it?" Tony guffawed, too.

And they burst into a mutual belly laugh, the two old friends, sitting side by side in the black Mercedes as the countryside neared, Harry happy for his friend's pleasure, some R&R after all those tedious meetings.

Nine holes would have been pushing it, so Tony stopped after seven, allowing time enough for a solid meal of lobster and a filet mignon in the clubhouse at the Horsley Commons. They also made the best seven-greens and toasted walnut salad, animated by little more than a tossed whisper of raspberry vinaigrette dressing. And in the best English tradition, the club's name was a devilish little lie, for no one 'common' was ever admitted.

Harry delivered Tony to the black-marble bank on Lime Street at a quarter to eight and then drove over to a favored pub just off the river, near the Old Billingsgate Market. As it was a Monday evening, the pub contained just a handful of regulars, recharging their engines after a long day.

This time, Sir Malcolm Goodge's secretary greeted Tony as he stepped off the elevator almost at the top of the obsidian tower. Nora escorted him down the long green hall, far past the sales posts of the mutual-funds staff, and shortly Tony found his chief, surrounded by the familiar rare, oiled woods of his isolated office, the antique tickertape on its pedestal and the gentry on horseback still chasing the fox on the wall.

Nora smiled, leaving them. Tony noticed the sunny pink nail polish of her fingers against the bright brass of the doorknob as she pulled it in silence, her eyes reverently on her boss in his desk chair, his eyes closed beneath the famous bushy white eyebrows. A click signaled she had left.

Tony took up his customary seat, a large winged thing made of deep green leather, and waited for those eyes to open on him.

There were moments of silence to wait through, a hush of spies, an aphony of vigilantes, before a muffled voice intruded.

It said, nearly beneath the sound spectrum, "This is a terrifying quarry, Captain. I almost hesitate to commit you." Tony saw the tiny pupils in the muted light, saw them upon him, like laser beams.

The word 'almost' stuck in his mind.

He looked as serious as a mortician back into those laser eyes.

"Why is that, sir?"

Goodge unfolded his hands. They had shielded his nose, their fingers interlocked like those of the children's Sunday School game about the roof and the steeple. His white moustache barely moved as he told Tony:

"Our Alexandra Allgood has not shrunk into a corner somewhere in the north of Ireland. Our mole has let us know she's assassinated her suspect, no warning, no questioning, just cold-blooded murder..."

"She believes the shot came from one of her own?"

"She killed her own half-brother, right in front of his father, her father. Shot him ten times in the face and thorax. With a forty-five ACP."

"My God," Tony could only say.

Goodge sat up then, his lips moving beneath the moustache, his tongue touching them, Tony could see, as if licking away a bad taste.

"I'm counting on you, Captain." It was the quietest order Tony had ever heard. Maybe the toughest, but not to Tony's mind. He said back:

"I'm a recycler of souls, sir. This one needs it bad."

Goodge cleared his throat, showed no reaction to Tony's statement, said without emotion and with a calm that might better be used talking about an illustration in a computer manual: "We'd already had our little confab, before I learned of this incident. The go-ahead had already come down from the highest authority, the very highest."

He looked still into Tony's wide blue eyes, nodding to himself. Tony knew it was best to say nothing at this moment.

"I'm even more keen on it now, Captain. You understand?"

Tony's body looked lashed to the back of the high chair, bolted to a stiff board, held in place.

"No misses next time, sir. Not even good misses," Tony replied in a voice so quiet he would not have recognized it as his, had he heard it.

All Goodge had to say was a curt, military-brief "Right, then." He got up with a slow deliberation, went over and tapped the top of the antique tickertape, its blown-glass bubble, standing in a corner of his office, stood to Tony's back so as to look at his assassin's head from the rear. Tony knew better than to face him. He just listened, staring on at Goodge's desk.

The voice behind Tony hinted at chilled determination as it said: "Our plan, Captain Spool, will form quickly as events continue to unfold. You are to go home tomorrow. Communication will be by encoded e-mail, confirmation by cell phone to this number. You will always hear Nora's voice, day or night, until we conclude. Use the usual codes when speaking."

Tony just listened, not even nodding, eyes straight ahead of him.

Again, a long silence as Tony waited. Finally:

"Shall we give it a try, Spool?"

Tony ventured an answer that would go beyond acceptance. He said:

"There's a saying I like, sir. From Sun Tzu."

"Yes?"

"'If the enemy is reckless, he can be killed.' Allgood is reckless. And I shall kill her."

Goodge smiled, his eyes lit up, but he stood out of Tony's sight. He said to the back of Tony's head:

"Another of his truths is a favorite of my own."

"Yes, sir?"

"Describing you, Captain, many centuries before your birth, Sun Tzu wrote: 'Subtle and insubstantial, the expert leaves no trace; divinely mysterious, he is inaudible. Thus he is master of his enemy's fate.'"

Tony turned about now, stood out of the winged chair, to face his chief, address his eyes again. He continued the Chinese passage, paraphrasing: "I'll come like lightning, and go like the wind!"

Sir Malcolm Goodge advanced towards Tony, the son he never had, and embraced him. Tony returned the embrace, the first time ever.

Just then, a horrific noise came from outside, and the windows of the secure office shook as if hit by a hurricane gale.

The two men broke partly apart, stood as though frozen in place by the wind from outside, and in moments heard the sound of sirens. They went to the heavily tinted window and could see, in a ghoulish orangey green, rather than red because of the window's tinting, the leaping flames of a fierce fire, maybe a mile to the west, in the heart of London.

* * *

The duty officer on the desk of the Metropolitan Police bomb squad picked up the jingling phone after it had rung on and on, perhaps for a minute, coming back from the window where he was watching the fire.

"Greet-ins from Belfast," he heard, the last syllable singing high.

"Who the bloody hell is this!" he demanded back into the telephone.

"Could yuh pass on a message to your P.M. for ush?"

"Did you do this!" the officer yelled into the phone.

"Ashk him, if yuh woold, fock with the INLA agin, real soon like."

"How's that?"

"We love explosives, and we've got a bit outta practish..."

EIGHTEEN

The world had toppled upside down.

A faraway shrieking pierced the night air, deathly screams and a horrible, unending roar. The black air was hot and thick with humidity, acrid in taste and smell. It burned in his mouth as he sucked it in.

Much as he peered into the dark, Tony couldn't discover where any of the noise was coming from. It echoed all around him, invading the gloomy veil, drilling ceaselessly into his ears.

He had a sense only of a low rolling fog, devoid of form or substance but carrying the awful rumble along with it. Even the moon had fled, hiding behind heavy clouds.

Rain began falling in a sudden rush, a torrent of water crashing invisibly through the heights of the rainforest, its rubbery trees more like gigantic broad-veined ferns than anything resembling familiar growth. The ground became all mud and puddles, muck.

The shrieking filled the air with mystery till the moon broke cover and Tony could see a most peculiar vegetation rising through the steam, taking forms like nothing he had ever seen before.

Out of nowhere, too, as if in a movie scene, a couple of lumbering beasts struggled in death's clutch, and Tony watched the T-Rex ripping the throat out of a fallen sauropod, vegetation in shreds flowing from its howling mouth in a bloody stream, its limbs thrashing, all a jumble...

But as it died, a strange metallic beeping perforated the prehistoric scene. *Beep, beep, beep...*

Tony's eyes popped open. Morning light glanced through the curtained windows, making them blink. He recognized his bedroom. The dinosaurs were gone. But the world was still upside down—the boxelders in his backyard were inverted, the pale dawning sky sat where the lawn should have been. He squeezed his eyes. *Beep, beep, beep...* What the hell?

As his eyes opened again, this time to stay open, he realized his neck was arched back, his throat had lain exposed to the razor teeth of the T-Rex in his dream, and his head was twisted back into the pillow.

He put his hand to his throat, as if to protect it, then straightened his spine and rolled over. Okay, now the sky was in the right place. The boxelders weren't topsy-turvy, not any more. And Susan was right there next to him, sleeping on her side, her hips outlined under the sheets. *Beep, beep, beep, beep, beep...*

He realized he was still holding his hand over his throat, felt stupid now that he was awake, and took it away.

Then he heard the noise of the shrieking dinosaurs again, but it was a shrill hum of motors and the clanking of dense metal he recognized now, coming from across the neighborhood, vibrating Tony's house. Modern monsters whose bellowing strafed the peaceful morning of suburban Virginia, invading Tony's ears and thoughts. Warping his subconscious mind.

Developers, cheap credit and low interest rates, these were the modern terrors which had stolen the quiet Tony had known when he bought the place. Tract houses, built for spec, being thrown up, oh, a mile away. Bulldozers and enormous land movers were the T-Rexes of America today, beeping to an inane federal safety mandate every time they backed up, beeping and beeping, a noise which seemed to carry for miles.

Especially at seven in the morning.

Tony cursed them under his breath as he slipped out from beneath the covers. Susan moved, just a little. How did she sleep through it?

Maybe she was dreaming of Jurassic beasts, too. He'd ask her over breakfast. He'd ask her.

He crossed the hardwood floor to close the window on the far side of the bed, slipping it quietly down its guides, not to disturb Susan, and the beeping outside faded quite a bit. The metal window frame felt cool to the touch, pleasantly cool and familiar.

But the muggy prehistoric night, and the heat, and beating rain of his dream—where had they come from? Or gone, for that matter.

As he walked naked to the center-hall bathroom, he rubbed his upper arms with his hands, and found them still moist. Then a strong musky smell reached his nostrils from his armpits. And his mouth tasted bitter, like yesterday's cold coffee. Oh, he thought, vaguely recalling his dream, fading already to nothing. Oh yeah. Looking for his toothbrush.

One of his few simple pleasures, wasn't it? The window open at night for the fresh air. But the night's pleasant air nowadays became the morning's irritation. No wonder so many neighbors lived in air-conditioned isolation.

Gad, he reflected of himself in the mirror. Ageing sucked! Was that another crease in his skin across his abs?

He touched his chin in the vanity, scratchy with beard growth. He needed a close shave today. Nothing electric. A badger-bristle brush, English lavender lather, a good sharp razor blade. His face was rough enough this morning to drive off even that T-Rex; bastard could break a tooth on this stubble.

As he shaved he stared at himself in boredom. Friday, wasn't it? Sometimes the days got lost. Yeah, it was Friday. Home Tuesday: he'd wanted to go to bed early but Susan was glued to the telly all evening. Wednesday it was bills and accumulated mail to sort through. What a pain. Once an hour he'd checked for e-mail. Nothing came in.

Thursday he got all the bill payments in the mail, logged first thing in the morning onto his e-mail file, and then again before driving to the post office—still nothing from London—decided to call Nora on his cell phone from the parking lot at the country club. All she had to say was a few words: Haberdasher should wait for the new measurements. Then clicked off.

Tony retreated to the club lounge to read the papers. The American 'news machine' was depressingly consistent: first the financial pages informed him once again that inflation had been killed by Washington since the price of cream cheese or whatever hadn't really risen much. While he read this, CNBC was playing on the TV in the lounge, where one commentator declared that gold funds were no longer functional realities, which sounded strong but Tony wasn't sure what it meant, and then another financial sage, all of twenty-five years of age, she looked, was very adamant in the opinion that bonds—or rather, mutual funds of bonds—made the best sense if you thought inflationary pressures might threaten stock prices. That's right, Tony thought. Switch funds, that's all; but keep the money in mutual funds, don't ever sell. And don't buy gold, wasn't that the first commentator's message? Go figure.

He spent three minutes on the sports-talk in the papers, mostly golf. Then flipped to the first section. The London-bombing story was nowhere to be found. It had been replaced on page one by glaring pictures and big headlines about a shooting in a school somewhere in rural Indiana. Five dead, all under twelve. One normal-looking boy arrested with what the media had decided was a 'small arsenal' consisting of a brick of twenty-two longs, a plinking rifle of the same calibre, some cardboard silhouette targets, and a stack of *Soldier of Fortune* magazines. Which made him a terrorist, of course, and a maniac. Sad.

But the story did contain an item of interest to Tony. The local sheriff was quoted by one reporter as saying that parents should have a new priority, a 'need for vigilance' over their children, should monitor their youngsters' exposure to violence. Some realistic assignment that was.

The sheriff went on to tell the reporter that the threat of violence was 'like ocean waves: you can never turn your back on them.' That was the bit Tony liked. He remembered the young English mum with her two tots on the beach at Minehead. Sure got those waves right, didn't he, that reporter?

As he put down the papers, Tony heard the school-shooting story come on the lounge TV. Lots of gory pictures, and footage of the child being led away by authorities, in handcuffs. They sure had him now, okay.

The broadcast reporter seemed almost orgasmic in her enthusiasm for the story. First-hand reporting. What did they used to call it? Social responsibility? Maybe she should read the sheriff's comments herself.

Tony trudged over to the club's dining room, trying hard to keep a frown off his face, and ordered chicken salad made with yogurt and pineapple, half an order of onion rings, and diet Pepsi with a lime sprig. He sat alone, eating and staring out at the greens. Slowly his mood lightened.

After lunch he spent two and a half hours on the back nine. First time he'd used his own clubs in weeks, and they still worked fine. That took care of Thursday, pretty much.

Friday morning, and what to do today? He was just scraping the beard off the left side of his chin when Susan said:

"Nothing in the papers today! All that horror—"

"Yesterday's news," Tony said over his razor. Susan had the *Washington Post* in her hands, running through the front section. Shaking her head in disbelief.

"It's a big story. How could they drop it already?"

"They say," Tony said, throwing cold water in his face, "the public's attention fades quickly. The thirty-minute TV melodrama? And what is it, three seconds you have to make a good first impression?"

"But, Tony," Susan scowled, folding the paper, "this is a big story. I mean, thirty-eight people died when that bomb went off! And the damage—it was like Oklahoma City... almost."

"It's not an American news event. What's on page one this morning?"

"The school shooting in Indiana."

"*Two* days for the school shooting! Wonder what it'll be tomorrow?"

"Disgusting," Susan mumbled. Her face was blank, her mind elsewhere.

Tony dried his face with a fluffy towel of pale blue. It had 'T.S.' monogrammed in one corner, in darker blue. Susan noticed the towel stop moving, framing her husband's face. He was staring at her.

"What?"

"Do you realize you have next to nothing on?"

She knew what it meant, his eyes like that.

"Want to?" he said.

"Tony, this is serious! How can you be in the mood right now?"

"Just am."

She shoved an arm beyond the shower curtain and twisted on the Cold spigot.

"Ice down, boy. I have to get ready for work."

As she padded back into the bedroom barefooted, her fanny shimmering in her silk panties, Tony dropped the towel, touched his tongue against his teeth, and climbed into the freezing shower.

First dinosaurs, he thought, his skin going all prickly. Now the ice treatment. It was going to be one of those days.

He made her French toast and put fresh strawberries over it, and before Susan left for the office he did get a nice kiss and a hug, with a pouty "Sorry" and a promise for tonight, but it didn't help much.

So he fixed himself grapefruit and oranges with sliced bananas. Hot black coffee. French vanilla. Not decaf either. He sipped at it. Too hot.

He picked up the papers from the last three days, waiting on a kitchen chair for the recycling bin. What did Susan expect? It was all over the front page of Tuesday and Wednesday's *Post*. And they gave it a few inches on Thursday, too, back on page eleven.

CNN had shown pictures every half hour on Wednesday. Pretty much the same pictures they were running when he got home Tuesday afternoon, Susan watching them over and over, till late in the evening.

Thursday they aired more video of the destruction: debris around the torn-up Royal Courts of Justice building, a big hole in its corner, by an alley, and workers picking their way among the rubble, the commentator said looking for bodies and evidence. Gray dust and trash, what it mostly looked like, with two tall yellow cranes in the alley. It had become all too familiar a scene; they could almost get away with file footage by now.

The news shows also aired some walk-by comments by the British PM, along with some file tapes on the IRA and an assortment of meaningless commentaries. And of course the usual awful interviews with relatives of the victims. Dreadful. Tony'd had enough by the third run-through.

As his French vanilla full-leaded cooled down, Tony reflected on how the new civilization would require a lot of patience, an awful lot. But waiting was so hard—

Just then the doorbell rang.

The mailman had two yellow slips for him to sign, one Certified and one Registered. Then handed Tony an envelope and a package.

Tony smiled to himself. Friday would be okay! The package was from Simon in London. King James would be inside. He went into his study to get a scissors to open the package, but as he put the Certified envelope down on his desk he saw the return address across the top of the back flap:

'Office of the Vice President of the United States, Old Executive Office Building, Washington, D.C. 20501' it read in three lines.

Tony opened it and just couldn't believe his eyes.

Here it was, not only the when but also the where he'd been waiting for. He'd send Percy Dithers a postcard from sunny Southern California!

*   *   *

Tony spun the tumbler on his safe; he was so excited about the letter, he decided to save King James for later. He put the package, unopened, on the top shelf of his safe and pushed the heavy door shut, spinning the tumbler again.

Friday was turning out to be a topping day, it really was. Plans spun through his mind. He'd work them all out on the golf course, that's what he'd do. Were his clubs still in the car? Yeah, they were. He hurried to leave the house, but as he turned the key to lock the door between the kitchen and the garage he remembered he hadn't checked for e-mail this morning. Better do it.

A single message. Oh brother, what a day this was turning into! It said:

'Haberdasher convocation.'

Good old Nora. 'Convocation'!

Halfway to the country club, Tony pulled his jet-black Beamer coupe over to the side of the road, beneath some maples whose red leaves mostly decorated the ground, and flipped open his cell phone. He dialed 011-44-171 and then Goodge's private number in London.

"Yes, hello?" came Nora's cheery voice.

"Is this Anglo-Saxon Funding, plc?"

"It is indeed, sir. Have you an account with us?"

"Yes I do."

"We're just closing for the day, sir. May I have your account rep ring you up on Monday morning?"

"Well, I'll ring him back. But I was just wondering, for my account, where are you directing funds these days?" Tony's voice was cheery, too. Games, he thought, how Sir Malcolm loved these games.

"Wall Street," came Nora's answer.

"Ah." Tony thought a moment, then said: "Why's that?"

"We expect a big run-up, sir. Sometime next month, we calculate."

"Next month, you say?"

"Middle of November, more than likely. Not much later."

"An autumn rally, then?"

"Yes, that's right."

"Is that so? Perhaps a month off?"

"We can almost guarantee it, sir. Ring us back Monday, all right?"

"Sure will!" Tony said, hyped now, more than ever. He snapped his cell closed and drove on to the country club, smiling all the way.

* * *

Susan kept her word Friday night. In fact, it was an odd session. She'd insisted on lights out, which was peculiar. Usually she crawled all over him, whispering to him how much she loved what she called his 'delicious body' and giving him everything of her own body, knowing how it delighted him. But not this time. This time, she scratched at him in the dark, beneath the covers, and did it hard, swift and hard.

As they humped silently in the dark, Tony pulling on the power she put into it, enjoying it physically, he suddenly thought, how utterly different this time was from all the others, rough like, sort of savage.

Thinking, it felt great. But not like it should.

Next morning Tony had the peripheral house alarm on while he studied his splendid gold coin. He was in his study, thinking about King James's soul while inspecting his picture under magnification, when Susan suddenly charged in to the room. Tony looked up to see anger on her face.

"What is it?"

"Damn them!" she cried. "Damn those filthy, two-faced traitors!"

Tony put down the coin and got up to hold her. Something must be terribly wrong. Susan never swore. It wasn't God's way, she always said. Her opinion in this matter had stopped an old habit of Tony's. It was one of the good changes she had made in him.

When he touched her bare arm she pulled away.

"Suz?"

She relented and held him. "Come, see the TV," she told him.

Not talking, they went to the kitchen. The TV on the counter was on.

"There," she told him. "Look at it yourself. See what I mean?" She had her arms crossed, as if in defiance, glaring at the screen, the tips of those perfect little white teeth just showing between her taut lips.

CNN was running footage of the damage to the buildings of the Royal Courts of Justice and of a police spokesman holding a license plate and pointing to a strip of sheet metal, both charred nearly black, the sheet metal revealing some faded red letters: 'ONMONGERS' they read.

Susan flipped off the Mute button so Tony could hear the commentary, but all he could take from it was the idea that the police might have suspects in the bombing.

He said, "What is it, Susan?"

"Shish," she told him. "Not this part. Keep watching."

The footage switched now to another scene, also of a building, or what used to be a building, a hole in a row of buildings, brick houses all in a row with a hole in the middle.

The voice of a reporter explained: an explosion in Londonderry had killed all five members of a Protestant family, all of them well liked in their community, a barber and his wife and three kids. They lived in a mixed neighborhood of Catholics and Protestants. The kids were fifteen, thirteen and seven. Two girls and a boy. The wife worked in the neighborhood bakery shop, and taught Sunday School. The husband had been a great guy, had cut everybody's hair, had no known enemies, had been on the winning bowling team and had been a scouting leader. Photos showed proud people from a poor neighborhood. They all had smiles on their faces, in the photos televised to the world today, smiling out of the TV at Tony and Susan, the smiles of the dead.

Tony just looked at Susan, standing there with her arms crossed.

Now the reporter on the TV was talking to a neighbor boy, a Catholic the reporter told them, and he said he had liked them but they were Protestants and they should have known better. They were living in a Catholic neighborhood, he said. They had put themselves in danger.

The reporter asked the boy how well he knew the dead kids.

He said he knew them all, he lived just across the street, that the oldest girl was very pretty and he found her attractive.

The reporter asked the boy if he knew the father.

Of course, said the boy. The father always cut his hair.

Why would anyone want to hurt this family, the reporter asked the boy.

Well, they were Protestants, weren't they, the boy responded.

Would the boy have hurt them, asked the reporter.

He would if he had to, the boy said. They were Protestants. He wasn't.

Susan looked at Tony, and Tony said "Oh, Suz."

"I guess the President won't be talking about our negotiations for peace in Ireland, will he?" she said to the TV. Then she looked at Tony and added: "All that work. That nice luncheon. All their nice smiles. . . "

"I'm so sorry, Suz."

"They've ruined the whole thing. Rotten liars!"

"It's been going on a long, long time, Suz. Decades. An old blood feud."

"The whole trip was a waste, wasn't it?" she asked, turning now to Tony, letting him hold her, starting to cry.

"No it wasn't," he told her gently. "You can only do what you can do. You tried, that's what counts."

Susan looked into his eyes, close to them, tears in hers, said in a very low voice, "Thanks."

"We all do only what we can, Suz. The rest is destiny."

Thinking, things went on as usual, didn't they? On as usual. At least for the moment.

NINETEEN

Like a sea anemone's tentacles, reaching into the drift current for sustenance, Tony's fingers played in the chilly draft of air coming from the vents by his window. His mind was far, far away. The vibrations of the jet motors and an indistinct humming were the only sensations, and they were much too subtle to interdict Tony's thoughts.

His eyes had settled upon the blank blackness through the portal, had been unfocused for over an hour as he had lost the present to thoughts of yesterday and tomorrow, but now something caught them, causing them to focus again, to regain the moment's reality.

It was the lights of the capital, twinkling up ahead in the distance, to the right and towards what would be the horizon if it were visible, but it wasn't in the dark. All was dark. The night sky. The cabin of the jetliner. And Tony's mood. Dark as the deep, empty expanse of space above the airplane.

Tony touched the window's trim and felt the vibrations of the jet engines as they torqued down to a lower speed. The trim had a chill to it, from the air hissing past, and a texture of very fine pebbles. Its color, if it could be called a color at all, was neutral gray, fading to nothingness in the low light of the cabin.

Tony's eyes now sought the stars of the heavens, but they were few tonight, overhead but mere dull pinpoints. There must be high cloud cover.

Below, and getting closer now, the Virginia landscape crept by, in that odd way land does as seen from an airplane at night, an isolated light here and there coming and going, immobile yet moving, the lights of houses and of spotty street illumination in the country. And little trails of moving lights, some white, some dull red and faint.

But soon the lights became more regular, patterns to them, squares and bigger white dots, and rivulets of moving lights going in many directions. The city fast approached beneath the jet's wings.

Inside the plane only dim illumination invaded the shadows of the sectional seats. These weren't the rows of narrow seats of a commercial jet. Here the shadows played over special blocks of seats, a larger one up front, another in the plane's mid-section, and two opposing groups of padded swivel seats aft, where Tony sat, on the right side of the plane.

In this faint light, Tony's odd half-smile was invisible.

Suddenly the rows of lights up and down each side of the cabin lit up, destroying the comforting shadows, and revealing life within. And death.

Tony glanced around. He saw the tall man, Bobby, up at the front, saw rather the rear of his head, bent forward a little as if reading. He alone sat at the complex of plush seats in the front of the cabin.

The slim man of patrician bearing and poise, Ira, occupied one of the sofa-like seats at mid-cabin. He appeared to be asleep right now, his head sunk back into the pillows of his plush bench.

The end of the coffin peeked out from beyond the back of another sofa, in front of Ira, stashed there, wedged in against the padded seat so as not to shift to the plane's movements. A heavy brass, elegant coffin.

Tony stared at it. Nodded his head ever so slightly. His lips tight.

Now the cabin staff reappeared, from the rear of the plane, from their own quarters, moving up the aisle. Six of them. And two marines moved into a guarding position beside the coffin. Useless but vigilant at its side.

The captain announced arrival at Dulles airport, and the staff checked with each of the passengers. Tony showed two attendants in a row that his seatbelt was indeed fastened. The cabin lights had eradicated his odd smile.

Three of the staff seated themselves near the man at the front, Bobby. One of them appeared to be chatting amiably with him as the plane touched ground, continued talking as the plane taxied over to the VIP military gate. Tony looked out his window at it. Could see the red carpet. The fancy boarding stairs. Same as they were—what was it, only yesterday, when they had all left together. There was levity then: jokes in poor taste, lots of excitement, and a loud-mouthed senator from Idaho. He wasn't loud-mouthed tonight, though. He was dead.

The parting a little while later was somber. Everyone shook hands, rocked their heads as if in sadness over the whole affair, and departed their own ways quietly. Bobby in his black Cadillac limousine with the little flags fluttering above the headlights. Ira in his dark-blue Rolls-Royce. Tony in his 850 coupe. And the senator in a black hearse. Tony was the only one who drove himself.

As he left the airport behind, the hour closing in on midnight, and the early-November air crisp, with a cutting edge to it, Tony opened the rear of the electric sunroof and dropped the windows a couple of inches, to let in the night. Slowly, now he was alone, the odd smile reappeared on his lips.

Out on the parkway he slowed down and pulled over beneath the trees. Their branches were bare. They streaked hither and yon, vaguely, almost invisibly, into the black sky.

Tony opened the roof all the way, put up the windows, made sure the doors were locked, and turned off the engine. Sat there in the still dark, looking through the open roof at the mute heavens. Feeling comforted and fulfilled. He couldn't go home yet. Susan would be sound asleep if she did what he had told her and didn't wait up.

Tony listened to the lovely silence of a world getting nearer and nearer to the peace promised by the new civilization. It was surely a day to remember. To savor. And to give thanks for.

An evil man had been purged. A soul recycled. The Lord's messenger had even delivered awareness, as a sort of sacrament or last rite, to the soul just before it departed the body which had imprisoned it.

Tony's own soul had been transported once again into that saint-like state of supreme wellbeing. He felt the delicious trill of blood flowing through his brain, the rapture of the destroyer. His lips had formed into that grotesque smile which no one had ever seen. No one. The smile of a holy killer. And no one saw it now, in the black of night.

Alone again. The good alone. Alone with his memories of the day of judgment.

* * *

He tried to recall every detail, but many were lost in the jumble of events which had led up to the past forty-eight hours.

What was first? Oh yes, the Certified letter.

Its very arrival had been a cause for joy. It verified one of his long-held beliefs, that God spoke to him through the gift of coincidence. Most people might see coincidence as the mere vagaries of chance, but not Tony. He knew that such events were not freak caprice, but were signs of holy ratification. They were God's vapors. He knew they formed part of the clarity of the new civilization calling to him. Knew it.

And they frequently came in twos, didn't they? Lucky numbers. Today, the day of judgment for Senator Winterbern, had been exactly twenty-two days after the shot fired at Alexandra Allgood. Why, Tony hadn't set the schedule. It was set for him in the letter. He merely attended as requested. He was simply the messenger, the deliverer. Following God's plan. How do you explain that kind of coincidence, if not of holy origin?

And what came next? The laugh, wasn't it? Pondering the sheer power of this coincidence, standing on the VIP red carpet at the military gate at Dulles, the day they left, yesterday, he had inadvertently laughed out loud. Unfortunately, the good senator had noticed it, then prodded him for a cause, more out of boredom than anything else, awaiting the arrival of the big man himself. The senator and the banker, Ira Greenblatt, asking him questions out there on a sunny morning, on the VIP carpet on the tarmac.

The senator: "What is it, pardner?" The fat man tugging at him, reacting to that laugh. "A good joke, Tony? You got somethin' on Mr. Clean?"

Tony looked away from the Air Force jetliner, not even knowing he had laughed, his eyes squinting in the sunshine as it glinted off the airplane's fuselage. Reading again the long lettering in red, white and blue on the airplane's side, not quite believing that he was actually here.

He didn't answer the senator. Didn't really understand the senator's question, distracted like.

Ira Greenblatt, the banker of patrician bearing, beautifully dressed today, elegant in Italian worsted, evidently mistook Tony's silence for reluctance, so he got interested too. Said: "C'mon, Tony, tell us! You have something on the Veep we should know?"

Tony shook his head vaguely, realizing now he must have let out a tiny laugh, standing there looking at Air Force Two in front of him. *Two.*

Sam Winterbern persisted: "Christ, Ira, it's gotta be good, huh?" The fat man nudged Tony's arm. "Load us up, baby! Load us up!"

What could he say? He hadn't meant to laugh. Didn't realize he did. Just had. Gotta be more careful. The senator's words popped back into his head, and he said:

"Mr. Clean?"

Fat face forgot what he was asking about then, hearing this, his lips ready to burst into laughter themselves in anticipation of a juicy tidbit of nastiness about the Vice President, but instead of laughter now he giggled, like a schoolboy, slobbering to Tony: "Yeah, Mr. Clean... what we call Bobby when he's out of earshot. Our little joke, Ira's and mine!" Giggling more.

Ira Greenblatt began to giggle himself. Tony stared at him, trying for some sort of pleasant smile on his own face, stared at this beautifully dressed, expensive man, this whipshot banker giggling like a child who has just seen his first naughty photograph. "Oh, God!" Ira gurgled at Sam.

"Mr. Clean because of his perfect reputation in Washington?" Tony asked them both, looking from one face to the other. Innocent question.

Ira the banker laughed even more wickedly, hearing this.

Sam the senator put an arm over Tony's shoulders, a gesture of confidence, little bubbles on his lips Tony noticed, and whispered towards his ear, not in it but only towards it, so Ira could hear: "No," he spluttered, looking at Ira, "not that kind of clean. Clean as in squeaky clean. And squeaky clean as in uptight. And uptight, as in, he's so uptight his ass squeaks when he walks!" Haw haw haw.

So Tony thought, looking at these two he thought, What the hell! And laughed out loud as his eyes took in the tall, colorful letters running along the fuselage of the Air Force jet: 'THE UNITED STATES OF AMERICA.' All shiny and pretty, officially beautiful. He'd laugh at his joke; they could laugh at theirs.

"God's sake," Ira the banker said to Tony, finally, getting over his fun as he watched the black limo with the little fluttering flags approaching. "God's sake, Tony, don't let Bobby know you know our little joke."

Sam said, "He'd just shit! Then he wouldn't enjoy our golf game, would he? And we wouldn't want that..."

Ira the banker put a slim, manicured finger to his lips, for Tony to see.

Tony's laugh changed to a nice smile now, a smile at the lovely irony of the whole thing. Getting invited by the Vice President of the United States to play golf with him and two friends out in Beverly Hills. Just the four of them. A nice little getaway from the hectic pace of Washington. On the taxpayer, of course. That was a given nobody would even mention.

And what was next? Oh yeah, the conversation on the plane while they crossed over the country in five hours of luxurious accommodation.

"Thanks awfully for inviting me, sir!" Tony had said to the tall man with the nice face and good suit. Official blue with hairline silver stripes running up and down. A good suit but not an elegant one. Just the proper reserve. The tie was dark blue, too. Sharp and glossy. Standard white shirt from Brooks Brothers. They were all alone, the four of them, aside from the Secret Service agents and the cabin attendants, who sat off in the rear of the jet, vigilant but not unnecessarily so. Everyone had been cleared.

The tall man told him without delay, "No sirs here, Tony. For this trip, it's just Bobby and Sam and Ira... and Tony, okay?"

"Yessir," Tony said. "I mean, Bobby!" And smiling a lot. They were all smiling a lot, so Tony figured he'd get in a little schmoozing, said "I hear you're good enough for the PGA Tour, Bobby."

The Vice President, Bobby, hearing this, looked over at Sam, who shrugged and said "See what I told you!" Bobby got a funny little look on his face at this, then changed it, like a card shark could change a drawn card, and gave Tony one of those sincere, right-in-your-eyes politician's looks, while he said, right in Tony's face: "Tony, I play with lots of the pros on their days off, and I can tell you, I'm simply in awe of them. Just in awe! Do you hear what I'm saying?"

"Yessir," Tony just said, realized it, so he said: "Me too... Bobby."

The browning farms beneath them gave way to light gray clouds as mixed drinks and refreshments got served up on AF2. Fatso Sam, the influential senator, hadn't changed a bit since Tony and he had spoken at the summer party at Ira's place in Georgetown. Not a bit. Soon had three drinks in him, and maybe four thousand calories in fancy, dainty hors d'oeuvres. Shrimp and crab and cheeses and other evil tidbits. 'Horse dew-vers' he kept calling them, each time he swept a bunch off a silver tray onto his fine-china plate with the Vice Presidential Seal in the center. Haw haw. 'Horse dew-vers.' It got old after the second time. Tony kept on smiling.

They talked about sports and Beltway traffic and Ira's various mansions and the senator's girlfriends and food and more sports, and inevitably money. Mostly about Ira's money. Not a word about governing. Tony said he enjoyed physical landscapes, kept looking out the window and commenting on where they were, he thought. Fatty Sam said the only physical things he liked were eating and sex. Big laugh all around. Tony noticed the Colorado River below them, the sky big and clear again now that the West got nearer.

Then things got nasty. Well, raw.

The four of them huddling around the seat grouping up at the front of the cabin, Bobby the VP and Ira the banker and Sam the senator and Tony the—

"What do you do?" asked Bobby.

"Retired investor, occasional bank consultant, nearly full-time golfer," Tony said with a straight face.

Greenblatt informed Bobby with a long, serious countenance: "Tony's big league. International banker!"

"Tell us about it, Tony," the VP ordered. Ordered as in, Would you be nice enough to bring me another iced Perrier, saying it to a cabin attendant.

Tony sighed inwardly. But kept on smiling, in that banker way of smiling. Smiling as in, I'll give you only what I want to.

He got modest, said "Oh, hardly big league. Years ago, I worked for an investment banking house in London, back home. Retired from it now."

"Back home?" asked the VP.

"Tony's a Brit," Sam let them know, as if his accent were totally gone.

"Oh?" from the VP.

"An American citizen these half-dozen years, Bobby. Grew up in the north of England. Worked all over the world, for the bank, when I worked. Retired here to Virginia, right after I met my wife."

"She's a peach!" Fatty Sam sang gleefully, nodding at Tony, a polite insult. "A real sweet peach, I can tell you!"

Tony's smile stayed in place.

He said, "So, no longer a Brit. God bless America!"

"Golfers *are* retired, the pros I mean," pronounced Ira, "but most bankers aren't. Not at your age anyhow. Where'd the money come from?"

Only an American would ask you a question like that, Tony thought. He kept the smile in place, though, said: "I've got a few bob, it's true, Ira. But I'm hardly in the big league, and I have to watch my pennies in order not to work. Modest living, that's the ticket to having plenty of free time."

He smiled wider now, at Ira and at Sam. Wrinkled his nose at Bobby.

"Banks in Europe must pay pretty damned good," said Sam. His kind of putdown. He got a smug look on his puss, guzzled another rum and Coke.

Bobby was just looking, sourly, at Ira. For the remark about golfers. He let it go, though. And looked Tony back in the face.

Tony said, "It was an *investment* bank, Sam. A private bank. We had our little rewards for outstanding performance. In my case, I knew about lots of things that were about to happen... if you see what I mean."

"We call that 'insider information' here in the States, Tony," responded Sam, jocularly. "Better watch your ass if you do it here!" He looked for approval at Bobby, got nothing in return, just a stolid face.

"Better have friends in high places," Ira rejoined, also looking at Bobby for a response, still getting none. "High fucking places!"

Bobby's eyes winced at this. He said to Ira, "You know I don't approve of language like that, okay Ira?"

"Yessir," Ira said, not to Bobby but to Sam, who winked back at him. Ira looked at Tony and said, "Do please forgive the lapse into French!"

Earning him another look from Bobby, but nothing more.

Tony thinking, *What* have these two got on this guy?

But Tony put a stop to the whole thing by saying "No fear of any of that, my friends. I don't invest in anything but myself anymore..."

Sam took a long breath while rubbing his belly. Tony noticed out the window they were just leaving the western end of the Grand Canyon behind, figured there wasn't any point at all in mentioning it to any of them. Who'd look?

"What was it then, you did, Tony?" asked Bobby with sincerity in his voice. Tony couldn't read him. Was he kidding, covering, or naive?

Much as he peered into Bobby's eyes, he couldn't read them. Blank. Glazed. The consummate politician. "Mutual funds?" asked Bobby, ending the thought.

"No," Tony answered. "No, mutuals were never for me. I was earlier than that. I was a sheer speculator, pushed it to the limit, borrowed on hunches. I did IPOs on, what shall we say, 'forward information to special clients' of the bank. Rumors, deals in the making. Threw everything I had and could razz up at them, every time—"

"Done a bit of that ourselves, haven't we, Ira?" from Sam, stuffing little crackers hosting olives on mounds of cream cheese into his face. He was sweating from the rum, little beads all over his forehead and cheeks.

"I realized I was living in an extraordinary time," Tony went on, for Bobby. "A time not likely to be repeated in my life! Something going down in Australia, I'd hear about it in Pakistan. A London merger, that might hit my ears a week ahead of time, in Argentina. I went for it!"

"So you've done little more than golf these past half-dozen years?" Bobby asked him. Looked at the other two, said "Gentlemen, we're in deep trouble come tomorrow, out there on the fairways!"

"No sir. Bobby, I mean." Tony said, "I've only been retired, fully, a few years now. From the market, I mean. It was when the Dow hit eight thousand, see. And the Nasdaq snuck across fifteen hundred. Got to the point I couldn't sleep at night. The PEs were absurd. And the euphoria on TV told me all the final suckers were being drawn into the market. Throwing their savings and earnings into those mutual funds. Take away the mutuals... well, it'd be over, wouldn't it?"

Tony earned a blank stare for this from Bobby, the VP of the USA.

"Are you suggesting," Bobby said at long last, while Ira the banker looked out the window and Sam the senator kept touching one of the air hostesses, friendly like, called her over for another rum and cola but wouldn't let go, Bobby's head working at it "... are you suggesting that our economic expansion isn't genuine? That stocks aren't the ideal place to put your investment dollars?"

Ira kept looking out his window.

"I'm not suggesting anything, Bobby," Tony told him. "I'm telling you that my own portfolio got big enough for me to retire on it. I was a bull for a long time, but I cashed out. I am definitely not a pig..." looking over at Fatty Sam.

"Well, I'm of the opinion that the market will be a Bull market for most of my life," said Bobby, sitting straight in his comfy chair, his suit immaculate, his smile sincere. Or so it appeared. "We both are, aren't we, Sam?" Sam had let go of the air hostess. His drink was pretty drained already.

"You may have enough bucks to say no to most people, Tony," Sam informed him, a gentle flush over his face now, "but you got out too damned early, boy! You left a fortune on the table." His tie was loosened. The rings of fat at his neck pushed out at the collar of his shirt. He said, to get his buddy back in the conversation, "And Ira and me picked it up, isn't that right, Ira? Isn't that god-damned right!"

"Please, Sammy," Bobby said to him, for the expletive.

Ira looked at Sam, displeased. Said only "We did indeed, Samuel."

"Sorry, Bobby," apologized fatso. "I've had too much to drink." Getting up, unsure feet taking him towards the back of the cabin, headed for a sofa.

"You really think these market drops aren't temporary corrections?" Bobby asked Tony. He actually believed all this stuff he heard on TV.

Tony paid all his attention to the VP now. How many men had a chance like this? He said:

"Bobby, sir... my old daddy, bless his heart, had a favorite expression. He often said 'Ignorance is bliss.' You don't hear it much anymore. Maybe there's too much ignorance, I don't know. What I do know is I usually recognize propaganda when I hear it, and that anything that goes into a hyperbolic curve—straight up—eventually falls to earth. Anything! You can't change the laws of physics. When my own investments got to a certain height, I sold. Every last share. I was out. Period."

"Period?" asked Bobby.

"Period, sir. So now, I never think about stocks or money. I don't collect dividends. I mostly collect life—and interest."

"How touching," said Ira through his knuckles.

"Maybe it's just smart!" answered Bobby.

"Sure keeps my mind clear, to concentrate on my golf game," Tony said back to Bobby, smiling now, and meaning the smile.

"We'll see tomorrow morning," said Ira through his own kind of smile.

"You know, Tony," Bobby told him, relaxed now in his padded seat, "Ira's one hell of a player! He may indeed beat you, Tony."

"It's because I'm a strategist," Ira told them both. "And *nothing* interferes with my concentration."

Bobby the VP picked up an icy glass of tonic water, gestured with it, and said Tony's direction, "Cheers!"

* * *

And what came after the continental crossing? The golf game, yeaaah.

Well, breakfast came right before that. It wasn't something Tony ordinarily thought a lot about, although he usually enjoyed breakfast, but that breakfast at the Sun Palm Court, well, that was memorable. And so outrageous that maybe it added to the plausibility of what happened later on.

The Sun Palm Court. Just off the back end of the Beverly Hollywood Hotel, where lots of celebs liked to be seen. Owned by a big, very big, celeb.

Nine the next morning, but it seemed earlier. No, it seemed kinda timeless. Out among the palm trees, under that big striped umbrella, almost like Italy but not Italy, definitely not Italy. Tony remembered how white the underside of that umbrella was, almost starched white, but nobody starched umbrellas, did they? And those crisp blue stripes through the white.

Ira the banker kept waving to people he evidently knew. Guys in these neat Armani jackets with diamond studs on their collars where a tie usually sat. Where had Tony seen that last? Sunny foreheads with pretty curls. Guys. Talking on their cell phones. Movie deals, like.

Sam the senator would motion to someone to come over and see them, every now and then. But the Secret Service guys wouldn't let most of them get anywhere near. Fatso Sam would make funny little apologetic faces and shoulder shrugs when that happened. You know, Well we'll talk next time, sorry about that, I'm with the Vice Prez, see.

Lot of posturing. Not so much from the VP, though. He was talking about golf. All he talked about. Tony said, No, fraid he didn't play with Jack Nicklaus. No, not with Nick Price either. No, not with any of them. But it wasn't name-dropping; Bobby really did play with them, frequently.

No, what Tony remembered most about breakfast at the Sun Palm Court was how outrageous it was, the food. Especially the food consumed by Fatty Sam.

Lessee, two very big orange juices with maraschino cherries, huge ones, in them, floating over the ice, with mint sprigs in there, too. Luscious rolls called bialys, something like that, wonderful Jewish things with onions and seeds and who knows what else. Swathed in butter, thick with butter, maybe half an inch thick on them. And three eggs sunny-side up, big orange yolks, two inches across those yolks, doused in salt. And the filet mignon, God what was it, three inches thick? And the asparagus, yeah the asparagus, a pool of that hollandaise sauce covering the tips. And of course dipping toast and more butter, and strawberry jam.

Tony watched Fatty Sam consume it all, right to the last morsel. Tony eating his citrus sections with some cherry juice, and black coffee, and one of those bialy things, without butter. Just amazed, watching the senator scarf it down.

A wonder he didn't have a heart attack right there, right at the breakfast table.

They had a ten-thirty tee-off at the Beverly Hillsdale Country Club, over on Century Boulevard. Ira the banker's club. Got there in a red Rolls-Royce.

Tony didn't really remember all that much about the golf game itself, each and every shot and like that. Beautiful course, just beautiful. He played well but most of his own concentration was on his mission. If he missed a shot he still had a broad grin on his face, thinking of what was coming.

Out on the fifth green Tony got a little fit of sneezing. Dry air nettled at his sinuses for a few minutes, hot dust, then passed. Tony suddenly remembered the same thing happened to him as he drove into Nice.

"You all right, Tony?" Bobby asked him.

"Yeah, all right. Get it once in a while. Don't know why."

"The Santa Ana winds," Ira told him. "Time of year."

Ira and Bobby played brilliantly. Bobby took his time, had a wonderful natural swing, putted well. Ira played to win, a competitive golfer. Sam cheated. Sam had no idea how to move his shoulders in unison, how to putt, how to sight the ball, nothing. He tapped rim balls into the cup with his toe and counted the holes a shot short, Tony noticed.

Mostly Tony noticed Fatty Sam huffing and puffing, just walking from the golf cart. And gulping ice water, lots of it, on the back nine. They had these cute little ice-water stops, in the shapes of old-time hand pumps, at each tee. And it was warm. November but in the eighties. Nobody but Fatty Sam minded it. They all walked the fairways, all but Sam in his electric cart.

At one point, the fourteenth hole Tony remembered, Fatty Sam was huffing so badly that Bobby asked him if he was all right. No problem, said the senator.

So the scene was set, really, for Tony's move.

They hit the nineteenth hole about three-thirty. Really hot by then, high eighties. But the "hole" was almost freezing, from the AC. A dark little cocktail lounge with members' photographs all around the walls. Movie stars and producers, singers you'd see in Vegas, guys like that, all up there next to politicians and suits Tony didn't recognize, but all of them with big gleaming mugs. Being on that wall was *it.*

Senator Sam plopped himself down wearily on one of the big fat easy chairs they had arranged in nice little, cozy groups.

Ira ordered a gin fizz. The VP had an iced cranberry juice with a twist. Tony asked for a Younger's Scotch Bitter, and they had it! The senator ordered a lime daiquiri. Tony couldn't believe it. Well, yeah, he could. God's vapors, right?

And a tray of 'horse dew-vers' as well. Fatty Sam was stuffing one in his face when he got a funny look on it and asked Tony to hand him his daiquiri. Looked like he was choking.

Tony had palmed Percy Dithers' clear-gel poison pill, the one the chemist had popped into his mouth. Tony had it tucked between his third and fourth fingers, invisible in the dark lounge, and just let it drop, a silent little plop, right into Fatty Sam's lime daiquiri as he handed it over to him.

Senator Sam took a big gulp from his daiquiri, looked better, smiled at them all—"Better now, guys, thanks Tony!"—then swallowed the rest of it in two more gulps. Sat back and ordered another, yelling over to the cocktail girl to come over, probably gonna fondle her too.

Ira and Bobby sat back in their stuffed leather, relieved that Sam got over choking, resumed chatting to each other about the eighteen holes they just did. Tony said he had to visit the gent's. Excused himself. "Be right back."

In the gent's, all done up in marble, a gleaming creamy tan and black marble, gold-plated faucets and handles, Tony went in a stall and dumped the other gel capsule into the toilet, flushed it twice, wrapped Percy's little glass tube in some toilet paper and crushed it with his shoe on the marble floor, then flushed the whole thing down another toilet, flushed it twice too.

Washed his hands in nice cold water. Splashed some in his face. Saw that *look* looking back at him in the vanity mirror, winked at himself, and then got serious. Dried his hands on a linen towel with the crest of the country club sewn on it, in gold thread.

When he came out of the gent's there was a commotion. Fatty Sam was flat out on the floor, on his back, making a fuss. The Secret Service guys, they were keeping everyone away from Bobby, had him cordoned off, waiters and waitresses and a bartender and a couple of women in nice business suits, little gold tags on their lapels, all worried about Senator Sam Winterbern, lying there on the floor, gasping for breath, moaning.

"What happened?" Tony asked Ira, kneeling next to Sam on the floor. A real look of concern on his face. His voice sounding worried.

"Heart attack, what else!" Ira shot back at Tony.

"My God," Tony said, looking over at Bobby, oh twenty feet away, asking him "Anybody called the parameds?"

"On the way!" Bobby yelled over the shoulders of his bodyguards.

"Jeez, what can we do till they get here?" Tony saying to Ira.

"Just stay out of it," Ira ordering. "God! Look at him!"

Fatty Sam's face was really flushed now, red like a cranberry, dark red, his skin looking like it was gonna pop, and his eyes were wide open, straining in fright, and complaining loudly that nobody was helping him. Yelling at everybody, at nobody, rude and nasty.

Cranky, Percy had said; the victim gets cranky.

But then he stopped yelling, those eyes wide open, his pupils huge Tony could see as he leaned down nearer to him. Had that white rime on his lips, dried spittle. Went into a convulsion, his chest heaving. Eyes squeezing closed. The end was near.

"My God!" Bobby cried, "can't we do anything!" He broke through the Secret Service agents and got over next to Tony and Ira, leaning over the senator.

"Let him get enough air," one of the waitresses told nobody in particular.

"That's the thing. Enough air!" shouted the bartender, behind her.

But Fatty Sam was into the tremors now, his limbs stiff, like starched shirts, funny looking, but tremors showing in his rolls of fat. His puffy neck all red and stiff.

His eyes opened suddenly, he recognized Tony, said in a terrible strained voice, terrified now, knowing he was dying, said "Toneeeey, help me, please help me—"

But the next convulsion shook him in a deep shudder, his eyes forced shut with the pain, Ira and Bobby looking terrified as well.

Tony took a linen hand towel, one of those with the gold threads of the country-club's crest on it, dipped it in his beer and wiped Senator Sam's forehead with it. Lifted his head gently, putting one hand under it, comforting him like, dabbing that cool towel against his forehead. Straining with the convulsion, Fatty Sam opened his eyes, narrowly, one more time, and choked out Tony's name in a little spitting sound.

Tony bent over him, put his ear to the senator's lips as if listening, then put his own lips to Fatty Sam's ear and whispered into it, as softly as he could, whispered "Die, you bastard, die!"

Those greedy little eyes opened one more time, just a fleeting glance at Tony, Tony up on his haunches now, over the body, then the eyes closed as a final twitch convulsed the carcass.

Tony stood up, still holding the cool linen hand towel.

"God!" Ira proclaimed. "God, that was awful!"

"What'd he say?" Bobby said to Tony.

"Huh?"

"What'd he say to you? What'd he tell you, into your ear?"

"Oh," Tony said quietly, putting the right look on his face for the Vice President, sort of confusion mixed with sadness, and then saying to Bobby softly, with a question to end the words, "He said he was sorry..."

Well, the paramedics got there, two minutes later. The VP was already ushered away by his bodyguards. Ira was telling Tony they should have seen it coming, the heart attack, probably started when he looked like he was choking, Tony saying back, Well you just never knew did you, standing there by the corpse, rocking his head side to side all the while, in sympathy for the poor deceased.

Thinking, what was it the senator had said to him at Ira's party? *The proper people were above the law, just above.* That was it, wasn't it?

After the coroner got there, Ira took the red Rolls-Royce back to their hotel, where Bobby probably already was he told Tony, and Tony walked out of the country club, down its long green lane to Century Boulevard, crossed the street and just strolled for a while, in a little bit got a cab to take him back to the hotel, where he bought a postcard in the gift shop, and an airmail stamp, and sat down over in the center of the luxurious lobby. On one of those round, velvet things.

The postcard showed the famous Hollywood Bowl. Tony thought Percy Dithers would appreciate that, remembering all the prints of French Impressionist paintings Percy had taped to his laboratory walls. A man of culture.

Tony addressed the card to the street in Southwark. In the card's message square, Tony wrote, in tiny letters:

'The banana daiquiri was cool and sweet. Cool and sweet. Wish you could have been here!'

Tony turned the postcard over and his face froze into an odd, twisted smile as his eyes danced unseeingly over the picture.

He never said he was sorry, did he?

TWENTY

A still, gray sky cast its spell over the heather moor. Birch and conifer and oak alike poked spindly branches into the grayness. A November damp suffused the air, silent now even as morning came, for the mole crickets had perished with the cold, had returned to Hell.

His long white sideburns softened the appearance of his rough face, as did his windblown unruly hair—fluffy white tassels crowning a face made pink by elevated blood pressure. But it wore a mean look.

He stood holding onto the wooden rail on the cabin's porch, listening, straining to hear a distant motor whining through the stillness. Gradually it became louder. It huffed and chugged. Finally his steel-colored eyes saw the old, beaten Volvo come through the bare trees, the thick forest, come out of the dirt lane into the clearing in front of the cabin.

Those steely eyes, set in that rouge face, watched her leave the car and come determinedly towards him.

She hopped up the wooden steps by twos and unexpectedly hugged him, clapping his back, then each thumped the other's back as two men might do. She sat on the top step. He went inside and emerged shortly holding two mugs with steam coming off them. He sat beside her on the stoop but not facing her, both of them looking out towards the still, dense forest, their eyes hunting the view as if searching out something, awaiting a ghost maybe. But in reality their search was one of avoidance of each other's eyes.

They sipped at their coffees until the old man said:

"Yewh've changed yurh hair agin, Allie."

"Aye."

She ran a hand through it, cut short and bristling like a soldier's just out of boot camp. Redder than the old man's face, an orange red like a fresh carrot. "Me true self," she added, and the old man ran his knuckles through it, smiling oddly at her, but an unseen smile. She didn't look back.

He returned his attention to his coffee mug, sipped at it, the coffee piping hot, just made.

"They done well, dun't yew think?" she said then.

"All we could've wanted, and then shom... be good to see 'em. When're they back then?"

"Not fur some taihme yet."

"Done their duty. Bring 'em back."

"Not yet. Sending Seamus and Peadar tuh join 'em, right soon now."

The old man put his mug down on the step, rubbed his beefy hands together briskly. "And why's that then?" he asked gruffly.

"Nother bit a' duty cummin'," she said back, still searching the empty trees, though her eyes darted his way a moment, to judge him.

"More of a plan, is it? More to blame on Patrick and Maere and their INLA, is it then?"

She threw the dregs of her coffee out into the dirt, dropped the mug onto the wooden stoop, and stood down in the dirt to face the old man.

"Pups," she said to him, hard but without violence, "theihr INLA can go fock 'em selves. Weh'll take credit our *uhwn* selves, now on. Startin' with the upcomin' present... bit a' divershion, see. Bit a' divershion."

She stood not a body length away, facing him, her hips angled in old, soft purple corduroy trousers, a pink silk scarf between her neck and a gray turtleneck sweater, the usual brown boots, wearing black leather gloves, the kind cut off halfway down the fingers, a shooter's gloves, stood over him, staring at him. His eyes escaped hers still, looking past her out at the trees. The gray wood of the old cabin seemed to age before her, the tin roof to rust on, the earthy debris in the channels of its sloping roof to thicken.

He asked another question. "Still gewin' yurshelf, are yew?"

She stood glaring at him now, judging, then told him.

"Gewing alone, sure nuff."

"Same time?" He picked up the coffee again, to feel its warmth.

The look on her face said she was certain now. A knowing look. Still no eye contact from the old man.

"That's right, Pups. I leave tomarrah, same as planned."

He looked up at her at last, meeting her eyes, found them drilling into his, holding on. He set down his coffee mug on the stoop, got up and walked a few paces away from the porch, around her, putting his back to her.

"They'll call it madness, yuh knowh. And it is." No accusation in this, just somber, like stating a fact.

"Histhory'll call it genius, won't it?"

He turned to her now, a docile smile on his lips, dark and thick with age. The best he could manage. Seeking an answer from her.

His eyes crinkled at their corners. "It may well," he said gently. "It may well. My Allie..."

Her look was hard, though. Didn't alter one bit.

She knew, didn't she? So he asked, "And the divershion?"

"Oh that'sh fer the lads ta knowh. A good one, though!"

"Another bomb, is it?"

"Wouldn't yewh just like ta knowh then?" she said placidly, without emotion, to his eyes. Even to her they looked weary.

And then she turned and walked away, out of his life.

He stood there for some time after her motor died away, rubbing the cold out of his hands and the arthritis out of his wrists, staring into the dead forest, the damp taking its toll on his joints and the still gray air spilling into his soul, decimating it.

* * *

A few days after he got home from killing the senator, Tony's e-mails started to come in thick and heavy. They also became increasingly abstruse. He had to download each encoded message, load the translation software he kept in his safe, run the encoded e-mail through it, memorize it, then trash the software and the message from his hard drive. For three days he got up to half a dozen of these e-mails a day.

He'd then take a ride and call Nora on his cell phone to confirm, each time from a different spot away from his house.

What was taking shape was an astonishing plan. And it was taking shape rapidly, so that in only a few days Tony knew what he would have to do. Sometimes he felt as if he might be fighting a shadow, though. An enemy so unreal that his only physical impression of it was a head of yellow hair that had miraculously escaped his bullet.

Sitting in his darkened den one afternoon, about an hour before Susan came home from work, Tony got a sudden shiver as he read the latest e-mail from London. That ancient shrill wail came to his ears, chasing him around the house, looking for a source. None to be found.

He came back to his PC screen and retrieved the e-mail from Sleep mode. As he stared at it, memorizing the latest detail Goodge had sent, the shiver returned, robbing his thought.

His eyes glazed over, staring at the screen, and he remembered...

He saw himself at nineteen, corporal in the Royal Marines, saw himself in youth as if peering into a mirror, his rug-like black curly hair trimmed close to his scalp, his muscles with a definition he'd never been able to regain, determined to win promotion and distinction, thinking even then of commando school. He could see himself now in the dark reflection of his PC screen on weekend leave up in Fort William, in a hostel room with a pixyish Scottish lass, two years his junior, short and petite with raven-black hair, curling thickly over her shoulders, teasing him with her tongue and eyes, walking pitapat in her bare feet from the bathroom to the little balcony, looking back over her shoulder, her body outlined against the pale sky beyond the balcony, toying with him, oh how she'd always wanted to meet a soldier, just a schoolgirl on holiday in the middle of June... but when she'd said no, Tony pushed her onto the bed, fought with her, slapped her, no idea she really meant it, and the more she resisted the more he was driven, till she gave in and he had sex with her, again and again, till he exhausted himself and he left her crying there on the rumpled bed. Left her...

She was the first of many, but the only innocent one. He had come to regret it, finally understanding what he had done, wanting to find her again but never able to. She had disappeared forever, taking something from his soul along with her.

Coming out of the memory, Tony caressed the sleeping PC screen, seeking to touch her again only for a moment, a gentle moment, and his fingertips felt a faint vibration as she faded once more into his dark past.

Thinking, what *was* power without control? His was now a soul of goodness in a wicked world. He would keep it that way.

* * *

Late morning, the silver and white Gulfstream jet taxied down the narrow runway, turned at one end, sat there briefly, then sped past the truncated trees, taking off with a roar and rapidly gaining altitude. In moments, it seemed, Northolt fell behind, the high-security Royal Air Force airport outside of London shrank back into the rolling landscape, disappeared.

Two RAF pilots at the controls. Soon even vast London shriveled, faded beneath the cloud cover as the jet turned west, speeding and climbing.

It carried just three passengers. And some specialized assault gear.

* * *

As the Gulfstream passed over Dingle Bay at the western tip of Ireland, heading for the North Atlantic, five men rode in two old cars up along the River Mersey, on the south side of Liverpool. The day was cold but clear, a rare bright spot in November. They drove in caravan along the A561, north and away from the water, coming soon to a market square with an ancient church spire in the center.

Vendors were set up all around the square. It was late morning, and the bakeries would soon be putting out the morning's breads and rolls. Hundreds of people shopped in the stalls, and queues began to appear by the doors to the bakeries. It was market day.

The two cars pulled into the square, drew up near a busy group of vendors, and with no hesitation three of the men jumped suddenly from the cars and opened fire on the crowd. Three AK-47s spewed out the Russian bullets, rapid fire, striking the old darkened stones of the church spire, smashing windows, invading stores, thudding into parked automobiles, glancing off cobblestones to fly in every direction at once. Alarm and panic came from the crowd, a mass screaming. In under a minute, the shooting was done, the two old cars sped off northward through the city towards the motorway, and dozens of shoppers lay dead and dying in the market square.

The peal of sirens began. Out near the suburb of Kirkby, by an industrial estate, one of the old cars pulled to the curb while the other continued on its way out of the city.

A door to the car opened. A red telephone kiosk was nearby.

One of the three men in the car said, "Yew do it, Peadar. Here'sh the number to call."

The man named Peadar climbed out of the car, walked briskly to the kiosk and shoved some 10p coins into the pay phone.

He heard a man's voice say, "City desk."

"Yeah," he said, in his heavy brogue, "and who woold yew be thinking thish here might be?"

"What is it?" the voice said back.

"There'sh been a shooting, down the city center," in Irish brogue.

"Are *you* the ones!" came the voice back to his ears.

"Us agin. Same as the courts bombing!" He was yelling gleefully.

"You the INLA, you filthy swine?"

"Fock 'em! Washn't *'em!* Thish is the *true* IRA, same as done them stinkin' courts, down Lowndon!"

"You dirty bastards, I hope you—" but the man with the Irish brogue slammed down the mouthpiece, then grabbed it again and used it to smash the phone box, hitting it until hunks of hard plastic broke off, smashing the mouthpiece again and again at the touch buttons, then dropping it, letting it hang from the cord.

He spat violently at the phone, then jumped into the open car door, and the car sped away.

* * *

The old Volvo plugged on, the woman at the wheel smoking steadily. She drove the scenic country roads south and eastward, seeing nothing more than blacktop. It was a tedious business, going day and night without rest other than petrol stops, until finally she reached the ferry port on the south side of Dublin, Dun Laoghaire. But she'd missed the sailing, so found a B&B a short distance off and stayed the night.

Next morning she drove the car onto the ferry in the cold air and light drizzle. For the next three and a half hours, she smoked cigarettes out on the fore deck as the ferry crossed the Irish Sea to the port at Holyhead, in Anglesey. Only as the western tip of Wales came into view did she go below decks for a cold pork pie and a tepid bottle of orangeade.

As soon as possible she got on the A5 and headed east towards England. She passed over the bleak Cambrian Mountains with their arid climate, then through the quaint little villages of Shropshire, and drove on through all the roundabouts, hour after hour and near to exhaustion, following the highlighted route on the map on the seat beside her, until she finally found New Street train station in Birmingham.

She left the Volvo in the carpark, bought a day ticket to London, and had to wait a good two hours for the train. She spent the time smoking and watching those she hated so deeply, strangers all of them.

She tried not to look, but couldn't help it. A group of children, preschool, five or six they looked, over there, crawling over the benches, guarded by some mums. Goin' somewhere on the train, weren't they?

A tear came to her eye. She swiped it away and took a drag on her Turkish cigarette. The nicotine bit into her tongue. She inhaled another heavy cloud, and as she let the smoke out on her breath she could see it all over again through the gray air.

She was five, too. With her momma, at the pub, Heart of Darkness they called it, in the black of night, too late for a child but Pups was upstairs at his meeting, some of the ladies were down in the pub, waiting for their men, drinking quietly, talking in whispers, not bothering anybody. She had a ginger ale. With a big red cherry in it. She'd been pushing the cherry around in the glass with her tongue when the soldiers came.

It was so sudden, so confusing. They made a lot of noise. It hurt her ears. She watched one of the British soldiers push momma down, slap her, heard momma crying, from behind her little bench saw the soldier doing something to momma, hurting her bad, and she rushed at him and stabbed at his back with a fork, wanted to make him stop hurting momma. He turned and pushed her away, and she saw he was doing *that thing* to momma. She picked up the fork again, her eyes reddening, but then another soldier was there, and he hit her in the head with the butt of his rifle.

She didn't remember anything else, except that Pups' hair turned white in the weeks after momma disappeared. White as new snow...

"You all right, miss?" the voice said to her, making her shudder, and she came back to the train station, looking up at an elderly man, stooping towards her. She realized she'd been crying. The man looked so kindly, concerned like. She stared at him, got up abruptly, snatching her bag, got around him somehow and walked quickly over to the ladies room.

She looked at her face in the mirror in the toilet. Put her bag down and ran the cold water tap, still staring at herself. Damned fool! She sloshed water onto her face for a good half minute. Looked at herself again. Anger came back. With the first two knuckles of her right hand she struck herself on the bridge of her nose. Hard, repeatedly, till it hurt.

Then she dried off her face, picked up her bag, and walked back to the waiting room, over to the far side, away from those kids, those damned kids still crawling over the benches, bothering people.

She sat down and rubbed the dent in her head. The dent the soldier made all those years ago with his rifle.

All she had with her was her bag, a student's backpack. In it were three things. A thousand dollars in twenties. A false Irish passport showing a recent photo of her in carrot-red hair, short cropped, and identifying her as Mary Kelly, born in Dublin in 1969. And a roundtrip economy ticket on Virgin Atlantic Airlines from Heathrow to JFK Airport in New York. She didn't know it, but the return ticket was a waste of money.

* * *

Sir Malcolm Goodge stuck a finger in his right ear and tugged at the canal, twisting his finger. With his thumb he rubbed the back of the ear, and yawned. Then he did the same to his left ear.

"Trouble, sir?" Tony asked him, seeing the ear work.

"Damned old noise," Goodge explained. "From my years at Sandhurst. Classrooms too near the firing ranges. They'll never be right."

"Sorry for you, sir."

"Well!" Goodge exclaimed. "Nothing to be done about it. Lots of work ahead for us, though. C'mon."

They walked briskly down the tarmac in the early light to a building that looked like a soundstage on a movie lot. But it wasn't a movie lot. It was a top-secret base the CIA kept near Quantico, in the Virginia countryside.

They left the gray, chilly morning behind as the Marine guard admitted them to the hangar.

Inside, it was all one gigantic room with walls that rose to steel girders and an arched roof, a good hundred feet up. A Sikorsky MH-60L VelcroHawk special-forces helicopter stood in the middle, painted dull black and bearing no markings of any kind. There appeared to be nothing else in the hangar.

Goodge led Tony over to it, and as they came around it they found two men waiting, dressed in black and standing near a pile of military gear.

Tony suddenly got a big smile on his face and one of the men spread his arms and said in a heavy Scots brogue, "Shon of a bitch! Tony Shpool!"

They hugged each other, thumping their backs. Goodge smiled.

"Angus, you old bear!" Tony coughed at him happily.

"Put things right, don't I, Captain?" Goodge said.

"That you do, sir, that you do!" Tony smiling at him, still holding on to the man named Angus, who now pushed him away, grabbing him by the shoulders, saying "Look at you! Just look, will ya!"

"Angus, God *damn* it!"

"Tis a fine thing, Tony me lad! Just a fine thing!" He slapped Tony on the cheek, and Tony laughed at it, and slapped him back.

They stood there just beaming at each other for a minute or so.

As they calmed down, the other man in black fatigues, Jack Rush, looked to Goodge for an explanation, threw him a puzzled face.

"Sit down, gentlemen," Goodge just said, and they took up places on two long benches which faced each other, a few feet apart.

Around them the hangar lay in a dim light on its peripheries, brightening towards the center where the helicopter sat.

Goodge looked to Jack Rush. "Old comrades in arms, these two. Nothing like a reunion in time of need."

"Yes sir," Rush said.

The man named Angus beamed on at Tony, then looked at Goodge in a manner of saying thanks, the crow's feet at the corners of his eyes deepening in appreciation, his head nodding just slightly at Goodge and a happy twist to his lips.

Major Angus Lukins was a big man, lean and sinewy and powerful in build despite his sixty-two years, his curly gray hair thinning, a wide moustache on his lip, gray sideburns growing down past his ears, something of a perpetual grin on his mouth.

Tony looked at Rush and told him: "Angus and I go back twenty years—is it, Angus?"—getting a new smile from him. "SAS paratroopers together, but Angus was jumping outta planes way before my time. Even coached the lads of 2 Para for the Falklands invasion, didn't you, Angus?"

"'At's right, Tony lad! And without 'em, the 45 Commando Royal Marines wouldn't a made it halfway to Two Sisters."

"One of the most successful assaults of the Falklands crisis," Goodge filled in for him, looking at Rush.

"And what else, Angus?"

"Aw, the odd job, is all . . . " Angus Lukins had that grin on his mug.

Goodge continued for him: "You were in 22 SAS Regiment in sixty-four and sixty-five, weren't you? In Borneo."

"That's right, sir. In the 'happy time.' Then came Northern Ireland in sixty-nine. Grim business, that."

"And in seventy-seven," Goodge continued recounting, "Angus went to Mogadishu. That dreadful German airliner hijacking."

"And Tony and me finally came together back in May of eighty, when we took the Iranian Embassy back for you Brits!"

"Friends ever since," Tony added. "Constant partners till we had to split company when Angus went to the Falklands and I—"

"Well, enough of that," Goodge interrupted suddenly. "Suffice to say, Angus has been successfully lent to ASF from time to time."

"That I have, sir. That I have. Always enjoy working with the best. What is it we have thish time, if I may ashk?"

"You may indeed, Major. Let me fill all of you gentlemen in . . . "

* * *

Three hours and a bit later, Goodge asked Tony to stay after the briefing with the other two men had concluded.

He said: "Bring you up to speed, Captain. No need for anyone else to know this intelligence, though."

"I appreciate that, sir," Tony said to him as he fingered the safety on the black Heckler & Koch silenced MP5 submachine-gun in his hands.

It had a stubby appearance, with a round grip beneath the silencer. "Fantastic, these guns," he said, laying it down. Then he looked Goodge intensely in the eyes, giving him his undivided attention.

"It seems they're intending to work out some sort of deal, our Miss Allgood and her new associates, at this meeting we're going to prevent," Goodge told Tony. His voice was quiet, the old look back on his face.

"What sort, exactly?"

"It's still unclear, I'm afraid. Immediately we heard of it we reckoned it would be arms. Then money. She and her group, as usual, are short of both. Our mole, though, has just let Freddy know that, yes, it's arms and money of course, but these are ancillary, mere add-ons. It's more, much much more, I'm afraid."

"Can you tell me, sir?"

"Yes I can. You should know the gravity of this mission, and so I'll tell you their intentions, so far as we know them. As I've said, the details of these relationships have remained an annoying mystery. But we know enough to *need* to be successful in this mission."

Goodge pulled at his white moustache with the fingers of his right hand, smoothing it over his lips, as if in reluctance to speak. But he spoke.

"We don't know if it's pure bluff on Allgood's part, if she intends to mislead them, even hit them at the meet. She may have something they want in return, some intelligence perhaps. Possibly, they intend to provide her needs simply in exchange for an obligation—or, helping her may just serve their goals, in an indirect way."

"And who is this 'they,' sir?"

"Ah, well that's where we owe you immensely, Spool. MI6 may not have all the clues in yet, but they've linked your deceased Mr. bin Qibla to a particularly nasty terrorist group in Qatar."

"On the Persian Gulf?"

"Right. Nothing to do with the governing family or its ministers, evidently. In fact, something of a stone in their shoe. It's all sand dunes and salt pans, but unfortunately harboring one of the world's biggest reserves of natural gas, and quite a bit of oil as well. OPEC member. It undoubtedly figures in all this somehow. A little pustule in Saudi Arabia's armpit, far as we're concerned."

"This terrorist group, has it got a name?" Tony asked.

"Call themselves 'God's Faith.'"

"Cute."

"Theatrical turds! I'm certain the Amir of Qatar would as soon be rid of them as we would. Fundamentalist bastards!"

"And what's the plan we're going to bust up, sir?"

"So ungodly it's... well, suicidal desperation. Our mole assures us Allgood is dead set on it, though. Dead set."

"And it is?" Tony could see the reluctance in Goodge's face.

Goodge let out a long, slow breath. Then he jiggled a finger in his right ear. The look on his face was one for the record books.

At last he said: "At this meeting, our Arab friends will be handing over to Miss Allgood an international sight draft for twenty-five million French francs—"

"*French* francs?" Tony said.

"That's right. Nearly three million in real money."

Real money. Tony knew what he meant. Sterling.

"This she intends to carry to Marseilles, where she will exchange it with a certain French-Algerian terrorist faction for a certain small bomb, which members of this Frog group seem to have stolen and will deliver, in parts, to an unknown location in or near London."

"A certain small bomb?" Tony asked.

"A neutron bomb."

A long, breathless hush came between the two as the significance of this intelligence sank in.

Fate hung like a vapid apparition, ethereal and drawn out, in the colorless air around the two soldiers of mankind's pale fortune.

At long last, Tony stood up and said, "So the mystery of our Dahoum bin Qibla continues, but the mission is a go?"

Goodge stood too, and looked with a father's faith into Tony's eyes, those blue pools shimmering in the dim light of the hangar.

"That's right, Spool. A *definite* go!"

In a few minutes, Tony emerged from the CIA hangar to find the noon-hour sky had lightened. The air was crisp and the morning's dullness had turned into an inviting pale blue with high, wispy clouds. Windy up there.

He headed towards the building that would be their home barracks for the next couple of days and saw Angus in the parking lot, loading their clubs into a government Lincoln Town Car. Angus saw him coming and waved.

They had a two-o'clock tee-off.

Tomorrow, before light, would begin two rigorous days of drilling.

As he approached the car, his mind started reviewing the timetable. Let's see, he thought, this was Thursday the thirteenth—and suddenly he stopped short. A peculiar expression gathered on his face, as he realized the mission was to occur exactly thirteen days after Senator Winterbern had surrendered to the new civilization.

Thirteen days. *Lucky* thirteen this time! It was positively inspiring, God's plan for him. Positively inspiring.

TWENTY-ONE

As though guided by the dead, the shadow crept steadily down one gray wall of the dim passageway, a faint specter stretching out before him.

It belonged to a special place... a place of rude voices and wailing terror where all motion became slow and hard, a place buried beneath familiar landscape, a place of decay and demons.

Was it his own shadow, or some phantom's?

Tony remembered it always as something else, a memory which must vanish again and again, only to return on the blackest nights, to haunt him into eternity. It moved without warning between the living and the dead.

The narrow oak boards, smoothed by countless small feet, reached out before his shadow. He ventured a careful step, but a creak came back to his ears. He halted, a foot raised, holding his breath, but no sound came from the room, so he placed the next foot down, soundlessly this time.

It was that time of day, just before dark, when shadows marred the world, distorted vision and perception, a time when the moon slowly evolved from nothingness into vague outline and finally into a spot on the sky, and its witchery called to the souls of the tortured to come forth from hiding.

Tony could see vividly in each nightmare the cracks in those smooth oak boards, stretching out down the passageway, the crooked grains and streaks of the floorboards, seamed together yet each strip distinct, unique in its nature, spotted and scratched and gouged, and worn over again.

His passage to his future.

The phantom gathered form, came from the void, as he gained the edge of the doorway. It ceased. It became a young commando. In the odd, poor light of the passage, cast on the colorless wall before him, he saw the shadow of his hand holding a slim triangle ending in a stabbing point, sharp as the tip of a razor. From the shadow of the thing on the wall, his eyes jumped to the thing itself, and the glint of bright steel reflected back at him. Jagged notches ran along both sides of the dagger. His hand gripped a thin, black handle made of finely carved ash wood, itself hard as stone.

An ancient weapon. The right choice. Known as the *skean dhu*, the 'black knife' of the Scots—and of SAS commandos.

Now he saw the hulk of the old man in his room, drowsy on his sofa, crossed the threshold in silence, drawing not a squeak from those floorboards which had echoed the howling terror of so many tender boys brought here for punishment.

Tony stood before him, deep in the room now, and saw only an old man with a hulking frame, once huge in the little boy's eyes and terrifying, but now powerless, old, used up.

He looked around the bleak room which had once so mortified him, saw again those cold walls into which his terror had faded, hollow and indifferent to his calls for Mummie. Mute witnesses still.

The old wallpaper, once of shiny blues and yellows, had long since browned into dingy mustards. The gas fire in the corner glowed as before, meager and dull and unwarming. Dust coated shelves of things, lined the frames of pictures, hung in high corners as it might in some ancient tomb.

The past flooded back.

Tony could see the huge man with the long, thin whip all over again, standing over him, dominating him, punishing him for his defiance, for his bravery, excited by a festering cruelty.

For a long moment Tony endured the pain of the thin whip lashing at his bare backside, felt the old rawhide strips rasping at his wrists and ankles, recoiled at the stabbing tears in his flesh, heard once again in silent anger those words which had rung in his ears year after distant year:

"This is between you and me, boy, between you and me!"

The demon drowsing on his worn-out sofa seemed so pathetic, there in front of the grown boy, his dagger poised to inflict revenge.

As Tony held the weapon, ready to strike, other shadows rapidly came at him, made him lose the moment to forgotten memories, coming out of nowhere... the little boy shivering violently and then his dad's strong, hairy hands holding him, rubbing his head, those arms wrapped about his small frame, pressing their bodies together for a final embrace, murmuring to him about his mum... never see her again, Tony, she was lost... and how could he take proper care of his little son not, oh the boarding school it was for the best just the best... the right thing... and then his dad's cold ears against his face, the clearest memory he had, he clung to it... clung to it as it faded, faded through all the years...

But the huge man with the long, thin whip never faded, standing there over him, bound to the bench, lashing him, again and again. That voice hissing against the hollow walls: "You leave 'mummie' out of this, you hear me, boy? This is between you and me, just you and me..."

Standing there, dagger in hand, looking down at the pathetic hulk within his chill walls, that ugly face somnolent as dark crept down the passage of the old boarding school and into his room, the dust suddenly nettled at the commando's sinuses and he let out a shallow sneeze.

The ancient face came alive again, the body jerked out of sleep, and those horrid eyes met Tony's.

"What is it, boy?" the body on the sofa snapped, without hesitation. "You back again?"

"You remember me?" Tony's voice had said to it.

"All the same, the same..." came an answer.

Tony's eyes suddenly flashed around the room, searching for the shrill cries that reverberated at him again. The wailing of a lost little boy, alone within those hollow walls.

Then just as suddenly the shrieking vanished. Silence came back.

Tony bent towards the hulk on the sofa, only inches away from that hideous face, said "Not all the same—not at all!" in a vicious, hoarse whisper, and the hulk dared to look into the bright, terrifying light of Tony's blue eyes, and gasped... as the dagger pierced his heart and Tony repeated a single word over and over until blood covered his hand as it twisted the blade:

"*Shend! Shend! Shend!*"

TWENTY-TWO

ETA: dawn.

In the pitch black, Tony couldn't tell if it was fear that hissed like a thunderhead in his brain, squeezing out the rest of the world, or just the steady vibration of the helicopter's rotor blades, whirling overhead.

He fought to keep from thinking of the peril he was about to face, but fear had always hidden in the night for Tony, and this night was as black as they came.

"Pieche o' cake, thish mission, right Tony lad?" he suddenly heard, the slurring Scots brogue breaking into his thoughts. It clarified in his brain, and suddenly the spell upon him was broken, and he laughed out loud.

Angus Lukins laughed then, too.

And Tony heard a slight rustle of fabric as Angus moved, then felt a sharp smack across his cheek, squarely placed despite the dark.

The Scots brogue came at him again. "Shmile, old son, you and me're abowt to shend thish little Irish lassie shtraight to Hell!"

"You and me, Angus, you and me!" Tony yelled back at his friend, over the noise of the helicopter.

"Good as done! Now sit back, and don't think o' nothin' or I'll have to shmack you on the haffet again!"

Again there was just the noise of the rotors.

Tony eased back into the harness that strapped him into the hard seat that faced his friend across the gangway. His fingers felt the ice-cold metal of his webbed seat. The helicopter shook all around him, vibrating thickly in the cold night, and now Tony thought he could smell sea air. That would be from the Chesapeake Bay. Then the salt smell disappeared, and Tony knew they must be over the peninsula now, heading due east, low over the terrain.

He still couldn't see more than a vague outline of Angus's body, only a few feet away. Without ambient light, their black body armor was night itself—invisible. They wore slick, close-fitting trousers and titanium flak-jackets, Browning 9mm High Power pistols and two spare clips each strapped to their right legs, a slim knife mounted upside down in a tension slide-sheath on the left upper arm, throat mikes and tiny headsets inside helmets that sculpted their heads, paratrooper's boots, and a compact nylon parachute on their backs. Everything dull black in color.

The deep of night seeped away around them, and as the sky lightened ever so slightly Tony began to make out his old friend's face, watched it gradually emerge from the black. It seemed to be at rest, as if asleep.

Now the sea air came back to Tony's nose and the sound of the heli blades changed vaguely. Tony knew they must be over water again.

The Sikorsky in fact flew straight out to sea as it passed over the tip of Cape May, and three miles out it turned abruptly north, going at close to its maximum speed of one hundred eighty-four miles per hour, two CIA pilots up front, and carrying Hellfire missiles just in case.

As they flew northward, just off the coast, the sky continued to lighten far away to the east. The aircraft remained all but invisible, dull black and flying low over the vast gray ocean. A ghost emerging like a vapor from the dark nowhere.

Tony thought he saw movement below the goggles on Angus's forehead, saw his wide moustache twitch, so he said:

"Do you know what Shinto worshippers do for luck, Angus?"

"What'sh 'at, Tony lad?"

"They clap their hands, before they pray. Four times."

"Couldn't hurt, could it?" Angus's moustache broadened, a smudge across his upper lip.

They rode hushed by the whirling power of the rotors for another twenty minutes when all of a sudden Jack Rush, sitting to the rear of them, announced:

"All right, gentlemen. We're on the countdown now."

Angus fastened his air-pressurized face mask, with its frog-eye goggles, into place, began breathing through the rubber respirator, pulled on his tight-fitting gloves, and picked up the silenced Heckler & Koch MP5 SD5 submachine-gun. The standard SAS weapon. He pulled the slide and checked the safety.

Tony did the same.

"Sandy Hook down there now, gentlemen," came Jack Rush's voice into their headsets. "We're approaching the lower bay."

Each warrior nodded across the gangway at the other.

The helicopter dropped in speed but gained altitude. It flew high over the center of the Verrazano-Narrows Bridge, only a few headlights of cars and trucks on it at this hour of Sunday morning.

Then the Sikorsky dropped to less than a hundred feet above the broad upper bay of New York harbor and flew directly toward the tip of Manhattan, passing just to the west of Governors Island and the U.S. Coast Guard base there. At that moment, the sun broke over the distant horizon to the east, and New York burst out of darkness. The intense new light glanced into the warriors' eyes, muted by their goggles.

One of the CIA pilots said into their headsets, "Two choppers ahead of us, gentlemen. Been tracking them on radar. Appear to be our targs..."

Jack Rush slid open one door, and freezing air streamed into the chopper. Tony and Angus released their harnesses and crouched before their seats.

"First chopper's just touched down, six men away," came the CIA pilot's voice. The Sikorsky swooped to the right of the Statue of Liberty, gaining speed as it passed over Battery Park.

"All six are armed, gentlemen. Pistols only. Waiting at the antenna."

Tony looked at Angus sharply as the Sikorsky jarred them, whirling in the air, and the icy draft from the open door whipped at their bodies.

Again came the pilot's voice:

"We have the second chopper in our sights now, a Bell... coming in from due west. Coming in high and level... *Here we go*, gentlemen!"

Tony brought his gloves together four times in the symbolic gesture. Angus laughed through his respirator, his bright eyes peering like a bird of prey's at Tony through his goggles, and then he reached over and slapped Tony's cheek sharply with one black glove.

The massive twin towers loomed directly ahead, like the Alps.

The Sikorsky buzzed rapidly now around the south tower of the World Trade Center, at mid height, and climbed like the wind up the steep wall of the north tower, its twirling blades angled so as to throw out a gale. As it came over the lip of the roof, a hundred and seven stories up, Tony and Angus saw seven figures near a gray steel door at the base of the huge white antenna jutting from the center of the roof—caught in the gale of the Sikorsky's blades, trying to protect their eyes from the stinging wind.

Tony saw a tan gravel roof through his open door, with short, white antennas sticking up, dozens of them, and immediately beneath him, on the southwest corner of the roof, he saw a yellow outline to a white square with a red circle inside it. A helipad.

It was a spot devoid of antennas, and the Sikorsky's wheels just grazed it as Tony and Angus stepped out of the helicopter and onto it as gracefully as dancers, at the same time firing their silenced submachine-guns at the figures on the roof. Some of them got off a few shots from their pistols, held lamely pointing at Tony and Angus, but the rapid fire took down all but one of them in seconds.

The Sikorsky lifted off and now angled its rotors away from the roof. It disappeared down the side of the tower, as stealthily as it had come, and calm abruptly returned, stillness out of a storm. Six bodies lay on the roof.

For a moment, nothing moved.

Then a shot rang out. Tony looked over to see Angus go down, face forward, saw a figure holding a pistol, firing it repeatedly at Angus as he fell, watched as the slugs slammed into the back of Angus's flak-jacket.

Tony swung his submachine-gun at the shooter, tripping the trigger as the muzzle came right, but it was already too late. The figure had leaped to cover beneath what looked like some sort of gray metal chute, raised about two feet above the roof's surface. His shots kicked up the gravel.

Tony began to advance on the chute. Just then, his eye caught Angus getting up awkwardly but waving an okay to him.

It was only a moment's distraction, but enough for the figure beneath the chute to lunge at Tony in a wild run, and as Tony brought down the H&K's muzzle again he was caught by the leg and tumbled.

The figure grabbed for his submachine-gun, wrenching at it, and it flew from his hands as fingers ripped at his goggles, tearing them from his face—and he saw an Irish beauty close up, as she tore at him and he struggled to keep her fingers from gouging his eyes. They locked bodies and rolled towards the outside of the steel lip which separated them from the roof's edge. She was pounding at his head and arms with savage fury.

He could see only quick snatches of close-cropped, carrot-red hair above arching eyebrows and a delicate nose. Skin that was pure and fine. But this face of beauty was horribly contorted into a hateful mask, a severe ugliness.

Tony realized who this must be, even though the previous yellow hair was missing.

She kicked viciously at him. She was fierce but small, and quickly Tony wrapped his arms around her body, pulling her back in to him in a tight grip, and slipped the slim black Viking knife from its sheath on his upper arm, drawing it across her throat, but before it could cut into her windpipe she twisted a shoulder into his neck, slid around in his arms and suddenly faced him, her eyes inches from his own, glaring death's own fury, hissing at him. But he held on tight, so she snapped at his face with her teeth. Tony recoiled this time. She caught the skin over his windpipe and bit down hard, drawing blood.

As she did this, Tony worked the blade in his hand through the tough material on her back, some sort of jacket, and she let out a scream and let go of his neck as the knife sliced between her ribs. Tony ripped it inward towards her backbone and started to thrust upward, but once again she twisted, forcing her body against the blade so hard that it fell from Tony's hand and skittered on the gravel of the roof.

In an instant she jerked free and slipped down between Tony's arms, punched him in the groin as she fell to the deck, and as he recoiled she leaped for the knife. In a heartbeat she slashed at him with it, catching the tip of the blade at the seam of the flak-jacket by the neck. She yanked down on the blade, slicing through the titanium fabric, cutting into Tony from the collarbone down towards the left nipple, ripping open the bulletproof jacket.

Tony flung his forearm at her, catching her wrist, and the knife fell onto the lip of the roof.

As she grabbed it, Tony heaved himself at her, locked her in his arms, pulling her back in towards his chest as tight as he could manage, and together they swept off the roof as one—and began tumbling.

In a moment of pure terror, Alexandra Allgood froze, and as she did so Tony clamped a hand, like a wrench, at the base of her skull, at the back of it just at the atlas vertebra, unlocked his leg hold and shoved her head down hard and away from his body with all the force he could muster.

She twisted around to face him as she fell away, thrashing viciously at him with the knife but only cutting the empty air. Tony tugged his ripcord, and as she began to fall away rapidly she hurled the knife at him in a last, desperate attempt to kill. But it merely passed, harmlessly, in a slow-motion arc under Tony's feet, glinting brightly for a moment in the day's new light. Then it disappeared.

As Allgood's body fell away from him faster and faster, getting smaller, the wind that had whipped at the tower's top floors suddenly lessened into a mere breeze tempered by the sheer size of the tower's massive walls, and Tony began to float, it felt like. Had the odd sensation of drifting inward, as if into the side of a pyramid widening out beneath him. An optical illusion. And then, a warm dry updraft met him halfway down, slowing him even more as he dropped vertically, swaying gently.

At that very moment, the light mist around the tower, caused by the cool and warm drafts merging in the new sun, reminded Tony of the mist around the fountains in Nice, and instantly he understood the meaning of all the signs that had pestered at him. All the birds, and his encounter with the odd little man at Agincourt, came back to him as the mysterious words buzzed with a sudden brilliant recognition through his brain:

I soar, I am a hawk!

Looking around him, he realized Alexandra Allgood's body had gone completely away. He looked up for a moment at the dizzying height above, but couldn't see the tower's top stories now.

What he saw, looking below him, as the ground neared rapidly, was a round dome and to its right a pyramidal one, both green, on the tops of two buildings across from him, getting bigger by the moment. Immediately below him he saw a grass plot to the left of a footbridge across a wide street. Three lanes were painted in each direction, to left and right, and in the center of them, coming close, he spotted several green circles to the left of a semicircular blacktop driveway. He realized they were large concrete pots holding plants. Beside them a white van was parked, with an American flag painted on its roof. Two men stood beside it.

Tony worked the parachute's draw cords, and in the nearly still air he maneuvered with ease the last couple hundred feet of drop towards the van. As he neared the ground it came directly under him, right between his boots as he looked down.

The two men watched in amazement as Tony thudded into the roof of the van, crumpling metal and the painted Stars and Stripes. As they looked up at him, Tony quipped, "How's that for a safe landing, gents?" Then he rolled off the roof onto the pavement, tumbled to the ground in a single movement.

One of the men quickly busied himself, rolling Tony's parachute into a compact ball.

"First time I've seen anything like that!" the other man said to Tony. "We watched you all the way down, in our binos. Couldn't believe it when we saw you come over the edge up there! It's a quarter of a mile up, you know!"

Tony stood there, beside the van, leaning forward, hands on his knees, his eyes wild as he realized what he had just done, breathing deeply now, trying to slow down his heart, and bleeding.

Then he straightened and stared at the man. About to say something. All of a sudden, an odd grin dominated Tony's face, as he thought *No wings to fly from God!* She didn't have them, did she? Holy punishment. A soul recycled.

But the man only said, "Christ, you're a mess, sir. Blood all over you!" He handed Tony a towel, and it turned bright red as Tony touched it to his neck and patted his chest with it.

"Where's my friend?" Tony asked, looking at the stained towel.

"On his way down—in the elevator! Called on his headset."

Just as he said this, the other man ran up to them, holding the balled-up parachute with one arm and a hand cupped over a headset on one ear, yelling, "We have to leave—now! Go, go, go!"

They all jumped into the van. Tony jumped in back, holding the towel to his neck to stay the bleeding, and the van jerked to a start and sped into a driveway leading down to the parking lot in the basement. Up ahead they soon saw Angus.

As he got into the van, Angus was grinning that grin of his, and he said to Tony, "You know, old shon, it's a hell of a lot eashier if you take the elevator!"

Then he slammed the van's sliding door closed into Tony's stare.

"You okay?" asked one of the men from the front seat, to Angus.

"Right as rain, laddy! Right as rain!" And he handed Tony's submachine-gun back across to him, saying "Thought you'd want thish... left it up there on the roof, you know. Can't have that!"

As Tony reached for it, the van jolted into motion again, and the blood-soaked towel fell off his neck.

Angus said in alarm, "Christ, Tony boy, what happened to you!"

"She bit me!"

"She bit you? The bloody bitch!"

"They all dead up there?"

"Oh, they're deader'n the Prophet Muhammad! But, unlike him... they're not holy men—all their shecrets are locked up tight!" Flashing that grin again at Tony.

"Such a pity!" Tony grinned back at Angus.

The van was moving fast now, and as it sped through a tunnel the CIA man in the front passenger's seat kneeled between the van's bucket seats with a hypodermic needle at the ready.

"Pull off that flak-jacket, Captain Spool," he told him. "You can use this."

"What is it?"

"Enkephaline. It'll stop the pain real quick." He jabbed Tony's arm as the jacket sleeve came off.

"Where we headed?" Tony asked him, as he winced in pain.

"We're in the Brooklyn Battery Tunnel right now, and in five minutes you'll be reboarding your Sikorsky on Governors Island."

Just then the cell phone rang in the front of the van. The CIA man picked it up, listened a second, and handed it to Tony.

"Somebody wants to speak to you, sir," he said to Tony.

Tony took it, listened, began to smile, said into the mouthpiece, "Like lightning, sir!" and handed the phone back.

"What'sh the upshot?" Angus asked.

"Sir Malcolm says CNN's on their way. The city police are already on site, and within the hour there'll be a press conference. The world will learn some upsetting news. Another Arab terrorist bombing of the World Trade Center's been attempted, but it's been successfully thwarted by the NYPD's anti-terrorist squad, you see... before any harm could be done."

"Ish that sho?" Angus said back at him. "Evidently Sir Malcolm mished the free-fall! A grand bit o' *harm*, that!" He clicked his teeth and then said, "What about you, Tony lad? Did ya shee that bitch hit the grouwnd? I reckon that was one for the record bouwk!"

"Fraid I missed the landing. Think they'll manage to figure out who she was, in the newspapers?"

"Doubtful, Tony lad. Doubtful!"

Just then the van emerged from the tunnel onto the little island off the tip of Manhattan, proceeding quickly to a grassy spot at the center of the island, where the Sikorsky helicopter waited.

Tony and Angus hopped in, and as the cold sun glinted on its blades the chopper lifted off. It flew over the field and the low buildings at the southern tip of the island and in moments was lifting over the choppy dark waters of New York harbor.

Inside, Tony and Angus stared at each other beneath the whirling blades in silence as the impact of what they had just done hit them.

The helicopter reached the narrows at the end of the lower bay, swooped up and passed over the center of the gigantic suspension bridge, heading out toward the Atlantic Ocean. Soon it would be flying south along the coastline.

Tony sat rigidly, strapped into his harness, as Jack Rush tended to his neck wound and the knife slash Alex Allgood had made down his chest.

Angus looked at the crimson slash, made a funny face, and said quizzically to Tony, "You don't expecht that wee cut'll interfere with your shwing any, do yuh, Tony lad?"

Tony saw the gleam in his old friend's eye, and laughed out loud, saying, "Angus, you mad rogue!"

"Well... you come up to Drumnadrochit then, laddie, shoon as can be, and I'll shew you some *gowlf!*" He reached over and slapped Tony gently across the cheek, grinning that grin of his.

And all of a sudden, for the first time in a long while, Tony felt completely at peace. His body relaxed, easing back into the webbed seat, its metal no longer cold to the touch, and smiling broadly back at Angus, he finally allowed himself to think of Susan. At long last.

He said to Angus, "First, you're coming home with me, and we'll have us both some R&R and a *proper* meal—roast beef with all the trimmin's!"

"'At's it, laddie. 'At's it," Angus seemed to murmer through the muting noise of the whirling above their heads. "Champion idea . . ."

The Scots grin and voice faded away, got all caught up in the noise and shaking of the chopper skimming fast over the whiteheads of the Atlantic seacoast, and gradually Tony lost his focus, sinking completely into his safe seat, going home again.

After a little while, the sound and vibration of the rotors softened as land came out of the distance. Tony sat up and peered past the pilots, through the armored windscreen, and saw it approach—a protected place at peace under a clear, cold sky.

And so, Tony Spool was a civilian again, for the time being.

The End

www.ingramcontent.com/pod-product-compliance
Lightning Source LLC
Chambersburg PA
CBHW060555310726
48982CB00008B/1126/J

* 9 7 8 0 9 3 7 9 1 2 6 1 4 *